ALL TOO HUMAN

ALL TOO HUMAN

A SAGA OF DEADLY DECEPTIONS
AND DARK DESIRES

KAREN WILLS

FIVE STAR
A part of Gale, a Cengage Company

Farmington Hills, Mich • San Francisco • New York • Waterville, Maine
Meriden, Conn • Mason, Ohio • Chicago

LIBRARY OF CONGRESS CATALOGING-IN-PUBLICATION DATA

Names: Wills, Karen, author.
Title: All too human : a saga of deadly deceptions and dark
    desires / Karen Wills.
Description: First edition. | Waterville, Maine : Five Star, a part
    of Gale, a Cengage Company, [2019]
Identifiers: LCCN 2019002602 (print) | ISBN 9781432855086
    (hardcover : alk. paper)
Classification: LCC PS3623.I577435 A79 2019 (print) | DDC 813/
    .67—dc23
LC record available at https://lccn.loc.gov/2019002602

First Edition. First Printing: September 2019
Find us on Facebook—https://www.facebook.com/FiveStarCengage
Visit our website—http://www.gale.cengage.com/fivestar/
Contact Five Star Publishing at FiveStar@cengage.com

Printed in Mexico
1 2 3 4 5 6 7 23 22 21 20 19

For Jerry, who supports me and my work
with unflagging wisdom and love.

ACKNOWLEDGMENTS

I am grateful for my critique partners, Janice McCaffrey and Bonnie Smith, for the constructive criticism that pushed me to make my writing better than what I first shared with them. Thank you as well to readers Debbie Burke, Shirley Rorvik, Ann Minnett Coleman, and Bev Zierow. Thanks also to my wonderful editors Tiffany Schofield, Gordon Aalborg, and Erin Bealmear at Five Star Publishing. Most of all, I thank my husband, Jerry Cunningham, who suggested I set *All Too Human* in the post–Civil War era of Montana Territory, as well as in 1905, after the territory had achieved statehood.

Many articles provided information for the writing of this book. Particular mention should go to:

Bridgeman, Kim. "The First Time: 1865 Christmas Sketch Shows Garden City in Its Infancy." *Missoulian,* December 24, 2015.

Lutz, Peggy Ann. "Food and Females: The Taming of the Oregon Palate?" Thesis submitted in partial fulfillment of the requirements for Master of Arts in History, Portland State University, 1991.

Two books that provided especially valuable information are:

McKay, Kathryn L. *Looking Back: A Pictorial History of the Flathead Valley, Montana.* Virginia Beach, VA: Donning, 1997.

Overholser, Joel. *Fort Benton: World's Innermost Port.* Fort Benton, MT: Joel Overholser, 1987.

CHAPTER ONE

Kalispell, Montana, October, 1905

Guilty? Not guilty? The jury had been deliberating for six hours. *Why?*

Rebecca Bryan, attorney at law and part of the defense team, shifted in her wooden chair and inhaled the beginning of a discreet sigh. The new Flathead County courthouse still smelled throughout of tacky paint and fresh-cut wood. The scent mingled with the stuffy odor of men and women spectators who'd crowded into this courtroom for the drama. Uncle Max, a successful attorney, hadn't disappointed. Rebecca, meticulous in her attention to detail, had assisted him throughout the proceedings. She exhaled and glanced at the empty jury box, then at Max, lead counsel for the defense.

She pondered the trial, and three questions emerged: What fact disputes in closing arguments caused this long wait? Had she missed something in her trial preparation work? Or couldn't jurors understand the judge's instructions?

If her uncle shared her tension about the trial's outcome, the veteran litigator didn't let it show as he chatted with their portly client. The two men contrasted in appearance. The perspiring client's sack coat had rumpled, his collar wilted. Max Bryan wore a formal black frock coat and a burgundy tie and vest. Silver hair reached just to the top of his collar in back. He carried no extra weight and could fix any witness with his trademark penetrating stare. Rebecca had heard more than one compare his features to those of a hawk.

The defendant had soft features in a round face. Nervous and pale after months of languishing "in durance vile" on embezzlement charges, he sat on Max's other side chewing one side of his bushy moustache.

Just as the courtroom clock's ticking became unbearable, Rebecca heard the double doors to the hallway open. The court reporter, prosecutor, bailiff, and spectators came back. The defendant jumped when Judge Aiken entered from his chambers. All present stood. The judge took his seat, then said, "It is my understanding that the jury has reached an agreement." All but the attorneys and the accused sat back down.

Rebecca studied each member of the all-male jury as they filed back to their seats. She looked Pete Barker in the eye. He owned the Barker Hotel. Pete gave a small smile and, to her amazement, winked at her. She scrawled on one of the papers in front of her the single word "Victory" and slid it toward Max, who gave an almost imperceptible nod. He'd seen the wink as well.

Fifteen minutes later, after the foreman announced the "not guilty" verdict, Judge Aiken thanked the men of the jury and dismissed the proceedings.

Max and Rebecca each shook hands with their client. Rebecca knew he would leave ahead of them, then vanish from Kalispell forever on the Galloping Goose spur line. No one would or should miss the fellow, she thought. If he'd been more likeable, his employer might have been less inclined to jump to conclusions.

In any event, the prosecutor had failed to prove that their client was guilty beyond a reasonable doubt. Max, with the help of her research, witness interviews, and organizational skills, had presented a solid case of innocence for the defendant. Thankfully, the accused wore the great cloak that protected every American at the start of a criminal trial: the presumption of innocence.

Rebecca gathered up the notes she'd compiled in trial preparation and shoved them in her briefcase. She'd taken notes and handed Max exhibits and documents from her pre-trial preparations. Pausing to gaze around the room, she wondered when her time to be lead counsel would arrive. A woman even assisting in court remained a rarity in 1905, even if that woman were a member of the Montana bar who'd studied under Max Bryan, Esquire.

She squared her shoulders, walked into the hall, and on toward the entrance doors. She returned nods to those fellow members of the bar who deigned to acknowledge her. There were a few more willing to do it than when she'd begun to work with Max. She downplayed her bluestocking and suffragette leanings except when with her enlightened uncle or in houses of Kalispell's more progressive citizens. She meant to attract her own clients to the firm as well as help with Max's caseload. While she intended to further the cause of votes for women, the firm had to come first. She owed that to Max.

Not seeing him, she turned to look out the windows that took up the doors' top halves. Her reflection gazed back from the panes: pale skin, chestnut hair rolled below her narrow hat brim with one modest feather for decoration. She stood straight and slender with searching dark eyes, mouth set, altogether a no-nonsense sort of person. That's how she wanted to face a world capable of crushing the frivolous, ever doing its best to discourage ambitious women.

Her thoughts returned to the case they'd won. Because the vanquished prosecutor knew he'd lost for good reason, he wouldn't appeal. That meant no arduous trip to Helena for oral arguments before the Montana Supreme Court. Max always collected a more than adequate retainer before a trial began, forestalling messy outstanding fees at its end whether he won or lost. She'd store the case file in a box that would accumulate dust for decades.

She looked again for Max. He might well be weary, but in a fine mood tonight as they dined, served by their housekeeper and cook, Mrs. Bracken. He'd open a bottle of champagne. They'd toast their success.

Just then the released former defendant rushed past with a quick nod, not meeting Rebecca's eyes. He'd now be one of the many former clients who appeared seeking help and, after receiving it, usually vanished from their attorneys' lives forever.

Max appeared next. He smiled and offered his arm to Rebecca. Grinning back, she took it. "Well," he said. "That couldn't have turned out better. It does a man good to see justice done. Nothing more exhilarating."

They went outside, and Rebecca breathed in the earthy scent of late October in the Flathead Valley. She welcomed the crisp air after the day spent in the stuffy courtroom.

Max, with other county commissioners, had chosen this site for the courthouse, just south of town and surrounded by open land. Surveyors' stakes revealed how adjoining land would soon be divided into lots. Kalispell would continue to grow as befitted a county seat.

He stopped, and they both looked around their setting with obvious satisfaction before he continued. "Do you feel ready to take one of our next cases to trial yourself?"

Rebecca's quick smile gave way to her usual more serious look. She took her time before responding. In the pause before she answered she heard the light winds whispering in tawny grass and the soft applause of golden aspen leaves. "Yes, I'm ready."

Max smiled and nodded. "How about the Peterson divorce? We'll start you out with the ones that won't be so publicized and move on to higher stakes cases as you gain confidence."

Rebecca remained unsmiling. "People accept me in the role of your Girl Friday, but I so want to plan and decide strategy on my own cases. That's the only way I'll gain my own reputation. I mean to be a respected trial attorney soon, Max. Like you. I want our firm and my practice to grow along with our town."

Max patted her hand. "You've got the ability. A colleague's sex doesn't matter to me as much as her mind and education. I've known some brilliant women. Gender shouldn't matter to anyone else. You're not flighty. We won't put up with outdated nonsense about women's limitations. Time you females assert yourselves. It's a new world out here. You'll become a bright light in the courtroom. Lady Justice."

Rebecca gave his arm an affectionate squeeze. "Lady Justice is blindfolded, Max. I want to see everything as it is. All the time."

"Well, what we see here is worth seeing, isn't it?" He paused and made a sweeping gesture with his free arm.

Mounded blues of the snowy Columbia Range lay to the east, and behind them glacial mountains that rivaled the Swiss Alps, where she'd often skied with European classmates during her boarding-school days. A slight cast of pink, the alpenglow Rebecca loved both in the European Alps and here, spread like a silken shawl on snow-covered peaks both close and distant.

They strode on to the three-story, white Victorian mansion that Max's logging and mining interests, along with a successful Kalispell law practice, had built. Once inside, they hung up their coats and hats and parted until dinner. Rebecca went up to her room, smoothed her wavy hair in front of the mirror, and removed her corset. As a rule, they didn't dress in formal dinner clothes. She changed into a wool skirt, pleated shirtwaist, and loose jacket. Her stomach rumbled. There'd been no time for lunch.

Uncle Max had decorated her room for a little girl when Rebecca came to him as a grieving, shattered, distrustful thirteen-year-old. At a loss as to what to do with her, he sent his niece to study at an elite girls' school near Geneva, Switzerland, then to college in New Hampshire. Although he could well afford to redecorate to make it a suitable boudoir for a young woman, both felt sentimental about change. She'd been back for three years. The room remained a pink and white little girl's dream space.

Rebecca heard a knock at the front entrance before she started downstairs. Mrs. Bracken's voice followed, then the sound of the door closing. As Rebecca rounded the landing, she saw that Max's stocky housekeeper held a telegram.

"For Mr. Bryan." Mrs. Bracken held the envelope out to Rebecca as if wanting to be rid of it. Telegrams were suspect at best. "From those people up near Jennings."

"The Cales," Rebecca murmured. "Max has probably been in touch about his annual elk hunt up there."

"Just so long as the meat comes butchered proper for our meals," Mrs. Bracken responded. "Will you see he gets it? I've to do the finishing touches before I serve your dinner."

Rebecca held, but didn't open, the telegram, its color like that of aged ivory. What could it portend?

She'd always found something a little mysterious in Max's relationship with that family. He labeled them his oldest and dearest friends but never introduced any of the family to her. He disappeared a few times each year to stay at Eagle Mountain. The Cales' remote hunting lodge turned permanent home sat near the mining town of Jennings, northwest of Kalispell. The family had suffered tragedies, but Max declined to elaborate on them. Rebecca knew from Mrs. Bracken that he'd been present at one terrible event. A longtime Cale guide died after a bear mauled him at their hunting camp.

She'd deduced that Max had long been in love with the widowed matriarch of the Cale family. But even though years had passed since her husband's death, Lucinda Cale never agreed to remarry. Probably wise, Rebecca thought to herself. Lucinda, whom she'd never met, had been left in control of a fortune. The woman stood as an ideal model of an independent progressive, a successful artist, an astute businesswoman. Altogether as rare as a practicing female attorney. Rebecca admired anyone who pushed aside society's attempts to keep women from advancing.

She carried the telegram to Max's office at the front of the house, tapped on his door, and stepped in following his brisk, "Enter." Max swiveled his wingback chair around from the fast-darkening window behind his long pine desk to face her. His hawkish expression showed effects of the theatrical, combative day in court, but every silver hair gleamed in place as usual. Dark, paneled walls lined with shelves of law books bespoke dignity and order, or so it always seemed to Rebecca. A desk lamp cast a golden glow around the man and his niece as he reached for the telegram.

She settled outside the light into a smaller wingback chair facing the desk. Her eyes rested on Uncle Max. He read the telegram, then let it drop to his desk. He forced a violent swing of his chair back to face the window and said, "Lucinda Cale died this morning—this morning while I focused my attention elsewhere. I would have thought I'd sense such a loss, but I didn't."

"Oh, Max . . ." Rebecca half stood.

"Her dear heart failed her. Mine beat for her always. I waited long, futile years for her to return my feelings." When he turned back to Rebecca, his face had contracted into an ashen grimace.

"I'm so sorry, Uncle Max. I know how much you cared for her." Rebecca's brown eyes met his wounded, gray ones.

He nodded. His voice thickened with grief. "I once proposed to her. She hesitated, and I tried to fill her dance card for the whole evening, but my friend Garrett Cale beat me to it. When they married three weeks later, they broke half the hearts in New York. Beginning with my own."

Rebecca sat back, then leaned forward. "Garrett must have been clever indeed to outmaneuver you. But after his death you could have courted Lucinda all over again. I've never seen you give up the pursuit of something you wanted."

Max ran a hand over his eyes. "Oh, Rebecca. The hunting, fishing, all those trips to discuss our business partnerships . . . I grasped them as excuses to see her, to try to convince her to marry me. The thought of our becoming man and wife consumed me at times. But she discouraged any real courtship."

"So Lucinda remained intractable?" Rebecca asked.

"Yes. I sometimes discerned an unfathomable darkness surrounding her. But no matter how implacable she remained in her refusals, I hoped someday she would agree to marry me.

"Then, too, Garrett had been so close a friend. Perhaps Lucinda and I both felt we'd be committing a betrayal of sorts. And there were her boys. Tension abounded in that household, although I didn't know its source. I did doubt that Damon, the oldest, would welcome me as a replacement for his father. His parents had carried a romantic aura about them, you know."

Max fingered the telegram, reread it more than once, then sat in silence for several minutes. "I'm curious as well as saddened," he said, looking up. "Aside from the great tragedy of Lucinda's death, something Damon added to the telegram doesn't sit right." He frowned, rolling his silver pen in the fingers of his right hand, a sure sign of him mulling over an enigma.

"You don't think Lucinda was—"

"No, no," he cut off Rebecca's question. "Dear Lucinda died of a heart attack, apparently in her sleep. Heart trouble haunted her for years. Besides, she lived surrounded by devoted caretakers. No, foul play doesn't concern me, but I am puzzled. Garrett hunted money with as much passion as he hunted game. He and I made our fortunes as partners in logging, mining, and other investments. He left all he had to Lucinda. She and I became partners in business, though never in domestic life as I so hoped."

"But you are puzzled?" Rebecca had never heard Max speak so much about the Cales.

"She wrote me that she made out a will after Garrett's funeral and kept the original at Eagle Mountain. She hinted at some personal disclosure in the document. She used her lawyer in the nearby town of Jennings. Once Lucinda became seriously ill I told Damon about its existence, but Damon adds in this telegram that he can find no such document. Furthermore, he says his mother never mentioned one, nor did he bring it up to her. He doubts its reality."

"Wouldn't Lucinda's lawyer still have a copy?" Rebecca asked, leaning forward.

Uncle Max nodded. "Excellent. You're quite right. There should be one, except her lawyer in Jennings died trying to put out a late night fire in his office building. It took out a whole street in that booming riverfront town. The inferno destroyed everything it contacted, including him. I knew him; a good, honest, small-town practitioner, but prone to take his time. Sadly, even by the day of his death, he had yet to file Lucinda's will in the courthouse."

"You don't suppose Lucinda kept a more recent original at Eagle Mountain?"

"No." He dropped the pen to his desk blotter and rubbed a

hand across his forehead. "Nothing significant changed in the family since she made her will other than the boys becoming men and leaving home. There would be no reason for regrets or doubt on her part. Lucinda was never one to change her mind. And, if she had, she would have told me."

They heard a soft tap at the office door. "Mrs. Bracken must be waiting for us to have dinner." Rebecca rose.

"I can't eat. I need to be alone with my old man's memories. With this news, I feel used up and worn out. Dine by yourself. Bring me tea when you've finished, dear."

Rebecca could have eaten in the kitchen with Mrs. Bracken, but it had been a long day filled by the firm's peak of success and Max's valley of grief. She needed to be alone, to calm herself. Books always offered peaceful distractions. She selected one from the library, Edith Wharton's *House of Mirth*. Its plot and characters reminded her of another way Max had rescued her. Thanks to him, she wasn't tied to custom, groomed only for marriage to some society Brahmin. Max wanted her to experience life as a free-thinking, knowledgeable human being. And so she would.

At the table, she pushed the book aside at first, letting her thoughts rest on Max and their respective futures. She loved Uncle Max and owed him a great debt for becoming a wise, affectionate father when she lost her own.

But years of fierce adversarial competition had aged and hardened him. At times the courtroom arena consumed Max until he seemed to live no other life except for his profession and investments. His relationships with clients were intense, high-stakes ones that flared hot, then burned out after decisions and verdicts concluded the work of interviews and preparations followed by the theater of trials. She sometimes wondered if his unrequited love for Lucinda Cale might be a romantic way of freeing himself for those dramatic, but finite, attorney-client dealings.

Rebecca intended to be one of the standard bearers for women's progress. She wanted to be enfranchised, and she wanted the same for others, even women who didn't yet support voting rights for both genders. Perhaps one day she'd run for political office herself. She might become the state's attorney for Flathead County. She wanted what men had: no limits. That would be worth any measure of the loneliness that a life of leadership, of standing out, might include. She turned to the calming escape of Edith Wharton's astute prose.

After dinner she closed the novel with a sigh, placing a velvet ribbon where she stopped. She poured Max's tea and carried it to his office. When she set the cup and saucer on his desk, she noted that his color remained ashen.

She paused before asking the rhetorical questions, "Do you want me to do something about the will? Isn't it possible she hired another attorney to draft a replacement? Some new attorney might have the original or a copy in his office."

He regarded her with avuncular appreciation. "You've worked with me until you can read my mind. Yes, represent me at Lucinda's funeral. Then stay with Damon and his family for as long as necessary. See what you can discover about Lucinda's missing Last Will and Testament, be it the old one or a new document. Find out whether there is a second one."

Rebecca paused. "But don't you want to be there? I know how long you loved her. I see the depth of your grief."

"At twenty-four you can't possibly understand, my dear," Uncle Max answered with a smile that turned more like a grimace. "But at my age the memories are best left undisturbed."

With that, Max's face contorted into a frown of pained confusion as he dropped his head in his hands. He swung in the chair, bending forward and to one side as if he might pitch onto

19

the floor. Rebecca cried out for Mrs. Bracken and rushed to Max, supporting him in her arms. He rested there, half-conscious.

Mrs. Bracken flew into the room and gasped. "I'll stay with him. Rebecca, get Fred to hitch up the wagon. I think it's a stroke. I've seen this before. He needs to be in the hospital."

Rebecca raced to the carriage house where Mrs. Bracken's son lived. She pounded both fists on the carriage house door, rousting Fred in short order, relieved that, although she could smell alcohol on his breath, the gangly man wasn't passed out or unsteady. Only his hands trembled.

In short order, Fred stopped the horses pulling the wagon before the front door, then carried her helpless uncle outside with Mrs. Bracken giving directions. Rebecca had climbed into the back where they usually placed luggage or boxes, and Fred put Max in with her. She sheltered her uncle's head in her lap.

They raced through the streets to the new medical building. Once there, Rebecca answered the doctor's questions as best she could. The stocky, bespectacled medical woman, half of a husband and wife team who ran the hospital, eventually confirmed that Mrs. Bracken's diagnoses had been correct. Max Bryan had suffered a severe stroke, the same disaster that took the widow Bracken's husband years before. But Max still lived.

The Fergusons were longtime friends to Max. Amelia, a rare professional woman who'd gained the community's gratitude and respect, had become a close ally and example to Rebecca.

Max appeared so fragile as he lay in his narrow hospital bed.

"How bad . . . ?" Rebecca stopped, unable to continue.

"We'll know by morning. Go home now, Rebecca," Amelia advised. She turned to Rebecca's driver, who'd come into the room. "Fred, you stay off the drink tonight. Miss Bryan will want to see her uncle early, I'm sure."

Fred nodded. Rebecca noted his hands still shook, but she trusted his loyalty. Rebecca trembled, too, at the thought of leaving Max there so pale and helpless.

CHAPTER TWO

Rebecca spent the night in misery. No matter how she tried to picture other things, her mind jumped to images of a stricken Max. She couldn't bear his dying in that stark, white room. She dreaded finding only the naked ticking on his stripped bed the next day. As Rebecca lay staring at the ceiling, tears slid across her temples into her hair. She wiped at them with the heels of her hands.

Max, her father's elder brother, became her guardian after her father's suicide when she'd just turned thirteen. Her mother had died of a tumor, leaving Rebecca desolate at twelve years old. Her father soon moved them, two unmoored survivors, to Granite, Montana. He planned to make a fortune in the rising demand for silver. When the market for silver crashed, taking the banks down with it in 1893, the boom town became a ghost town overnight.

Her father then became a real ghost. He died by his own hand, abandoning Rebecca to cope as best she could.

Max, all the family she had left, rescued her. As she came to know her uncle, she grew to admire his canny and sometimes ruthless brilliance in business and law. Astute, Max took care of the people he valued and the possessions that he wanted to increase in value. Rebecca determined to do the same. She'd never forgiven her father for what she and Max both judged as the suicide's weak, irresponsible behavior.

Lying there, she felt a growing dread. She pictured herself

walking next day from the hospital to the undertakers. She'd taken such a walk once before, a frightened thirteen year old making her way through Granite's all but deserted streets. When she finally fell into an exhausted sleep, she picked up where the images had taken her. She revisited the nightmare sight of her father's body, the charred mark of the bullet hole in his temple.

She awoke at 1:00 a.m., her thoughts whirling in fears of how serious the stroke might be, how much it might affect the rest of Max's life. Could he even survive? He must have suffered severe damage. When she left him, his mouth drooped flaccid on one side; his eyes had a glassy look. Would he walk again? Would he see? Would he have to be in the hospital for long? She could care for him, of course. She could obtain continuances for trials on the docket for the next several months.

He'd asked her to go to Eagle Mountain. That wouldn't happen now. She'd telegraph their sympathy to the Cale household.

She fell again into troubled dreams that mixed the two brothers, her uncle and her father, in various states of illness and death. Both stared at her out of gray faces, melancholy and helpless. Both terrified her when they receded into dark storm clouds, not responding when she bid them to stay, to tell her what to do. Her entreaties whipped away on a swirling wind.

Rebecca awakened before dawn. Giving up on any further night's rest, she dressed and went into the office to clear the way for a few trial-free months. Just after sunrise, she told Fred she wouldn't need him. She wanted to walk to the hospital to clear her head before she saw her uncle and whichever Doctor Ferguson might be in attendance.

The air felt frosty despite sunshine. The last aspen and oak leaves twirled in a shuddering dance from tree limbs to the boardwalk. She passed big household gardens where pumpkins sat burnished in morning light among yellow and green squash and rows of dry corn stalks. Ferns and hollyhock stems had faded to yellowish brown. A cold, damp tang hinted that snow might visit Kalispell ahead of schedule this year.

She strode to the courthouse to file necessary documents and inform concerned parties of Max's illness. After that she hurried toward the hospital inhaling deep breaths, trying to shake free of apprehension and fatigue, the detritus of distraught sleep.

She rushed toward Max's room. Doctor Amelia Ferguson caught up as if wanting to offer support. The woman's presence did reassure Rebecca, a kindred spirit in the lonely world of professional women. They nodded to the nurse who stood when Rebecca and the doctor entered.

"The stroke has affected your uncle's ability to walk and speak," Amelia said, brushing back a tendril from her prematurely graying hair.

"He can't speak at all?" Rebecca looked to Max. His eyes pierced her from his face that sagged on the right side. She realized her uncle could understand all they said. She moved to the bed to take his hand, as cold as her own. "Uncle Max," she said, pulling the chair close to the bed and sitting so she faced the stricken man.

Max, known as a most eloquent attorney, struggled to speak. She heard him say, "Yes."

Amelia stood across the bed from her, a dark, stolid figure against the light from the window. "As you see, Max can say a few words. 'Yes. No,' but little else. We'll keep him here for the next two weeks, then see what you can do for him at home."

Max raised a hand.

"Uncle Max, should I send our sympathy to the Cale family? I won't be away from you now."

The answer came immediate and harsh, "No." Then a struggle resulting in a guttural, "Go. Yes. Go."

"You want me to leave you like this to go to them?"

The "Yes" was as emphatic as the weakened man could make it. His distress and Rebecca's long habit of trying to please him led her to capitulate.

"Is he out of immediate danger, Amelia?" she asked.

"These things can always turn, but I believe so."

"Are you sure, Uncle Max?"

He glowered, his voice louder. "Yes. Yes. Yes." Uncle Max wanted her to go to Eagle Mountain, represent him, find Lucinda's will. Nothing had changed in that respect. His brilliant mind, trapped inside a failing body, still held the power to command.

"All right," she agreed, her words slowed by reluctance. "I'll leave tomorrow, although I'd rather stay with you. Don't worry, dear Max. I remember all you said. I'll take care of everything. Mrs. Bracken will visit you here until Fred brings you home."

In the hall, she told Amelia, "I'll leave word of where I'll be. Send a telegram if his condition worsens. I wish he weren't so insistent. I'd rather be with him."

The doctor bestowed a reassuring smile. "Max will rest easier knowing you're doing as he wished. It makes him feel he still has a measure of control. Send Mrs. Bracken to me, and I'll speak with her."

Rebecca spent the rest of the day closing the file on their liberated client, writing a few letters, and packing for her journey. At the depot, Fred obtained her train ticket on a spur line from Kalispell to Jennings. Once there, she'd have to hire a coach from the livery to take her the twelve miles to the Cale lodge, Eagle Mountain.

Soaking that night in the claw-footed tub, Rebecca considered what faced her. It would be an exciting journey, but difficult. She'd have to meet the Cales by herself while fretting every minute over her uncle's condition.

She stepped out of the bath and stared at her misted reflection in the lamplight. Although tall and slender, she'd rounded into womanhood. Her years in Switzerland, in the company of wealthy girls from England and the Continent, had taken away any false modesty about women's bodies. There'd been no secrets about the pleasures and purposes for which breasts, hips, and all the rest had been made. She learned early about the affairs of her friends' parents, mothers and fathers often taking lovers, not a puritanical thing about any of them.

Her teachers, heirs of the enlightenment, had been forward-looking men and women. Regardless of the romantic or frivolous concerns of young girls, their teachers focused on their minds. The school turned out young women who spoke French, read Latin (later a great help to Rebecca in the law practice), knew world history, and studied scientific discoveries. They attended plays, read novels, and learned how to navigate everything from directing servants, to creating table settings, to presentation at court, and the etiquette of debutante balls.

Rebecca had taken one lover, a classmate's striking older brother. She expected they'd become engaged, but his parents threatened to disown him if he married the orphaned American. They'd heard of her father's suicide and wanted no such taint on their unstained family crest. After the feckless young aristocrat caved in to his parents, Rebecca wrote to Uncle Max that she wanted to come home. She'd turned seventeen with a broken and disillusioned heart. Turning cynical as romantic youth can do, she determined never again to trust in her own heart. Or in anyone else's.

Uncle Max insisted that she come back to America but must then earn her degree at a college in New Hampshire. After her graduation, he summoned her to the beautiful, raw West. Once there, she left despair behind, losing herself in legal work and studies.

Young men tried to befriend and court her, but she refused them with exquisite courtesy. She wanted only to live a challenging intellectual life with her uncle. No youthful men could match his courtroom dramatics and business ambition. Not in Rebecca's eyes.

But sometimes at night, memories intruded, memories of passion, of moments in a marble gazebo radiant in moonlight, and the young man's hands . . . Sometimes she missed that urgent heat. Sometimes she missed finding her own needs met by a man who swore depthless love while exploring her with his own burning eagerness.

At the end of the day Rebecca climbed into her brass bed expecting another awful night. But it seemed only an instant before she awoke to dawn. Time to dress and have Fred drive her and her things to the depot.

Rebecca worried over leaving Uncle Max even in the competent hands of the dedicated Ferguson medical team. But Max's insistence had so taken her aback and weakened any efforts she perhaps ought to have made to argue against the idea. Besides, Mrs. Bracken and Fred had been running the house for years, long before Rebecca returned from New Hampshire, so there could be nothing except her own need to be close to Max to keep her in Kalispell.

By afternoon, she relaxed into guiltless enjoyment of watching forests, mountains, ponds, and lakes appear and vanish as the train chuffed past them. Foliage had turned every orange, yellow-gold, pink, red, or purple that autumn in its prime could provide, but nature had also begun subsiding into muted colors. Rebecca loved the tumult of the russets and golds and greens that continued to appear from time to time. Still, when the train finally reached its late-afternoon stop at Jennings, Rebecca clutched her luggage and disembarked with relief.

Charred rubble remained in some lots on the east side of

Main Street. Jennings had suffered one of the fires that so often spread out of control to devastate forest towns. But construction sounds, metallic clanks and hammering of nails into wood, even a boat builder's enterprise signaled rebuilding. A row of thriving businesses stretched along the undamaged west side of the street. Paddlewheels and steamboats lined nearby docks on the Kootenai River.

Passengers and freight came and went, people disembarking, loading, and buying tickets. Rebecca overheard enough conversations to know that many of the men were going to railroad camps, smelters, and undertaking journeys north on the Fort Steele trail to the mines of British Columbia. All wanted work, wanted the prosperity that the frontier promised. Rebecca felt a surge of pride that her uncle had a hand in developing all this enterprise.

Her immediate concern involved hiring a driver with a coach, or buggy, or if nothing else a wagon, to take her the twelve miles to Eagle Mountain Lodge. She gripped her suitcase and Max's documents case and strode into Jennings in search of its livery.

She found the rough-hewn building as much by the odor of horses as by reading its identifying sign. She called out. No one answered, so she let herself through the gate, entered the barn, and called again.

A paunchy man, none too clean by the look of his clothes and grizzled yellow-gray beard, stepped out of a stall. He leaned a manure-caked pitchfork against the unpainted wall and looked her up and down with bloodshot eyes. She'd seen that look on Fred. Her spirits fell.

She tried not to sound rattled. "Do you own this place? I'm in need of transportation up to Eagle Mountain Lodge." She succeeded in using a firm tone that would have done her well in a crowded courtroom. Here her only audience, the unkempt codger, appeared unimpressed.

"Bill Sauer. I own it. I'll take you, but I have business to finish first. I'll have to find someone to watch the place while I'm gone. It'll cost you. I don't hire on cheap, especially to go up there."

"I don't want to wait until tomorrow. If we start in an hour, I'll pay you a fair sum."

After fifteen minutes of intense haggling, they reached the sum of fourteen dollars. He said he'd pick her up at the nearby Kootenai Café in an hour and a half. Rebecca paid half his fee, the rest due when she arrived at the lodge.

She walked to the café and hesitated. Through the window she peered into a smoky room filled with men and only a few women. Realizing she had no choice, she pushed against the door with her shoulder, her hands maintaining their grip on her luggage.

Sets of eyes, predatory male or envious female, followed her as she made her way to a small table by the window. A sidelong glance told her the women were a hard lot. Rebecca sat with her back to the wall and cast frequent glances through the panes, hoping to see Mr. Sauer. A waiter took her order of coffee, steak, and apple pie. As she hadn't eaten all day, when the food arrived it tasted wonderful.

Nursing a third cup, she'd almost given up on Bill Sauer, when, shaded by early twilight, her unkempt driver appeared. At least she would be spared riding in a topless mud wagon. Slender poles on this vehicle supported a flat roof, but Rebecca noted her coach's open sides. She saw seating space next to Mr. Sauer, and only room for her baggage on the seat behind. He had already piled that space with burlap bags of unknown purpose.

The horses appeared healthy and well fed. Perhaps Sauer

liked animals more than people, more than Rebecca's gender anyway.

He didn't climb down. She paid her bill and walked out. She handed up her bags, which he, impatient as though she'd been the one to keep him waiting, slung to the rear seat. Rebecca climbed up to sit next to him and pulled a shabby blanket that smelled of horse over her knees.

She caught the odor of stale whiskey when Sauer exhaled. Hesitance to ride with an inebriated stranger brushed through her. Would he turn overly familiar? But he seemed to find the whole task distasteful enough that he probably just wanted to deliver her and get back to his livery.

The coach ascended the mountainside, the road made up in large part of switchbacks over steep ground, interrupted by rocky outcroppings. As they gained elevation, aspen leaves turned from the brown of deer in late autumn to their gray in early winter. Bared tree limbs rose like lace flags against a dimming sky. The resigned horses plodded upward as twilight darkened.

Transition to night happened fast in that old-growth forest. Temperatures dropped with equal speed. Then the season's first snowflakes appeared, wandering with blatant indifference down onto discarded leaves and larch needles. Rebecca shivered. Freezing mud turned slippery as the temperature fell.

"Cold, aren't ya? It's winter, so what'd youze expect, little city slicker?" Sauer pulled a bottle from his pocket. Rebecca could hear his gulps even over rising gusts and the hiss of snowflakes coming down faster. He held out the bottle.

"No. I don't want it. And address me as Miss Bryan."

Sauer belched. "I s'pose you just want to drink with the city uppity-ups at the fancy lodge. They carry on with each other up there and shoot game just to brag on when they go back home. No doubt they'll all be drinkin' to the old woman tonight.

"Have to say she was a beauty back when we were young. That red hair and those wild green eyes. Dead beautiful she was. Fatal, you might say. First her high and mighty husband, then good old Seth. He worked as hunting guide and caretaker there. Both departed from our midst before their time. What the coroner called accidents."

Rebecca faced away from the driver as he hiccupped. If local gossip existed about her uncle's lost love, she didn't care to hear it. She hugged herself, not wanting to give away how much the increasing cold and Sauer's spiteful company caused her to shiver. They drove for another hour with only sounds of coach wheels on the rutted road along with the protesting roar of tall pines tossing in the rising wind. What were they protesting?

Occasional gusts rose to become a wind that whooshed through all it touched. With no warning, the coach lurched. They'd lost the rear wheel on Rebecca's side. The coach collapsed, pitching her back. She grasped the closest post. Even gripping that for support, she leaned at an awkward angle. Gravity had taken charge.

Sauer didn't get down but muttered an oath, then tipped his bottle for precious last drops. His head lowered. In horror, Rebecca heard thick snoring.

She poked his snow-dusted arm. "Wake up, you worthless excuse for a man," she ordered. "Rouse yourself. Don't you dare pass out and leave me here."

No response. Sauer had started drinking early in the day, and she couldn't revive him now. "Serves you right if you freeze to death, you damned old reprobate," Rebecca muttered.

The horses stamped and blew, their breath making white clouds. One turned his large head and gave Rebecca an impassive look, then turned forward again. Snow spattered a ghostly white blanket on the team's broad backs.

Rebecca struggled to sit up. Straightened, she peered down

the road ahead. She thought for a moment a light glimmered. Could it be? Eagle Mountain Lodge must be somewhere up there. She reached back for her leather suitcase and the matching documents case. Thoughts of walking alone on the forest road ahead daunted her, but she had no wish to become a frostbite victim next to odoriferous friend of demon rum Mr. Sauer.

"Your name sounds like you smell, you good for nothing," she declared to him. She wrapped and tied the ratty lap robe around her shoulders. She clambered down, the coach rocking precariously. She set her luggage beside her, refastened the hood of her coat, picked up the cases, and started past the horses. They gazed at her, accusatory and woeful.

"Don't go anywhere," she ordered them through clenched teeth. "I promise to send help if—no, when—I find any." She began to hum the "Hallelujah" chorus, defiant as she walked, grateful she'd decided to lace up sturdy leather boots instead of chancing that light shoes would be enough for the journey.

The snowfall ceased. Then moving clouds interspersed with emerging and vanishing stars in the vast night sky. Struggling not to feel insignificant and vulnerable, Rebecca trudged on, losing her sense of time in the blackness of heavy forest under the lowering, gathering, and scattering clouds. The wind blew against her, and, when it briefly let up, fog drifted in and hung in the branches ahead.

Rebecca glanced behind her and to both roadsides. She ached from cold and the uneven burdens she carried. The dress case proved much heavier than the lighter documents case. She put both down, opened and closed her fingers, then switched sides to vary their burdensome weight.

She glanced back at intervals. There must be bears, mountain lions, moose, or anything in this abysmal night. She heard what might have been a growl and tried to boost her walking speed.

She'd never experienced such an uncompromising absence of light. Not a lamp's glow to show her what lay ahead, clouds now obscuring the stars in that infinite black sky. The Cales didn't even expect her. Only her stricken uncle and a few others in Kalispell knew of her plans to attend Lucinda's funeral. Snowflakes increased, a descending army of pallid invaders.

CHAPTER THREE

Rebecca shivered even as she tried to keep up a brisk pace. How long does it take, she wondered, before a person begins to freeze to death? She stumbled in a rut and caught herself. As time wore on, the discouraging road with its ascending switchbacks threatened to reduce her to tears of exhaustion. She fought off that urge to weep while surrounding forest dwarfed and terrified her. Unseen threats lurked everywhere.

She had to keep hold of her wits. No good would come of crumbling into a wretched state of self pity or fear. She'd seen firsthand the results of giving up. She'd seen her father on the undertaker's table. She would fight to survive. Always.

Again she thought she saw a light glimmer ahead. She forced herself not to break into a panicky run toward it. After all, she didn't know what it might reveal. Traversing the switchbacks she slipped and slid, struggling on. The light disappeared and reappeared to her several times. She began to think this whole night a timeless hell in which she'd been condemned to keep putting one frozen foot before the other while moving through stinging snow.

Bowed from exhaustion and anxiety, she finally arrived at the glimmer's source.

A cabin sat about fifty feet from the road. Yellow light burned through uncovered windows, although limbs of towering fir still blocked a complete view. Just as Rebecca paused to catch her breath and study the cabin, the relentless wind quieted. This structure couldn't be Eagle Mountain Lodge but appeared, nevertheless, as a haven from winter's onset.

Rebecca crunched over snow-crusted pine needles toward the grail of warmth. Twigs snapped under her boots. She speculated on what or who might be inside. Off balance from lugging one heavy and one light case, she fought not to slip. Her fingers felt rigid. She wasn't sure she would be capable of letting go of her luggage.

Maybe the cabin served as a guesthouse for visitors wanting privacy. After all, Max said the Cales entertained the rich and famous from American metropolises as well as European capitals and trade centers.

A magnificent rack of deer antlers spread like bony wings above the cabin's door. Rebecca set down both cases and drew a deep breath, searing her lungs with frigid air. She knocked. Nothing. She knocked again and waited, only an indifferent silence within. She tried the door's knob. Although it turned she couldn't force the door open.

She shifted from one cold-numbed foot to the other. "You must be there," she muttered. "Please be here. Be awake. Your lamp is lit, after all. Answer my knock. Answer, please. Oh, please, please, please . . ." On the verge of tears she leaned her head against the closed door and moaned. She pulled her gloves off to blow hot breath on her hands.

Something rustled in the trees behind her. What animal might prey on her? What hungered in those trees? Hearing twigs snap, she pounded at the door, wild with fear. Nothing. She moved in terror to the frosted window, raising her arm to break the panes with her documents case. She'd climb through to safety. Anything to be inside. To be out of harm's way.

Seized from behind, she felt her raised arm caught and held against a bristling, furry body. Rebecca screamed once and wrenched free, reeling around to land her documents case against the head of whatever grasped her. With the courage of a prisoner bent on escape, she struck a second time.

"Stop that. Who the hell are you? Where did you come from? Why break my window?"

Her cheek had brushed fur, but this was, although gruff, a male human's voice. Facing a man in a fur parka, she blinked. Her eyelashes had stiffened from tears she hadn't realized had fallen. The wolverine ruff of the man's hood made it impossible to make out his features. The only certainty was that the broad-shouldered man facing her stood tall and angry.

Her own anger flared. "I'd have stopped if you called out. That's all you had to do. I thought you were some wild animal." She straightened the hood of her own coat and raised her chin, then reached to retrieve the case he'd wrenched from her. "Now where is the big lodge? The Cale family's Eagle Mountain? That is my destination."

"You'll have frostbite before you make your way to the lodge if you don't already. It's a good half mile yet." The stranger reached around Rebecca and tried the knob. He groaned. "Stuck again." He pushed the door open with his shoulder. Rebecca followed him inside. Air like a warming oven's enveloped her.

She could have fallen to her knees in relief.

The man shut the heavy door behind them, gestured her to move farther in, and pushed back his parka's hood. Rebecca studied her host. He was not unhandsome. Green eyes narrowed above high cheekbones framed by auburn hair that fell to his collar. His lips were full, but tight and unsmiling. "I can't abide disrespect for other people's property, especially when it's mine," he announced.

"Don't speak to me in that tone. You're the disrespectful one here." She pulled off the thick scarf and lowered her hood.

Their mutual glares led to silence. Unable to think of what to say next, Rebecca felt ridiculous. She summoned one of her uncle's favorite maxims: the best defense is most often a good offence. "Who do you think you are, behaving like such a beast when you could see my distress?"

"You should expect a man to resent it when you try to smash your way into his home. Have a care, miss. You're in luck that I didn't shoot you." For the first time she realized he carried a rifle. He continued, "You still owe me an explanation. Sit down while I build up the fire. I'm cold." He pulled a stool out from beneath one of several tables.

A powdery substance covered the seat he indicated. Rebecca sank onto it anyway, too drained from the night's perils to care about her coat. Unfastening the smelly blanket from her shoulders, she scanned the room. A stone wheel positioned horizontally sat in one corner. Bottles and jars with different labels stretched down a shelf-lined wall. Various forms of pottery—pots, bowls, and some sculptured forms—rested on the tables. One corner held a cot covered by a worn quilt. A stained sink stood nearby.

Rebecca peered into a smaller room. What appeared to be a brick furnace about her own height sat in its center. Fire danced through the furnace door's open slots. A collection of weird, fantastic clay figures, grinning goblins and monsters each only a few inches high, leered at her from its top.

Her host sat down on a second stool and confronted her. "Were you trying to steal something?"

Rebecca stood, willing away any feelings of intimidation. "I am Rebecca Bryan, attorney at law. My uncle, Max Bryan, was a friend of the late Lucinda Cale. I'm here to represent Mr. Bryan at her funeral and help the family sort through Mrs. Cale's estate afterwards. My uncle partnered in business with her as with her husband before his death. Mr. Bryan is also a well-respected Kalispell attorney, although you, no doubt, have never heard of him."

"I don't care what your uncle does. I don't care if your name is added to his shingle. It's two o'clock in the morning, and I'm tired. I just returned from the unpleasant task of searching for, and not finding, a loved old dog. He's dead, no doubt, killed by some predator. I'll miss him, and I'm cold. And I know who Max Bryan is. My dog never particularly liked him.

"Your story doesn't add up to me. If you're really moneyed old Max Bryan's niece, why didn't you arrive in style like a lady? Why all this floundering alone with your luggage in the late hours of a winter night?"

Rebecca caught her breath, remembering Bill Sauer. The intoxicated oaf might be frozen to death by now. And the poor horses . . . Her voice shook as she explained about losing the wheel and the offensive drunk passing out. She omitted how frightening and lonely the trek in the darkness had been.

"I have a horse and sleigh out back. I'll go save Bill Sauer's bacon. He's tough, but this is no night for old-timers like him to be left outside. You stay and try to stop shivering. And please don't smash anything."

In spite of the barb, Rebecca felt relief. "Thank you for your help if not your implications. Do you work for the Cales, or lease this place?"

He pulled the parka back on and then tossed the words over his shoulder as he turned to leave. "Hard to say. I'm Bretton Cale, Lucinda's youngest son."

Rebecca stood. "Sir, you might have said so in the first place. Not identifying yourself reeks of bad manners. Does being a backwoods artist bestow special privileges?"

He gave an exasperated groan, picked up a lantern, and strode out the door.

Rebecca moved near the fireplace, avoiding the sight of the evil little figures in the adjoining room. Exhausted, she sank to a rocking chair by the fire. The cabin's interior log walls had been whitewashed. She looked around the room, trying to fit the beautiful art nouveau forms filling it with their hostile creator. The pieces, mostly vases and pitchers, soared upward in ceramic thrusts of blue, green, gold . . . all the colors of nature.

But the hideous, mocking goblins were Bretton Cale's creations as well. His artist's mind conjured those weird beings from some place of darkness within him. She felt the need for caution in these strange surroundings.

Steam rose from snow melting on her wool clothes. The flames' murmur and shifting glow combined to make her drowsy. She fought sleep, not wanting to be startled by her reluctant host when he returned. She felt uneasy, alone in such a strange setting. He called it his home, but only the bed spoke of habitation. There wasn't a crumb of food or a bit of tea or coffee. Strange even for a single man, if that's what he was. Where did Bretton Cale eat? Why didn't he just stay at the lodge? Why did this place make her so apprehensive? Was it the place that disturbed her? Or was it the man who claimed it? She slid into deep slumber in spite of herself.

The sound of logs being thrown on the fire startled her back to wakefulness. Bretton Cale knelt with his back to her. She took a moment, watching the shift of his shoulders as he crouched before the fire. He'd rolled up his sleeves, and firelight played on his forearms. The thought came that she could just reach forward to touch him. It had been such a long time since she had felt a man's bare skin in other than a stranger's handshake or an avuncular peck on the cheek from Max.

Annoyed with herself, she interrupted her awareness of the man's physical proximity and sat up straight, smoothing her skirt. "Did you find Mr. Sauer alive?"

"They say the Lord looks after fools." Bretton stood and faced her. "Got the wheel back on, and the old rascal insisted on turning around and heading back without even a thank-you. He didn't have anything good to say about you, just sang a bawdy song to his horses as they moved off."

Bretton paused and gazed down at her. For the second time the two studied each other. Rebecca recognized the dangerous pull of attraction, although she hadn't felt it as strong since her European affair. Men noticed her often enough, but she'd felt no response except pleasure in being thought attractive.

Both now chose to avert their eyes.

"Time for us to move off, too," Bretton said. "Only without Sauer's infernal singing. I'll give you a ride to the lodge."

Rebecca hated to ask, but nature demanded. "I've been here for some time. Before we start is there a—"

"Behind the cabin. Help yourself to a lantern. It's not light enough yet to see. Have a care how you step. It's warming a little. There's heavy ground fog. You won't see your feet or the ice coating the path beneath them."

Rebecca nodded.

The door opened to a world of eerie shadows. Spires of ancient trees silhouetted against a smear of charcoal sky looked almost as indistinct as they had in full dark. She steadied herself against the outer wall of the cabin with one hand while lifting the lantern with the other. Her skirts were the fashionable shorter ankle length, for which she felt grateful. When would women be able to don practical trousers like men to go about life's requirements?

She heard rustles outside while she finished her business in the dank outhouse. It took a moment to summon the courage to leave that shelter, such as it was. When she'd made it halfway to the cabin she heard an unearthly scream. A woman screaming in this opaque fog? Rebecca stopped, her heart thudding against her throat.

Bretton Cale came from around the cabin to meet her.

"Mountain lion," he said. "It's not too close. Wait inside while I see to the horse, and we'll start for the lodge."

Chilled through again from only those few minutes outdoors, Rebecca stood close to the fire. She considered that she might never be truly warm out of doors again. Then Bretton opened the door and beckoned. After carrying her luggage to the sleigh and placing it behind their seats, he helped her up and tucked a buffalo robe around her skirts before he climbed up beside her, took the reins, and urged the horse on.

Neither spoke as the sleigh shushed through fresh snow and ice. Feeling sluggish from her long journey, chills, fright, the hike to the cabin, and the aftermath of finding it, Rebecca had no more will for conversation than her silent companion. The leaden sky lightened a bit, but fog tendrils lingered. It occurred to Rebecca that they approached a house of mourning in a befitting, somber way.

The lodge made of stone and huge logs materialized in that mist-shrouded daybreak. Time and harsh weather had darkened the Cale lodge, which formed a massive presence even in this ancient forest that dwarfed all within it. Rebecca found the lodge's impact oppressive, with nothing comforting in the sight of it. Upon closer examination she could see that much of the building needed maintenance. Cracks ran along the foundation. Cedar shingles hung loose or had fallen from places on the roof. Why would a family of wealth allow decay to advance on their home?

Melting ice and snow dripped from the roof. Someone inside had pulled heavy curtains across the big windows. If lights illuminated the interior, none outside could see them. A door, dark from heavy varnish, interrupted a wraparound veranda.

Bretton climbed down and reached to lift out Rebecca's cases. He assisted her to the ground before he climbed back to his driver's seat. "They're at home. Just knock. My brother's an early riser." He clicked to the horse, tapped its back with the reins, and, turning the sleigh around, headed back toward his cabin.

Dismayed, Rebecca watched as he abandoned her. This whole journey felt like one abandonment after the other. She turned to the lodge and considered what to do. Even though no light showed, an early riser could be up inside. And she could hardly stand outside in the cold. She sighed, picked up her documents case and the larger suitcase once again, and moved with cautious steps to the entrance. Even so, she slid once and struggled not to fall on the ice-covered stone walk.

The massive old knocker chilled her hand even through her gloves. She shivered and waited, straining to hear footsteps. Without a sound from within, the great door swung open.

Remembering the unpleasantness of her arrival at Bretton's cabin, she determined to appear calm and pleasant. A visitor should appear so when arriving at someone's home at dawn, or any other time, especially an unannounced visitor. Pushing back her hood, she made an effort to smile, though she knew her face must be pale and drawn with fatigue. Any smile she could muster would appear tentative at best.

A tall man in his mid-thirties stood before her. From his narrow, almost gaunt, face, pale-blue, heavy-lidded eyes stared at her. A shock of blond hair fell over his high forehead. For just a moment she felt apprehensive. Something about him, maybe a sullen look, or perhaps one of annoyance, repelled her. Then to her relief he flashed a welcoming grin that transformed everything. Her first impression must have been the product of weariness.

"Well, who might you be?" There was no hint of irritation at his having been called to the door even before full daylight.

"I'm Rebecca, Max Bryan's niece. Uncle Max told me of Lucinda Cale's—I believe she was your mother—your mother's death." Rebecca paused to consider. How much should she reveal of Max's reaction to Lucinda's death? How much should she admit that his feelings for Lucinda caused the stroke? She decided to be honest.

"My uncle collapsed from the shock after telling me, and I'm here on his behalf to attend her funeral. His doctor tells me he has suffered a stroke. He'll need time to recover before coming here. I'll stay on after the funeral service and help in any way if I can be of service to the Cale family. I'm also an attorney."

The man hesitated, serious once more, but then his quicksilver smile returned and broadened. He held out his hand. "I'm Damon Cale, Lucinda's eldest son. It's wonderful of Max to send you. We'll need your counsel, I'm sure." Despite the smile, his eyes appeared wary.

He motioned her into an entry hall with coat trees, one of which soon bore Rebecca's damp coat. She wiped her soles on a heavy, old rag rug before Damon escorted her into the warmth of a high-ceilinged great room. Big logs burned in a massive fireplace. Flame light danced against solid furniture strewn with fur throws. Trophy mounts of deer, elk, and moose hung on the walls. The hearth's stone mantle completed the elegant ambiance of a long- and well-established hunting lodge.

Despite her host's smile, uneasiness hovered in his eyes. Damon swept his arm in an expansive gesture. "We've tried to preserve what I've always believed to be Eagle Mountain's charm. Hunting lodges have a sort of romantic aura, don't you agree?"

Rebecca nodded in appreciation, noting the great staircase dividing the hallway above them, lined with several doors.

Damon followed her look. "That's where our guestrooms and family bedrooms are. Right now, between Mother's death and the lack of enough snow for winter sport, we're quite alone." His smile vanished as he mentioned Lucinda. "Sit down. Tell me about Max. How bad is he? And tell me how you arrived. I didn't see any means of travel with you."

Rebecca recounted Max's stroke, her train journey to Jennings, Bill Sauer, and the broken wheel. She omitted details, but told Damon of her nocturnal trek to Bretton's cabin. "Your brother took care to fix Mr. Sauer's wheel, sent him off, and brought me here in his sleigh. But I have to say, he could take lessons in hospitality from you."

Damon laughed, a bitter sound. Anger threaded through his tone when he spoke. "Bretton has managed to be the blackest of black sheep. I can't even begin to understand why he's come back, except for a share of Mother's property. God knows how that will turn out. So far, even though Max believes she wrote a will, we can't find any such document."

Rebecca noticed frustration had crept into his voice. The estate would be large, and Damon might have pressing financial needs. What bearing might this have on the lost will?

Her host continued, "My brother broke Mother's heart, and it's too late for him to make it up to her." He cut the words off with an impatient shrug. "Ah, the devil take it. I'm sure your uncle filled you in on some of our family history. Anyway, that's enough for now. Best just stay out of Bretton's way. He seems to hurt anyone who ventures close enough to brave his thorny moods."

"I'll remember your warning," Rebecca murmured, shivering with her clinging chill and the memory of that odd meeting with Lucinda's younger son. She didn't tell her host that in truth she knew few details of his family's history. Her uncle had kept the Cales mostly a mystery. What hadn't he told her, and why?

"Now I'm the only one up, except for the probable meanderings of my daughter Amy, a solitary child. She often sleepwalks or wanders wakeful in the night. We consulted doctors, but they proffer only vague opinions as to her restlessness, no helpful solutions. Well, I'll fetch you tea and toast. Just warm yourself here by our fire."

Grateful for Damon Cale's kindness, and realizing how weary and hungry she'd become, Rebecca walked to a huge leather chair before the dancing flames. Sinking into it, she put her feet up on a matching ottoman and sighed in relief. She glanced at the firelight, but gloom in every corner and hallway drew her eyes more. She hoped to find this missing will and get back to Uncle Max without spending much time in this strange, unsettling place. She rested her head against the back of her chair and closed her eyes.

A sudden draft and the sound of someone moving down the staircase startled her.

CHAPTER FOUR

Rebecca turned her head to see a pale girl of thirteen or fourteen in a dress the gray-green of lichen. The child's white-blonde hair hung straight to her waist. Round spectacles magnified grave eyes.

Although the girl didn't smile, Rebecca sat up and made an effort to be pleasant. "Good morning. You must be Amy. I'm Rebecca Bryan. I'm here for your Grandmother Cale's funeral. My uncle Max is a longtime friend of your family."

The girl stared. She neither moved toward Rebecca nor answered. She continued to study her as though Rebecca were some unidentified specimen, an insect pinned on a board. Rebecca also had the feeling she had a yet unknown test to pass before this one would accept her. This girl's cool perusal betrayed no shyness, no bashful timidity. What prompted her to stare so?

Rebecca said nothing further, only met the girl's gaze with her own. After a long moment the child stepped forward. "Yes. I'm Amy." She spoke in a firm tone, the words slow, unhurried, as though they belonged to a language that wasn't native to the speaker. Perhaps Amy spoke easily only to those she knew well. Something in Amy's solemn approach belied the trappings of childhood.

She continued, "I expected someone to arrive this morning, but I didn't know who. I anticipate such things. I woke up very early and waited. We haven't had any guests for awhile, but your knocking didn't surprise me."

Her shift in tone with its calculated disdain annoyed Rebecca. "Why not? Don't tell me you have a crystal ball?"

"Close." With that response, Amy walked to the fire and jabbed at it with a poker. The logs collapsed with a hissing flare. "I can't stand how Mother sleeps through everything. Father and Mother are so tedious. They need protection from the world, from themselves, too. I'll watch out for them both until I can leave them."

Frowning, Amy turned to face Rebecca. "How did you know my Grandmother Cale?" She sat down on the ottoman's edge, peering into the newcomer's face. Her unflinching eyes reminded Rebecca of a cat's focused on prey.

Disconcerted, Rebecca felt a flicker of irrational fear and then chided herself into irritation. She was no mouse about to be some tabby's breakfast. What made everything in this place so odd? She forced herself to remain composed in the face of this child-sized interrogator. No normal girl, Amy weighed every syllable. Rebecca had interviewed too many witnesses to mistake a secretive demeanor. What had Amy seen or experienced to render her so guarded?

Rebecca responded, "I didn't have the honor of knowing your grandmother. My uncle, Max Bryan, knew her and your grandfather when they were young. Later, he joined in a partnership with them in mining and logging enterprises. He thought so much of both of them that he asked me to represent him at her funeral."

"I know all that. Why didn't he come himself? He loved her, but only I know how much."

Surprised again, Rebecca decided against pursuing that remark, although it sounded somehow like a challenge. Amy's words added to Rebecca's growing disorientation. Was everything in this place somehow out of kilter?

She didn't respond except to go through the story of her uncle's stroke once again. When finished, she added, "I think it would have been hard for him to come even if his health had been good. He cared for your Grandma Lucinda so very much. I believe he felt sad that . . . well, that he's the only one left of all the friends who knew each other so long ago."

A furtive little smile hovered on the girl's lips. "Yes, Grandmother used to say, 'Death is certain, so why try to figure it out.' I always think how someone died, and especially when or why, is interesting. Sometimes death happens at the perfect time. I wonder if your uncle thinks about why he's the only one left alive."

Rebecca wondered why this child couched questions in statements. The notion also struck again that Amy appeared to possess secrets, and not nice ones. No young girl should speak of death with such cool detachment.

Amy stood and pointed to a portrait above the fireplace. "That's my grandmother a long time ago."

The painting depicted a striking young woman in a riding costume. Long, auburn hair escaped from a loose ribbon at the nape of her slender neck. Piercing, green eyes searched the face of the viewer.

Rebecca's own eyes widened as she stood to better study the subject. So that wild, beautiful woman was why Uncle Max had never taken a wife. If her portrait showed only a shadow of her essence, in life she must've been unforgettable. Even her image signaled a woman of deep passions. Lucinda's confident eyes conveyed an invitation. What man wouldn't have sought her company? "What an arresting face," she murmured.

"Yes," Amy responded, no vestige of the crooked little smile remaining. Her expression tightened. "She had many secrets. So did Grandfather Cale, but you don't know. I don't imagine you ever will. She said I was the only one she could talk to about her life. Grandmother and I were close. No one else really knew her. I know everything. She often told me that people are seldom what they seem."

This final statement hung in the air.

Rebecca wanted to draw Amy out further, but Damon returned carrying a tray with a tea pot, toast, and a bowl of preserves.

"Why, Amy," he said, "my little early bird. She's up at the slightest sound, night or day. When do you sleep, dearest?"

Amy flicked a sullen glance at her father. "Your brother doesn't sleep, so I don't want to either. His cabin lamps are always lit."

"How do you know that?" Damon reached to ruffle his daughter's hair, but she ducked away from his touch.

"Because I can see his light from the attic. Why can't you tell him to go away and leave us alone? Uncle Bretton doesn't belong here. He isn't wanted here. He should go back to New Mexico Territory to make his ugly pottery. He should be the one who's dead."

"Amy," Damon's voice betrayed his shock. "Your uncle Bretton is a difficult man, but he's also my brother. I won't tell him he can't stay at Eagle Mountain if that's his choice. Besides, I don't believe anybody but Seth could ever stop Bretton from doing as he pleases. To want someone dead is an evil impulse. I wish you'd stay out of the attic. Is that where you think up such things? Don't go up there unaccompanied. Now, Daughter, there's breakfast waiting for you in the kitchen."

"I don't feel unaccompanied up there, Father. Evil has visited Eagle Mountain before. Others bring it; I know they do. The attic has nothing to do with what I know. I know because I know." Amy stalked off in the direction her father had just come.

Damon looked shaken but shrugged as he turned to Rebecca. "She'll grab a book in the library and read while she eats. Amy can be a difficult child. Sometimes I think she's never actually been a little girl. I'm sorry you had to hear her as haughty as that."

Rebecca shook her head in dismissal of his apology and said, "Amy's at an age for strange notions. I must have been a strange girl at her age. At least I think I made that impression on my classmates."

She'd become ravenous. Her last meal at the café in Jennings had been hours ago and in a different world. Damon excused himself to speak further with Amy, leaving Rebecca to her breakfast and the turmoil of her thoughts.

When Rebecca had eaten, she followed Damon, who'd returned to carry her cases to her room. He puffed up the stairs while she followed, puzzled by why Amy had such an aversion to Bretton. But Rebecca's own first meeting with that discourteous recluse hadn't gone well either.

A huge chandelier hung from the ceiling at the top of the stairs. When Rebecca commented on it, Damon laughed. "It's a little out of place here, I'll grant you. But my parents entertained Swedish nobility. One of them had this shipped all the way from Stockholm to Eagle Mountain after a hunt that earned him a six-point elk."

When Damon opened the door to her room, Rebecca sighed with pleasure. She would sleep in a perfect rustic setting. Night tables topped by brass oil lamps flanked a brass double bed. Braided rugs covered most of the pine floor. A cedar dresser's fragrance greeted her. A fireplace with a blue and white ceramic tile mantelpiece graced one wall, and, thanks to someone having lit the fire in it much earlier, the room temperature felt cozy and comfortable.

Damon indicated an interior door. "Your private bath is just there. Open the door, and it will warm shortly. I suggest you rest awhile. Your difficult night must have exhausted you. I'm pleased you're here. Come down and join us but not before you feel up to it."

Rebecca offered her hand. Damon squeezed it and stepped out, closing the door behind him.

"Thank you," Rebecca murmured, even though her host had already gone. She sighed in relief at finally reaching a private resting place. She unpacked a few clothes, undressed and washed using the pitcher and basin in the chilly bathroom, then scurried back to stand nude before the fireplace, letting her skin absorb its heat while she studied the charming tiles. Putting on a nightgown and wrapper over that, she pulled a down comforter up from the foot of the bed, turned her covers down, and nestled under them. She fell asleep before she had time to wonder about the Cales with their secrets and sorrows, their hatreds and loves.

When Rebecca awoke, midday winter sunshine brightened the room, which still felt comfortable. She rose and, going to the window, peered into forest and mountains. A raven swooped across the scene, its shadow a dark movement across the new skiff of snow beneath. She shuddered. She'd actually walked in that wild country the night before. Alone. She turned away and gave the logs a shift, then replaced the poker. Had Bretton Cale risen yet? Had he gone to bed at all or just resumed his work?

Rebecca frowned as she sat and contemplated the reluctant host who'd brought her to Eagle Mountain. What a man he'd have been if he'd combined both the outrageous good looks he inherited from his mother with Damon's warmth. What could have made one brother a hermit, simmering with bitterness, and the other so adept at pleasing others? Or so each appeared on this brief acquaintance.

She started to apply the word "open" to describe Damon but stopped. There'd been that moment when he stood inside the door. Had he looked worried? Or threatened? Or annoyed?

Something about him had held her in check. Something hard to identify. What a bewildering family.

She thought again of the great beauty who'd broken her uncle's heart so many years before. Bretton resembled her. Yes, Rebecca admitted to herself, in spite of his behavior the previous night, he had a magnetic male attraction. She frowned. Better not let two generations of Bryans be tangled for life in the Cale web of ruinous charm.

Light footsteps in the hall pulled Rebecca out of her reverie. They paused at her door, then trailed away.

But she mustn't forget her purpose here, she considered, climbing back into the warm bed to cover herself in case someone wanted to come in and speak with her. She hadn't dressed yet, but her thoughts turned to her purpose in being at Eagle Mountain.

Why would the woman whose portrait hung above the massive fireplace have written a will and then destroyed it? Or had she? She didn't appear to be a woman who'd change her mind. Had she drafted a will to replace the one lost in the fire?

And what about Amy's allusions earlier this morning? A dart of unease rose within Rebecca. She'd have to investigate Bretton Cale. Indeed, she'd have to put all of the Cales under scrutiny to prove to Max that no one in the family had hoped to gain from hiding or destroying Lucinda's last testament. If she couldn't find it . . .

For a second time, footsteps interrupted Rebecca's thoughts. Now the person not only stopped outside her door but tapped on it.

Rebecca sat up calling, "Come in."

A lovely blonde woman entered, her hair piled on her head in a disheveled, but charming, way. Her dress, hanging free below the breast line, did nothing to disguise her pregnancy.

She carried a steaming mug in one hand, which she held out

to Rebecca. "Good afternoon. I'm Claudia Cale. I didn't even hear your early arrival. I'm the world's heaviest sleeper, especially these days."

Rebecca took the coffee and smiled. "Thank you, Mrs. Cale. Damon and Amy welcomed me."

Claudia's face clouded. "You must call me Claudia. Damon told me of Amy's bad manners. I'm sorry. Our young lady can be a trial at times. She spent much time with her grandmother. They formed a bond so tight that I lost control of my own daughter. To be honest, Lucinda took over many of a mother's prerogatives, shutting me out. I didn't challenge Lucinda Cale, though. No one challenged her except Bretton."

Rebecca's eyes widened at Claudia's frank words on such immediate acquaintance. "Bretton. I met him last night. I can believe he'd be a match for anyone."

Claudia turned and walked to the window. She spoke in a tumble of words, as though she'd been holding in a host of thoughts, just waiting for a confidante. "I shouldn't speak of Lucinda so. We all adored her, of course. Your uncle did as well, I believe. How could any man not? It's just that she had such a strong will and definite preferences. . . . I long to return to the East Coast. I had friends there. A life of culture and social events. I've missed it. But we have good reason to be here, at least for awhile."

The last statement with no following explanation hung suspended between them. Rebecca guessed Claudia referred to the settling of Lucinda's estate. Claudia took a seat by the fire as Rebecca, still sitting up in bed, sipped from the mug. Steam warmed her face as hot coffee warmed her inside.

"It must have been a great change for you. I went through a bit of that when I came West, although I'd been here as a child. Still, Lucinda must have been a captivating, forceful woman to know. I don't believe Max ever stopped being in love with her, even though he always admired and respected Garrett."

"Oh, how your uncle yearned for her. Just yesterday I found letters from Max Bryan among Lucinda's papers. He'd written them before she married Garrett. Your uncle could be so persuasive even then. I don't know how she resisted him. But everyone says Garrett was handsome and turned women's heads with his charm. Damon remembers him as volatile and . . . physical, an accomplished marksman and hunter. He liked to kill things and keep trophies of his conquests. I suppose in a way Lucinda became his greatest triumph. He used to call her his lioness."

"They sound romantic," Rebecca felt renewed surprise that Claudia could be so open about personal matters when they'd just met.

Claudia lifted her shoulders as though she guessed Rebecca's thoughts. "Oh, I shouldn't tell you these family things, but I'm so alone here. It's wonderful to have a friend to talk to, and you are Max Bryan's niece. That makes you almost family. You're so generous to offer to help us sort the estate and property issues out. Ethan McBride practices law in Jennings, but he's been called away for the next few months, so we couldn't consult him even if we wanted to. It's such a comfort not to have to rely on the advice of a stranger."

"Were Lucinda and Garrett always content?" Rebecca asked.

"Heavens, no. They had terrific battles. Damon says he remembers their loud voices from his boyhood. Garrett had a temper. Damon says he didn't spare the rod with him or, from what he heard, with Lucinda, either.

"She seldom spoke of Garrett when I knew her. She turned her face from anyone who asked questions. Of course, she'd been a widow for decades. I think she probably spoke of him to Amy. Amy has strong opinions about everything here, past and present. Where else could they have come from?"

Rebecca set her emptied mug on the night table. "I spoke to her downstairs. She did have a strong bond with her grandmother. How did Garrett die? Uncle Max told me something about him being lost in a blizzard."

Claudia shook her head. "Yes, it was sad and . . . horrible."

"What happened?" Rebecca leaned forward.

"Lucinda had gone into labor with Bretton here at Eagle Mountain. A tremendous storm came up, a blizzard lasting for days. We haven't had one as destructive since, thank goodness. Lucinda's labor went on and on. She endured horrible pain. Damon says he remembers her screams even now."

"What did they do?"

"The nearest doctor lived four miles down the road, and Seth, who already worked here as a guide and skinner, announced that he'd fetch him. But Garrett couldn't stand anyone else being the hero. He went out into the storm with Seth. Somehow they became separated. Garrett didn't answer Seth's calls. Perhaps the wind snatched Seth's voice away or drowned him out. Garrett must have become lost or disoriented. He didn't survive. They found him frozen to death in the woods days after the blizzard ended."

"What a terrible legacy." Rebecca smoothed her comforter. The thought came that every family legend could be told in different versions. Of course, the dead left no version behind, at least not their own. An unbidden memory of her father's lifeless body made her wonder what version of his end he'd recount if she confronted him now.

CHAPTER FIVE

Rebecca noted that Claudia sat in silence, just as she herself did.

"Yes," Claudia finally replied. "Neither Seth nor Lucinda ever spoke of Garrett's death. Damon told me about it. Lucinda somehow blamed Bretton, or acted like she did, for the tragedy. We discussed it and guessed she thought if he'd never been born, the tragedy wouldn't have happened."

"Strange," Rebecca said, frowning. "Unfair as well as illogical."

Claudia nodded. "It didn't make sense, but Lucinda's coldness toward Bretton never thawed. Seth helped raise both Damon and Bretton. Damon caused no problems. Basically, as I understand, he behaved like a normal boy with a normal child's energy.

"Bretton, though, differed from the outset—a wild boy who tested everyone including himself. No one could reach him, at times not even Seth, although he managed most often."

"Was it always so strained between Bretton and Lucinda? Is that why he left?" Even with Claudia's candor something eluded Rebecca about the mother and son.

"Bretton and Lucinda had some ongoing conflict even though both her sons must have adored their mother at some level. In the end, Lucinda and Bretton had an awful quarrel. He left for years. He's only come back since Damon sent him word that Lucinda was dying. He arrived with crates of his work the day after she passed away."

"But what about his studio? It looks as though it's been set up for much longer than a few days."

"Oh, yes. Lucinda created ceramics using the kiln just as Bretton does now. Bretton is like her in that as well as in his handsome looks. She had her pottery studio set up in one of the guest cottages. Art critics back East praised her work. Twice a year she sent her best efforts to New York. Her ceramics appeared to glowing reviews in a lot of shows. She did teach Bretton to be a potter. Damon says they worked long days in the studio."

Rebecca hugged her wrapper against her. She chanced a question that might be considered odd since she didn't really know Bretton. "He must have enjoyed that part of his life here, didn't he?"

"She gave him harsh criticism and negative judgments. If Bretton broke anything or made a mistake she raged at him. Maybe that's what went wrong, at least in part."

Rebecca studied the other's face. "No wonder he keeps to himself. He's so closed off," she murmured.

"Damon says difficult doesn't even begin to describe my brother-in-law. In a way my husband is in awe of Bretton. In spite of Damon's good nature there seems to be awkwardness between the brothers. From what we know of Bretton's adventures after he left Eagle Mountain, he served in Cuba during the Spanish American War, then in our war in the Philippines until he received a bullet wound in his leg.

"After his recovery, he traveled. He wrote Damon that he traveled in Latin America, Italy, and even France. As Lucinda's heart condition became more serious, Damon tracked Bretton down to an artists' community in the American Southwest. I don't know whether Bretton studied pottery during all those years away or just in New Mexico."

"So many experiences. Any of them would be daunting." Rebecca returned to her seat.

She studied the woman before her as Claudia continued. "Bretton seldom speaks to us. My family's wealth comes from armament sales during the same war that left him scarred.

"He just spends hours out in the studio and pops into the kitchen now and then for food. It's unfortunate, but his nearby presence has disrupted our entire household. And Amy! I've never seen her so high strung and irritable. Perhaps it's her age. The only one not affected is Teddy. And, speaking of my Teddy, here he is!"

A round-faced little boy of about five with tousled hair and merry blue eyes that echoed his mother's stood in the doorway. With no hesitation, he ran for the bed and dove into the warmth beside Rebecca.

"Teddy!" His mother patted the wriggling lump under the bedclothes, trying to drag him out, while he protested and Rebecca laughed.

"Well, hello, young man. I'm Rebecca." A giggle sounded under the covers. Then Teddy's happy face emerged.

"It appears that you're soon going to have another addition to the family." Rebecca smiled at Claudia.

"Yes, a little caboose. Damon is delighted, and I will be, too, as soon as the baby is here. Right now, I feel like I've been in this state all my life. That's another thing. I wish Lucinda could have been with us to see her third grandchild. She loved Amy and Teddy so. How ironic that she's the one who's left us. She felt so uneasy about me and this pregnancy, as though I were in danger. I think I made her remember her own experience giving birth to Bretton during that fatal blizzard."

"Does that make you apprehensive?" Rebecca asked, turning her covers back and patting Teddy on his uncovered nose with her index finger. Her reward was a delighted chortle.

"It would, but Damon is going to take me to Doctor Munson's home and infirmary two weeks before my delivery date. It sounds silly with the sort of weather we're having, so little snow except what drove down in the squall last night, but a serious blizzard, the kind that lasts for days, could come up, and none of us wants to take chances."

"What a wise decision," Rebecca agreed.

Teddy popped out to stand next to the bed.

Claudia grasped her son's hand and took slow steps toward the door. "Let's give you time to get dressed. There's bread and cold meat in the kitchen downstairs. The funeral will be tomorrow morning. Come join us when you've eaten."

Rebecca put on a thin shift, then fastened the hooks and eyes of her stiff corset. She pulled on stockings and slipped a petticoat over her head before donning a white shirtwaist. She adjusted a green wool skirt and jacket as her ensemble's final layer. As she brushed and piled her hair into a dark crown, securing it with hairpins, her mind spun. What a family history!

And Bretton's heartrending start to this life with his mother's near death and his father's actual death while Bretton arrived during a howling Montana blizzard. Apparently from birth nothing had ever been easy for him. Except, she thought, perhaps by the time he reached manhood women gravitated to him as men had to his mother. Rebecca focused her thoughts. She didn't intend to become involved in the burdens trapped behind those hard, green eyes.

She pondered Claudia's story. Did it bear on the matter of the missing will? If Garrett left Lucinda a fortune, and she had only two sons, it would follow in the normal course of estate settlement that each should inherit half of what she owned. That meant a considerable amount provided she'd continued to handle Garrett's investments with the shrewdness Max had admired. He'd hinted her fortune included at least hundreds of thousands in property, investments, and savings.

However, Lucinda had violent quarrels with her youngest son. If he'd rejected her and bolted out of her life, she might have left everything to Damon. After all, he'd served as a dutiful son, looking after Lucinda and, she assumed, assisting her with her property since he and his family moved to Eagle Mountain three years before. If anyone stood to profit from the disappearance of Lucinda Cale's will, it might well be her prodigal son, Bretton.

Perhaps Bretton destroyed a will that left everything to Damon. On the other hand Damon might have discovered that Bretton inherited everything by some whim of Lucinda's and in his bitterness destroyed a version of the will that operated against him. Stranger things had happened with estates. Or Damon may have felt he should inherit everything and believed an early version granted him that wish.

Rebecca tested ideas as she descended the great staircase. If Bretton had the will, it might be in his studio. Or did it still exist? How easy it would have been for Bretton to burn it in the kiln under the gaze of those wicked little figures.

At the foot of the stairs Rebecca turned left and walked into a huge room flanked on all sides by shelves upon shelves of books. Another fireplace, larger than the one in her room, with more elaborate green and white tiles, stood at the center of one wall with bay windows on either side. Amy, in a moss-gray dress, had curled up in one of their window seats, staring out at the day.

"Excuse me, Amy, could you direct me toward the kitchen?"

Amy gave Rebecca a sharp look. "Oh, you saw fit to get up and dress at last. We'd begun to wonder if you survived your journey, or if it was all just too much for you. Not that anyone here would mourn you, a complete stranger. We grieve for Grandmother, of course."

"As you see, my stroll in the dark did me no harm," Rebecca said, folding her arms and taking a firm stance against this rudeness. "The kitchen?"

Amy blinked. "Go through that door and the dining room and one more door." The girl turned back to the window.

"Thank you." Rebecca followed Amy's directions and soon found herself in a large kitchen. A black cast iron and nickel Majestic range took up much of one wall, a slightly steaming water reservoir attached to one of the big stove's sides. A fragrant pot of perked coffee warmed on it. The kitchen was warm and welcoming. Copper and iron pots hung from low beams. She opened cupboard drawers, noting them well stocked and organized. She made herself a lunch of bread and cold cuts from an ice box. Mulling over Amy's rude remarks, Rebecca prepared to carry her plate to the trestle table in the room's center.

The outside door opened. Bretton Cale strode in, accompanied by wintry air.

Before he noticed her, Rebecca studied Bretton's face, his mouth in a tight line, his eyes somber. Dark circles under them betrayed weariness and perhaps a touch of his susceptibility to normal human troubles. She hadn't guessed that of him the night before.

His shaggy, auburn hair still lent him a wild, adventurous look as he shrugged out of his parka and stood in workman's pants and a woolen shirt. Realizing he would discover her at any moment, Rebecca stepped out from behind the counter where she'd been hidden behind canisters and hanging towels.

"Good afternoon," she said, keeping her voice even.

"It's you. Late to bed and even later to rise, I see." His tone could only be described as surly. Rebecca checked any sharp rejoinder, remembering Claudia's story and that Bretton and the rest of the family had to face Lucinda's funeral the next day.

"Pour me a cup of coffee, will you? Even a refined lady such as yourself can be useful. I've been wondering; why did you come? It's a long, arduous journey in near-winter when your uncle could have sent a memorial gift and been done with it." His gaze pierced her.

Rebecca turned to the coffee pot. She poured two mugs and handed one to him without asking whether he preferred black. "Max was your mother's dear, longtime friend as well as business partner. But he's too ill to come himself. The news shocked him. I'm here because he asked me to represent him and offer help to all of you." She met his gaze with her own direct look. She wanted to catch his reaction to her next words. "I've been my uncle's law partner for the past six months. Some of that concerns working with estates. He thought I might be able to help your family straighten out Lucinda's documents. I told you some of this last night."

Neither a defensive nor respectful response came from Bretton, only a quick, indifferent shrug. He sipped his coffee, then spoke. "I guess that would be up to Damon. My mother never discussed her financial dealings with me. Damon shared her interest in—no, her passion for—money. They both wanted lots of it just for its own sake as far as I could tell." Casual, he leaned against the counter. Only his voice betrayed tension.

Was he lying, she wondered. "But you learned to be a potter from her. You must have spent time together in the studio. Wouldn't you like to have your own studio on your own land in the Southwest? Never worry about supplies or having to do anything but create your art? Have enough to promote your own work? Never need patrons? Of course, you're such an unfriendly sort, I'm sure you'd love to be free to do as you please, especially in your work."

For the first time, Bretton looked uncomfortable. He finished his coffee, slammed the mug on the counter, and challenged her. "You've been gossiping about me? With Claudia, no doubt. I don't know what Damon will say about your staying on after the funeral to pry through our family's business, but I don't like it. My privacy is and always has been my most prized possession. I protect it. How does the old saying go? 'Curiosity killed the cat,' my dear." He grabbed his jacket and turned to walk away.

Rebecca grabbed his arm. "Don't you threaten me. Your trite insults are small potatoes compared with real disdain I've faced from arrogant men like you. Remember this: I am still standing."

She forced herself to hold Bretton's gaze until he turned away. A small victory, yet a necessary one.

But then he turned back and snarled, "I don't make threats, Miss Bryan, but neither do I compromise what's important to me. You or any other had best tread with care when you poke into matters that don't concern you. I'll respect you when you respect my privacy."

His eyes searched hers as if for confirmation that she understood.

She slammed her plate down on the table. "Tread with care yourself, Mr. Cale. It's not your business alone, but your family's and my uncle's. Your brother has welcomed me, as has Claudia. I'll stay until I'm satisfied that I've accomplished what Max sent me to do. You're the only one who doesn't want me here."

"Stay away from me and my work," he muttered, putting on his jacket. "I should have let you fend for yourself last night. It's clear you think you can do as you like when you like, even stumbling around in the dark." He picked up the plate Rebecca had prepared for herself and charged out the door with it.

Rebecca gazed after him. Did that sharp anger auger deception? What might Bretton want to hide? She detected no love of family, including his mother. That could only leave money as the magnet that drew him to Eagle Mountain. She realized how hard she'd struck home by mentioning his need for the money that would leave him free as an artist.

She allowed herself an inward smile as she made another plate and ate with a hearty appetite. She knew there would be more conflict with this difficult man. She'd won, or at least hadn't lost, the first round. She'd keep her wits about her and be just as ready for the second.

That night, the family gathered for dinner in the dining room. Rebecca hadn't met the housekeeper and cook, Mrs. Bell, before, but the robust woman served a fine chicken stew with homemade bread.

To Rebecca's surprise, Bretton joined them. He nodded to her but didn't engage in dinner conversation. He departed as soon as he'd eaten. After he left, Rebecca wondered whether he'd just come to keep them from speaking of him in his absence? If so, he had the right idea.

The moment he shut the door behind him, Amy groaned. "Why did he have to come tonight? He brings nothing but trouble. I've felt what's in his mind. He's come to grab what he doesn't deserve. The end will cause our family such pain." Putting her napkin on the table in an abrupt gesture, she rose and left the adults rendered speechless, staring after her.

Rebecca made a mental note. Amy might hold the key to this strange family's significant, perhaps vital, secrets.

"Uncle Bretton just wanted to eat," Teddy observed with a frown. "Everybody gets hungry."

"Of course, they do," Damon said in a hearty tone that, to Rebecca, sounded forced.

Claudia turned the conversation to the order of things for next day. Breakfast would be a casual business in the kitchen.

Then the family would gather at 10:00 a.m. under Lucinda's portrait and leave in separate carriages for the funeral. If it snowed in the night then the Cale sleighs would be in order. "Be sure to dress in warm clothes, Rebecca," she advised. "Our stone chapel chills us to the marrow once winter arrives."

Later that evening the children carried mugs of hot chocolate while the adults took glasses of cordial or brandy into the great room. Rebecca and Claudia carried only their cordials. Damon, however, picked up a full whiskey decanter and carried it along with his glass. He sat before the fire and refilled that elegant glass with liberal doses. Rebecca eyed her host. It occurred to her that heavy drinking often sprang from heavy burdens. Liquor often loosened tongues, and she'd listen for any slip Damon might make.

Rebecca raised the issue of her role in the matters of Lucinda's estate. To her relief, both Damon and Claudia said they understood that she offered them her services as a family friend, as Max would have done. They wanted her help in searching out the will. They hadn't done more than a cursory search so far. Both declared they hadn't felt ready to search beyond Lucinda's office, her bedroom having been Lucinda's sanctum sanctorum, no others welcome there.

To Rebecca it seemed strange that finding the will wouldn't be the heirs' first priority.

At one point Damon stood, wobbling a little, and raised his glass to his mother's portrait. "Lift your cordials, ladies. In fact, be cordial. We must toast to Lucinda Cale, the woman who made all we see here possible."

Claudia's nervous laugh followed. She raised her glass in the toast but afterwards turned to Damon. "Well, darling, your father had a hand in it all, too."

"Ah, Garrett Cale, lord of the manor. What could he have done to deserve his iced and untimely fate?"

Damon, Rebecca realized, didn't have any affection for his father at all and might be as puzzling as his difficult brother.

Amy spoke in a low voice. "Grandfather loved Grandmother. He should never have died in that storm. Grandmother and I talked every day. She shared her thoughts and taught me what she'd learned in her long life. We agreed we'd never reveal each other's secrets to anyone else. I feel her presence with me often, and I learn more every single hour. Grandmother talks to me in my dreams. I even feel her thoughts when I'm awake."

Claudia put her arm around Amy. "You have strange dreams, darling. You've had them since we moved to Eagle Mountain. We know how close you were to your grandmother and how much her death is affecting you. But these are mere fancies."

Amy glared at her mother with disdain, squirming from her touch.

"It's time for bed, children," Claudia said in a firm tone, resting a brief, cool look on her daughter. "Tomorrow will be difficult. We need to sleep well. No wandering tonight, Amy. You'll stay in your room. If slumber doesn't come, you may read awhile. Let's pick out a book before we go upstairs."

Claudia's tone of authority impressed Rebecca. Perhaps this lovely woman had strength that one missed at first meeting. Max had often counseled his niece to assume nothing about anyone, that everyone had dark, always-closed rooms in their past. Rebecca wondered what Claudia's locked rooms might contain.

Amy and Teddy followed Claudia into the library. The three emerged with books in their arms before bidding Damon and Rebecca good night. Rebecca watched them go upstairs, then turn into the nursery down the hall. Amy seemed to glide on her way like a pale ghost while Teddy bounced and giggled.

Damon had nodded off, his head thrown back, the empty decanter on the floor by his chair. Rebecca eased the glass from his relaxed hand. His face looked strained even in sleep. A small frown furrowed his forehead. Strange, people didn't often appear older when they slept, she thought. But Damon did.

Since she still felt the tiring effects of the night before, Rebecca left her drowsing host to his slumbers. She picked up a burning candle to light her way up to her room.

CHAPTER SIX

Someone, perhaps Mrs. Bell, had come in before her and turned down her blankets. Rebecca washed, then pulled on her warm nightgown and slipped under the covers. She said a prayer for Max and in gratitude that nothing fatal had befallen her on the road to Eagle Mountain.

She fell into a dreamless sleep until a vague noise startled her two hours later. She lay awake until the grandfather clock downstairs chimed 1:00 a.m. Details of the day before paraded across her mind's eye. She found herself unable to fall back asleep in the gloom-shrouded lodge looming in the cold night's stillness.

Her thoughts returned to Lucinda Cale's missing will. So much remained unknown. Rebecca had no answers, or even clues, yet. Damon's and Claudia's finances had yet to be explored. It seemed logical that Damon would manage Eagle Mountain and the family business interests. But Claudia yearned for their lost metropolitan life in Washington, D.C. Why did they never speak of making the actual move back East?

Amy obsessed over her grandmother. No matter how disturbed Lucinda's granddaughter might be, she held information that could prove essential.

Maybe there never had been a will. Had Max been misinformed? No. Uncle Max never based an opinion on guesswork. Rebecca couldn't go back to him without logical explanations. Somehow she must find the truth about how the mysterious will, or some new one, had been spirited away or destroyed or, best of all outcomes, found.

Rebecca sat up and lit the candle that had guided her to bed. By the low light, she rose and pulled on her wrapper and woolen slippers, then opened the door a crack and peered into the dim hallway. She crept back, picked up the candle, and tiptoed out. For this time at least she had the house to herself. As she descended the staircase she caught her breath at the creak of an old pine board threatening to betray her. After that, she tested each stair step to find the places that didn't complain under her feet.

She paused at the bottom of the stairs. Her candle's flame cast looming shadows over the high-beamed room. Bear heads on fur rugs grimaced at her. Their glass eyes seemed to see something far beyond the gloom. She shuddered. Maybe growing up here wouldn't have been so much fun.

Now where to start? Rebecca thought of the library with its rows of leather-bound volumes. It would be easy to slip a document between the pages of one of those. It could hide there for years if someone wanted to secrete, but not destroy, it. Damon didn't strike her as a reader, although Claudia had collected books to take to the children's rooms.

On the way to the library she picked up an oil lamp. Once there, she set it on one of the long tables, struck a match, and held it to the wick until that, too, ignited. She shook out the match and replaced the lamp's chimney. Lamp and candle together cast enough light for her to see what she needed.

Rebecca scanned the rows of books. Well, the smaller modern ones would never hide a thick document between them. It would have to be in or between the big, old, leather-bound volumes, the classics. Rebecca pushed the library ladder, grateful that it slid almost without sound, climbed it, and started at one end of a shelf ten feet above the floor. She began riffling through yellowed pages of Shakespeare, then Dickens. Faint vanilla scents wafted from the foxed pages. She sniffed, reminded of the old law tomes Uncle Max collected.

After half an hour she began to doubt the wisdom of her method. Rebecca rubbed the back of her neck, then eyed a three volume set of Gibbon's *Decline and Fall of the Roman Empire*. She picked up volume I. Its heft felt different in her hand from previous books. Gold lettering on maroon leather announced the title. Spines on the three volumes showed first an intact pillar, erect and beautiful on volume I. Volume II revealed the pillar half disintegrated. Only a jagged stump of the ruined column remained on the spine of volume III.

"Interesting," Rebecca whispered to the shadowed walls. She held volume I. A premonition sent a frisson through her. Rebecca opened the heavy book to scan the pages and murmured, "Oh!" She held not a book, but a book box! Someone had hollowed out the center from the Gibbon.

A smaller book rested inside. Gold leaf on its flowered cover proclaimed *Diary* in a delicate script. Rebecca inhaled a slow, shaky breath.

The diary had a tarnished brass lock with a leather strap going across. Rebecca tried the latch, surprised when it opened. Whoever wrote the diary hadn't locked it, or had someone else used a tiny key? Did someone else already know about Rebecca's discovery? But no family member had mentioned a diary. Rebecca replaced volume I of *The Decline and Fall*. On a hunch, she took volume II off the shelf and made a similar discovery. Another book box and inside a second diary. Rebecca pulled down volume III, her hands shaking, and found a third. Three diaries. Rebecca removed them all, replaced the larger volumes, and carried the smaller books to the heavy oak table in the library's center.

The silence in the old lodge felt oppressive. Then she heard a sound. Light footsteps approached from the hallway. Rebecca turned down the lamp, blew out the candle, and stood unmoving. She mustn't be seen. She grabbed the diaries and backed into deep shadow cast by an ancient statue. She tried to breathe without sound. The footsteps never slowed. At an even pace their maker entered the room.

Amy seemed to float into the library. She didn't appear in a child's nightgown, but in a negligee of thin material and lace. Its train pooled on the floor. The girl seemed to be sleepwalking. Dressed this way Amy appeared older, a girl on the cusp of womanhood.

She stood in the room's center and extended her arms from her sides. The pale lashes of her closed eyes quivered. Amy spoke in a lower register than her usual soft voice. "Grandmother, I am here. I've kept my promise. Please, help me find the answers we need."

After a span of chilling silence, Amy lowered her arms. She glided out, an otherworldly vision in the negligee, her face free of the schoolgirl glasses, her eyes closed, their lids fluttering.

Rebecca waited several minutes after Amy had slipped from the library before relighting the candle.

She compressed her lips and hesitated with the awareness that in moments she'd be probing into a private, personal record. The Cale family might not appreciate her reading Lucinda's thoughts and dreams, perhaps even secrets. But a clue to Lucinda's treatment of them, and their reactions to that treatment, might be here, perhaps leading to a revelation about the will.

Rebecca stacked the three journals and carried them under one arm. She left the unlit lamp on the table, then raised the candle with its wavering flame to light her way. At the foot of the stairs, she paused and walked over to Lucinda's portrait, lifting the candle in its holder to illuminate that exquisite, intense face. "It's all right, Lucinda," she whispered. "I have to understand you and what you might have done with the will. I won't use your writings to cause any harm." Even as she said it, she realized she could make no unbreakable promise. So often the outcome of a will's probate wounded an unsuspecting heir.

She turned and, again avoiding creaky spots, moved without sound up the stairs. No one had stirred. She slipped into her room and eased the door closed behind her. The clock on the mantle showed 2:00 a.m. The tired family would sleep for hours she hoped, but, to be sure of privacy, she turned the key, locking her door. Setting the fat, still burning candle on the stand by her bed, she braced up her pillows and climbed in, pulling the comforter around her. She opened the first diary and began to read:

November 20, 1865, New York, New York

The heading simply read, Journal of Lucinda Bordeaux Cale

I, Lucinda Bordeaux Cale, begin this journal. I am twenty years of age. I have been a married woman for five blissful days. My husband is Garrett Cale. He is excessively beautiful and sinfully rich. Everyone envies me. I am also quite beautiful, although I doubt a woman can ever be excessively so, but am sinfully poor as well. Or that's how I would describe myself until I married Garrett. I have auburn hair, green eyes, and an eighteen-inch waist when in my corset. I'm vain, I suppose, pleased by such crucial lures as a slender waist.

My family has been marked by tragedy. Four years ago, a letter written by my brother Peter's friend and fellow soldier arrived with the terrible news of Peter's death. He died at Bull Run fighting for the Union. My parents might as well have died with him. Certainly the life we'd led received a fatal blow. Stricken with grief, they found themselves unable to govern their sorrow.

My mother has become a recluse. She resides in her room, in her bed, the curtains drawn. She refuses to see anyone except those of us who share her grief over dear Peter. Oh, my beloved brother, how could Providence take you from us?

Peter was everything . . . at the top of his class at Exeter and valedictorian of his graduating class at West Point. The blind horror of this war between North and South! My father took the loss in quite a different way from Mother. Always a bon vivant, he tried to escape Peter's death by drinking, finding comfort and pleasure in the company of much younger women, and gambling. He lived that reckless life for months, becoming wilder and foolish and more and more out of control. I strove to reason with him and with Mother. But their extremes destroyed us.

Everything turned terrible, a black time of mourning and loneliness for me. Even now I can hardly write the words. My father lost his fortune gambling. He lost everything. There was nothing left for him to wager. When his last shameless fortune hunter of a mistress grew bored and saw there would be no more parties and gifts, she abandoned him alone in a cheap hotel room.

They found him there hours later. Dead. He must have fallen against the mantle and struck his head in a drunken stupor. Mother's sister took us into her home in New York. Now Garrett and I have plans to send Mother to a place where she can be cared for while she lives out her distracted days grieving for Peter and her lost husband. They say Mrs. Lincoln is much the same in her widowhood.

Everything we had left of any worth has been sold and my family declared bankrupt. We who were once among the most sought-after in society . . . The handsome men who used to stand in line for one dance with me disappeared as if by magic, all but a special few. Dear Max Bryan remained faithful. But he has nothing. I have no doubt he will one day be a success, but that day is years in the future. In order to maintain Mother in the institution to which I intend to send her I need money.

To be honest, I need to have money for myself as well. I want fine things around me. I'm an artist, and I need to create and be surrounded by beauty. I want servants and fine food and travel.

I met my husband on the night Max proposed. I went to a ball to raise funds for the Union veterans. That might not have been considered the proper thing for me to do when just out of mourning for my father, but all the sorrow and dreariness of this past year threatened to smother me. I craved a breath of the heady air from our old, carefree life before the war. Before President Lincoln's assassination.

Max occupied himself writing his name over and over on my dance card when the most exciting man I'd ever seen snatched the card away. I thought Max would be furious, but when he looked up I saw from his smile that they were friends. Garrett Cale and Max Bryan went to school together before both served in the New York Regiment under Major General Daniel Sickles at Gettysburg.

The night we met, Garrett wore his officer's dress uniform. His blond hair fell over his forehead, and his blue-gray eyes held a readiness for mischief. So many men coming back looked dulled, as if war had burned the life out of them. Not Garrett. His flame never burned out. The war seemed only to have added to his zest for life, for excitement. He promised me adventure.

He swept me away, and we danced together all night. We danced most to Strauss waltzes, but "Aura Lee" became our song. My only regret is that in finding love's fulfillment we caused pain to a dear friend. But Max has taken it all with such kindness and generosity. He even served as Garrett's best man at our wedding.

I love Garrett with all my heart. He's like Peter, bright and capable with that passion for exploring all the world has to offer that I admired so in my brother. He makes love to me with wonderful passion. I am fortunate at last after that desert of poverty and sorrow.

We leave New York in May for St. Louis. Then we'll go on by steamboat to Fort Benton in Montana Territory and even further to the Cale family hunting lodge in northwest Montana, where Garrett's company is looking into mining possibilities. Garrett's family, his father and uncles, increased their already sizeable fortunes by manufacturing steamboats to carry freight in the fur, liquor, and gun trade, along with other items up and down the Missouri River through the still partially untamed West. The cargo includes government annuities the Indians depend on to live. The boats return loaded with gold from mining camps in the Wild West.

I must add that the Cale family also invested well and turned the recent war to their significant financial advantage. I don't care how they earned it; it's glorious to have money again.

Garrett says gold may have already been found near the family's Montana hunting lodge. That's one reason he wants to live there. He predicts that as rail travel extends west there will be commerce there. Towns will be built and with them the need for lumber, which is plentiful in that forested country.

Both Garrett and his father before him gained wide
reputations as hunters. Garrett seems determined to excel
in all he attempts. He calls me his lioness, and sometimes I
think he savored capturing my heart when he knew Max
wanted to so badly. That's something I won't think of. A
guilty conscience can only lead to unhappiness.

Anyway, once again I'm well-to-do, as they say. I have
new dresses for day and gowns for evening. My maid, an
Irish girl named Peggy Flynn, will come with us on our
journey.

The Cale lodge, Eagle Mountain, is high in the Rocky
Mountains. Garrett says the forests are deep and wild,
filled with waterfalls, lakes, and wildlife. He described how
he once shot a bear within fifty feet of the lodge. It will be
so different from my life here.

I'm a bit uneasy about such a change, and yet I want to
leave New York, the place of my family's sorrow and public
disgrace. Garrett says we have to wait until spring to begin
our journey. In the meantime, we've rented a rosewood
and brocatelle-decor suite at the Fifth Avenue Hotel. This
is the address to have if one is, like us, in society. It's all
red brick and white marble. Ulysses S. Grant even stayed
here.

It's even the first such hotel to have an elevator. I love
riding up and down to and from our apartment. I sink my
toes into our thick carpets and take relaxing bubbly soaks
in our private bathroom's claw-foot tub.

All the powerful and elite meet here at the Fifth Avenue.
Investors like Garrett even do their after-hours trading
down in one of the main rooms in the evenings. Sometimes
he works until very late in the night. And we've spent hours
planning purchases that include all we'll need in Montana

Territory. We'll go by train to St. Louis in early June, then start our journey upriver to Fort Benton.

Garrett anticipates life in the wilderness with an almost hectic eagerness. He speaks very little about the war, but I know some of his military experiences must've been bad. At least one friend died next to him at Gettysburg. He and Max both fought there. Garrett only makes curt references to that time though. He doesn't talk to me about his past but makes clear that my place in his future is of paramount importance.

I wish that he'd share his ghosts from the horrors of battle. He sometimes awakens in the night with a start. I know he's relived some terror in sleep that I know nothing of. Perhaps in time he will confide the details of his nightmares. Perhaps, I could help him bear his memories.

I'm glad to have Peggy. She's a survivor of the potato famine in Ireland, came over as a child, and knows the value of hard work.

Garrett promises I can set up a studio at the lodge and continue with my ceramics. What began as a school girl's interest progressed to a hobby and is now an obsession. I had one show here in New York, and the critics wrote encouraging reviews. I will work hard and experiment with form and glaze in those isolated forests. Until then I'll sketch my way into the Wild West. Paper is more easily carried on a steamboat than a kiln.

Rebecca stopped and sat up straight, staring at the diary. What a discovery this turned out to be. She swung her legs to the floor, pushed her feet into slippers, and pulled a shawl around her. She went to the window, staring out on the black spires of pines across the road. This young bride with her breathless excitement for the future had broken Max's heart, but Rebecca still found herself liking her.

CHAPTER SEVEN

If only she could reveal the journals to someone, share her discovery. What would Max think? Rebecca could tell no one here, at least not until she'd read them through. Not yet, and she still had much reading to do. She climbed back into bed and, spellbound, picked up Lucinda's story.

June 1, 1866
I write from a desk in our suite at the Southern Hotel in St. Louis. If it isn't the Fifth Avenue, it's close, both built in the elegant Italianate style of architecture. The main floor has pillars, and one side is lined by stores. We have a lovely corner suite on the sixth floor and can look down on busy streets filled with freight wagons, coaches, and swarms of people: Irish, freed slaves, men and women of every sort from everywhere.

We poise at the edge of civilization here. This city on the Mississippi River is the jumping off point for those of us going west. So far, I can't call our journey by train a hardship. Garrett arranged for us to have a private car all to ourselves, even when we had to change trains. My husband pampers me to where I feel almost guilty about how easy life is for us, knowing as I do the torments of poverty and privation.

Many of the men I've seen here and from train windows on the journey have returned from war missing limbs or are scarred in some other way. Their gaunt faces show the brutality of what they endured in battle or prison camps. We've also seen depots with waiting families crowded together to welcome home sons and husbands finally recovered enough from wounds or disease to travel. It's a fine, joyous, hectic time for some families. For others it is the beginning of sorrow that will haunt them to their last day and hour. Their adored son, brother, husband, or father will never come home. I know that agony.

I confided to Garrett that I feel guilty at times at our great happiness, but he laughed. He said he went through hell in the army. He reminded me that I lost my whole family in one way or another to the damned war. He said he has the power to protect us both from any new bitterness or melancholy. Then he closed the curtain where I'd stood gazing out the window and gathered me into his arms so that I soon forgot to think of the troops, their families, anything but our happiness.

June 2, 1866

Making our way to the landing to board proved challenging and noisy. Steamboats hissed like giant geese, and for the first time I smelled that lingering scent of wood burning, which, I know well now, is part of steamboat life. Teamsters shouted and cracked whips at their long-suffering horses and oxen. People pushed and shoved to wind through crowds, stacked boxes, and barrels to reach waiting boats, or to greet or say farewell to those just arriving or leaving.

What a thrill as we approached our floating palace, and I saw my name in bold letters on the side. Garrett hadn't told me but saved that as a surprise. *The Lucinda* is a new boat. This will be the maiden Missouri voyage for both of us. I feel a kinship with this vessel that is my namesake. I feel as though nothing can harm us on this best of all honeymoon journeys, although Peggy, not fond of being on the water, muttered that she hoped it wouldn't turn into a "honey-moan." I glared at her. Appropriately enough, our home on the water reminds me of a wedding cake, white and three tiered.

It was a joy to finally board. Captain Fry greeted us with courtly respect. It is wonderful to be in our comfortable staterooms on the second tier. We are well and truly on our way. We will journey on this, our own "Missouri steamer" for all 2,385 miles to Fort Benton. Captain Fry says that if we make good time with no accidents or other disasters, we'll have been on the Missouri sixty to seventy days in all from our departure until we reach Fort Benton.

The lower tier is for the boiler, freight, and less fortunate travelers who must sleep on deck. They would be the first to die if a boiler were to blow up as happened near Memphis to a boatload of released Union veterans. The poor souls had survived Confederate prison camps only to die in flames.

Up above us is the pilot house. *The Lucinda* is a stern wheeler, built to make good time on the Missouri. Even so, we depend on the water level staying high from spring snow melt, and on ready wood supplies along our route. Garrett reassures me with his joke that the Cale steamboats are so well-constructed they would keep running just on "light dew."

We are also told some of the natives, the Blackfeet in particular, are restive to the point of being a danger to "wood hawks," the men who cut the cords of wood our ship consumes to keep us moving. Garrett looked thoughtful at hearing that. Does he have some premonition of trouble? Should I?

Anyway, it's lovely to step out and sit in a deck chair, sketching the scenery and other boats as they go by. Although I prefer working in ceramics, I'm sketching with pencil and charcoal on the boat, another way to record our journey into the wilderness. This is no place for a potter's wheel.

We stroll on the decks for exercise. *The Lucinda* stops for the occasional handkerchief-waving person who signals, with desperate vigor, a wish to board.

Garrett and I talked last night as we lay in bed, the moon pouring creamy light over us through the door open to the deck. He spoke of his plans to organize hunts in the West. He's invited royalty from Sweden to be our first guests. Governors and senators and businessmen and their wives will also come to hunt and fish. Life will not be as isolated as I'd assumed it would be. Perhaps one never escapes society when people have wealth enough to pursue their own pleasures whenever they like and wherever they may lead.

Garrett says I must learn to shoot and hunt. I tried to discourage him from that idea. I've known enough of death and its sorrows. Guns claimed Peter's life. If I never saw a gun again I would be pleased. I've tried to explain my feelings, but Garrett doesn't acknowledge what I say. He doesn't even seem to hear me. I wonder if we will have our first quarrel over the matter.

He remains implacable.

This is new behavior from Garrett. I felt a flash of uneasiness. What else do I not know about my new husband? I pushed this silly concern away. Like any man, my Garrett has bad days along with the good ones. He loves me, and he has wealth enough to keep me safe. That is all that matters.

June 4, 1866

Something preys on my mind. We left the Mississippi River to join the Missouri just a few miles north of St. Louis. A strange thing—we saw an alligator at least ten feet long just before we turned to our new river highway. What a send off by the South! Those indifferent reptilian eyes suggested an adventurous, perhaps dangerous, beginning for a bride! Silly, but it sent a chill through me.

But I push such fear away. I, who love nothing better than to immerse my hands into and work with clay, never tire of looking at the colors of the river banks. The water's edge is fringed with long grass and bright yellow, white, red, and blue, even purple, flowers, the light ever shifting on water that at times appears to be the consistency of mud. The earth rises, sometimes strewn with rocks or with hard cliffs on both banks, to contain this river. I love the call of raptors and the deep song of croaking frogs. We catch occasional glimpses of wildlife such as deer. The sky at night is blue-black patterned with stars so bright they seem to pulse, the constellations emerging like white bouquets for the gods. This is such a glorious beginning to our married life.

Garrett, lacking the satisfaction I derive from being occupied with my drawing, is sometimes restless. He's taken to sleeping late into the afternoons. Then, after dinner, which we take at the captain's table, he joins other men below to drink and play cards far into the night.

I find his late hours with cards, liquor, and gambling unsettling, but I shouldn't complain. Memories of my father's behavior are with me too often. Garrett continues so kind to me, and I don't want him to be bored. I fear he is, though, as in his tedium he's taken to calling this wide, muddy river "the Misery."

Pausing, Rebecca lifted her eyes and considered. Had Lucinda married a man like her father? A man ruined by his own weaknesses for cards and liquor? Did women tend to seek out husbands similar to their male parents? Ought she be wary of anything that hinted at depression in any man who courted her? She gave a little *hmmpph* of recognition. Why did these diaries provoke thoughts about her own future? Were Lucinda's diaries to be a cautionary tale? Should she learn from them?

She'd once heard that men chose women similar to their own mothers. Bretton seemed to have only dislike for Lucinda. And yet he'd come back for her funeral. Had he come back for answers that might be found in Lucinda's journals about the missing will? Did he or anyone else even know about the journals? Their latches had been unlocked after all. She rubbed her temples for a moment, then moved the candle closer and continued reading.

June 14, 1866

We stopped for a day in Kansas City. Known as "Bleeding Kansas" since the years of John Brown and the conflict over whether to accept or abolish slavery, the state will take some time to recover from violence that tore it apart even before the war. But recover it will, according to Garrett.

We disembarked to shop while *The Lucinda* took on additional provisions. Peggy and I went into the few stores, rough and with limited inventory compared to what we're used to, but we are on a western adventure. I bought the board game checkers for us to play during the long hours on the boat when I can't sketch any longer because of the waning light. And when Garrett is otherwise occupied.

What a mix of humanity we saw: whites, including veterans from both sides, freed Negroes, aloof Arapaho Indians still alone somehow even in the crowds, and boyish cowboys. Yet, even among this colorful throng I saw the marks of poverty and abject need. Many wore clothes that were little more than rags. I find it odd that my beautiful husband has no compassion for the sufferings of poor fellow humans. He says they need to learn the value of hard work. How would hard work have helped me? Beauty and charm and my husband's own competitive nature won me my present life.

My fingers twitched, I so wanted to start sketching right in the middle of the crowded street. Garrett, more interested in commerce and profits, says there's some talk of making this a location for stockyards where beef will be sold and slaughtered. How ugly.

I felt happy to return to *The Lucinda*. Our rooms have become our snug home on the great Missouri.

We proceed now along the Nebraska-Iowa border. The days are hot, and we seem to glide in a dream world at times, floating past willows, cottonwood, and alder clumps that shimmer in the blaze of midday sun. I'm grateful that *The Lucinda* moves in the wide river where the breeze across water gives us occasional relief from the heat.

We must avoid sawyers, those lovely trees that bow down into the water from the bank, looking so peaceful and cool, but with the deadly ability to put holes in passing boats. The captain has to be alert to watch for both sawyers and snags. The latter are dead trees that lurk just under the water at times so their unseen branches can claw and tear into *The Lucinda*.

We feel more isolated. The Indians here in the eastern

part of Nebraska are mostly the Omaha. Lakota Sioux also have a presence. Most are on reservations but may still be seen here and there. We watch for them on the ridges and escarpments. We listen to the boom of prairie chickens in the grasslands near the water and spend much time trying to distinguish their sounds from those of unseen savage drums. I sense a growing, unspoken tension among passengers and crew as we continue northwest toward Dakota Territory.

Our steamboat seems to devour wood. We stop often as cottonwood, the most common fuel to be found, burns hot and fast. We consume forty or fifty cords of wood a day. Garrett told me a cord is a stack four feet by four feet by eight feet. In high winds, Captain Fry pulls us over rather than fight a headwind that would mean our boat would have to practically inhale enough wood to power us so we could keep going.

July 4, 1866

During the day, we move past long, pale, feathered grasses, wild roses, yellow blossoms on shrubby plants called cinquefoil, and brown-eyed Susans. As evening brings relief from the sun's glare, deer come to the water to drink, so tranquil in appearance in the day's final glow. Then they turn wary as they lift their heads to watch us continue past.

I've also seen wolves, big, watchful, intimidating. Once a herd of shaggy, proud, wild horses ran along a ridge, tossing their heads, manes flowing like flags as though challenging us to race them in a playful contest they would surely win.

The sunsets and sunrises are almost too much grandeur to bear. Dawn spreads before us as if the day is being raised by wildfire. The sunsets call to us in shades of red, pink, and orange, scored by ribbons of azure and violet fading to blue, then to star-encrusted black. The prairie seems so peaceful from the boat. Although I do wish for more attention from Garrett, part of me wants to reside on *The Lucinda* forever . . . on this wide, muddy river as the solitary, anonymous traveler. A woman of mystery.

Setting the diary aside for a moment, Rebecca sighed. Lucinda seemed so young in her belief that Garrett would in time be more attentive. Yet the young newlywed also wanted to be her own person, an artist in love with the adventure spreading out before her. But was there something insidious creeping into that marriage? Would there have been such a thing in her own life had Rebecca's former love, the class-ridden European aristocrat, had the courage to marry her? She picked up the diary and continued.

July 9, 1866

Finally weary of drinking through the nights and sleeping all day, Garrett and a few others have taken to leaving our boat at landings where the wood choppers disembark to do their hard labor. The former carousers hunt prairie chickens, rabbit, whatever they can, even the occasional wild turkeys. They also provide us with welcome venison, and sometimes fish.

There's another, ominous, reason my husband takes his gun and sometimes stays near the "wood hawks." We've had word of Sioux attacks on the Missouri's banks. It's dangerous work these choppers do, exposed as they are while they wield their axes and hatchets. Besides hunting, Garrett and others stand guard, watching for danger while the wood hawks make our progress possible by providing fuel. I'm proud of my husband and relieved that he's found a brave and useful purpose as we proceed toward Fort Benton.

August 1, 1866

We've reached a milestone on our journey, Fort Union trading post. As such installations go in the West, it's a longstanding fort with walls, watchtowers, and a great main building along with officers' quarters and barracks. John Jacob Astor's fur company did business here.

I gripped my parasol as we disembarked in relentless prairie winds. This is no place of gentle zephyrs. The grass is sun-sered and browned by the merciless dry heat of midsummer, but sage, a lovely gray-green, softens the slopes, hollows, and swales below the buttes. Willows sway and show us the silver undersides of their leaves, a reminder of the strength of survivors on the plains.

Fort Union is well maintained. Tribes like the Crow and Blackfeet, the Hidatsa and Lakota still trade here, bringing buffalo robes and other furs. We, in turn, have unloaded part of our cargo: blankets, knives, mirrors, calico, beaver traps, cookware. And whiskey. Always whiskey.

We dined with the officers, so good to visit with new people, and they so admiring and chivalrous. Garrett's military experiences show more on this long journey than in New York. He sometimes gives me orders as if I were a lowly private under his imperious command. I remind him, trying to keep my tone light, that I am his wife, not a subordinate soldier. He apologizes, but it seems the farther away from civilization we proceed the harder it is for Garrett to be civil. Something in his temperament has begun to smolder.

I managed to push anxious thoughts aside as we joined the others in the evening's gaiety.

I wore a teal, silk evening gown that set off my eyes, and I think the officers' attentions made Garrett see me anew. He became aware again that he has a wife other men admire.

As Garrett and I strolled outside together after dining, a strange thing happened. A woman with a scarred face, wearing only her nightdress and robe, her feet bare, her nightcap askew, rushed toward us as though being pursued. "Help me," she begged. "They're here. They'll kill us all."

A large man with an untrimmed beard ran from the building that we later learned was the Fort's infirmary. He grabbed her, turning her so that he hid her disfigured face against his chest. I couldn't tell for certain if he attempted to protect her or held her so as to keep us from seeing her scars.

"It's all right, Sadie," he said with a sort of rough desperation. "Come back inside now. These are good people." He picked her up and rushed back to the door. She began to shriek again before he had her inside the building.

An officer, probably the fort doctor, stepped out of the building and approached us.

"The prairie is a hard place for women. Even if the Indians leave them alone, some settlers see danger everywhere. That couple lost their little girl. She wandered from home. The wife, who'd been too long alone and afraid, took it in her head the child had been captured by Indians. Then she heard screams. A wolf had the girl in its jaws.

"The woman fought it off. Now she's insane, and her daughter is dead. We need to send the poor soul back East, but it will be hard for her husband to do that and maintain his farm. I believe one of her sisters is making the long journey to fetch her back to Vermont before winter."

I'm ashamed to admit I felt relieved to hear a solution had been found that didn't involve us. Her terror snapped at my own nerves. Her confusion threatened me. A woman alone in this vast prairie would be so vulnerable.

Sometimes I feel a growing sense that I, too, am alone, not the mysterious solitary beauty, but a woman in some sort of danger. It sneaks up on me like a stealthy wolf when Garrett spends too much money and time with his drinking and gambling. The more he does it, the stronger my insecurity is. When I spoke to Garrett about this he just laughed. He said we would have all the time in the world to be together at Eagle Mountain. I hope it's true.

Rebecca rose to change her candle to one of the room's oil lamps, thinking of the travelers' long and hazardous journey. For her, the West was a place of opportunity, but really little personal danger. Lucinda had seen it in the truly wild days of early settlement. But the young bride's growing sense of unease seemed to be caused more by changes in her new husband's behavior than by natives, other humans, wild animals, or the currents of the great river.

CHAPTER EIGHT

August 7, 1866

The Missouri is lower and wood more scarce. We've spotted Indians on the bluffs above us, those cliffs so drenched in colors that the great artist Turner would want to paint them, I think. I prepared to sketch the Indians, but Garrett ordered me to come inside from the deck. At night we hear wolves howling their harmonious compositions on the bluffs. But are they really wolves? Or are they humans who would have us dead? This country shifts until we don't know what is real. Let me not become like the madwoman at Fort Union.

August 12, 1866

Trouble here in the Missouri breaks. Yesterday the wood hawks worked thirteen hours, cutting wood from 6:00 a.m. until 7:00 p.m. Garrett and a few others stood guard, as there are rumors of hostile Blackfeet in the area. Today we became stuck on a sand bar. The men on board strained at ropes but could not budge *The Lucinda.* Captain Fry, looking grim, ordered that every stick of wood from yesterday's work had to be thrown off on the sand bar. Then, lighter, we finally moved, but tomorrow will have to begin the work of chopping and loading all over again. We are discouraged and weary.

August 17, 1866

A figure on a rocky outcropping, perhaps more than one, fired down at us today. Captain Fry said it probably was Blackfeet, but, with the light behind the snipers, we couldn't be sure. Thank God the silhouetted figures and their bullets hurt no one.

August 21, 1866

Fort Benton tomorrow. Unlike Garrett and Peggy, I'll leave *The Lucinda* with regret. I felt safe on our boat despite the hazards from natives and nature. The cliffs with their ever-changing light gave me idea after idea for my art; both sketches and ceramics will pour from my hands once we're settled. I didn't feel bored even if Garrett did neglect me. I felt peaceful and finally free of the scandals and sorrows of my family's past.

Life is opening onto a big, wide, panoramic stage. So far, I haven't missed New York society. I face the future armed with Garrett Cale's name and fortune. I only wish the memory of the madwoman at Fort Union didn't haunt me so. God forbid that I lose my very self as she has in this wild country. Or turn into someone I wouldn't choose to be. I don't want to wind up acting the fool on this great prairie theater, nor like a character in a Greek or Shakespearean tragedy.

August 22, 1866

Well, we most certainly have arrived in the Wild West. We anchored at the Fort Benton levee. Blackfeet in larger numbers than I've seen, gamblers, mountain men with furs for trade, and the saloons outnumber the stores.

I'm writing in a great hurry as we'll soon be on land with no return to *The Lucinda*.

Garrett stayed with me all night. He reminded me of a boy, so excited to be disembarking. I feel a bit sad that this part of the journey has ended, or perhaps it's that I'm a little frightened of the long overland journey ahead. It feels as though we'll be much more exposed and vulnerable than we've been on *The Lucinda*. Garrett has returned to his best manners, and I remind myself of my good luck to have such a husband.

Garrett says as of this year travelers call the Missouri the Golden Highway. "We'll make a fortune from the sale of our freight, and even more from the gold and buffalo hides *The Lucinda* will carry back to St. Louis. I believe we'll make seventy thousand dollars or more," he said.

We made love, giddy with our progress thus far and the excitement of starting the second stage of our journey.

Peggy is ecstatic just to soon be off *The Lucinda*. If anything she found the journey more tedious than Garrett did. She flirted with the boatmen and wood hawks just to pass the time, I think. I ignore this for the time being. I do realize that seeing to our clothes and keeping our quarters presentable or listening to me read or playing hours of checkers must have grown tiresome. I thank God for my faithful art . . . always there to intrigue and engage me.

The clock in Rebecca's room read 4:00 a.m. Time had flown. She determined to keep reading even if it meant a sleepless night. This was a woman who'd undertaken even more challenging journeys than her own when Uncle Max sent her, chaperoned of course, to Switzerland.

August 23, 1866
Remembering the officers at Fort Union, I dressed to draw admiration in Fort Benton. I wore a blue-and-cream-striped linen gauze day dress instead of the simple cotton

gowns I'd worn on *The Lucinda.* This would remind my
darling Garrett that other men find me beautiful here as
they do everywhere I go. He took the hint and showed me
off with the pride he'd show if a prize horse walked at his
side. I don't like that my husband at times treats me as a
possession. I look forward to being a person of standing,
the mistress of the manor at Eagle Mountain. Garrett and
I will return to our unstrained affection and passion once
we're in our permanent home.

We disembarked from *The Lucinda* and made our way
amidst mining equipment, barrels, and innumerable boxes
at the levee. And men. Fort Benton is small and rough but
has the strain of excitement of throngs of men heading to
the goldfields, places like Virginia City and Last Chance
Gulch, Bannock, and points further northwest where we
are bound. Just the names of these places shimmer with
the promise of riches, or at the very least adventures, to
come.

There is, of course, a fort, constructed of sod and
timber, to give this place its name. All in all, this is a settlement strung out along the Missouri, facing the high cliff-
like bluffs across the great river. A man named I. G. Baker
deals here in furs and trade goods. Near his is the T. C.
Power store, still under construction, and, further on down,
the old North Western Fur building.

We went past these as we rode to the log hotel owned by
a character named Jacob Schmidt. It's really three businesses—a hotel, a restaurant, and a butcher shop. We
ventured forth to the restaurant once we'd freshened up in
our rustic little rooms. It was as full as it could be with
hungry, unkempt men eating like starved predators, but no
women! Peggy and I retreated, and Garrett arranged for
dinner to be sent to our rooms. It took a long time, but the

steaks, bread, and greens were cooked well. There was even apple butter for the bread.

After awhile we heard a commotion from the directions of the diners. Jacob Schmidt's shouts arose amid the unmistakable sound of breaking dishes. Garrett, who had opted to eat in the restaurant, came back gasping with laughter. When he caught his breath, he reported that Jacob had lost his temper when a hungry miner tugged at the overwhelmed proprietor's coattails as he attempted to serve his other impatient customers.

Peggy joined in his laughter. I summoned up a smile, but the image of men wolfing down food, our innkeeper shattering his own china, and our rough little rooms threatened to pull me down. I missed our little world of *The Lucinda*.

September 1, 1866

We've departed Fort Benton. We'll travel awhile with a large wagon train. The other wagons belong to men headed to the gold mines of Fort Shaw, or elsewhere. We will split off to be on our own then. For now, all of us are moving out together in fear of an attack by Blackfeet should we travel in isolation.

September 2, 1866

Fear and excitement vie to fill me to my brim. I ride in the Concord with Peggy and the young man, little more than a shy, blushing boy, hired to drive us, care for the horses, and help with other stock. But we also have two covered wagons, one with a bed for Peggy and me, along with all the things I packed for life at Eagle Mountain. The other is full of provisions to sustain us on the Mullan Road and beyond.

The provisions are better than many have in the wagons of families or single men who make their way in the train behind us. We have cheese, coffee, tea, flour, salt, sugar, vinegar, molasses, dried apricots, apples, prunes, parsnips, potatoes, rice, beans, bacon, and jerky. A milk cow is tethered behind the wagon. Cans of her milk bump along, tied at the wagon's sides. By evening the continuous jolting gives us balls of sweet butter floating in buttermilk. Our cook also has use of a Dutch oven and a sheet-iron stove with a reflector on each side. Garrett thought of everything.

Our cook, an old Frenchman who once canoed and trapped for furs in Canada, doesn't say much but certainly seems to know what he's about. Garrett will hunt and keep Cook supplied with prairie hens, ducks, venison, antelope, and what else, I'm not sure. The men will fish when we make camp beside streams at night.

The wagons are immense when you add on the bovines that pull them. The oxen are double yoked, four pair to a wagon. Their pace is ponderous, slow but steady. We also have pack mules and, of course, the four horses that pull the coach. What dust they raise! I've learned that our pace is determined by the slowest animal. This distinction goes to our stoic oxen. We're so fortunate to be at the head of the wagon train.

The sky is so vast here, varying from a pale blue, almost white, to a bright royal blue. The light is at all times of day an artist's dream. It makes me long for paints or watercolors rather than my charcoal or pencil.

Sunrises promise clear days that by midday become so bright we have to squint. At the close of such long days brilliant orange to red to violet to indigo sunsets cast down from the hills across the panoramic green, buff, and ochre prairies. I must remember the colors for my ceramics.

I sketch by lamplight in the evenings, as the road we travel during the day is often too rough for an artist's sketching. And I get out to walk on the rough earth, which clacks with grasshoppers, Peggy sometimes marches along with me, enjoying the breeze until heat sends us both back to our covered coach. She's also afraid of snakes. I believe she's seen life's dangers more often than I. We join in expressing our amazement at the vast panorama of prairies, hills, and distant mountains.

September 7, 1866
We travel on the Mullan Road, more rightly said to be the Military Road, but most call it by the name of the engineer who, with his expedition, brought it into being. We'll go first to Fort Shaw, near the great falls discovered by Lewis and Clark. If we survive that initial leg of the journey and its dangers from possible Indian attacks or violent robbers, we turn south-southwest toward the place first known as Last Chance Gulch, now as Helena, a booming mining town that's also a point for trading supplies and gold to take to Fort Benton and our steamboats. Garrett says those bandits we fear are often renegade Confederate soldiers, skilled in shooting and worse.

Garrett hired five men at Fort Benton to ride alongside us as armed protectors all the way to Eagle Mountain, along with Louis the cook and our young driver and packer. The protectors are hard men. I've never seen even one of them smile. None have spoken to me or Peggy. I'm accustomed to men flitting like moths to my flame, so this indifferent behavior unsettles me.

I admit it. Male lack of interest is new, and it stings my vanity. Did the war burn away any ability they once had to appreciate womanly charms? Did it leave their emotions hard as metal? Cold as ashes? Peggy declares herself insulted by their unconcern for her flirtatious approaches. She protested today, "How can they protect me if they can't see me?"

Garrett made sure when he hired them that all five fought for the Union. I'm wary of them even as they fascinate me. In the circles I frequented back home I seldom conversed with or met any lower ranking enlisted men. Plain to see, these hard souls who ride with us withstood merciless use in horror-filled battles.

I study them when I suppose they aren't looking but suspect they note my artless spying. They're ever alert. Their eyes must miss nothing.

When one of them does flick a rare glance at me, sadness rests in his bleary eyes. Each carries a brace of revolvers and long knives in their boots as well as his own rifle. Although their clothes are shabby and often carry several days' worth of dust, they keep their weapons spotless and shining from well-oiled care.

Thoughts of my brother's death in the horrors of battle haunt me like Mr. Poe's raven haunted him. I think my grief will never leave me. Nevermore. Was it possible that cheerful Peter would have returned volatile as Garrett, or dour as these bitter men, their faces lined before their time? Would my own brother have been a stranger to me after being seared in the heat of bloody conflicts? I pray not. I hope Peter is with God and at peace.

My future is bound to my husband's regardless of all else. I hope our lives will be secure and filled with love and happiness once we reach Eagle Mountain. I'm growing used to this vast open country, to the hawks and golden eagles that soar overhead, to the song of the meadowlarks, to the coyotes yapping at night. What will the world of shaded forests and steep mountain peaks be like for me? I've been a city mouse and now am adventuring in the increasingly wild West.

To my surprise I like it. We all just bring ourselves, and no one really cares what we do or what befell us in the East. I've discovered that New York society can be abandoned and almost forgotten in this boundless land. My relief is tangible.

A memory returned to Rebecca of the effect learning about her father's suicide had on her European fiancé's aristocratic parents. "Don't be so sure, Lucinda," she whispered. "Don't be so sure you're leaving your past behind." She returned to the diary.

September 8, 1866

Garrett pushes his men. He's determined that we must arrive at Eagle Mountain as soon as we can. Our original plan had been to reach our home before the snows and ice of winter. Because of delays on the river, we may have to deal with wintry traveling. If he sees a man appearing to waste time he upbraids him in a humiliating way. The veterans take any of Garrett's loud rebukes with no change in expression. They know and carry out their duties with cool independence.

Garrett disappoints me in one respect. He indulges in what I can only term bullying. This side of his nature disturbs me almost more than the drinking and gambling I put up with on our passage from St. Louis. I've committed to share my life with a man who fails over and over to control his temper. What other ugliness hides in Garrett's heart? I pray this being quick to anger is a passing phase due to relentless heat, dust, and responsibilities that drain his energy and leave him with bad headaches. Do I worry more than I should? I don't know. I don't know what lies ahead as we journey toward our remote home.

September 12, 1866

Yesterday evening, Jeremiah, one of our hard-edged veterans, took a break from preparing camp to draw on his pipe, straightening his back while gazing about at the countryside, the river, and mountains. The day had been blistering, and we were all dealing with discomfort and frayed nerves.

Jeremiah is a short, thickset man whose face belies the fact that he's still in his twenties. He has dark-brown eyes and, unlike some of the others, keeps himself clean-shaven. He has a way of glaring at nothing, which unnerves me when he turns his empty stare in my direction. I don't know what Jeremiah stood pondering when a blustering Garrett took a stride and stopped in front of the man, inches from his face, and barked orders that he see to his work at once.

Jeremiah took a step back and looked down at his scuffed boots for a moment as if to reorganize his thoughts. Then he scowled with murderous eyes up into Garrett's face. "If you ain't happy you pay me off right now, or I believe I will kill you right now. Your choice."

He said the words bold as brass, his hand hovering over his revolver. A chill overcame me as I watched that steady hand with its stubby fingers. Jeremiah had turned from our hired protector into a murderous enemy.

Garrett amazed me. He stepped back. His eyes shifted away from Jeremiah's. "That's not what I meant. I want you to stay on."

I couldn't move. My husband's life hung in the balance.

Then the oldest guard, Ben Smallwood, a tall man with

long, black hair who limps from being shot at Fredericks-burg, stepped between the two. He spoke in measured tones to Jeremiah, who turned his back on Garrett and walked away with no further words. I pretended not to have seen the effect of Jeremiah's threat on Garrett.

Mr. Smallwood, stroking his whiskers as he spoke, talked for some minutes with my husband. I don't know what they said, but Garrett hasn't hectored the men since. He leaves former Sergeant Smallwood to deal with them most of the time. Like most bullies, Garrett only puffs up and gives threatening orders to those he perceives as weak. I pray he'll become more steady and thoughtful when the hardships of Mullan Road are behind us.

To my surprise, I've noticed that one or the other of our five guards tends to hover nearby when Garrett turns angry and difficult. Can it be that these severe men are watchful for my safety? Surely, Garrett would never harm me. I am his beloved wife.

CHAPTER NINE

September 14, 1866

We are heading toward the boomtown of Helena, built up around Last Chance Gulch. It's the most recent gold mining camp. Four men discovered gold in the creek there last year. The road becomes more used by wagons, horses, and mules and is even dustier as we near our destination. There is a growing, contagious sense of urgency . . . of excitement.

Glassing the hills above our road, Sergeant Smallwood spotted rough looking men riding parallel to us. I understand now Garrett's wisdom in hiring extra guards. Two of the five ride close to the coach, cradling their rifles. The rest ride alongside the wagons.

Occasionally one of our veterans stopped and studied our unwelcome watchers. Inevitably our man spit tobacco. Apparently that showed his contempt to the distant riders. Our veterans showed no fear but were watchful. Peggy and I did not alight as we've done other days, to walk when the jolting of the coach grows too tiresome.

September 15, 1866

The possible highwaymen took off out of our sight, perhaps to find more vulnerable prey.

September 16, 1866

Garrett cursed in what I saw as disgust and justifiable wrath when we came upon the ruin of a lone coach that had been attacked by robbers, probably those we saw scouting the road from above days earlier. They'd apparently given up on us because of our guards and ridden hard to catch the more vulnerable lone coach miles ahead of us.

What we found made Peggy cry, "Mary, Mother of God, and all the saints preserve us."

We both retched and held handkerchiefs to our faces. The prairie wind carried an awful stench of decay from bodies on the ground near the ruined coach. Those aboard, all men, appeared to have fought with courage, shooting at their pursuers from the windows, but now the unfortunate travelers and the driver's remains lay bloated in the sun. I'd seen pictures taken by the photographer Bailey of the dead, twisted and grotesque like these poor men, on battlefields such as Antietam and Gettysburg.

Sergeant Smallwood remarked that the victims might have made it had they been able to get out of the coach, but the attackers surrounded them and shot through its back. They killed them, then dragged their bodies onto the dry prairie grass, now stained the dark red-brown of the poor victims' blood. So much blood soaked into the dry earth. How little these strangers' lives meant to the highwaymen. Life, their own or that of another, means nothing to some men after they've lost everything.

The corpses had stiffened, all in the positions their murderers dropped them in, on their backs, probably to make it easier for the killers to go through the pockets of their clothes that were now torn as their mortal remains swelled and stiffened. Ravens flew off as Garrett and our men approached the bodies, waving their arms and shouting to make them go. The black scavengers had been making a repulsive meal of the dead.

Of course, the poor victims had been stripped of their watches and wallets, and their bags and trunks left opened. All that wasn't valuable lay strewn on the ground or had blown away.

One of the robbers also lay dead, killed by a well-aimed shot by one of the four passengers. The remaining murderers deserted their comrade's remains with no formalities such as burial. What rogues would do such horrible deeds? The recent war must have left many of such violent, displaced men, predatory as hungry wolves, to roam the west. For the first time, I felt afraid. I began to shake and had to grip my elbows tight to try to control my reaction. I must be strong. This is no place for the weak. In the end, here, I must look to myself in a sort of primitive way that didn't arise in the snubs and gossip of the East. This world threatens life itself, not just reputations.

The prairie wind whipped over the victims' bodies. Garrett, his jaw clenched, joined the men as they took shovels and began to dig graves. I ventured close enough to ask if anyone had found anything that would help us learn the deceaseds' names at least. Nothing remained in their wallets or bags to identify them. I wondered about the lost dreams held by these dead who would soon lie under prairie sod. Were they leaving disappointing pasts? Did they look forward to the future?

Garrett said he would report the crime to the authorities in Helena. He added, though, that it seemed unlikely the murderers, with such a head start, would be hunted down and brought to justice.

It took some hours for our men and those in wagons

coming along behind to dig the graves and say the 23rd Psalm for these men. The dead outlaw lay in a shallower grave some distance from the passengers he murdered.

As our parties saw to the dead, another wagon went around us, further infuriating Garrett. We camped just a bit beyond where we discovered the dead. The mourning doves sounded sadder than ever as the sun gave way to a night sky brilliant with stars. I thought of Longfellow calling them "the forget-me-nots of the night." Who would remember the men we'd buried? I would never forget what befell them.

Garrett and I walked away from the circle of our campfire, leaving Peggy to trade views of the day with our cook. Garrett calmed in the still night air. He made an effort to comfort and reassure me. "It won't be like any of this at Eagle Mountain," he said. "It's peaceful there. Cool and quiet and beautiful. We'll have the harmonies of wolves rather than this endless yipping of coyotes."

I shivered and didn't tell him that such reference to howling wolves did not create the soothing effect on me that he intended.

Sept. 21, 1866

We've arrived in Helena at last. A rough but most lively place! Near where gold filled the stream of Last Chance Gulch, now runs the wide, unpaved Main Street. Mules, freight wagons, and bullwhackers crowd it in the hundreds if not thousands. The noise is of men agitated by the promise of wealth via gold or commerce. Oxen and mules carry freight to and from Fort Benton and the mining camps along the way to where we find ourselves.

Helena has the rudiments of civilization. The structures are squat log cabins or frame buildings. There are a few homes. I've seen both respectable and fallen women in the stores. As for Peggy and me, we checked into a rustic hotel. Garrett and I will share a room at last, and Peggy has hers across the hall, which suits her. We've gotten on fairly well but both of us are ready to be apart by at least the width of a hallway.

Before anything else, Peggy and I took all our clothes except those we wear (and our finer things, packed well and deep in our trunks until we can hang them in the armoires at Eagle Mountain) to a Chinese laundry down the street. I so look forward to clean, pressed garments. We also took baths and washed our hair.

Garrett and I dined at a steak house next to our hotel. I don't know what Garrett paid to get us in, but it must have been a great deal. We had a table by the window and watched the endless parade of wagons and colorful characters standing, striding, or just milling about outside.

Later, Garrett and I made love, only a little distracted by continuous shouts, cries, and laughter from Main Street below. We slept for awhile in each other's arms.

We awoke to a knock on the door. A hotel maid informed us that our laundry had been delivered to the front desk. Once she'd brought the clothes to our room, I exclaimed in delight at how clean they smelled.

Afterwards, Garrett dressed in his pressed frock coat and the rest and excused himself to find a card game. I felt too tired and pleased to be in a real room to worry. Perhaps a game and some whiskey would keep him in a cheerful frame of mind. I locked the door behind him before falling into a deep sleep. When I woke at dawn, he'd slipped in with his key and lay, still dressed, beside me.

I rose and sketched him lying rumpled as he was. I felt tempted to title the portrait "The Drunkard," but thought

better of it. He looked so handsome even as he slept off
the effects of his night's debauchery. I stilled my pencil
and simply rested my eyes on him.

Sept. 28, 1866
We've been in Helena for a week now, stocking up on supplies, mending and strengthening our wagons and coach,
and attending to all else required for the next part of our
journey. Garrett gave our veterans a bonus to stay on with
us, as they were becoming restive. He told them in detail
about the gold fields in British Columbia. They've decided
to stick with us to Eagle Mountain, then ride on north to
make their fortunes.

Although Helena is a noisy place, it has a powerful
energy about it. Again, this great Western adventure shows
me a world where class or backgrounds don't matter much
at all. Garrett says that will change. He's predicting a great
future for Helena. Indeed, crews are building more frame
stores and businesses along both sides of Main Street.
We've gotten almost used to how noisy it is from shouts of
men and cracking of whips over oxen. How smelly and
also how colorful its denizens and visitors are . . . outland-
ish as any onlooker could desire.

I love to sit at the window and sketch the natives,
prospectors, businessmen, and women of every moral type
who walk beneath me. Peggy loves to be sent on errands
just to be out in the midst of it all. I hope she doesn't
decide to stay. I've grown used to her wry Irish observations. And she's a patient model when I need a figure to
enliven my sketches of the endless landscape we'll soon
travel into once more.

Oct. 1, 1866

Today, we left on the last leg of our journey, still traveling the hard way known as Mullan Road. We returned to its bumpy surface but not to so much heat. Only the afternoons have any heat in them now. The nights are cold, the mornings and evenings increasingly chilly. Tomorrow we climb to the Continental Divide.

The prairie hills are sprinkled with ponderosa pine and cottonwoods by the burbling creeks, and the rest is the tawny grass of autumn. Hawks fly over us—red-tailed, and other birds I don't know yet. The songbirds have deserted us.

I'm glad to be away again, as Garrett has been sliding back into too much of his old ways. He's happy to be on horseback in the open now. He's maintaining good relations with Ben Smallwood. The men are happy to be on the move, I think. Our coach driver sings to himself in a soft voice, gentle songs like "Sweet Lorena."

Oct. 7, 1866

The pass proved to be slow going on the approach, but amazing when we finally paused to let the animals and ourselves rest. I saw the mountains, range after range to be seen from the summit—an artist's dream. I'm not as anxious about our survival as I was. How many women have the opportunity to see the frontier as it is now? How many artists will have the chance to benefit from its inspiration? It truly is God's country.

Oct. 22, 1866

We've arrived at Missoula Mills, just a few miles east of the trading settlement once called Hellgate. Garrett knows the two founders, Frank Worden and Captain Christopher

Higgins. Although they started their business endeavors with a trading post, they've set up a two-story store, used as mercantile, courthouse, dance hall, and Masonic Hall—whatever the day's demands require.

They've also built a working saw mill, soon to be joined by a grist mill. Lumber and flour are perhaps the two most indispensable things here for settlers' survival. Most important, Missoula Mills has the civilized touch of the Cottage Hotel, a small, squat, but cozy inn. I enjoyed the first full hot bath since we left Helena. Ah, the luxury.

Garrett and I have our privacy while Peggy shares a downstairs room with a hotel maid. She's learning all the local gossip and passes it on to me. We humans are ever curious. Garrett is more intrigued with the settlement's history and future.

Oct. 28, 1866

I've seen and recorded in my sketches history being made where gold waits for the adventurous to wrest it from earth and rock to send downriver to St. Louis. This adds to the Cale fortunes as our boats carry gold to civilization.

Garrett is proud and satisfied. He so enjoys visiting with Captain Higgins and Mr. Worden about their plans for the future of this Missoula. Garrett is a remarkable man, and I love him, but I wish for safe passage from here. It snowed for the past few days. Winter crept up on us, and we still have long, hard miles to go.

I've discovered that I hate oxen. They are slow beasts and would be of no use if we had to flee from trouble. I'm reassured by everyone, though, that the Salish and Flathead Indians we'll see on our journey north are much more peaceful than the Blackfeet and other tribes of the Great Plains we've left behind us.

I met the most interesting man. Granville Stuart is a longtime friend of Frank Worden's. He's an author, and historian, and he draws to preserve a record of what he sees on this frontier before it all goes away. I hadn't thought of it all going away, but Granville has a sense of urgency about recording all he can. He's delighted by my efforts on our trip.

I came upon him sitting in the snow on the south bank of the Missoula River, drawing the twelve buildings and corral that make up the settlement here. He hadn't paid too much attention to me when we'd been at dinner with the others, but today he noted my sketch book and took an immense interest in my drawings. At his request I suggested how he might improve his own work. He was most impressed with mine. We chatted on happily in spite of the cold. In the end, I promised to send him some of the work I hope to do from Eagle Mountain.

But in truth our trip has stopped dead. Instead of traveling on to Eagle Mountain with the other parties, even as winter threatened to arrive with chilling temperatures, Garrett insists on staying in Missoula to inspect and buy land in the valley. He claims the value of property here can only see a drastic increase as more of the West opens up. The businessmen he's come to know and admire believe this rustic county seat will one day boast a railway depot. They say people will want to settle and make their homes and livings here where tribes used to fight each other to the death.

What can I say or do? He is my husband and my sole financial base. I'll support his endeavors as a wife should. On nights when I wake in our little room and he's not with me, my heart pounds in panic. I fight giving in to growing anxieties over this headstrong man I married. He is an entrepreneur being advised by other entrepreneurs.

Yet, with every passing day his behavior changes before my eyes. He drinks with other ambitious men who live or stop here on their way to fortunes elsewhere. I tell myself that his business interests are important to both of us.

He's instructed our veterans to make a cold camp near the Missoula River while he retains locals to show him the area. Now that I'm used to them, I often feel safer with these rough men than with Garrett. On some days Garrett is the dashing officer who swept me away in his arms. When Garrett is in this mood he makes wonderful love to me and treats me as if I am royalty. After our times of intimacy his eyes and thoughts are those of an excited boy who wants to show me his wonders. This is the man I married, not that moody bully who replaces him at times with no warning. That's the frightening man with the short temper. I don't believe he'll ever strike me, but he glowers at me with impatience . . . or some other ugly emotion I cannot identify.

I try to share in his visions for our future in hopes his dark moods will abate never to return. As we turn north, there will be three other parties and their conveyances with us. They are miners intent on following the rumors of gold in the Northwest. Garrett says there is strength in numbers, and our chance of being raided by villains or Indians is greatly reduced.

November 1, 1866
Thank God we are on the move again toward Eagle Mountain. Each endless day in Missoula Mills with bored and boring Peggy came close to driving me mad. She fidgeted when work was done, then flirted with any man who glanced her way. And, unlike our hardened veterans,

assorted miners and salesmen did notice her, hungry as they are for the company of women. I had to remind her more than once of the dangers that might befall her if she lost her head over one of these traveling, rootless fellows.

Garrett purchased several hundred acres but took an endless while to close the deals. Many of his days ended in his drinking with newfound local friends. I despise this drinking, as it makes him churlish. Then I become a pouting, nagging wife. I cannot forget the ruin of my father, who thrust his family into the deepest hardships and the most desperate poverty. That is not what I intended to relive when I married Garrett.

When I remember those horrible times caused by Father, I shudder that my future is now tied to this difficult man who is my husband. I pray daily that the man I married will return to be the cheerful, happy person that I've loved so dearly. However, I cannot—no, will not—return to the old depths of misery.

My parting gift from Granville Stuart, Frank Worden, and Captain Higgins was a lovely buffalo robe for keeping us warm in the coach. They expressed concern that I keep myself from actual frostbite. We also left with plenty of smoked meat, flour, sugar, and coffee. We butchered our milk cow, so no more milk for awhile. Garrett deemed it unlikely she'd survive the long journey in snow. Since we won't have her milk, we've also packed what we hope will be enough butter and cheese for most of the way. In many ways, I know this will be the most arduous part of our journey, but we'll reach the end of our travels by Christmas. I do so want to see Eagle Mountain.

CHAPTER TEN

November 10, 1866

After a stopover at Fort Connah to buy items and food, we've left the Jocko Valley and now travel along the west side of Flathead Lake, the graceful Mission Mountains on our right. I'm going to turn my sketches into paintings some day with the varied blues and grays of winter and the deep greens and blacks of the pines. The palette of colors we see at sunrise and sunset, always with rosy alpenglow on the snow covered peaks, is lovely. The mountains call me more than any other landscape I've ever seen. I think Garrett is right. We'll be living in paradise. And it's nearly untouched. What will we make of it? The present may be difficult, but the future holds promise.

November 18, 1866

We have reached the broad Flathead Valley. It's largely unsettled, but Garrett says someday within the next fifty years it will already be farmed and civilized with towns and perhaps even a city or two. For now, though, it's a great, flat, snow-covered expanse ringed by mountains that have stood for thousands upon thousands of years, much of them without the tread of human feet on their steep slopes and wild drainages. I so hope that I'll feel that I belong in the mountains we journey toward in the Northwest.

Thanksgiving, 1866

We made a winter camp on the banks of the Fisher River and sat out another snowfall that fell like a soft curtain on the lake and us Thanksgiving Day. It was still, but the temperature dropped steadily. We bundled up in furs, grateful for the plentiful hot food and drink. The days are shorter and ever colder as we meet the challenges of this hard trail north. By "we" I mean all of us, including our animals. It's a struggle for the oxen, horses, and mules shuffling at times in snow up to their knees and worse. I can say the same for us. We've purchased snowshoes from friendly Indians, and they help but take time to master. My legs shook from cold at first, but now I put on a shortened pair of Garrett's trousers beneath my coat and make progress as well as the men do when I choose to walk.

At midday Cook served us fresh wild turkey with his own recipe of bread stuffing. He even managed a pumpkin pie. It heartened us to know we could still eat well and hold to our President Lincoln's proclamation of a day of Thanksgiving for the Union victory at Gettysburg two years past. Our veterans, some of whom were there, bowed their heads as Garrett said a heartfelt and sincere prayer.

Progress has slowed due to snowfall that fills and hides the ruts of the trail we follow, much rougher than the Mullan Road that I once complained about. We've seen Indians—Flathead, Kootenai, and Salish—both in their settlements along Flathead Lake and out hunting on their own. They seem peaceful and are all in all a handsome people. We follow what was once an animal trail, then an Indian trail, and now a trail for settlers on their way to the Flathead Valley and beyond. I vacillate between feeling the glory of this wonderful adventure and self-pity over my chapped face and roughened hands.

In spite of the soaring magnificence around us— sometimes the mountains merge into the sky and snow swirls around the peaks—we're weary with constant cold and damp. The starry mysteries of our clear nights compensate for the almost endless succession of gray days. The sky and the mountains tell me how insignificant I am with my worries and physical discomforts from this arduous, but wondrous, journey.

November 28, 1866

Peggy and I bundle ourselves against the cold, except when we're required to get down and wait while the men struggle with the coach or wagons being stuck in drifts. All surrounding us is some shade of white or green. Under a pastel gray sky, fir, larch, and lodge pole provide relief with their forests.

Garrett grows more determined to reach Eagle Mountain soon, no matter how hard we must struggle. The stress of winter travel brings back his unpredictable moods. I help those who experience frostbite, their fingers or toes painful and sometimes discolored. Peggy helps Cook with preparing our meals. We'll make it to Eagle Mountain, but, even with proper winter clothes and decent food, we progress each day at the price of our well-being, skin raw and bathing impossible.

December 3, 1866

Our arduous adventure has ended at last. No stranger now to hardships and dangers of rivers, Indians, robbers, deep snows, and icy mountain summits, now that we've arrived I feel like a princess in an enchanted forest. Perhaps like a princess in a Russian fairy tale? I could be a royal member of the Czar's court.

Last night we left the coach at a mining camp called Libby after some miner's daughter, near the confluence of the Fisher and Kootenai Rivers. We climbed down from the coach. Garrett smiled and draped his homecoming present around my shoulders. To my delight, I wore a long ermine cape.

Our new environs displayed cold magic. Snow-covered pines, "snow ghosts" Garrett called them, glowed white under a full moon. Even stars crowding the night sky reminded me of glittering frost. As a romantic surprise Garrett arranged for his own horse-drawn sleigh to take us the last several miles to the lodge. Garrett introduced me to our driver, Seth Dubois, a man about Garrett's own age. Garrett says he's the best hunting guide in northwest Montana.

Seth is handsome in an unkempt sort of way. Garrett and he grew up here together. Seth, half-Kootenai and half-French, lives near the lodge like a poor relation. His father, now deceased, worked as a hunting guide for the Cales before Seth also signed on with Garrett's family.

Seth stared at me as though thunderstruck. I feared Garrett would be offended, but I don't believe my husband even noticed. Peggy, who'd been complaining in an irritating whine about the cold, perked up at the sight of our handsome driver, but he treated her the way the horses would treat a summer fly. He just flicked away her attempts to get his attention. She's a pretty thing, too, not dumpy, since the long, hard journey to arrive here made us all lean and fit, but a girl with a bouncing bosom of the sort men notice. I saw my dearest Garrett pat her bottom once. I disliked it but didn't reproach him.

We climbed into the sleigh, and Seth tucked bearskin

robes around us before the horse trotted along, the bells on his reins jingling into the night. I snuggled against Garrett, who seemed boyish, so proud and eager to show me everything on our way to the lodge. He knows the area well. He told me that some of the lands above us have never felt a human tread; true mountain wilderness, every inch virgin forest.

The lodge is big and rustic, closed in by towering old-growth pines. Garrett assures me a sizeable mountain lake is only a short trek away. In the morning I'll take a walk to investigate.

Light footsteps approached in the hallway. They paused outside Rebecca's door and something or someone brushed against it. Rebecca slipped the diary under her covers and stood, wondering if she should give in to her urge to grab the poker for protection. The knob turned. "Who's there?" Rebecca cleared her throat and asked again.

The footsteps grew fainter as Rebecca's unwanted visitor moved away, down the hall. Rebecca considered again that all was not peaceful in this rustic structure. She waited a moment, then climbed back into bed, taking up the diary once more.

Seth and Peggy unloaded the sleigh while Garrett carried me over the threshold. Flames blazed in the fireplace.

I know already that I want to make changes. The lodge needs a tasteful woman's touch. Mounted elk heads with what Garrett says are six-point racks have been placed high above the fireplace. Great bear rugs on the floor crowd the room. I hate their snarling heads. They give Eagle Mountain too savage a look for full-time residence. I want our home to be a haven of safety for us and our children to come. I didn't say a word last night, though. Garrett is so in love with everything about his life here.

We drank brandy in front of the fire. Garrett imbibed a bit too much; I'm afraid we both did. Peggy retired early, and Seth sleeps in a guest cottage we passed on the way to the main lodge. It was Garrett's and my first time to be alone in this, our own home. He made fierce love to me on the rug before the fire.

The way he took me became almost too rough.

I felt as though he had me with little thought of my own wishes, and, if I'd protested, it wouldn't have made any difference. I think he actually wanted me to struggle against him. He bit my breast so hard that I cried out, and when I tried once to pull away he covered my mouth with his and entered me with a violence I did not realize could exist between us. I felt an awful fear. Afterwards he laughed in satisfaction, and we went upstairs to our huge, high-ceilinged bedroom. Spent, Garrett fell asleep at once, but I lay awake watching his oblivious slumber. I realized how alone I am on this mountain.

No one had ever been rough with Rebecca, who now tried to imagine travel-weary Lucinda's isolation in this forest primeval. Sympathy for the bride rose and coursed through her. She shivered.

December 4, 1866

When I awoke this morning and reached for Garrett, he'd already gone. I lay alone remembering the night before until first light showed pink behind our frosted window-panes. Then I rose in the chill to brush my hair, wash, and go downstairs. No sign of Peggy, so I decided to explore.

Upon reaching the kitchen I discovered the person I

believe will be my greatest help here. Our cook, Mrs. Hedvig Anderson, is a large-boned, cheerful woman. She arrives before breakfast and leaves for her little cabin just behind the lodge after dinner. I introduced myself. To my relief she seemed sincere in her warm welcome.

She speaks with a heavy Swedish accent with frequent references to God. Between Peggy's brogue and wry expressions, Seth's silence, and Mrs. Anderson's Lutheran references, I feel grateful for Garrett's plain English. Without it, in a year heaven knows what I might sound like.

Mrs. Anderson said that Seth and Garrett had already gone out. Seth had set mink and marten traps, and Garrett wanted to go along to check them. There also had been talk of wolves, and they intended to investigate for confirming signs.

I ate a huge breakfast of toast, eggs, and meat that I took for ham, until Mrs. Anderson informed me that I'd breakfasted on smoked bear. Lazy Peggy finally came in. I introduced her to Mrs. Anderson, and we spent the next hour with our heads together checking through their duties. Mrs. Anderson will have complete responsibility for the kitchen. Peggy will have primary responsibility for the rest of the house, with Mrs. Anderson doing light cleaning to help when she can.

Next, Peggy and I unpacked Garrett's and my clothes. I put on the warmest jacket and skirt, and the heaviest coat I own, along with lace-up leather shoes. Then I went hiking. In daylight it's all even more breathtaking than in last night's enchanted moonlight.

My shoes crunched on snow as I walked the road that runs past the house until I found Seth's cabin. I'm afraid we'll have to move him, as it would make a perfect studio for me. Then I took another path and found the lake frozen over. Its snow-covered ice is the only level expanse here. The sky gleamed so bright that the sun's glare on everything hurt my eyes. Squinting, I made out still forms on the lake. I must ask Garrett what they are.

I returned to the house to find Peggy scrubbing the living room floor while protesting that, "Sure, it would be too much for one woman to keep up with this lot."

The old lodge does need attention. Seeing that there was too much for one maid, I rolled up my sleeves and joined in the work. Once the first thorough cleaning is done, Peggy will be expected to do it all. We cleaned and dusted and waxed until lunch. Mrs. Anderson served us trout cooked to perfection. We still saw no sign of Garrett or Seth.

Peggy and I continued to restore cleanliness and order all afternoon. Even though it's a hunting lodge, I'm even more convinced the interior is too wild, too much the masculine retreat if it is to be our home. I believe that influence must've overwhelmed Garrett when he became so rough in our lovemaking last night.

January 1, 1867
New Year's Day. We are at the start of a new year, but for me this beginning has proved a miserable and humiliating one. Garrett becomes more and more a stranger to me. Last night, New Year's Eve, Mrs. Anderson fixed us a lovely roast goose dinner. We dined alone before the fire. Garrett brought superb champagne from the cellar and insisted on Peggy, Seth, and Mrs. Anderson each sharing a glass with us before they retired or went home.

Seth's demeanor remained distant, yet I sensed him studying me from the shadows. I can believe he's a gifted

119

hunter. At times I feel as though he's lying in wait, although his attitude is always one of complete respect. Peggy became silly, giggling and flirting with Seth, who seemed as immune as ever to her forays. She behaved almost the same with Garrett, who kissed her on the mouth. He patted her broad bottom, too. Furious, I showed my anger.

My father, at his worst, knew better than to carry on even the lightest and most harmless flirtation with a housemaid. It shows disrespect to me. Mrs. Anderson fidgeted, uncomfortable and disapproving. She wished us all a Happy New Year and bustled on her way. Dear soul; I would be lost here without her.

After her departure, I offered my hand to Seth, who took it and looked at me with the strangest expression in those depthless brown eyes of his. I wished him a good New Year, and he, too, departed. Peggy soon became so tipsy that Garrett had to help her to her room.

When he returned, I began the talk I'd planned with great forethought. I told Garrett first that I hoped soon to set up my studio as he promised I might. He shrugged and said he had no objection to my pursuing any hobby I fancied, but soon he'd teach me to hunt so I'd be a credit to the Cale family name.

That angered me. I retorted that, to me, form and color and creation were more important than any hunt—that I wasn't even sure I could kill a living thing.

His scowl turned his face to a sinister mask. He told me if I wanted a studio I'd damn well learn to hunt and love it. I responded that I'd try, although I couldn't promise, that I hadn't realized my becoming a wilderness hunter had been a requirement of being his wife. Then, and this part is so difficult to write, Garrett flicked out his hand and slapped me across the face. I fell on the bear rug. In blind fury I pushed myself up and sprang at him.

"You are a little lioness." He laughed and pinned my arms behind me. "You're mad enough to kill right now. Your struggling is wonderful."

In spite of my protesting and struggling against him, he pushed me down on the rug, and, with my head against a snarling bear's stiff fur, he forced himself on me. He tore at my clothes like some madman. When I pushed him away he pressed me back.

"You're mine. You'll do as I tell you." He gripped my breasts so hard purple marks of his fingers are on them today.

I'm so lost, so frightened. Where can I go? What can I do? This morning Garrett, tender and sorry, apologized. He's promised to move Seth into the house and give him orders to help me set up the studio with the equipment we shipped here. It will take time, but he promises to let me keep Seth at the job until I have a work space.

I'm bruised and sore but must keep my head. If I leave Garrett, there will be no money at all for Mother's care or for my own existence. Raised to be a rich man's wife, I know how to be little else. I don't believe my pottery would pay for all Mother's and my needs. In the meantime, I'll try to keep Garrett happy. I cannot forget the suffering that poverty visited on my mother and me. It killed my father. I swear I'll do anything to keep from returning to that precarious, degrading state.

Tomorrow we expect guests, a party including a senator from Massachusetts and a tycoon from Boston. Garrett plans to ice fish with them. There's much to be done. Peggy, Mrs. Anderson, and I will be busy with arrangements.

After the guests leave, I'll instruct Seth to begin work on my studio.

CHAPTER ELEVEN

Rebecca shook her head and set the diary aside. She slid down into her bed and closed her eyes, thinking of poverty and what she'd experienced of it. Her desperate father killed himself when he lost everything. He left her. Did Lucinda truly sacrifice herself to wealth and propriety? If not for her mother, would she have left Garrett? How much grew from a woman's helplessness, how much from the status of women in Lucinda's time and Rebecca's time, too?

She felt even more gratitude than usual for Uncle Max and his progressive views, as well as his generosity. What would she do without her legal training? Independence must be treasured, but what price might be too high to pay for it? Lucinda craved financial security, and she accepted the sacrifice of her person to achieve it. Rebecca sighed for the hopeful girl who had arrived long ago at Eagle Mountain on that glittering winter night.

Unable to sleep, she sat up and continued to read.

January 15, 1867
I haven't been able to snatch a moment for writing. Our guests proved a wonderful break in this strange winter. The senator behaved in an attentive and charming manner toward me. As Garrett watched us, I think his pride competed in equal parts with jealousy.

The shipping magnate from Boston waxed loud and blustery, but both men had great stories to share. I learned an unanticipated amount regarding politics and commerce during their stay. Even more unexpected, I found those subjects fascinating. The businessman and Garrett closeted themselves away at times. They're working on a contract for his company to purchase lumber from our forest.

Garrett seems pleased. He did insist that I go ice fishing with the men, and I went. We sat on wooden crates and dropped our lines through holes in the ice. I enjoyed it. We pulled up huge walleye and northern pike. We had them with dinner. Delicious.

Garrett is charming once more. He can be a delightful husband, and I long to please him. He hasn't made love to me again. His meetings with Mr. Cox, the Bostonian, run late into the night. I pretend to be asleep when he comes to bed.

That awful night when he forced me to submit to him lies between us, perhaps forever . . . a memory that won't quite die and decompose.

January 20, 1867

I hope and believe that I am to have a child. I felt nauseated this morning and so weak that I couldn't manage to descend the stairs. At midmorning I felt fine, but the sight of a bucket of walleye guts left on the back step after Seth cleaned the fish made me ill and dizzy. Gentle and competent, he saw my distress, supported me to a couch, and covered my forehead with a cool, damp cloth.

I'm going to wait a bit longer before going to a doctor.

February 1, 1867

It's true! I am to have a child! What great delight. Garrett is ecstatic. He already plans hunts, travels, and schools for his son. I only have the ancient hope of any expectant mother that this baby will be well. Garrett puts me under less pressure to hunt, for which I'm grateful. I hope against hope that he'll relinquish this demand altogether.

It's difficult, though, for me to escape the house alone. He wants me always to have Peggy or Mrs. Anderson in tow. I laugh at him, but I'm also careful. The birth of this baby means everything.

February 14, 1867

My Valentine's present is the start of work on my studio. Seth seems impassive even about moving out of his cabin. My respect for him grows daily. He's a large part of Garrett's success here, although I don't believe my husband is altogether aware of that fact.

Seth knows the forest and mountains here as others know their lovers, their homes, or their own reflections. He has intimate knowledge of the animals, the plants, the streams. He comprehends what the weather will be and where to set traps, drop fishing lines, or hunt. He remains somewhat distant from us, but I don't believe he misses a thing. Mrs. Anderson adores him. Peggy, on the other hand, has developed an open dislike for Seth. I think it's because he's been relentlessly unresponsive to her earthy charms.

Since the doctor confirmed my condition, Garrett stopped his foolishness with Peggy. It's as though he's been transformed back to the wondrous, vital, and energetic, but gentle, man I loved when we married. He's away long hours between business and his sporting pursuits, but when he returns to me he's contented.

I hate to add that twice he's come home unsteady and smelling of whiskey. I pray we are safe now in our life here, although I can't help but worry. I remember my father and the sorry state to which his imbibing reduced us. I'll be watchful of Garrett's drinking and try to keep him from exceeding safe bounds.

He is adamant in refusing to discuss any changes to the lodge. He turns stony or walks away when I urge it. The one exception is that the big room next to ours will be converted to a nursery. Seth is building shelves in it for books and toys. We've ordered a lovely crib from New York. I must believe that everything will be good and right in time.

Rebecca scanned accounts of life at the lodge and of Lucinda and Garrett hosting other important visitors. Lucinda continued to detail the changes pregnancy brought to her body. She described the beauty of the summer and Garrett's long hours hunting, fishing, and conducting business with guests. She worked at her pottery when time permitted.

Some comments indicated Lucinda's aching loneliness. Garrett seemed distant again, although proud and delighted over her expectant condition.

Then came the entry dated September 1, 1867.

I am devastated. How shall I describe my revulsion? I can write only to this diary. I cannot confide in Mrs. Anderson or Peggy, least of all Seth. None of them will ever know how I suffer. I am wild to leave this miserable outpost, but concern for my unborn baby limits all options. Penniless as I would be without Garrett's money, I don't know what to do. Divorce is out of the question. I can bear no more scandal or soul-crushing, body-tormenting poverty. My circumstances imprison me.

The Plessmans returned a week ago. Garrett and Senator Plessman's wife, Amanda, are lovers.

Garrett has ordered me to curtail any forest rambles because of my condition. But yesterday, weary of being housebound and always in the company of a guard in one form or another, I slipped out and set off by myself to gather white and pale green snowberry branches. I felt as happy as I've been for a long while, our child moving inside me, and Garrett being ever more solicitous. Basking in blessed solitude completed my contentment.

I walked toward a clearing behind my studio. I heard the two before I saw them. They lay together, embracing on a blanket surrounded by gold and blood-red leaves. Unseen behind marsh willows and aspen, I watched them kiss, saw Amanda unfasten her bodice.

I felt nauseated. I hurried back to the studio, where I actually was sick. I felt so ugly. I told myself Garrett must have thought me beautiful before. Now he must see me as clumsy and fat. The unwanted cow. All he wants is the cow to produce a good calf while he sports with this desirable new mistress.

To make matters worse Seth found me soaked with tears and perspiration. He asked no questions. He fetched water and a towel and talked gently about such subjects as the weather, animals preparing for the change of season, and setting his traps for the winter. I'd never heard him talk so much. Once I appeared somewhat refreshed he helped me to the cot and went to the lodge. He returned with the buggy and drove me back.

I pray Seth doesn't know what I saw or, if he does, won't speak of it. No one must know. I went straight to bed, claiming truthfully that I felt unwell.

Garrett came in later, the very model of a concerned

husband. I behaved so that he suspects nothing. I have too much pride to let anyone know of this. When our little one is born I'll decide what I must do. In the meantime I smile and am sweet as honey to Amanda. Mother of the heir to the Cale fortune, I can afford to bide my time. After all, what choice do I have? I know the instinct of revenge is wrong, but I can think of little else. Amanda seems to bloom on a daily basis, which disgusts me. I pray that, when our guests depart at last, Garrett will forget her.

October 1, 1867

Amanda and her husband, along with the rest of their party, have gone. I believe no one suspects what took place during their visit except, possibly, Seth. Seth is my mainstay. I can bear his company better than either Peggy's or Mrs. Anderson's, who chatters about Amanda's beauty and style.

Without ever having spoken of it, Seth and I share a secret. He is so kind. He's never far away, and, when I need him, he appears. He carried Amanda's bags to the wagon when the Plessmans were leaving.

Amanda leaned toward me as we stood on the porch and whispered, "I can't think why, but I don't believe your guide likes me."

I bit my lip to halt a scornful laugh and then told her Seth is a quiet man. I believe he does know about the affair, although Garrett and he seem as amicable as ever.

The thought that my husband has engaged in infidelity before gnaws at me. How can I ever trust Garrett again? How will I suffer him to touch me?

Footsteps again. This time heavy ones. Rebecca pushed the diary under her pillow, casting a glance at the poker. The sounds didn't stop by her door, but she heard the stairs creak as someone, probably the early rising Damon, descended. As the steps faded she reflected on the strangeness of Eagle Mountain. How could anyone feel at ease here? She'd be so happy to settle all accounts, go home to Max, and rejoin civilization. She picked up the diary with renewed purpose.

October 5, 1867

Garrett and I have the joy of a healthy son. We named him Damon Garrett Cale. He's blond and beautiful like his father.

Damon's birth came harder than I could have imagined. Doctor Gillette, who lives four miles from our lodge, attended me. I wouldn't have believed such pain possible, or, if it were, that I could endure it. Mrs. Anderson proved a pillar to lean on as always, a help to me and to the doctor.

I am so proud. In spite of all my recent hurt and bitterness, I know that I do love Garrett, and I adore our son. I am committed to try to be a good wife and mother and forget past troubles. Garrett has been so tender and sweet. I believe it's a new and better beginning for us. I've finally given him something he wanted more than he ever wanted anything—more than any woman, or business acquisition, or trophy. I've given him an heir.

November 1, 1867

These past weeks have been busy, but happy. Our son is ever a delight. He gains weight and sleeps well. I felt exhausted at first, but Peggy has shown herself adept at something at last. Peggy had several younger brothers and sisters, so handling Damon is second nature to her. She meets his wants and needs with practiced ease, while I'm terrified of making any mistake that might harm my precious boy.

Garrett dotes on Damon. He already plans which schools our son will attend, when and how he shall take on business matters, and, of course, the everlasting hunts.

We expect guests again for deer season, so our days will be occupied. Another problem I'd hoped was behind us is Garrett's renewed insistence that I join the hunting parties. I've tried again to explain how I'm not meant for such sport, that guns remind me of Peter's death in battle. Garrett, his eyes cold, only says, "The lioness of the pride must also be its huntress."

I dreamed last night of Peter, Confederates shooting guns at him, screams around him, or were they from his own throat? I don't believe I have it in me after his death to take aim at a living creature and pull the trigger hoping to kill.

Rebecca put aside the diary and stretched. Her muscles had tensed as Lucinda's troubles multiplied. But at least the baby seemed fine. Rebecca hadn't thought of motherhood for herself, now or in the future. Yet, could she someday combine marriage and its usual outcome with a career? Doctor Amelia might offer some insight. There was no one else.

November 16, 1867

What a wretched day. Garrett woke me at dawn, cheerful and full of energy. He laid out a set of hunting clothes he'd ordered for me. I told him that I didn't want to join the shooting. I truly preferred to stay at home and tend Damon. Garrett grabbed my shoulders and shook me. Then he asked if I would dress myself or if he would have to rip my nightgown from me.

I told him to get away, but that wild look that I've tried so hard to forget returned to his eyes. He grabbed my gown at the throat and tore it down the front, then yanked me out of bed. I stood naked in the room's dim cold.

He pointed to the clothes, and I dressed knowing he would not accept anything else. He'd selected a red jacket and heavy skirt and leather boots. He ordered me to follow him downstairs. As we reached the door he gripped my shoulder hard. He ordered me not to act as though anything were wrong in front of Mr. and Mrs. Philbrook and Count De Sica. I followed him into the room, trapped as if in a nightmare.

Mrs. Anderson served us a huge breakfast. I ate nothing. Seth sent me a curious look but remained silent. He speaks little in company. The talk at breakfast centered on the hunt, where we would go, and what the hunters bagged last year.

Our party set out from the lodge, Seth in the lead. We tracked near the clearing. I hadn't been there since the day I saw Garrett with Amanda Plessman. I felt ill once again in the pewter light of this hoarfrost-laden dawn.

Seth positioned us all. He sat near me and noted my trembling.

"You didn't want to come," he whispered.

Wretched, I shook my head.

"Why didn't you stay home?" he asked.

I couldn't form an answer without tears starting.

Garrett moved over to me and whispered with a wolfish grin, "The first shot will be yours, Lucinda."

As he finished his sentence, a lordly buck broke into the clearing. Its antlers spread against the sky like the bones of huge wings. I froze, as if paralyzed.

"Aim," Garrett whispered. "He'll get away, you fool. Shoot him."

Garrett had taught me target shooting, but I found the

thought of ending that breathtaking creature's life revolting. I crouched motionless. Sweat poured into my collar. Garrett turned white with frustration. I think he wanted to strike me, but just then a shot sounded. The ground shuddered as the great buck crashed to earth.

I don't know whether Seth did it to lift the pressure from me or not, but a bright red spot in a little circle on the buck's chest testified that an expert had fired the fatal shot.

Garrett stared at Seth, dumbfounded. My husband raised his voice to Seth for the first time in my memory. "That was Lucinda's kill."

"Lucinda wasn't ready. Anybody can get buck fever. I give him to you as a gift, Lucinda." Seth made a little bow, his smile gentle.

"God damn," Garrett said. "I ought to fire you here and now, but you're the best guide in Montana Territory, so I'll let this pass. Next time though, Lucinda makes her own kill."

The others each brought down a deer, although none as stunning as the monarch Seth shot for me. To show my gratitude, I've asked Seth to put the rack above my studio door. He's also tanning the hide. I'll have deerskin riding gloves made, because Garrett has promised we'll have riding horses soon. As much as I wish the buck were still alive, I'm too grateful to Seth to treat what he did as anything but fine. And so very kind. Kindness is something I've not seen much in this rustic Montana prison.

I fear the next hunt. What can I do? I believe I'll have to join in it or leave Garrett. I doubt if I left that he'd allow me to take Damon. And, strange as it is, for the times that he's gentle and good, I still love my husband. When he turns cruel, it's as though a stranger entered that body that

I desire so when he's the man I fell in love with in that old life. I am afraid of lovemaking. I once enjoyed our private times but now only remember his repeated cruelties.

I fear Garrett's rage.

Reading more eagerly, Rebecca continued to scan entries as the troubled history of Damon's and Bretton's parents unrolled. The candle sputtered and died. She found a new one on the mantel and lit it. Once she jumped, thinking she heard light footsteps again just outside her door. She couldn't be sure of what she heard. In the end she concluded nothing but house noises had disturbed her. As dawn heightened into full daylight, she blew out the candle and continued reading.

November 30, 1867

I shot a deer today. Seth pointed it out. Garrett watched, but Seth directed me. I fired at his order, but closed my eyes before the bullet struck. I had to force away the image of Peter, taking the bullet and falling to the bloodied ground. I felt as though Seth, not I, pulled the trigger. Garrett crowed in triumph. I'm only weary and relieved that it's over.

I feel contempt for Garrett, for his bullying and stubborn insistence. I hope to claim any excuse not to repeat this animal killing. Seth seems to understand, although he never says a word.

Chapter Twelve

December 25, 1867

Christmas Day. At two months, Damon can't understand that this is his first Christmas. My husband gave me an Appaloosa filly, a wild, graceful animal. I'll love riding her. Seth promised to train her to be a trail horse for me in the spring. His Christmas gift to me turned out to be the deerskin riding gloves. I think he feared I wouldn't like them, but they are very fine. Shy when I thanked him, Seth looked handsome today. He's growing a mustache, and it suits him. He looks the part of the mountaineer that he is. At times I find myself watching him. Is it my loneliness that leads me to do so, or perhaps our growing friendship?

January 1, 1868

Another New Year. So much has happened since our arrival. Here I am in remote mountains with a little son and a complicated, difficult husband who, despite everything, says he loves me. I hope it's true. Trust has all but vanished. Yet hope remains.

January 15, 1868

Last night Garrett and I had a terrible quarrel. He simply will not hear of any changes to the lodge. I want to make it mine as well as his. We raised our voices until I'm sure the whole house heard us. Damon cried, but Garrett blocked me from going to him. He said his son would never be a mama's boy. He'd shut him in the closet if he didn't stop soon. I fear he meant it.

February 2, 1870

I've written nothing in this journal for two years. Life has not been easy, but I've managed well enough.

Now I find that Garrett and Peggy are carrying on an affair. I must write to ease my poor bruised heart. And my pride.

I thought that foolishness had passed, but I saw them embracing in the kitchen. They didn't see me. Somehow I'm not so shaken this time. I hope to dismiss Peggy in time. Until then I'll endure this latest humiliation until an advantageous moment arrives to break my silence. For now I'll return to confiding only in these pages.

February 7, 1870

I lack the power to dismiss Peggy. Garrett refuses to end their nonsense. In a flat tone, he said he controls our lives and will bed anyone he wants for as long as he wants. His own father had that freedom. His mother accepted the inevitable.

I stormed toward the stairs in disgust shouting that I was neither his mother nor his slave. He shouted after me that I am a fool. I am certain the entire household heard our ugly words. I know Damon did. He started crying as he does when his parents do battle.

Garrett grabbed our son's little arm and dragged him upstairs with me following. He opened the nursery's closet door and shoved Damon inside. Garrett bellowed that if he heard one more sound from Damon he'd leave him there all night. After five minutes of silence he opened the door. Damon's face was white and contorted in terror. I swept him up and took him to the kitchen to comfort him.

I want to run away but again face my own weakness. I've no funds to leave here. Who would take care of my mother and protect my child? I must endure for them. I pray God will be merciful and somehow release me from this sham of a marriage.

Peggy is smug just short of rudeness. She must know that I'm aware of her betrayal. She no doubt wants to maintain her privileged status as favored mistress. The foolish girl doesn't realize what a small role she plays in Garrett's thoughts and future. I'll rid myself of her in time, but the affair continues for now. Garrett's pride pushes him to flaunt any conquest.

I conceal my rage. They think me helpless, but in truth I'm planning my revenge and escape. I avoid Garrett. I suspect he enjoys betraying me so much that he'll do it again and again, even after he tires of silly Peggy. I won't always be helpless to stop him.

After making a quick trip to the adjoining room to wash, Rebecca put on her undergarments, including the tight corset. Then she pulled the wrapper over them, glancing at the clock. She had a little more time before the hour to leave for Lucinda's funeral.

Entries proceeded through the next three years. They chronicled Garrett's heavier drinking, wild quarrels over whether or not Lucinda would join in hunting parties, how Eagle Mountain's interior should appear, and Garrett's numerous dalliances.

Worst of all, he continued to bully Damon.

February 1, 1872

Garrett knows nothing except his own pleasures and seldom talks to me or little Damon. Business, drinking, and illicit pleasures eclipse his pride in family. My poor little boy shies away when he sees his father come near.

Peggy is not as pleased with herself as during the beginnings of her welcome seduction. Garrett uses her now and then, but he also uses other women, be they wives of guests, coy local girls, or whores from Jennings or Libby. And he is never subtle about such amorous forays. Nevertheless Peggy carries herself with the impertinence born of being her employer's mistress. What has Garrett promised her? I'd like to crush them as they have crushed and disregarded me.

Interspersed were entries that chronicled Lucinda's progress with ceramics. She sent more and more of her potter's work to the East Coast, where it appeared in galleries to favorable reviews. She never appeared at her openings, as Garrett wouldn't permit her to travel farther than Jennings.

May 1, 1872

Garrett has gone too far. He and I fought late last night about when Damon will start to ride. Our sweet boy is too little and fears horses. He's not a brave child by nature. He's sensitive, kind, and eager to please, but he cries too easily for his father's way of looking at the world.

I stood fast, determined to protect my son. Garrett, in his drunken state, tried to strike me, but I ducked away, putting the settee between us.

Then I heard him mutter, "All right, Miss high and mighty. I'll show you."

He lifted a deer rifle from our gun rack and staggered outside. Moments later I heard a shot from the stable. I threw a shawl around my shoulders and ran there. Once inside, I saw Garrett standing over my horse, Scout. Garrett had simply gone out and shot her dead because I loved her.

"Now," he snarled, slurring his words. "When Damon is old enough for a horse of his own, his mother shall have a horse of her own again as well."

I flew at him, striking with my fists. He knocked me to the hard floor. I tore my skirt on a nail as I fell and scraped my knee.

Seth appeared in the doorway. He looked from me with my torn clothes and disheveled hair, to Garrett, and finally to the horse. For the first time I saw Seth's expression turn from his usual serenity to shock and disgust. He swelled with rage. I raised my eyes to Garrett. In that moment my husband feared Seth. I'd never seen Garrett afraid of anyone or anything since the strange encounter with Jeremiah on the Mullan Road so long ago.

The two men glared at each other.

I'd rolled into scratchy hay when I fell. When I scrambled to stand and brush it off, Garrett blinked and seemed to come to himself. He gestured to poor Scout and said, "I didn't want my wife riding this animal anymore. Next time we'll find a more suitable one for her. That is, when the right time comes. Get rid of the carcass, Seth."

"Get rid of it yourself, you son of a bitch," Seth responded. "I quit."

"No, Seth," I pleaded. "I need you here. Don't leave us."

Seth only gave me a long look, turned, and walked away. Garrett slumped down and passed out in the scattered straw and widening pool of blood seeping from Scout's carcass.

I followed Seth from the stable toward the house. How much a part of my life he'd become. His constant strength and serene nature had smoothed the days at Eagle Mountain in so many ways. When Garrett left me for days at a time, Seth remained nearby. When Garrett had had too much to drink, Seth stayed close at hand to help, even carrying him upstairs to bed.

The hunts succeeded because of Seth's knowledge of wild creatures and his guiding skills. With him as their leader, guests discovered and reveled in our wilderness. And, unspoken, but ever present from our first meeting, Seth gave me his loyalty and love.

I'd thought him devoted enough never to leave. How could he think of abandoning me now?

What could I do to make him stay? What should I give? What would I promise?

I went to his room, down a hall near the back of the lodge. I tapped on his closed door. Before that night I'd never gone there. It wouldn't have been proper, and, I now realized, it would have been dangerous. I must have wanted Seth all of this time in a way unknown even to me. But I admitted my attraction as I repeated my soft, but insistent, knocking.

If I were honest I'd known for a long time—I wanted him. He's not rich, nor is he powerful in the eyes of others, people like Garrett and Max. He's peaceful and kind and at ease in his world. Perhaps that is enough.

The door opened. Seth stood with the light at his back. He'd taken off his shirt. His chest was smooth, not like Garrett's, so pale with sparse curling hairs. A jagged scar on one shoulder stood out white as lightning against Seth's dark skin. The sight reminded me. Seth had been in the war, too. He'd been an infantryman, though, no officer's uniform for him. He received his wound at Gettysburg.

I gazed into his eyes as dark as obsidian. I made a nervous gesture with my hands. "I want to come in," I said at last. Even to my ears, it sounded like a plea.

He drew me toward him and closed the door behind me. "I've waited years for you to say that."

I burrowed into the warmth of his arms, where I discovered comfort I hadn't known for such a long time. Seth kissed me, and our being together felt good and right. I stayed with him for only a few hours, our lovemaking the most complete experience of sharing I could imagine. I hadn't understood before that such love and intertwining of spirits could exist.

By the time I left his room at dawn, I'd extracted his promise never to leave me. That, in spite of the fact that I promised him nothing.

Rebecca raised a hand to her heated cheek. She hadn't anticipated either the confession or such a description of passion and felt a physical response to the reminder of such feelings. There was the slightly guilty sense of being a spy as well. She shook that off as the reasons to continue persuaded her to keep reading.

Lucinda's going to Seth's room didn't happen as a result of her being sophisticated or through a lack of caring for society's opinions. Lucinda was no freethinker. Rather, she behaved as a desperate, lonely young woman reaching out to keep the one man she could rely on from slipping away. The last sentence, though, conveyed wonder and a hint of discovery of a power Lucinda hadn't realized she possessed until that night.

Much later that morning, Garrett stumbled into the room he and I shared. His movements showed how his body ached after a night on the stable floor, and he winced from a well-deserved headache. Pale and confused about my horse, unable to remember what he did in the stable, he looked ashamed when I told him. He promised me a new filly in the spring.

Certainly he doesn't remember Seth's declaration that he planned to leave us. Thank God for that.

May 28, 1872

Garrett suspects nothing. My fragile happiness continues. Seth and I meet in his old cabin, now my studio. I crave our times together, the hard smooth muscles of my wilderness love, his taste, his smell. I have never known such joy. If only Seth and I could live together. But that can never be. He's poor, and poverty won't meet my needs, my own and Mother's. Seth and I have our love and our passion. Our need for each other is like a craving. What will come of this?

June 5, 1872

My mother's health is fading. A letter arrived this afternoon. Mother doesn't recognize anyone now. She cannot feed herself or meet her bodily needs. She will have to be cared for at all hours of the day and night with no exceptions. That will mean at least two full-time nurses. I need Garrett Cale's fortune more than ever before. Besides Mother's helplessness, I can't face a return to the specter of want and the impoverished life that threatened to crush my very being.

There is also my darling, gentle Damon. I want him to have the best of everything. I need to be his buffer against life's cruelties, which can strike even the privileged. How well I know that death and betrayal and loss are no respecters of mere mortals. Garrett treats Damon as though he's a disappointment, as though Garrett deserved a rowdier boy. But he would die before relinquishing his son. He'd keep Damon to spite me if for no other reason. If I try to leave, I'll lose my golden child.

Seth makes no demands that I divorce Garrett. Seth is like the forest. He exists in the world as he finds it.

June 30, 1872

I will bear a second child. I'm two months along and certain this baby is Seth's. Garrett will suspect nothing. Seth must help me decide what to do. I am so torn. To stay with Garrett seems the basest dishonesty. I don't love him. There have been too many infidelities, too much battering of hearts and bodies. Our marriage is shattered as though it were one of my ceramic failures. My love for Garrett, like his for me, lies in shards.

In a way I thank Garrett for his heartlessness. Seth and I would never have discovered our passion—our love—if Garrett hadn't driven us to search out comfort in each other's arms. The man in uniform who swept me away from Max has degenerated into a brutal drunk who beats his wife, terrifies his child, and shoots defenseless animals out of spite. I feel nothing for my husband but contempt, pity, and hate.

I retained a daughter's love for her father even when mine imbibed to excess. I knew he did it because of Peter's death and my mother's self-burial. But Garrett has turned into a greedy, bestial monster for no reason that I can see. I've heard that the war made some men like this.

Garrett sometimes talks of it during his drunken rants. I've concluded that he enjoyed the power that he held over enlisted men like Seth. He boasts of sending his troops to their death even when no military goal could be gained.

He often ordered Rebel prisoners shot after he convinced them to lay down their arms and surrender.

He found satisfaction in those deaths. Listening to him I felt abhorrence and the shame of being his wife. Thoughts of Peter's death have never left me. Even though those dead Confederates fought against our cause, like Peter they sacrificed their lives in war. I see my brother with them in my nightmares. Stilled silence and sad eyes of all the lost young soldiers from both sides reproach me.

Garrett inhabits his own hellish realm. He's created a Hades for those around him. I tried so hard to be a good wife.

I am still beautiful. I see admiration in the eyes of men who visit us. My lovemaking with Seth is wonderful. Damon, my work, and Seth intersperse the misery of my life here with brief hours of liberated joy.

But my husband no longer sees me. He no longer resembles the man who desired me. Most nights he stumbles to his own room after drinking late. On black midnights when he does come to me I grit my teeth and suffer his fumbled lovemaking and the smell of spirits on his breath. I fear his violent temper if I refuse.

He'll take me by brute force if I try to stop him.

Garrett will believe he's my baby's father. His arrogance would never permit him to think otherwise. But if Seth wishes to have the child acknowledged as his, I don't know what to do. I do believe I love Seth.

I find myself praying for Garrett's death. I know Seth would love and treasure me, but he's unable to take Damon and me from here while Garrett lives. Even if Seth had the means, he's part of this place and will never leave. He's a good man, but he lacks the means and the education, the refinement I need to live as I prefer. I hate how callous I've grown here. My soul is deprived of its birthright of goodness and purity.

I want to give my son and his future sibling a love of nature, but more than that, the ability to live well anywhere. Culture ought to be part of their lives, too. I love Seth, but eventually our meetings may have to end. I write this even believing he would be devoted and care for us for the rest of my life if it were granted him to try.

I acknowledge certain differences between us. If left to ourselves, I wonder what we would converse about, whether we'd become mutually annoyed by our differences. Seth has no ambitions beyond living as he does. His formal education as a half white-half Kootenai has been limited. His natural intelligence, abilities, and masculine strength make him all I could desire now, but what might change in years ahead? How would society look upon us? Disgrace and poverty rear their monstrous heads again.

I cannot—will not—endure scandal and poverty for me or my children.

From outside a scream interrupted Rebecca's reading. She sprang out of bed and turned toward the window. She knew what it was, the mountain lion she'd heard at the cabin, or one like it. The scream sounded close, but in spite of its night-splitting threat, she knew herself safe within the old lodge's walls. At least from the cat on its hunt.

She sighed and went to look out on the forest, her mind returning to what she'd read so far. Lucinda had changed and perhaps hardened during the years of the diary. Did constraint make her cruel? Did she use her beauty as a weapon? Or for some merciless leverage? These pages read as the relentless fossilizing of a human heart. Still, Rebecca concluded that Lucinda Cale had become her own person, capable of . . . anything? A large animal shot from the snow-covered clearing in front of the house and into the trees. A smaller, limp shadow hung from its jaws.

Apprehensive, Rebecca turned back to the diary.

And what about my little Damon? He's made of both Garrett and me, and when we quarrel it breaks my heart to see him torn between us. Garrett demands too much of our son. If that is true now, what of the boy's future? Damon is so sweet and sensitive. Like me, he hates the idea of killing animals. Garrett is determined to "make a man" of Damon, and I fear the consequences.

Damon has come to me in tears when he displeases his father and Garrett's displeasure turns to rage. When a mother cannot protect her child what is she to do? I ask Damon to be brave and behave as Garrett demands. I hope Damon will find more ways to satisfy his brute of a father. He tries to be silly to make Garrett laugh. He tries so hard to win Garrett's approval—as much as a child's ability lets him.

I cannot tell Damon that, as time goes on, I pray daily for his father's demise. My little boy loves Eagle Mountain, but he's becoming sullen when his efforts to please Garrett fail. He's losing his love for Garrett as I have lost mine. I understand his fear and growing distrust. I'm afraid, too. My son and I have become companions and victims.

Seth teaches Damon much about the wilderness. We go on long rambles, the three of us. Damon has gained a precocious knowledge of native birds and plants. I don't know whether he'd be happy anywhere but here. Would I break his heart by taking him away, or would relief at being free of Garrett be enough? I stroke Damon's hair and pray for a miracle.

Garrett would never let me raise my boy, or the new

child, elsewhere. As I've always seen, the law is with the father in these cases. Garrett's influence, I fear, might buy any court run by men. It isn't fair, but I have to face reality. I must find a way to escape Eagle Mountain and the threats that haunt me here.

Besides, how can I stay and raise this new baby as Garrett's child in front of Seth? What if he should be dark like his half-white father? Garrett is blinded by arrogance, but the child will be part Kootenai. This is like some farcical stage comedy, yet it feels tragic.

CHAPTER THIRTEEN

September 15, 1872

I am not sick with this pregnancy as when I carried Damon. My hunger for Seth grows like a starving woman's need for bread. The touch of his rough hand on my breast is the food I require to live. I'm famished for his body as soon as we are separated. I feel a sense of urgency about everything as though this child's birth is going to alter us in some tremendous way. For good or ill I can't say. I feel both exhilarated and frightened at the same time.

November 2, 1872

Seth and I met last night at the studio to decide on vital paths for our child's future. How strange that with all our strains and problems passion only burns stronger, deeper. Does it blind us to dangers? Do we choose to overlook our peril? What is best for this baby?

We met at twilight, a time I love. Seth waited for me, then we walked together as we have so often by the lake, not touching, hardly talking. But I tingled with the awareness of his proximity in every nerve ending, every sense. I believe he did the same. I cherish our passion. His hands on my most private and sensitive places make me delirious.

Garrett Cale married a foolish, desperate girl. Seth Dubois's love has transformed her into a strong and seasoned woman.

We turned to the studio, walking through falling, golden aspen leaves. Inside, Seth kissed me with urgency, then slowed to tenderness. We made love as warm and enveloping as that first time, but with more knowledge of the beloved other. I am like the forest that he loves when I am in his arms. He is wild and dark. He knows me, and his love has made me bountiful.

Afterwards, we talked. We decided nothing will change. Seth is willing that this baby be acknowledged as Garrett's, reared with the obvious advantages of being a Cale. With another, I might have suspected weakness or an attempt to slough off responsibility in his decision. But not with Seth. He's as quiet, accepting, and proud as he can be. His pride is not in his name, not in what the world will see. He'll stay at the lodge to be near me. He will teach our child to know the wilderness much as he's opened the natural world to Damon.

I'm ashamed that I may be using Seth. More and more I seek him out to serve my desires as well as my yearning heart's needs, even though I have doubts about our prospects. I sense a dangerous future with Garrett if lacking Seth's love and protection. Somehow I must find the way to destroy my husband.

I've more than earned Garrett's money in the many times he's beaten me. I weary of hiding bruises and tender places on my scalp after he's pulled my hair or yanked my head back when I try to walk away from him. Nor can I forget the times he tore off my clothes and ravished me against my will. He revels in my helplessness. I conceal as much as I can from Seth. I fear he would fight with Garrett and leave, or kill him and be arrested.

Garrett taunts me with details of his amorous intrigues.

Hatred matches my humiliation. I'm determined that, when it's time, the Cale fortune will be mine. With it, I'll provide an education and advantages for my children far beyond just freedom from want and fear. I no longer feel guilty as I dream of Garrett dead. On the contrary, I anticipate his approaching death as inevitable . . . a benefit to me and my children.

What a strange life I've come to. Yet I want this baby as much as I longed for my little Damon.

To add to my happiness, Max has written that he plans to come hunting this fall. He'll stay with us for sport as well as business reasons. He and Garrett will spend time behind closed doors. But I'll learn the substance of their contracts. Max always discloses details of our shared business interests that Garrett refuses to explain to me. Max has built his practice into such a profitable enterprise, and he still loves me. I often wonder what my life might have been as his wife.

Rebecca lifted her attention to the window after hearing the new sound of a soft hoot. She gasped as a great horned owl swooped past in the setting moon's light. It didn't dive but kept going in a slow descent. Hunting. Had the cougar grabbed its dinner before it arrived? Life in the forest truly was "red in tooth and claw."

How would her own life have been different if Lucinda had married Max? Would they all have been happier? Lucinda's story seemed as poignant with "what might have been" as Rebecca's own. She thought of her father again. What if he hadn't been overwhelmed by despair? Lucinda's writing suggested what a desperate person might begin to consider, and how in her own desperation she might prey on someone made vulnerable to manipulation by love.

November 5, 1872

Garrett is pleased by news of this second baby. Just as I predicted, he suspects nothing. What sweet revenge it would be to tell the truth. I'd enjoy shouting it in his face. But I won't. I cannot have my children exposed, nor can I be absent from their lives. Fleeting happiness doesn't change Garrett's ways, of course. He still drinks. His attacks have lessened, but I never know when violence might rise up again.

I've asked him not to make love to me until after the baby is born. I hinted at medical reasons. Garrett still has Peggy as well as other women. I now feel some gratitude to these whorish vixens. When Garrett is using them he doesn't force himself on me.

I should be at ease now, but a sense of dread shadows me even though my condition proceeds well.

The diary continued with accounts of Lucinda's pregnancy, small events at the lodge, and the severe winter that marked that year in the locals' memories. She and Garrett endured stormy inner weather as well.

February 14, 1873

My Valentine's present is a new horse, a black mare with a white star on her forehead. Although my surprise was genuine, I only pretended joy. I'll never forget how Garrett destroyed my beautiful Scout. Whatever way my husband turns threatens hurt and pain. How long will this horse live?

I've noticed Seth's growing hatred for Garrett. Seth's eyes glitter when Garrett orders him about. During Max's visit, Seth and he hunted from a winter camp while Garrett had to deal with a business emergency. Max and Seth are longtime friends, so they enjoyed themselves. They spoke often during Max's visit, their heads together. If I didn't know his reticence as I do, I'd fear Seth might be confiding our secrets to Max.

This morning Garrett sat down on the edge of my bed and began speaking of his childhood. He told me how his father did everything on a grand scale. He kept beautiful mistresses. He owned thoroughbred horses and enjoyed high repute as a hunter's hunter. He founded the Cale fortune by successful mining ventures.

Garrett's father set aside his wife, a society belle, once she'd produced a male heir. He remembers how his father beat his mother. Garrett claimed his mother asked for it more often than not. Disgusting! As if any woman deserved to be beaten. His parents' private domestic life shaped the heated, defensive posturing of a child loyal to his adored father.

"I wanted to be like him, and by God I am. Mother should have been a more obedient wife," Garrett said in a warning tone. "Every woman has that duty."

I felt confused. Bewildered. What made him bring up his parents? Then I remembered. He once told me his mother and father drowned together in a boating accident on a Friday the thirteenth in February twelve years ago. Today is Saturday. Last night would've marked the twelfth anniversary of their death.

He came to me for reassurance. What has become clear to me is Garrett's cowardice. He abuses those under his power. In his stupors he told me how as a boy he bullied animals and even servants' children. He did confess that only one fought back. Seth.

I'd seen plenty of these confiding moods come and go. I braced myself, because beatings and insults often follow such confessions.

Rebecca read on, feeling both growing sympathy and rising distaste for Lucinda Cale.

Although I feel it fading, I will never regret what I've had with Seth. There. Did I really write those words? Is our love affair truly to come to an end? No. I love him, but in some ways we are so different.

I must think. If only there were someone to whom I could unburden my poor heart. I feel as alone—more alone—than I did before finding love with Seth. I think more and more about Max. How different my life would have been if I'd married him. I'm so confused. My desire and need for a man's love sent me to Seth's arms. What future unhappiness will I cause him?

I cannot override my need for Seth as I cannot escape from Garrett. I pray for Garrett to die. He deserves an untimely death, a departure that would free me and those I love. I've begun pondering how it might happen. I must find a solution to my situation or go mad. God help me. I have no fear of hell to come. I am in that dark place now.

I sometimes imagine seeking help from Max. I suspect he never married because of his feelings for me. Would it be cruel to tell the man I refused to marry that I've made such a mess of things? How different these three men are from each other! The deeper I sink in this quagmire the more I think of Max and my growing memories of those easy, pleasant times when he courted me. Perhaps I now love not just one, but two men? What is to happen to me? To any of us?

February 20, 1873
These past few days have been the hardest of my life. How can we solve the problem of Garrett? I unburdened myself

to Seth. He heard me out, every awful idea that tumbles over and over in my brain. He didn't seem shocked that my thoughts had turned to advantages of widowhood.

Then he asked, as he has before, "What would this mean for our child?"

I told Seth that I cannot continue living as we do. I emphasized how I feared Garrett's violence might result in my mutilation or death. Garrett's end is the only way I'll ever escape his violence and degradations and maintain the freedom from scandal and poverty that I've earned at such a price.

Then I gave Seth my promise to marry him after Garrett's death. My husband's estate would be settled as mine with the resulting liberation of me and my children. I begged Seth to help me do what must be done to save us all.

I expected him to be shocked and disappointed in me. I thought he might dismiss my plea as the hysterical fantasy of a woman under great pressure. I repeated that I wanted our baby to have his influence, his presence. But I added that to avoid scandal and ensure the child's entrée into a world of privilege, this baby must be raised as a Cale even if Garrett is dead.

To my relief Seth said he'd entertained similar thoughts. But his long boyhood friendship with Garrett made him doubt he could go through with the act. He'd never expected my offer of marriage. I saw in Seth's yearning eyes that he might well do anything necessary for us to be joined as man and wife.

In the end, he swore to help free me from the shackles of this marriage. At one point, though, he put his face in his hands. I had a flicker of doubt that he could actually see this through. He asked, "Is there no other way? I see well what he's become, but we were like brothers before the war."

I shook my head. "If you want us wed, you'll do this. Help me."

We were in the studio. Seth had been turning a goblet in his hands.

"The guilt," he murmured. "How will we live with the guilt?" He hurled the goblet across the room near the cot where we'd made love so many times. It struck the wall and shattered. Shards flew everywhere.

My finished piece can never be restored to the beautiful original I created. Nor, perhaps, when we've accomplished this awful deed will we be able to bear being together. I'd never seen Seth lose control. Would, he, too, turn to rash acts? Did I cause and even bring this out in those who loved me?

Yet I must escape this life as Garrett's possession. I reminded Seth that Garrett is not the man I married nor is he the friend Seth knew as a boy.

Seth grimaced. "Yes. He's more animal than man when he drinks, and he drinks too much. A wolf with rabies must be destroyed." At last I heard Seth say the words that meant my emancipation. "I will kill him to save you, to save us."

I nodded in speechless gratitude. We sat in solemn silence. Seth would kill Garrett. He would do this or anything else I asked. But poor man, his love for me had grown stronger than mine for him.

We turned to each other. His need for my body made him desperate. We lost ourselves in desire. As I looked to the future, I saw freedom mixed with guilt over the mortal sin I'd persuaded this good man to commit. Then guilt dropped away, and I felt only fierce and furious joy over what would soon happen to Garrett Cale.

Just as her mantel clock chimed 9:00 a.m., Rebecca heard Cale voices in the hall. A heavy knock sounded on her door. She closed Lucinda's diary with reluctance and flipped her bedding over it.

She straightened her wrapper, smoothed her hair, and opened the door. Damon stood before her, his hand on the outer knob. To her surprise, he pushed the door open farther and peered into the room. She moved a little, in case the covers didn't conceal the diary.

"I thought you might need a wake up," he said. "Can I help you with anything?"

"No. Thank you. I'll join you in a few moments." Rebecca tried to smile and closed the door. He had seemed rather forward.

She found herself thinking that Shakespeare could never have conjured more suspense than Lucinda Cale managed. And this story had taken place here at remote Eagle Mountain, not the capitals of Europe.

She muttered, "I'll learn more of this dark tale. My God, what went on in this forbidding place? What did Seth do for love of that desperate woman? In order to escape from one man, she used another. I'll know more after tonight."

She slid the diaries under her mattress, then rose. She dressed in a black wool suit with a pearl-gray shirtwaist. She piled and pinned her hair and topped it with a black, short-veiled hat. Her large coat hood could cover the hat in the event of foul weather. Mindful of her frigid trek the other night, she laced up her boots and picked up her fur-lined, black leather gloves. She felt ready for the weather if not another meeting with Bretton Cale.

Rebecca descended the stairs to join the family. They'd gathered in a forlorn group, their coats on. All stood beneath

Lucinda's portrait except Bretton, who stared out the window as the rest talked in subdued voices.

Damon looked strained but mustered a smile. "Ah, here you are, Rebecca. Did you want breakfast? I think there's time."

Amy shot Rebecca a look of distaste.

Ignoring the girl who didn't like guests, Rebecca only smiled and shook her head. "I hope I haven't kept you waiting."

"Not at all. Your timing is perfect." Damon took Claudia's arm. "We'd better start though. I'm afraid I only have room for the four of us in our coach, but there's a smaller buggy that will accommodate two."

"I can follow you," Rebecca responded, not wanting her presence to be a burden. "I take the reins in Kalispell on occasion."

"Bretton, why don't you escort Rebecca?" Claudia suggested.

Rebecca expected Bretton to protest, but he appeared indifferent. He nodded without meeting her eyes.

"Are Rebecca and Bretton going to get married?" Teddy's voice piped into the silence.

"No, little man." Teddy's father hoisted the boy up on his shoulder.

"Heavens," Claudia laughed. "What children won't say."

"Best be on the road," Bretton advised.

They proceeded toward the door. As she turned for a final look at Lucinda's fascinating portrait, Rebecca thought of Uncle Max lying helpless in Kalispell. The look on his face when he learned of Lucinda's death had revealed such long years of love, pain, and despair. Although news of her death brought on his stroke, the young Lucinda had stricken his heart years earlier. Rebecca thought with a stab of anger of Lucinda's way of referring to Max as a handy, reliable friend. He'd been so devoted. Would he, like Seth, have planned a murder to possess her?

Rebecca stared at the cool, green eyes. The captivating Lucinda held Max, Garrett, and Seth in her web for—how many years? Since well before Bretton's birth, and Seth had stayed in this primeval forest under her spell until his horrific death. Lucinda Cale. Who had she really been to have caused so much pain and inspired so much enthralled love?

Outside, Rebecca saw that the weather had changed. Clouds the color of dirty ice slid in overhead. A chill wind sliced from the north. Pines bent in protesting curves.

She shivered.

"Come on," Bretton spoke behind her. "I'll take the reins." He held out a hand to help her into the passenger's seat of the buggy.

"I'm more than capable of handling these horses, thank you." Ignoring his hand Rebecca started around to the driver's side.

For the second time that day Bretton looked vulnerable. "I'm sure you are, although your arrival at my cabin hardly fills me with confidence in your ability to handle anything. But the fact is, if I don't take the reins, I'll have to walk. It's an eccentricity of mine, I suppose."

"Not the only one." Exasperated, Rebecca walked back to the passenger side. "I didn't come all this way to make you late to your mother's funeral service. Just do a better job than Bill Sauer did."

He let her sharpness pass in his obvious relief at being in control of the reins. "Not a difficult assignment." He held out a gloved hand and assisted her up to her seat.

They proceeded through the forest in silence. As a hard gust rocked the buggy, Rebecca pulled the heavy buffalo robe over her lap and legs.

"We're in for a big one, all right." Bretton leaned forward to scan the leaden sky.

CHAPTER FOURTEEN

"Attending your mother's funeral is my main reason for being here." Rebecca picked up the conversation. "Although, I have to admit I used to wonder about this place. After my father died, Uncle Max sent me to school in Switzerland. Following graduation there I enrolled in college in New Hampshire. Finally, I returned to study law with Max. He could have taken me along on one of his visits to Eagle Mountain. The fact that he never did made me more curious about your family as time went on."

Bretton shook his head and made a wry smile. "Max. He loved my mother. That became obvious to all of us. She reduced him to near lapdog status. She had a way of doing that to men."

Rebecca cast him a sharp look. "I find it hard to believe anyone could do that to Uncle Max. It's clear you've never seen him defend a client in court."

"She held people's hearts . . . How shall I put it? Not so much in the palm of her hands as in her fists."

"That's a harsh judgment on a woman no longer here to defend herself."

"Lucinda Cale passed many a harsh judgment in her day. No one knows that better than I." Noting his anger, Rebecca wondered how deep Bretton's anger reached.

Rebecca considered whether to challenge him but let the conversation rest. He seemed almost weak to her now, close to self-pitying. After a moment, she asked, "What do you remember about Seth Dubois? He became like a father to you, didn't he?"

"Seth? Exactly like a father. No one could have asked for more. He became my father in all the ways that count. No better man ever lived. Mother should have seen that, but she had her snobbish class consciousness."

Rebecca reacted with discomfort to his speaking ill of the dead. She'd gained empathy, or at least sympathy, for Lucinda as she read her journals. Whether the diarist acted in self-defense posed a real question. Lucinda believed she did. Lucinda used the weapons she had, her beauty and her persuasive powers, to save herself. But Bretton spoke from his own beliefs.

How soon men resented a strong woman.

He voiced strong enough bitterness that Rebecca concluded he'd never seen Lucinda's diaries. Any reader would feel some compassion for the young wife victimized to near madness. Of course, like Rebecca, another reader might be shocked by Lucinda's calculations to murder Garrett. The diaries clarified so much about Lucinda Cale, both her manipulative powers and her vulnerability.

How many women ever pondered murder? What happened to one who lived in fear of physical violence? Of the dread of rape by a drunken husband? Who faced the horror of poverty and its relentless grasp? Should those who'd never floundered in waters as deep and treacherous as those Lucinda fought be capable of judging her?

Rebecca shifted the conversation, pursuing questions about what Seth had taught Bretton and the close connection the older man helped him form with wilderness. She tried to detect whether Bretton knew Seth was his true father, but he revealed nothing.

When not speaking of Lucinda, Bretton relaxed into explaining the area to Rebecca. He spoke of Kootenai history, the art of wilderness survival, flora, fauna, and even local geology. Bretton had knowledge Seth taught him and the insight of a well-read naturalist and historian. He explained how he intended his ceramic forms and colors to celebrate the world around them.

She comprehended Bretton's appreciation of Eagle Mountain and its environs. Could his appreciation have morphed into a desire for possession? That might explain the disappearance of his estranged mother's will. With no written testament directing otherwise, he would own half of Eagle Mountain regardless of who his natural father might be. Even if he didn't want it, he could sell his half to further his career. Who would turn down a fortune?

After three miles, Bretton pulled the horses up before a stone church in a clearing.

"My father had this chapel built here," he said. "It's easier for Cales to reach, although not for others in the community. They come to worship here nevertheless."

A graveyard lay to one side, measured off by a wrought-iron fence. Twenty-some tombstones leaned, and ten granite angels tilted weathered wings at awkward angles. Rebecca thought that on a milder day she'd like to read the inscriptions on those old graves. Now Lucinda would join those at peace there.

The wrought-iron gate with its pointed spikes sagged a little and needed to be lifted by anyone going in or out. It sat open now. Rebecca and Bretton paused, observing the rectangular hole in the earth waiting to hold Lucinda Cale's coffin.

Bretton helped Rebecca down and took her arm as they walked toward the chapel and Lucinda's waiting family. His hand cupping her elbow felt natural. Several local people gathered in the vestibule eyed them with curiosity.

"This is where I leave you." Bretton let go of her with a nod, took a deep breath, and strode into the church.

Rebecca entered the chapel and chose to sit in a rear pew. A big-boned woman at the organ began to pump its pedals and play with mechanical competence. The family filed in from a side room, taking their places in a front pew like ravens on a branch. Rebecca observed the Cales. Any behavior today might reveal useful information. Amy led, taking the innermost place. Bretton took the aisle seat. Big and tawny, he'd have appeared more at home in a jungle than in this peaceful church.

He wore a beleaguered expression. Was it Rebecca's imagination, or did his eyes sweep the mourners to flick against hers before he turned to sit with Damon and the others? Did she want to believe he sought her? She knew the power of physical attraction and what it could lead to for those in its snare.

But her thoughts drifted. She had to acknowledge her reaction to Bretton, reminding herself that Max had entrusted a serious assignment to her professional care. No weakness could or should put her career in jeopardy. Lucinda made no mistake when she wrote in her diary of the harm scandal might visit on a woman who became careless with her favors.

The minister spoke with simple devotion. He extolled Lucinda's many charitable gifts to the church and to its parishioners in need. He swept his arm toward the windows to his right.

"These windows and those across from them may well have been her most beautiful and lasting gift. She designed them and hired the workmen who made them possible. Of course, today the sun itself seems to mourn with us, so they don't shine as they do when the day is bright. In any event, they make our little church a destination for those in the larger parishes of even Helena or Missoula." He smiled ruefully. "I should, of course, mention that she gave us the remarkable windows in memory of her beloved husband, Garrett." The reverend added that Garrett had died too soon, leaving his young widow, mother of their two little boys, alone so many years before.

Amy turned her head to look at the windows and remained

fixated on them for the rest of the service. Rebecca made a mental note to return on a sunny day to speak to the reverend and study the windows, now dulled, as he pointed out, by the overcast day.

Two plump young women stood in the cold sanctuary without removing their coats. Eyes fixed on their hymnals, they sang a tremulous duet of *Nearer My God to Thee*.

Members of the family wept, all but Bretton. His broad shoulders didn't shake. His head never bowed. Rebecca found herself wondering whether Lucinda wept at Garrett's funeral. The next pages of the diary would reveal so much. She recalled how harsh Bretton had been in speaking of his mother. Rebecca pulled back from judging either of them until Lucinda revealed more of their difficult lives.

The thought also came of how, although she never spoke of her father, she judged him with no less severity than Bretton did Lucinda. Shouldn't an adult daughter show more compassion than an angry young girl? But he'd abandoned her. Not just emotionally, but to survive on her own. Unless . . . had he ever spoken to Max? At some point had Max committed himself to take her in if something happened to her only parent? She'd never asked her uncle.

After the service, Rebecca waited until the family followed the casket outside and others filed out behind them. She needed to ponder for a moment. What, if anything, might the grieving young widow and mother have revealed to the pastor years ago? Or what did she confide more recently as an aged woman all too aware of her weakened heart?

The sky had darkened to the color of tarnished silver, and rising wind caused an ominous roar in pines flanking the churchyard. Snow descended in white pellets that struck with stinging force, bouncing off surfaces before piling into growing drifts. Rebecca felt chilled in spite of her heavy wool coat. When the minister had spoken his final prayers and pallbearers lowered the casket into the ground, sorrowful family members stepped forward to drop hard clods onto the casket where flakes landed on them like frozen tears.

"Oh, Max." Watching them, Rebecca whispered, "You should have stopped loving her."

The minister canceled the luncheon scheduled to follow the service. Women of the congregation distributed cakes and breads among those in attendance to carry to their own tables.

Glancing at the ominous sky, guests dispersed into wagons, coaches, and buggies. Their drivers appeared intent on reaching home before the storm hit with full force.

Bretton looked pale, a sick uneasiness in his eyes. As he approached Rebecca, little Teddy broke away from the others and caught his uncle's hand.

"I want to go with you."

Startled out of his daze, Bretton reached down with a gentleness Rebecca hadn't seen in him before. His fingers stroked the little boy's eager, upturned face.

Amy ran forward to snatch her little brother back. "No! Stay away from him!"

"Amy!" Rebecca stepped forward, but Amy yanked Teddy's arm again.

Turning to Rebecca she said in tones as icy as the weather, "You stay away from us, too. You're not part of our family!"

Damon approached, his face reddened. "Amy! Apologize. What's gotten into you? Rebecca is Max Bryan's niece. Max has been a dear friend of this family for as long as I can remember . . . almost one of us."

Claudia put an arm around her daughter and spoke. "Darling, I know how much you loved Grandmother Lucinda. But she's gone. Turning against each other and our guest will never bring your grandmother back. Please, tell Rebecca how sorry I know you really are."

"I'm sorry," Amy muttered. But her apology sounded rancorous. Her face hardened. As if clinging to a grudge, Amy remained unapproachable. Nevertheless, Rebecca thought, this hostile child is hiding something. Some key information? She determined to break through the stone wall blocking her from Amy's secrets.

Rebecca studied the girl. What did she know, and what did she imagine? After hesitating, Rebecca smiled and answered in a kind tone. "I accept your apology. This is a difficult day. We should start back without the weight of bitter words."

Teddy looked sober, but he wriggled out of his sister's grasp to clutch Bretton's hand. Then he grabbed Rebecca's with his free one, swinging with lifted feet between them. "I want to go with Bretton and Rebecca," he insisted.

"Then you shall, my Teddy." Claudia smiled at Rebecca. "We'll see you back at Eagle Mountain."

Teddy sat on Rebecca's lap, chattering while the two snuggled their chins into the curly hair of the buffalo robe. The curious little boy fired one question after the other to Bretton, who responded in a distracted way. Watching them occupied Rebecca's thoughts. Bretton focused on guiding the horses through the worsening weather. Soon visibility extended only a few feet ahead. The storm's noise—creaking tree trunks, wind moaning through boughs—raged on.

At one point the buggy skidded on the iced road. Rebecca bit her lip but held back any comment when she saw Bretton's strained expression. After what seemed like hours, Eagle Mountain's blurred outline appeared.

"Take Teddy in," Bretton yelled, his voice almost drowned out from the shrieking wind. "I'm going back to batten down the studio and take the team into the barn."

"Wait for me," Rebecca ordered, remembering the story of Garrett's death. "You shouldn't go alone. I'll be quick."

Bretton stared at her. "I'll be damned. All right. You wait here. Keep tight hold on the reins. I'll carry him in. Come on, Teddy." Bretton put protective arms around the little boy. Teddy shielded his face against his uncle's neck.

Rebecca wondered at herself. Why had she offered to go with this difficult man to his studio? Why had it seemed the most natural thing in the world to do? Could she really be such an easy mark for troubled people? In spite of his tough persona Bretton did have troubles. There'd been a look in his eyes that surpassed ordinary uneasiness about bad road conditions, and she'd noted a flash of gratitude at her offer. Despite his tough persona, he could be emotional. He claimed to want nothing, and yet he'd come home. Why?

In truth, though, she acknowledged more than one motive to herself for going with him to the studio. Despite the pull she felt toward Bretton, he remained a prime suspect in the matter of the lost will. Privacy might allow her to learn more. But was that the most important reason? She remembered the feel of his hand on her arm. Could her offer have risen from another desire to be alone with him?

She shivered against the seat, hugging herself. "Oh, Uncle Max," she murmured. "This assignment is more difficult than you could have imagined."

The storm's lamentations drowned her words as Bretton climbed back in beside her and reclaimed the reins. "I told them to have hot chocolate or something stronger ready when we get back," he shouted. "Now let's see if we can make it to the studio and return without trouble."

The narrow road, though somewhat protected by pines and underbrush bordering it, began to fill with drifts. With effort, the stalwart horses pulled them to the cabin.

Bretton unhitched them and left them eating from feed troughs in the little barn. He turned to Rebecca, who'd clambered down and occupied herself with stamping her cold feet as she followed him. "Okay," he said. "Take my hand, and don't let go."

The blizzard made mere breathing an accomplishment. The struggle to cover the few yards to the cabin left them both puffing. Once inside, Rebecca panted and leaned against one of the tables.

Bretton said, "Sit over there."

She nodded and staggered over to plop down on the quilt-covered cot. Bretton disappeared into the adjoining room, which held his kiln, and opened its door. He gingerly removed a few bricks.

"Good. They're ready to unload. It's always a little like Christmas morning waiting to see how things turned out," he called to her.

While Bretton busied himself, Rebecca glanced around the cabin-turned-studio. This might be her only opportunity to search this place for the will.

She slid one hand under Bretton's pillow. No papers. What about the mattress? She stood and ran a hand between the springs and the thin mattress. Nothing. Summoning her returning strength, she walked to the shelf containing buckets, glass bottles, jars, and packages with brown paper wrapping, all labeled with names of varied chemicals. It didn't seem that someone wanting to hide a document would leave it there, but . . . She glanced over her shoulder and saw Bretton still occupied. That provided her the opportunity to check the shelves' contents. She shifted one of the packages and ran her fingers down the row, feeling between them.

"What are you doing?"

She whirled to see that Bretton, silent and surreptitious, had returned to the main room. His cold glare bespoke suspicion and hostility. He gripped an unglazed urn with a jagged crack running down one side.

Rebecca felt grateful for her cheeks being already, no doubt, scarlet from the cold. "Oh," she shrugged. "You were distracted so long I wanted to have a look around. I've never been in a potter's studio before."

"Did you expect to find something in particular? It looked like you were searching my cabin. I asked you before. Why did you come to Eagle Mountain?" He took a step toward her.

Rebecca glanced to the door.

Bretton continued. "I'm not as trusting as my brother. I haven't spent my life being sheltered. I know when somebody is after something. What do you want from us? I don't know what it is yet, but you're going to tell me."

"You impugn motives where I have none," Rebecca said, wincing inwardly at the lie. "I only want to help you. That's why I offered to come here. You seemed so troubled." She could tell him about the will, she thought. The others knew, but now his anger mingled with distrust might lead to . . . she didn't know what. Her mind full of Garrett's violence, she dared not risk finding out.

She realized her mistake in speaking of his mood. Bretton tried to appear secretive, aloof. For her to have spotted his emotion showed that at least to one person he'd become transparent. And his possible reaction to her perception could be anything. Melting snow dripped from his hair. He assumed a defensive stance like a wolf at bay. The fleeting thought came to Rebecca that that's when wild creatures are at their most dangerous.

Intolerable tension filled the cabin. The storm pushing at the walls added to Rebecca's apprehension. Then Bretton hurled the cracked urn across the room, where it shattered on the wall.

Shards landed, striking and bouncing off the cot that Rebecca had searched moments before. She gasped.

And so, she thought, like his father before him. Both Seth and Bretton were capable of losing control.

He laughed that bitter sound again. "What is it about this place? What was it about her? I should have stayed away. They can have it all if that's what she wanted. There are no honest answers here. Only lies. I thought you might be what you seem. What a damned fool I am."

"I'm here to help," Rebecca protested. "Don't cast aspersions when you don't have all the facts."

He glared at her. "Everything in this place is an illusion—or an act. And she could put on a great act . . . appear so loving, so concerned, so helpful. But I knew the person she turned into when we worked in here together. A frozen heart existed inside her. Her cold eyes . . . her icy irritation." He advanced a step. "I'm going to learn your secret. I know why I'm here. I know why the rest of them are here. But you have a different story. What is it? Why did you really come to Eagle Mountain? What do you want from us, from me?"

"I don't want anything from you." Rebecca stepped back. "Stop right there. I've told you: I'm here to help."

"I'm not going to hurt you." Bretton's shoulders sagged. As he turned, his eyes shifted from green to an opaque gray. Fatigue and sorrow showed in his drawn face. "I don't know. Perhaps you are telling the truth."

Guilt over her deception filled Rebecca. Should she confide her dual purpose to Bretton? No. Uncle Max would never advise it. "Always play your cards close to the vest. Secrecy is your main ally." Those words summed up her canny uncle's philosophy. She glanced at this volatile man standing before her. But at what price, Uncle Max? she thought to herself.

"Bretton." She moved forward to touch his arm. "I'm not

your enemy. Please, explain your work to me. The things I see here are so arresting. Besides, how can we trust each other until we're better acquainted?"

Bretton studied her again. Their gazes locked. Rebecca found herself as breathless as she'd been in the storm outside. Now she felt the turbulent weather within. She so wanted this intense, mysterious man to accept her at least a little.

"All right." He granted her a thin smile. "But I don't believe you came here to learn about vases or bowls or pots."

CHAPTER FIFTEEN

He spent the next while talking with increasing pride and eagerness, showing her beautiful forms he'd created, explaining glazes, rubbing away rough spots on the bottoms of fired pieces. Rebecca understood the passion he poured into his work.

When he finally wound down Rebecca asked, "How did you start with all this?"

"Mother worked in clay, a ceramics artist, a good one. Seth helped her turn this guest cabin into a studio just after she and Garrett Cale arrived. She spent hours out here, and I liked to hang about watching and learning."

"It sounds like a wonderful boyhood."

"That it was not. Mother had powerful ways. She controlled all around her. Well, enough of that. Sorry I ran on so. I haven't talked this much in months, certainly not about ceramics."

For the first time, Bretton didn't have his defenses up. Relaxed, he became much more compelling than when wary. Rebecca looked up at him. He trailed a finger along her cheek.

The gray-green of the eyes that met hers seemed to have deepened to a dark blue.

Then he enveloped her in his arms and pulled her against his long, muscular body. She felt the planes and contours of him, bone and muscle. She felt herself melting into him, her arms around him, her fingers buried in his hair. He smelled like wood smoke. Eager, returning his kiss, she floated warm and responsive. How she'd missed this. All of this.

His hand touched her breast. Returned to reality, Rebecca removed his exploring hand and stepped back. "I'm sorry. I can't become careless . . . My uncle is so ill. And you've just buried your mother."

She stopped to take a breath and tuck tendrils of hair behind her ears. "I feel as you, but America isn't the Europe where I came of age. Society here is so proper and strict, so puritanical. This is not the time or place for me to break from this unforgiving culture's idea of proper behavior if I want to live in it. And I do."

She pulled her shoulders back and gave him a fixed look. "I'm trying to establish myself as a woman in a man's profession. I can't let my heart guide my head. Still," she gave him a wistful smile, "if I had nothing more to restrain me . . ."

Bretton continued to gaze at her and then lifted his hands in a gesture of defeat. "I know," he said. "I know. But you felt something. You're not a conventional woman any more than I'm a conventional man. Why behave as though we are? Don't be afraid. Don't shrink from life with its unpredictable turns and twists."

"I won't. I intend to live a full life, all it can offer, but on my own terms. I'll never shirk my obligations. One is to help your family. They'll worry about us if we're not back soon."

Bretton looked at her for a moment more. "As you wish." He spoke in an uneven voice. "Perhaps we can continue this another time. For now let's start back. From the sound of things, we'll have even harder going outside than we're having in here."

When Bretton opened the studio door, a blast of arctic air struck Rebecca full force.

"Wait," he said. "Wrap this around you." He brought her the quilt from his cot. "You're going to need it. This is a storm of the century."

He settled the quilt around her shoulders, shards of the shattered urn hitting the floor in little explosions around her feet. Both Bretton and Rebecca pulled up their hoods before challenging the elements. Bretton started out first, and Rebecca hurried after him. She used his broad back to break the winds that sliced like malicious knives.

They reached the barn. Even opening its doors proved a struggle. Once inside Rebecca inhaled the still, animal-scented air. Bretton went to hitch up the sleigh in the walled-off space behind the horse troughs. He made an exclamation of disgust.

"Damn. Damon had the sleigh taken to the lodge this morning so he'd have it for carrying Claudia into town tomorrow. We're going to have to go on foot. There's too much snow for the buggy, and one horse is becoming lame. Both are exhausted."

Rebecca thought of Garrett Cale's death. She looked toward the door. "But can we? It's a long way."

"We'd better try anyway. I don't keep food out here. This storm could last for days. Come on. You'll be fine. I won't let go of you. In any event not until we get to Eagle Mountain. Then we'll have to avoid each others' eyes, or our improper behavior might show. Claudia sees everything."

"I'd say Amy does," Rebecca said with a rueful grin.

Rebecca followed him out of the barn, gasping as the winds threw her back against its outer wall. Bretton took one of her gloved hands, and they began the struggle to reach the lodge. They'd wrapped mufflers around their fur-ruffed hoods, pulled close around their faces. Rebecca stopped trying to see ahead. She kept her eyes open just enough to see her feet, or where she would see them if they weren't obscured by the whiteout. Bretton kept his promise. He gripped her hand as he led her forward.

There could be no point in trying to talk. With twilight descending they found themselves surrounded by snow that swirled from white to blue. Rebecca fell, and for a terrifying moment thought she'd lost Bretton. Then she felt his grip on her arm as he pulled her back up out of a drift. Her hands and feet numbed. Worse yet, her eyelids, burning from exposure, began to feel heavy. She slowed in resistance to Bretton's pace. If he'd let go, she could rest for just a minute. Then she'd be able to continue on. Her mind drifted.

She tugged against him, but he pulled her forward, merciless as the freezing wind in that blinding whiteout. It gnawed and howled, leaving her battered.

Her thoughts slowed to a sluggish mix where anger smoldered. Oh, but that Bretton, how brutish and mean. How strange that she'd let a person like that, with that animal charm, kiss her the way he had. She'd never let it happen again. Uncle Max would disapprove. Still, the kiss had been wonderful. She'd felt needed—warm. She felt her knees buckling and knelt in the snow.

"Rebecca! Rebecca!"

Was someone calling her? Bretton's eyes, his brows caked in snow, swam into sight, and the next moment he shook her. Hard. She protested. She wanted him to go on ahead and leave her, just let her rest. The shaking became harsher. She tried to raise her heavy arms to push him away. Then of all things, she felt a slap to her cheek. That monster hit her. Her eyes widened and focused on him. She tried to hit back.

"That's better. Now get up if you don't want to wind up like Garrett Cale, dying out here. Come on, Rebecca, we're two-thirds there." He shouted into her ear, his voice made faint by the wind's howl.

Rebecca wanted to cry, but found she lacked the energy. Bretton hauled her to her numbed feet and began to half pull, half carry her. Like an automaton, she put one foot in front of the other, leaning on him. Then her mind once again wandered into a blank whiteness. She felt Bretton shaking her harder, but her head just rolled on her shoulders. What difference did it make if Bretton Cale or the storm killed her? Craving peace, she drifted, soon enveloped in darkness.

She heard a voice say, "All right, darling, no more of this." At times in the next few moments, consciousness filtered through. She had the sensation of being carried. How strange.

Rebecca came to consciousness on a leather couch, aware of being in a place of light and sound and blessed warmth.

"Put her hands in heated towels." Bretton gave firm orders. "And get the hot chocolate."

Someone put the drink to her lips, and she swallowed. Her stomach warmed, and her eyes closed despite her decision to keep them open. Voices and pain penetrated her half-conscious haze as heat reached her hands and feet.

"Bretton, we worried so about you both." Claudia's voice conveyed real concern.

"At one point, I did, too," Bretton responded. "Rebecca's strength kept failing. Let's get some more hot chocolate into her. She'll be all right now."

Rebecca opened her eyes to see Damon hovering over her, his expression anxious, and worry evident in his tone. "Can you sit up?"

"Yes. I'm so sorry I caused such trouble," Rebecca murmured, directing her words to Bretton. Despite her doubts, her underestimating him, he'd saved her. Grateful she could breathe and move her hands she realized he'd been more reliable than her own instincts. Left to herself she would have lain down and died. He could have rid himself of her with no one the wiser.

"You gave me a reason to keep on, too," Bretton said. "I couldn't leave you."

Amy's accusing voice pierced the silence that followed. "You mean you wouldn't leave her to freeze to death like Seth did Grandfather Garrett. After all, you wouldn't want to be the cause of two people dying in blizzards. You caused one just by being born."

"Amy!" Claudia's shocked reproach came too late.

Bretton's expression turned steely and defiant. He strode out of the room toward the kitchen. How strange, Rebecca thought, that he made no sound on the wooden floor as he left. He just vanished. Perhaps he'd learned to walk that way during the war.

"Amy!" Damon sounded furious. "What's come over you these last weeks? Don't speak that way, certainly not to any adult. You're unfair in attacking your uncle to say the least. He's not at fault for your grandfather's death. You know Garrett Cale died trying to bring help for your grandmother. The blizzard killed him, not a person."

Damon shook his head. "Father always took risks. He died because of the storm. I know Bretton's ways can be hard to understand, but he is my brother. He's welcome here. Find him and apologize. Be the sweet child I know you to be. No dilly dallying. Then go to your room. Think over the fact that words spoken in haste still have consequences."

Amy cast her father a stricken look. "You don't understand. I did it for you. He should never have been born. Then Grandfather Garrett would still be alive. Then everything would be different." Amy lifted her chin and stalked out of the room.

It became clear there would be no apologies from Amy. In spite of her exhaustion Rebecca surmised that the odd girl held her cards close, cards that Rebecca intended to see before the game progressed much further. But for now, she wanted only warmth and hot chocolate.

Damon raised his hands, palms outward, and shrugged. "What's to be done? It's as though she's turned into a different girl in these past months. She used to be kind and loving. Now she seems obsessed with lashing out at Bretton and insulting Seth's memory. Seth did save Mother by bringing help. And my brother's never spoken a harsh word to my daughter. I'll try reasoning with her one more time." Damon shook his head and followed after Amy.

Rebecca resolved anew to talk to Amy herself when the opportunity arose. Perhaps the girl had some reason for her mystifying hatred. Or had she misunderstood something her grandmother said . . . or wrote?

Claudia walked over. "Are you able to stand, Rebecca?"

"Yes, I'm sure I can. I just gave in to cold and exhaustion." Rebecca stood and gave Claudia a shaky smile. "Yes. I can walk, too."

Claudia took her arm. "A bubble bath, then beef stew for supper, and you'll be good as new. What a day!"

As kind and generous as Damon, Claudia saw Rebecca upstairs and instructed Damon and Mrs. Bell to bring water for a steaming bath with plenty of fragrant bubbles. She even laid out a plum-colored bath towel.

"I'll bring you one of my flannel gowns and a goose down robe," she said. "I think we're about of a size. At least we would be under normal circumstances." She patted her rounded belly. "The nightie and robe aren't stylish, but when you've been chilled there's nothing cozier. I'll lay them on your bed. Then I'll leave you to bask in peace."

"Thank you, Claudia. You're all so kind." After Claudia left, Rebecca shook her head and undressed. She tested the water with one toe—heaven. She sank into the steamy bubbles with a contented sigh but wondered as she did which member of Lucinda's thoughtful family might want to frustrate the carrying out of her last wishes.

The door swung open. Rebecca grabbed the towel and covered her breasts as best she could. The intruder turned out to be a grinning Teddy, cheerful and oblivious that he'd invaded Rebecca's privacy.

"Hi," he approached and popped a bubble with one finger as he contemplated her. "Amy said you almost died. You didn't, did you?"

Rebecca laughed. "No, of course not, Teddy. Your Uncle Bretton took good care of me. He was a hero in the blizzard. He should receive a medal. Now, young man, you turn around and march yourself out of here so I can finish my bath."

"But I want to stay and talk."

Someone pushed the bathroom door farther open. Bretton stood before them.

"What is this? A Cale convention? Next time I'll send invitations." She challenged Bretton with not altogether serious eyes. His eyes sought her breasts, molded to the towel, for a second too long.

Bretton caught himself and looked into her pink face. "I heard Teddy and came to get him."

"Well then, please take him and yourself, too, away." She tried to sound stern as she scooped bubbles up to her shoulders, but ill-suppressed laughter gave her away.

"Off we go, little man," Bretton said, scooping Teddy up under one arm. As they left she heard Teddy's piercing little voice. "Rebecca says you're a hero, Uncle Bretton. Does she love you?"

The door closed, and Rebecca hurried to finish. She toweled dry and went into her room. Teddy's question rang in her mind. Did she love Bretton? Desire him would be closer to the truth, and now she felt gratitude as well as attraction.

She shook her head. Uncle Max had sent her to find an answer, and all she could come up with so far were questions and a temptation to misbehave with a handsome artist. To love someone with Bretton's moods would invite a whirlwind, and this brush with a real storm had been enough.

Rebecca pondered. Little Teddy adored his uncle, but Amy had some virulent reason for disliking Bretton. Children were often astute about adults' characters. In this case, which sibling was correct?

Bretton drew her to him with magnetic force. Yet she remembered him hurling the urn. How violent could he become? Lucinda missed sensing the violence in Garrett's character before they married. Such a lapse in awareness could ruin a woman's life, or end it.

Rebecca reminded herself of her purpose in coming, to solve the mystery of the missing will. Romance couldn't interfere with demands of that assignment. But part of her agreed with Bretton that life's pleasures should be enjoyed to the fullest. The memory of holding Bretton brought color to her face, not from modesty, but a flash of desire. A sensation long set aside.

She'd recovered from the ordeal of the storm except for a relaxed fatigue. Deciding the hour too early for the nightgown and robe, she set them aside. For the evening she chose a burgundy wool dress and a heavy shawl. She rearranged her hair and studied herself in the mirror. The face that met her didn't seem too much the worse from the day's trials.

Rebecca closed her door and walked down the great stairs, appraising the scene below her. The family had gathered around the huge stone fireplace, where a blaze leapt and crackled. The smell of burning pine added to the rare impression of familial harmony. Amy and Teddy toasted bread by the hearth. Damon sat on the floor at his Claudia's feet. But, from her portrait on the wall, Lucinda's disquieting gaze flowed over them.

Bretton sprawled in one of the large chairs, staring at the others with a look of mixed amusement and longing. Rebecca yearned to go to him, always the child shut out. She guessed that if he tried to join them Amy would protest, so he stayed on the edge nursing a whiskey and brooding.

Rebecca greeted the group. "You look so lovely in the firelight. I wish I could have brought my camera."

"So you count photography among your talents." Damon smiled. "Pull up a chair and join us." The generous fire in the hearth cast light into the room. "Let's light candles and lamps. I sent most of the help home before we left for the funeral. Mrs. Bell is staying here, but she's gone to bed." Damon headed toward the door.

Teddy walked over to Bretton, offering to share his buttered toast. Bretton pulled the little boy onto his lap. In seconds they laughed together, throwing shadow pictures on the wall. Rebecca noted the wavering outlines of wolves, rabbits, and giraffes made by hands, one set small, one large. Perhaps Bretton knew so much about illusions because he, too, knew how to create them so well. Amy watched the two with a detached coldness and then walked over to Rebecca to offer her toast.

"I wish we could play the Victrola," Amy sighed.

"We don't need to, angel." Damon looked at his brother. "Bretton, you used to be the best guitar player in the county. Let's be old-fashioned and return to making our own music."

"Not until after supper," Claudia said. "Stew's ready. We'll eat in here." She passed out heavy pottery bowls, made, she told Rebecca, by Lucinda. Damon brought in a steaming pot of Irish stew prepared by Mrs. Bell before she retired.

They visited as they ate, reminiscing about Lucinda. After everyone had finished, Rebecca and Claudia used heated water from the Majestic stove in the kitchen to wash dishes.

"Now we'll have music," Damon announced when the two women rejoined the others.

"Oh, Father," Amy protested. "I just wanted a song on the

gramophone."

"Bretton, please. I'd love to hear you play," said Claudia, frowning at her grousing daughter.

Bretton hesitated as though he'd rather decline. An eager Teddy interrupted the refusal. "Play me a song, Uncle Bretton. Play one song just for me."

"Well, how can I turn down my best friend?"

"You can't." Damon, who'd gone upstairs, returned with a guitar that he thrust at his brother before resuming his earlier place at Claudia's feet.

Amy turned her back to the group, poking with obvious irritation at the fire. A log fell, sending up a burst of explosive, red sparks.

Bretton tuned the guitar. When he'd finished, his long fingers brushed over its strings. Rebecca, glad to be in shadow, watched him. His dark lashes hovered over high cheekbones framed by auburn hair. She felt like a swimmer caught in an undertow not of water, but her own desire. Apprehension filled her. What if, like Max, she should become in thrall to someone too marred by life to love her? How had her uncle stood it? She must never make the mistake he had.

Bretton played first in a lively style. Some song he'd learned in Cuba? Teddy jumped up and did his best to entertain them with leaps and twirls before he flopped, out of breath, on a bear rug near the fire. Then, Bretton sang and strummed other folk songs of the Cuban culture. His voice, a full, sensitive baritone, swelled. He lost himself in the music. He didn't announce the songs but went from one to the next. Except for Amy's angry stabs at burning logs, the little group sat spellbound. In the darkness, Rebecca drifted into an admiration that approached Teddy's.

Bretton finished with a love ballad about a sailor whose young wife had died while he served at sea, yet he saw her in the stars and moonlit ocean. After the last chords, Bretton looked at Rebecca. Their eyes held until he stood. "Well, that's more than enough. Damon, let's play that gramophone."

"I want to dance with my wife. Amy, find us a waltz," Damon commanded.

Amy made no objection, but did as her father asked. In moments a Strauss waltz floated through the lodge. Damon held Claudia as though she were precious, fragile porcelain. The two entered into a slow and graceful dance.

Bretton approached Rebecca. "Well, here's your chance not to be a wallflower."

"Conceited, aren't you?" But she stood and lifted her hand to his shoulder. Bretton wore a wool shirt. His collar open, chest hairs curled just below his throat. Rebecca longed to touch them. She looked up. He smiled. The music had exorcised, at least for the moment, whatever ghosts haunted him.

Rebecca returned his smile. They circled the great half-dark room without speaking. At the end of each graceful waltz, Amy started another, the music evoking a time of happiness gone by.

"Well, we've lost one of the party," Bretton observed. Teddy lay asleep. Damon had covered his son with a sheepskin throw, and Teddy lay rosy-cheeked and dreaming in the firelight.

"We'll take him up," Rebecca offered to Damon and Claudia. "You stay here and put another log on the fire."

Bretton collected the sleeping boy. Rebecca preceded them up the stairs, a candle holder in one hand as she shielded the flame with the other. Away from the hearth fire, the house chilled, seeming bigger and darker.

CHAPTER SIXTEEN

"This way." Bretton nodded his head indicating a room at the opposite end of the hall from Rebecca's. The nursery held two single beds and shelves of toys and books.

"What a charming place to grow up in," she murmured as Bretton laid Teddy on one of the beds, pulling off the child's scuffed shoes and covering him with a down comforter.

"He can sleep in his clothes this once," Bretton said, placing the shoes side by side on the floor.

"Was this your room?" Rebecca asked.

Bretton's face closed as it had earlier when she questioned him about his life.

He answered with a noncommittal, "It was the nursery." He raised his shoulders as though shaking off a burden. "You might as well know, although you should've sensed it by now. My mother loved Damon. She put up with me. At night when she thought we'd both dropped off, she'd come in. She always bent over Damon, kissed him, and straightened his quilt, the image of maternal perfection.

"Then she'd come to my bed. She never bent over my pillow. She'd stand for several minutes, then sigh . . . a terrible, lonely, sound. And she'd walk away fast, as though leaving something vile."

"I'm so sorry." Rebecca reached out to hold and comfort the man who'd been the unloved little boy.

But Bretton shook his head. "No, you don't have to do that.

It happened years ago. It's all but forgotten except when I'm here. Now let's go downstairs before we compromise that respectable reputation of yours."

Rebecca set her jaw and followed as he left the room. She would reach him. He had started speaking to her of his earlier life. Soon she'd cut through the distrust he'd learned through long experience. But, she chided herself, she would never be Lucinda, using a siren's wiles to lure a man, then push him where she wanted him to go. Or would the diaries convince her not to close that possibility? Lucinda's pages were as much windows into the past as they might be doors opening to her vanished will.

Later that night, when all had bid their good nights and retired, Rebecca hurried through her preparations for bed. She put her hair in a long braid and flicked it behind her as she reached for the diary. At last she'd learn details of events that resulted from Lucinda's manipulation of Seth.

March 1, 1873

This morning I felt Seth's baby moving in my womb, and I wondered what fate awaits the two of us. That old dread of some unknown horror returned. I pray this baby will be well.

March 5, 1873

Damon and I sat playing checkers before the fire. We talked and laughed. Damon looks like his father but is so different. Damon gave me an extra turn when it seemed I teetered on the brink of losing. If only Garrett had as gentle a way of looking at life as his little son. What will my expected child be like? Will my second baby inherit Seth's natural serenity? I hope I haven't stolen that from my lover forever.

March 10, 1873

Seth is away, hunting I believe. I worry about him. It isn't fair the way I've used his devotion. Still, I think in time he'll understand that taking such drastic means to free me will be for the best.

March 14, 1873

Seth is back! He returned and told us that he went to Kalispell on personal matters. He stayed with Max Bryan. He reports Max is well and wishes us all best with the coming birth.

Seth also advised that a storm is coming. Garrett wanted to take me to stay with the doctor before it arrives, but I told him I wished to stay here. I couldn't tell him that I want Seth to be able to see his child as soon as it's born. I owe him that. Seth is and has been a beacon to me in the dark. Part of me will always love and be with him, even though I may not be able to keep all my promises, especially the one that binds him to our deadly plan.

March 15, 1873

The blizzard.

It's here. Seth's wilderness understanding held true. This morning we awakened to the rising wind even before pulling back the curtains. The baby is expected any time, and now, with the level of this storm, I confess I am frightened. Garrett's expression betrays his worry. Of course, his concern is not for me, but for his expected child. He hopes for a second son more like him than little Damon will ever be.

He probably wanted me absent, too, so he could resume dallying with Peggy. I can tell by her dejected attitude that he no longer makes love to her as often as she'd like. At times I observe desperation in her eyes. She's learning that Garrett is no respecter of persons. I take satisfaction in her failing efforts to hold him. What a bitter woman I've become. How well I know that Garrett must always be the hunter. He'll never lose his drive to take new trophies, trophies other men can only envy.

It's obvious that he's been ignoring the silly creature. For awhile she'd put on airs as though she thought herself my equal, if not my better. I marvel at her foolishness in believing he'd never grow bored and drop her. I almost pity her. I, too, once failed to understand what harm he could inflict on any woman who loved him.

We went downstairs for breakfast in our robes. Peggy worked in the kitchen alongside Mrs. Anderson. She fixed us a lovely breakfast of steaming hot coffee, thick slabs of bacon, and pancakes with maple syrup. Seth entered, and Garrett insisted he join us. Seth hesitated, but the aroma of Mrs. Anderson's cooking enticed him to stay.

We talked about the storm. Seth believes this will be a long one, probably lasting days. We have plenty of firewood and are well-stocked with provisions. The only problem is that my labor could start. Seth and Garrett discussed this as if I weren't present listening to them.

"It's too late to take Lucinda to the doctor now," Seth said. "If her labor starts we'll need to deliver the baby ourselves."

"I don't like it," Garrett answered. "What if the birth doesn't go well?"

He didn't look at me as he said it. As I wrote earlier, he doesn't think of me. His concern is for his second heir. He wants another son to mold into his idea of a man.

"If there are complications, I'll go for Doctor Gillette." Seth's chin jutted out in his determination.

"We'll see," Garrett answered in a grim tone.

I thought of the dangers of the blizzard. Then, as I looked through the window to the whiteout beyond, I saw the answer to our problems as if someone had written it across a blank sheet of paper. Did providence now offer Seth the opportunity to accomplish Garrett's end? Would the blizzard prove my salvation?

I'd assured Seth that Garrett's death would seal my promise to marry him. He sought that promise for so long. Seth, a man of the mountains, has knowledge enough to survive the raging storm where another might not. I studied the two of them. Seth had let his hair grow long and shaggy. His broad, powerful body suits his life as a guide and trapper. I think of touching that body. In unbidden moments the thought overpowers and leaves me shaken.

Garrett's hair hung over his forehead in that unruly way it had. He could have been a king in his purple robe, but a royal ruined by decadence. Lines branch beside his eyes to his temples. Dark, puffy crescents sag under them, too. He trembles if there's too much of a time lag between whiskeys. He sometimes requires sleeping powders or even laudanum to rest his nerves.

But like a king he seems to feel he can do whatever he likes to anyone.

Little does he know.

Rubbing her hand over tired eyes, Rebecca shuddered. Did Bretton's mother in fact commit a crime or, worse yet, incite his natural father to commit one? She read from pages trembling in her unsteady hands.

March 20, 1873
My baby is born. He's healthy, a well-formed boy with

dark-blue eyes that veer toward green and hair the color of my own.

Just after I put this journal away five days ago, I felt pains starting. I didn't tell anyone at first. We all sat before the fire visiting and drinking cider, the picture of snow-bound coziness. Soon, however, the moments of cramping discomfort turned severe. Mrs. Anderson perceived their significance. Garrett helped me upstairs. I turned and caught Seth's eye as he stood watching. I mouthed the words, "Save me."

Seth, Peggy, and Mrs. Anderson prepared for the birth. They put water on to boil and gathered extra linens. As a young girl, Mrs. Anderson had assisted her mother, a community midwife. That's why I felt secure even without Doctor Gillette. Or, I did in the beginning. My labor went on far longer than it should, the pains all but unbearable. Mrs. Anderson finally told Seth and Garrett it would be a breech birth.

My agony became unspeakable. I felt angry. What an outrage that I had been brought to this level of pain. It couldn't be happening to me. I feared for the baby and then began to fear for myself. I believed I'd never see my little Damon again, that my life would soon be over. I begged Mrs. Anderson to do something.

In the end I pleaded with them to fetch the doctor. It seemed a long time since I'd seen either Seth or Garrett. I felt the tenfold return of that apprehension that plagued me from the outset of my pregnancy. Something horrible might happen. What if my tormentor survived to come home, and Seth did not?

But with odd, absolute certainty I knew of a sudden that Garrett would be the one to die. I would never again be his victim. And Seth would live to save me. The outcome had been written in the white blankness of the storm.

"Where's the doctor?" I kept repeating as the wind screamed outside.

At last Mrs. Anderson shook her head and left the room. When the door opened again, she came to me and took my hand, her weary face flushed and strained. "Garrett and Seth are both going to bring back Doctor Gillette. They'll be safe together. Seth knows the forest so well. He'll keep your husband safe. I'll call upon my years of experience to deliver your baby if the doctor doesn't arrive in time. Peggy is helping them prepare, gathering what they'll need in the storm."

My mind conjured an image of the two men lost in the white roar of blizzard. "What will happen to us all?"

"Two strong men can take care of themselves. It's a bad storm, but all we can do now is wait. I'll try to turn the baby before the doctor arrives."

"Dear Seth, take care of Garrett," I murmured.

Mrs. Anderson misunderstood my meaning. "Seth will take care of your husband. Of course he will."

How I hoped so.

I slept a bit and dreamed of two indistinct figures lost in a howling storm, each calling my name. I couldn't see them. I could only hear their separate voices, calling and calling, over and over. I found myself in the whiteout searching for Seth, but his voice seemed to echo from everywhere. When I woke, the blizzard still wailed, pushing the curtains in from the closed windows. Mrs. Anderson dozed in a rocker near my bed.

I experienced another pain, then another and another. I had a dim realization in the following hours that the men should have returned with Doctor Gillette. I smelled blood and sweat and my own excrement. My scattered thoughts penetrating the haze of pain and exhaustion were of those gone into that endless storm as well as of my own desperate plight.

"What's happening?" I questioned Mrs. Anderson.

"I don't know. There's no use in trying to guess," she answered in her usual blunt and honest way.

Peggy entered my room with a pitcher of fresh water, her face drawn and tight lipped. Her few terse words showed her to be edgy and short tempered as she built up the fire and gathered soiled linens to take downstairs.

I supposed she suffered in fear for my husband. Only I knew what it meant to suffer in fear *of* him. If Garrett died, Seth's love for me killed him. And the baby, the result of Seth's and my clandestine love, will never know what brutality lived in the man whose name he'll carry.

At last, Seth arrived with the doctor, but Garrett did not return. The storm had eased, and they came by sleigh. Then Doctor Gillette saved my life. The good man worked, fought death, and brought Seth's and my son into the world alive.

I'm weak, but two great burdens have lifted. I'd worried over giving birth, fearing for the child's health. While I carried him I'd been pushed, slapped, and lived under threat of worse from Garrett. I can't show my great relief at being released from the prison of my marriage. But, thank God, and Seth, I am released from it forever.

Seth reported to the household that Garrett became separated from him during the blizzard. Seth called and called but heard no answer. Perhaps the wind blew his words away. He gave up trying to locate Garrett and forged on to bring the doctor to save me and the baby. Seth will rest a little, then search for Garrett. But, he adds, no man could survive long in that fury of blinding, icy wind.

I am safe. I am safe! Eventually I'll learn exactly what Seth did to rescue me.

Rebecca jumped out of bed and paced the room, ignoring the cold floor on her bare feet. They did it. They really did it. Or Seth did. Garrett's death and Bretton's birth. A pall hung over each. She climbed back into bed and read on.

March 25, 1873

Seth found Garrett's body today. He brought my husband's corpse, stiff and frozen, home on a toboggan. I came downstairs to reassure myself that my marital suffering is over. Peggy stood looking on Garrett's body as well. I expected to see her weep, but her eyes remained dry, her face a bitter mask.

Seth studies me more than I like. I return his gaze with no regret. Garrett had to die so my sons and I could live. I pray Seth won't succumb to remorse. He's promised that he loves me. He did the only thing one who loved me could or would do. He delivered me and his first born and Damon from a husband and father who possessed an uncontrolled, vicious temper, but no conscience.

Seth is building Garrett's coffin. When winter's hard earth thaws and it becomes possible, we'll take my husband's body to the church graveyard. We'll have a funeral. I'll play my part as grieving wife and mother. I'll act the sorrowing widow as long as is proper. I won't let on that after enough time passes I intend to be a merry one. I've had enough of misery, terror, and marital captivity.

I've resolved never to remarry. No. I control my life at last. Only a fool would relinquish that power. I won't tell Seth my decision now. I can't risk him reacting in any way that would endanger his life or my new-found liberty.

Seth and I avoided being alone since his return with

Garrett's body, but this evening he came to my room. He sat on the edge of my bed, and we spoke as I nursed our son.

He began, "Garrett is gone now. After a spell of mourning, we'll marry as we planned. I'll be father to the boys. Damon will need me as much as this little son of ours."

I squeezed his rough hand. "I want you. But, of course, I can't rush into a second marriage. Not for quite a long time. People will suspect something. Tongues wag at the slightest provocation. You understand. No one knows that better than I. We must go slowly, slowly. I'll still come to you. We can still meet as we did in the studio.

"Of course, I want you to stay here. I couldn't bear losing you, the only person who knows the truth. And you're right. Both my boys will need you. How very much they will. Together we can teach them what they'll need to carry on in the world as Cale heirs."

Seth's eyes gave away his shock at this new turn. He studied me for a long time. "I risked my life for you," he said. "I thought you, not just the boys, needed me. I won't be less than what we planned—your husband. Otherwise I did it for nothing."

I reached for Seth and kissed him. "Of course, you did it all for us, Seth. Of course, you did. You did it for our love. And I do love you. It will take time is all; time will make us safe."

He protested, "I thought Garrett's death made us safe. Now you say you need time." He looked so disappointed and sad. I kissed him again, but as I did my mind raced. If he began to think he'd acted in error, he might feel remorse. He might decide to confess to ease any growing guilt. I begged him to be patient, to wait for marriage. I promised that nothing else would change. I would be his in all but name as soon as I'd recovered from giving birth to our son. I insisted that I longed for our precious hours in each others' arms. I told him everything I knew he wanted to hear. His mind became passion clouded. Intimate caresses that followed gave me the time I needed.

I promised again that we would marry. He agreed, but with a look of lingering doubt I'd never seen before. I must use care, as much now as ever in the past. God forgive me. What have I become?

April 2, 1873

Bretton Bordeaux Cale is baptized. Unknown to anyone else, Seth chose his name. Seth spent some time as a young trapper in Quebec with native relatives. He remembers a town there that he liked so much he considered never coming back to Eagle Mountain. He named our child after it. The Bordeaux is for my side of the family.

Bretton didn't cry during his baptism. It's as if he already senses that a cloud hangs over him. His green eyes observe the world with a wary, intense focus.

May 5, 1873

Garrett's funeral took place today. The church filled with our solemn local neighbors as well as sympathetic people who journeyed over distant miles. In spite of Garrett's difficult ways, his charm usually won people over, or won them back. The exceptions were those of us who had intimate knowledge of him.

Seth stood at the rear of the sanctuary without speaking or moving during the entire service.

After its conclusion and the burial we returned home for refreshments. Several old friends approached. They expressed sympathy, then turned to admire Bretton. When

Max Bryan appeared I dabbed at my eyes with a handker-chief as if to dry nonexistent tears. We embraced. Mrs. Anderson took Bretton, now fussing to be fed and changed, away along with Damon, who stared wide-eyed at our guests.

Max and I could then speak in relative privacy. Max looked dapper in a black frock coat and, until he entered the lodge, a top hat. He'd become the image of a success-ful attorney. He gave me a searching look, guessing, I think, that I wasn't as grief stricken as he might have expected.

I turned the subject to my inheritance. We made plans for a business meeting in two days. Max and I will never be as he wishes, but he's invaluable in our shared interests, the lumber and mining concerns. I intend to keep his friendship and devotion. I may need them often. Besides, I enjoy my longtime friend's company.

Max knows nothing of my affair with Seth or of what Seth did for me and why. I won't tell him. It's perilous enough that Seth has become reticent, even sullen at times. He's an honest man. He couldn't have imagined that I'd retreat from what he considered a sacred promise of mar-riage. I hope that he still loves me enough never to give away what we planned . . . what we did.

He's grown quieter and quieter even during our meet-ings in the studio. We speak little of marriage since I've told him I can't think of it with so many demands on me these days.

After all, I've become a woman of property. I make busi-ness decisions I never dreamed I could.

CHAPTER SEVENTEEN

Throughout the service I'd held Bretton in my arms, and Damon sat beside us. Poor little Damon doesn't speak of his father, but he's not as frightened by sudden noises as when Garrett terrorized us. However, since we told him, Damon has nightmares about storms.

He looks so like Garrett. He'll be the image of his father just as Bretton will be my reflection. But neither may mirror us in terms of their behavior. Garrett beat most of the courage out of Damon. What will I pass on to Bretton? I think it better if he inherits Seth's even temperament, not my careening one. I'm growing more extreme in my moods. Is that what freedom does? Or do I feel remorse?

As a mother, I find joy in Damon, but my heart freezes into a cold, solid thing when I look at Bretton. I feel guilty over how I distance myself from Seth. I conceal my fading feelings toward him when we're together. I hope ardor's heat conceals my innermost, cooling feelings. My guilt over Seth makes me irritable, and our child wearies me. I find Bretton a source of annoyance.

I'm sorry to be tied to another infant when my art and journeys to the East Coast call.

Still, I well know that this baby is a victim as much or even more than the rest of us. That thought doesn't make me love him, though, even if I pretend I do. To me, his umbilical cord has its source in darkness and fear of scandal.

Max, like everyone but Seth, assumed that I would leave the lodge and return to New York for good. It's true Garrett left me a wealthy woman, and my work could appear in more shows there. But I can't tell either of them the real reason for my staying—that New York holds too many memories of my family and our tragic disintegration. In time I hope to feel otherwise.

Also, Seth will be here. Even though I won't be his wife as he still hopes, I don't want to take Bretton from him. I want both boys to know Seth as the strong, protective man he is. But I won't always be at Eagle Mountain. I prize this freedom I never had before. I'm finally at liberty to leave and come back or not, as I choose. In time I'll opt for East or West as it suits me.

I plan to make all the changes in the lodge that Garrett opposed. I'll make it a place I can come back to for my work, for respite, and to see my children and my lover, for I still want Seth's touch. That has never gone amiss with us. I may bring artists here. I'll never tell him there's no chance of our marrying. A man stripped of hope might turn vengeful. My father turned his anger against himself. Garrett's turned on others. I still care for Seth and wouldn't want to see his serenity or even his disappointment transformed to anger in any direction.

I am tender with him when we make love. I give him every pleasure. A satisfied man is easier to control. Oh, what has become of me? I care for Seth but will never again be under any man's lawful boot heel.

Besides, I anticipate reveling as an unburdened woman in centers of culture such as New York. There are so many interesting and interested men to be found in such a metropolis. But I want the boys to know the wild force of nature here, the skills of survival in a place where we feel the wilderness in us and around us. Seth will teach them of the natural world.

The house had quieted, but outside an owl called. Rebecca stilled and listened to the soft auger of death. Like a warning, a caveat. Then she heard the death cry of some rabbit or other prey. The owl had been the lucky one this night. She thought again as she shivered and picked up the diary that Lucinda had changed from Garrett's prey to a sort of predator in this place. Whatever Lucinda had become or would turn into would be revealed further.

A loud crack followed from somewhere below. She heard a voice muttering, then light, quick footsteps running up the stairs. She heard Damon's questioning voice and Amy's response.

"It's all right, Father. I just dropped a book while I looked for something in the library."

Rebecca sat still. Had Amy been searching for the diaries? Had she read them already?

She held the one she'd been reading as she would a precious possession.

May 7, 1873

After we finished our business meeting, I asked Max why he never married. He shook his head and smiled. "Lucinda, I've never found a woman to equal you."

I stared at him. Here stood another good man whom I could destroy. I could, but I won't. Dear Max is useful as a friend and advisor, and that's how I'll keep him. Ours is an uncomplicated and amicable bond, at least for me. I have to admit I enjoy his admiration as well.

How different things might have been if Garrett hadn't written in my dance card so long ago. But he did. And he is no more. And I am more alive than I have ever been.

Lucinda had changed so that Rebecca wondered at her. The candle flame sank and sent a line of dark smoke that dispersed as if it, too, had grown tired and confused. Rebecca pinched the flame, extinguishing all light but the hearth's red, glowing embers. It made her think, as she fell asleep, of how passion between men and women so often flames, tossing sparks in all directions, only to die down as the heart is consumed. What a cautionary tale Lucinda recorded. Rebecca considered whether she, too, could one day be consumed by her own passions or insatiable desires. No. She determined to protect her own course with reason and common sense.

In the morning Rebecca secreted the diary under her mattress next to its companion volumes. She rose, prepared for the day, and straightened the room. She wasn't surprised to hear familiar footsteps, followed by a tap at the door.

Rebecca opened it to greet Claudia, also dressed and carrying a mug of hot chocolate that she held out to her guest, who accepted it before lighting a fire to warm the room. Then each pulled a chair before the little blaze. The two women had been comfortable with each other from the beginning. While Claudia had chosen the conventional path of marriage and motherhood, she showed her admiration of Rebecca's choice to forge a thornier path. They'd fallen into a sisterly ease.

This morning, Claudia shifted in her chair, uncomfortable and weary.

"You should rest more," Rebecca said. "I don't want to be a

burden here. Let me help in any way I can, not just with the estate."

Claudia waved a dismissive hand. "We have a woman coming in to help. Everything in the household is in order. It's a relief to have Lucinda's funeral over. Now we must consider our next move. I want so badly to go back East, to be with my family. No one is left here but Bretton, and he's no sunny presence, as you may have noticed."

"I thought perhaps you might stay on here. Won't Damon take over management of his mother's business interests?"

"He wants to, I think. But we don't like how Amy has changed. In time, what will there be for her? As for me, I miss theaters, fashion, society in general. But we can't return to Washington, not yet."

"Why ever not? Forgive me if I'm being too forward, but Damon had a good position with the armaments company that employed him, didn't he? Doesn't he have any interest in going back to it?"

Claudia paused for a moment and ran a hand across her forehead. Without warning, her face crumpled like a child's. She pulled a handkerchief from her pocket and wept into it.

Rebecca rose and knelt before her, taking her hand. "What is it, Claudia? Can you tell me? I can keep a confidence. It's a requirement of my profession, you know."

"You must never tell what I'm about to share with you. Lucinda knew, and others in the East, but no one here except family."

Rebecca squeezed Claudia's hand. "Tell me. I want to understand what troubles you, my dear friend."

Claudia removed her hand and walked to the window. She stared out for a moment, then returned to her chair before the stove. "We had trouble in D.C.," she began. "Damon felt inferior to my father and other men higher up in the company. Insecure, he began drinking. He gambled as well. I think he had Garrett's weaknesses in such things but lacked his arrogance and drive. Anyway, Damon lost money, a lot of money. We faced bankruptcy."

Claudia turned and paced back to stand again by the fire. She stared into it, avoiding Rebecca's eyes. "He did something terrible. He embezzled from my father's company. The head accountant figured out what Damon had done and reported it in private to Father. Of course, he was furious. Somehow word got out. I believe Father confided to a close friend, and the friend betrayed the confidence to others.

"Anyway, we had to leave the city because of the disgrace. Father paid our debts, but with the understanding that we remain in the wilds of Montana for some time to come. He loved me and the children but couldn't bear the sight of Damon. He still can't."

Rebecca stared at Claudia, at a loss for what to say. Claudia turned away.

"And Lucinda knew?" Rebecca asked.

"Yes. My father wrote to her and revealed that she should be wary of letting her own son have control over her business matters. Furious, she ranted at Damon, called him demeaning names, and refused to let him have much of anything to do with the mining and logging concerns. She did let us live here, but under a sort of supervised status. She also took over Amy's training and leisure time. God help me, I grew to hate her and this place."

"But you stayed with Damon."

"Yes, I love Damon in spite of everything. Now that Lucinda's gone, perhaps my husband will become a stronger man. I pray so."

"Do you think he wants to manage the businesses now? Would you stay here?"

Claudia frowned. "It's not what I want, but we need to let more time pass before returning to D.C. We may send Amy to school abroad. Max did that with you, didn't he?"

"Yes. My parents had both died. That left Max flummoxed about what to do with a sorrowing thirteen-year-old niece. It was lonely at first at school, but I learned to fit in."

Claudia nodded. "Well, I'd better go and see to the children. Will you walk down with me?"

"In a little while. I need a few moments."

Rebecca wanted time to consider Claudia's astounding revelation. After the other woman left, Rebecca closed the door and exhaled. She sat on the bed, pondering.

What could be the significance of what she'd just learned? She locked her door behind her this time as she left. She would do so from now on.

Through the great room's window, Rebecca gazed at spires of pine that pointed to the storm-clouded sky. Claudia's revelations opened the prospect of Damon being the brother who'd destroyed or stolen the will. Damon claimed to doubt its existence. Yet Lucinda had told Max of her relief on making a final last testament. If only the elusive Ethan McBride would return so she could ask him if he'd drafted a new will.

And what of Claudia? She seemed more aggrieved than grieving. There'd been no closeness between Lucinda and her daughter-in-law. Or was there? Claudia seemed to fit in everywhere. She had some similarities to a chameleon.

But one so very ambitious? Would Claudia pretend friendship with Lucinda to achieve a lucrative end? If she failed, would she destroy a will if it left little or nothing to Damon?

Rebecca continued mulling over Claudia's disclosures.

With an effort, she assumed a neutral expression. Someone might have read the diaries before she found them. She didn't want that reader to suspect she'd learned any more about Cale history than what she'd gleaned conversing with family members.

Rebecca went to the kitchen. The Cales sat at the long trestle table. Bretton glanced up. His gaze pierced her, inscrutable and intense as his mother's in her portrait. Then Teddy distracted him. The little boy had chosen to sit beside his uncle, as usual. Amy, seemingly in a bad mood, flipped pancakes at the stove while Claudia poured coffee.

Damon smiled. "Rebecca, good morning. Come and enjoy an old-fashioned feast. Did you sleep well?"

"Perfectly, thank you." She sat next to Teddy.

"I thought I heard somebody wandering around last night," said Amy, turning her steady gaze on Rebecca. "Did you?" She brought two pancakes over and flipped them so hard onto Rebecca's plate they bounced.

"No," Rebecca answered, adding syrup and tucking into the food. "I even slept through the storm."

"You must have heard the house creaking from the wind, sweetheart," Damon said to his daughter. Then he turned to Rebecca. "I'm glad Max sent you. It's been helpful to have your friendship through the funeral, but I think Max had his mind on other ways you could help, too. We do need some assistance."

He turned to his brother. "Bretton, I haven't talked to you yet about how the estate should be settled. It will be complicated. Mother owned Eagle Mountain, of course, but there were the other things: stocks, bonds, and mining and logging interests. Why, she even owned an off-Broadway theater in New York. Max told me once that she made out a will, but I think he must have misunderstood.

"Mother made business decisions in these last years, often without discussing them with me. But I think she would have at least told me if there had been a will, even if she didn't divulge its contents. Anyway, her lawyer in New York knew nothing about a will. I exchanged telegrams with him. And the old lawyer in Jennings died during the fire that took half of Main Street. I haven't even met the new fellow; Mother probably wouldn't have even known him."

Rebecca made an instant decision to be honest. "Uncle Max is certain one exists, or existed. Lucinda told him so. He said it surprised him how pleased she seemed to have had one drafted and signed. He said she seemed relieved, as though a weighty burden had been lifted."

Claudia raised her head and sniffed. "Amy, look to what you're doing! You've burned a whole batch of pancakes."

Amy had been standing by the stove paying avid attention to the discussion between Rebecca and her father. She jumped and pried blackened pancakes from the griddle.

"It's all right. Just make us a fresh batch," Damon advised his red-faced daughter. He turned again to Rebecca. "Well, she should have had a will. I spoke to her about it a number of times. There's only Bretton and myself, and possibly the children, but with her other holdings I really felt she needed to plan for estate tax purposes. But you make it sound as though she had more on her mind than just taxes. What else did Max tell you?"

Amy slammed the spatula down on the counter. "I'm not hungry. I'm also not happy about this conversation. Everybody here, except Rebecca, knew her. If there isn't any will it's because she didn't make one."

Rebecca persisted. "But, Amy, she did make a will; she said so. A lawyer in Jennings made it for her. His copy burned in the fire where he died, too, but there has to be an original here or someplace, or possibly even another will. Uncle Max is sure of it. It is important that we find it."

Amy shook her head and left the kitchen. Claudia rolled her eyes and took over the pancakes.

"So that's what you came for." Bretton laughed, derision in the sound. "I knew there had to be more going on than just a gesture of respect. So that's what you looked for in my studio. You thought I might have hidden it."

"Good grief, Rebecca." Damon stared at her. "You're welcome to turn the house upside down now that Mother's funeral is over. In fact, we'll all help. I meant to ask you to help me put all the paperwork in order to settle the estate. They say the new lawyer in Jennings, Ethan McBride, is a good man. Mother may have had him draft a more recent will after all. I'd talk to him about it, but he's still off on some other business. When he returns we'll talk to him. He can file whatever we need if you and Max decide there's a conflict of interest, what with his partnership with Mother."

"We do feel that way, of course. I'm just here to help you reach that point and be organized. Why don't we finish our coffee?" Rebecca suggested. "Then you can show me where we need to start to assemble documents for Mr. McBride. Claudia, perhaps later you and I could go through the rest of the house to search for the will."

Bretton rose from the table when they'd finished. He carried his dishes to the sink, then strode out of the room, not glancing at Rebecca. She guessed he resented her hiding the truth when he interrupted her rummaging among his glaze powders. She excused herself to find him before she turned her attention to work.

He stood at one of the front windows, staring out at the storm that still pummeled and tugged at the house. Nothing but opaque white showed beyond the window.

"Bretton." She rested a hand on his forearm, feeling hard, tense muscles under her fingers. "Don't be angry. I just didn't feel ready to tell you what I wanted to find. I didn't know you well enough to be sure how you'd react.

"Uncle Max wanted me to find the will. It has to be here. For some reason someone is concealing its whereabouts . . . or may have even destroyed it. Yet now that I know all of you, I can't believe any of you would do such a thing."

"Don't you? I told you that Mother wasted no maternal affection on me. Maybe she cut me out of my inheritance. Believe me, that's likely. I'm the person with the perfect motive here. Don't play more games. I know you've thought of that by now."

"I did. I've thought about it a lot. You're right; perhaps Lucinda did disinherit you. But she wouldn't have let you know it before her death. No one else would want to hide the will or destroy it because you were cut out. Besides, they'd have had time to find it before you arrived at Eagle Mountain after her death."

"You might have a point."

"Thank you." Rebecca paused. In spite of his heroism he might have any number of reasons to destroy the will. How much did money matter to Bretton?

He stared at her, then walked a few steps away, rubbing his hand over his eyes in a weary gesture. "I came back for her funeral. I don't know any longer whether I felt anything for her beyond some respect, but there was that.

"And I missed this place. I missed it the most when I was fighting in the Philippines. Everybody missed home when they were overseas. I didn't come back after the war because Lucinda and I had had a final quarrel when I left . . . the kind that separates families for good.

"But, during the war, I felt the forest in my blood, in the marrow of my bones. I guessed that, like Mother, I'd have to be here to do my best work. I can't think why else she stayed. Anyway, it turned out not to be true for me. I've discovered New Mexico, the artists' colonies there. I want a life where I can learn around the best and then work in solitude."

Rebecca moved toward him. "You don't want to live here? To own Eagle Mountain?"

Bretton flashed a disarming smile. "Not any longer."

"Is there really so much solitude there? Do you plan to buy land?"

He gave her a quizzical look. "Why do I feel cross-examination has begun? Sure. I'd like to buy land. I'd like to sit in the dead center of a thousand acres. And that costs. Your suspicions have a basis. I'd also like money to promote my work, have gallery shows. But I don't have the will."

"I can't rule out anyone yet. Max wouldn't."

"Max is astute. We're a complicated outfit. Don't make quick decisions about any of us. Don't you think Damon wants money? Claudia's an expensive woman."

"I won't. I'd better meet Damon in his study. You've changed, Bretton. What's made you decide to accept me, even knowing why I came?"

"Oh, any friend of Teddy's is a friend of mine."

"Well, you come highly recommended by him, too, you know. Now I'd better go help Damon."

Rebecca smiled, but the smile faded as she walked away. Bretton had no love for his mother. Therefore, why stay on? Damon, no angel, had a criminal past. Claudia missed the socialite life. What about Amy? Could the child be capable of committing grown-up crimes?

The thought also came that Bretton planned a life far afield from her own.

Would the life Uncle Max had lived, of client connections that were briefly close and intense but soon broken, be enough for her? She might end with nothing permanent except memories of courtroom victories and defeats, or of settlements in various shades of gray. Would that really be enough?

She stopped in her room for a few moments to think before

meeting Damon.

Was she so different from Lucinda in her determination to pursue the goals of an independent woman? After all, both dreamed of a life of self control and personal freedom. A proscribed life had attractions. But, no. Lucinda's reasons were selfish once Garrett's death rendered her safe. Rebecca wanted justice for everyone, suffrage and dignity for women so they wouldn't wind up as twisted as Lucinda Cale.

Rebecca and Damon closeted themselves in Lucinda's office for several hours. When they emerged, Rebecca had seen yet another facet of Lucinda Cale, a woman in firm control of her mining, logging, and artistic enterprises. Lucinda managed her businesses from both Eagle Mountain and New York. Evidence showed that Lucinda maintained a thorough knowledge of her assets. Lucinda had cultivated the Cale fortune, considerable at the time of Garrett's death, with mergers and the expertise that comes from research and expert advice. Although the diaries didn't reflect or detail business acumen, Lucinda increased her capital. Any of the family stood to become wealthy, depending on her final will's disposition.

Chapter Eighteen

That night Rebecca excused herself early, wishing everyone a good night. With Damon and Claudia still downstairs, Bretton back in his cabin, and the children sent to bed, Rebecca had a thought. Wouldn't an attic full of trunks and bags and dressers be an ideal hiding place for a document? She took a candle from her room and walked with light steps to the end of the hallway.

She climbed the narrow set of stairs to open the attic door. Bright moonlight streamed in the windows of the frigid room above the storm that had collapsed into a ground blizzard. Rebecca could see well enough by candle and moonlight in the storybook attic, full of trunks and old lamps, old furniture, including what appeared to be an antique baby carriage. Tomorrow she would ask Claudia to let her sort through all of it.

Startled by a sound, she whirled to face Amy, who stood pale in the moonlight by the window, an apparition in her long, white nightgown.

"Amy! I didn't expect anyone else to be here."

"Neither did I," Amy responded with chilling calm. "What are you doing?"

"Why . . . I . . . Actually, I was thinking about how the road will be tomorrow. I plan to chat with Reverend Gilmore. I believe your grandmother may have spoken to him not long before she died. I'll ask if she spoke of a will. You mentioned a window up here, so with the moonlight so bright I thought I might be able to look out and judge my prospects," she lied.

From the gloom, Amy's cool eyes took her measure.

Remembering Uncle Max's tactic, "When put on the defensive turn the tables," she asked, "Why are you up so late, and in the dark at that?"

"Just thinking," came the unruffled answer. "And planning."

"Planning for . . . ?"

"Nothing for you to worry about. Well, I'm going to bed now. Are you coming?"

"No. I want to see what I can see first. Sleep well, Amy."

Amy slipped past. Rebecca listened for her footsteps down the stairs, then moved to the window. The ground blizzard had abated. Moonlight etched crystalline details. Swaying limbs thrust fleeting shadows across the cold ground. What dangers lingered in those forest deeps? What secrets existed in the human hearts and historic hallways of this dreary hunting lodge?

The road to Bretton's studio as well as the road leading from the lodge appeared passable. At the end of the studio road she saw that, indeed, a light still burned where Bretton created in solitude. She shivered. Perhaps a part of Bretton would always be closed even to those who cared for him. Did he only work on ceramics or did he stay awake nursing past injuries?

Her thoughts turned to Seth, loving Lucinda enough to murder for her. And Max, who gave her a lifetime of unrequited devotion. She shook her head. Being bound by love half denied would never be enough for her. She'd protect her future in every way.

A frigid draft put out her candle's flame. A frisson of apprehension ran up her spine. Turning from the window, she swallowed a cry. A man stood in shadow, facing her across the room. He wore a Union army dress uniform from the Civil War era. A shock of blond hair fell across the forehead of his aristocratic face, one with large, pale eyes and an arrogant mouth. Disdainful and amused, his eyes conveyed a hint of pain as well. He stood motionless. Rebecca stared, paralyzed by terror.

"Garrett Cale." Her lips formed his name without sound. Some self-protective instinct propelled her to strike a match and relight her candle, all while shaking so hard she feared dropping both. When the flame leapt up, the apparition disappeared. A mirror stood in its place. Across the room, beside Rebecca, leaned a life-size portrait of Garrett Cale as a young officer.

"Oh, Rebecca," she reprimanded herself. Then she leaned on the portrait's frame and gave way to nervous laughter. Her composure regained, she studied the portrait. "My, but you were a handsome devil," she murmured. "You could be cruel. Still, when the two of you walked into a room you must have cast quite a spell."

Rebecca blew out her candle, and the illusion of Garrett's ghost reappeared in the moonlight. Shaking her head, she pulled the door closed behind her and made her way down the stairs with care.

Stealthy, Rebecca hurried to her room where a fire burned low and welcoming in the cozy little hearth. She changed into her nightgown, her thoughts flying to the diaries hidden under her mattress. The diaries called to her more than ever. What had transpired between Bretton and his mother? How had the child shut out turned on Lucinda?

Rebecca locked the door, then washed in the next room. Slipping into bed she prepared to read what Lucinda's elegant hand revealed by the shifting candle flame.

As she read, moonlight glistened and sparkled off spectral crystalline frost patterns on the window, all ghost-white ferns and silvery leaves.

January 1, 1888

Years have passed since I last wrote in this journal. My life differs more than ever from what that naïve girl who arrived at Eagle Mountain so long ago imagined it would be. She anticipated living as an adored, pampered wife. Her dreams soon burned to ruins. Revisiting them, I catch only the scent of bitter smoke, the taste of ashes.

I'm independent now and, to be honest, have no strong emotions toward anyone. It's as if past experience tinkles a little warning bell whenever I begin to lower my defenses. What a pity I can't accept the love so many offer. Seth stays on here, my occasional lover and the man my sons see as the father Garrett never could have been.

Max has proposed more than once, but I've never encouraged him. I suspect, too, that Max knows almost as much as Seth about Garrett's death. I suspect Seth has spoken to him about it, but I can't be certain, or, if he has, in how much detail. In any event, neither has gone to the authorities. Their feelings for me will keep Seth from caving in to guilt, or Max to his conscience as an "officer of the court."

Raising two active sons, managing business matters most mornings, and spending afternoons in the studio keep me busy, especially with our economy as it is. I've kept up with my ceramics to a surprising degree. That's been a bonus. I've been able to do it because of our tranquil life at Eagle Mountain.

Unlike Garrett, I don't conduct all of our business from here. He did because his passion for hunting and fishing combined so well with his business negotiations. I've been grateful for those contracts signed behind closed doors here at the lodge. In spite of his faults as a husband, he made safe, wise investments. But I don't have his knack for combining business with pleasure.

It takes a long time to reach New York by stage and train. I travel back to New York and elsewhere for three to six months every year. Once there, I see to matters of business, meet on a day to day basis with those who work for and with me, and present my artwork to the world in gallery shows. My life combines two worlds. No one refers to the old scandals. I don't know that I'd care if they did. Time buries scandal like sediment at the bottom of a lake.

Damon will soon attend Harvard in Boston. I want him to go into business studies, as, eventually, he'll be handling our fortune. I think he hates to go, but I assure him that we'll visit during my sojourns in New York.

Seth continues to be invaluable, a man each of my boys can love and respect. He has, for the most part, reverted to the role he took when I first arrived at Eagle Mountain. He's nearby when needed but never speaks of the past. For the most part, he accepts my decision that we go on as occasional lovers and the closest of friends.

I am aware of changes in the world from my trips to New York. Here, little changes. Mrs. Anderson retired, and I have a new cook. Peggy married, but the logger left her a widow within a year. She went away to live with a sister but soon died of diptheria.

Seth has taught the boys all they could hope to learn about the outdoors. So far as I can see, he treats them as equal in his affections. I'm afraid, through no fault of Bretton's, that's more than I can do.

He's a difficult boy—moody—a loner.

Damon has always been just the opposite—still a nervous boy, eager to have friends, eager to please everyone he knows. He has his father's charm without Garrett's dark side. And Damon is bright. He'll do well if he doesn't fall into the drink and gambling that brought emotional ruin on his father and me.

Bretton is the male version of me, his coloring and his eyes a copy of mine, but he's big like Seth. He takes after me in one other respect. He loves to work in the studio, sketching and working with clay. With my inclination to isolate myself when working, sometimes I can hardly bear to have him near me. I see him as the result of past trouble, pain, and actual crime, of my long ago neediness and lapses. Still, I can see that he has my artistic talent. I'm never easy on Bretton, but he persists.

My natural acumen for business allows me to continue well in this man's world. I've succeeded in mastering control of our business interests as Garrett did.

I've also learned to take what I want in other spheres. I meet wealthy, powerful, creative men. I take them to my bed when I want them there. They always want me. I choose our trysts together as I do with Seth. Seth has even learned to accept that I sometimes bring male guests home to Eagle Mountain. One painted my portrait. It's a likeness that shows my bold spirit. I'll hang it over the mantelpiece. The woman in the portrait is like an older, harder sister of the happy creature who began these diaries.

I finally moved some of the bear rugs and head mounts back into the lodge. No matter how I changed the decor, its rustic origins called for them. I don't know if our family history reflects their ferocity and wildness, but I've decided they do belong here after all. My taste reverted after Garrett's death. Symbols of the hunt always served as a source of conflict between us. Perhaps we can only acknowledge the right of someone else's opinion when the opponent is vanquished.

October 7, 1889
Damon has written with fine news that will alter our lives.

He's engaged. The girl is Claudia Brecht. Her family owns a remarkable armaments factory . . . no, more than one. Factories. The Brechts are an industry dynasty. He described his fiancée, and she sounds sweet, conventional, and malleable. That's what I want in any daughter-in-law.

Damon discovered the local girls early, my only cause for worry concerning him. But even though they threw themselves in Bretton's path, he didn't give them the slightest notice. They flirted. He refused to acknowledge them. When they rode by the lodge he ignored them. No, he didn't stay as long as he did because of any youthful romance. Bretton loved the forest and his work in my studio.

Why speak of the difficult son? Enough. Damon and Claudia sound happy. He writes that for now they'll live in Washington, D.C., where Damon will work for Claudia's father. If rumors of war prove true, his work for the company will keep him out of the fighting, but with honor.

So be it.

Entries for the next years were sparse. Then Rebecca arrived at one dated August 1, 1892.

Bretton has gone. I wanted him away. I thought to send him to school in the East as I did Damon. My inability to love Bretton has never changed. He remains a flesh and blood reproach of acts done during a time I want to forget, a daily reminder of them. He's old enough to be elsewhere, and elsewhere is where I want him. We'll all be better off.

When he refused to go, my angry words almost destroyed the secret Seth and I have protected all these years. That secret must be kept, or disgrace and worse might follow.

Bretton tends to be quiet like Seth, but there's nothing in Bretton of Seth's acceptance of fate's decrees. Instead,

Bretton is unstructured, artistic, and headstrong. I also believe he sometimes intends to anger me. Last night he confronted me, saying that he was finished trying to meet expectations of a father he's never seen.

"He died trying to save your life," I said, or perhaps I snarled the words.

"No. He died trying to save yours," he answered. "And that's what you can't live with."

I shouted terrible things at him after that. I called him a failure. I said he didn't deserve the Cale name.

Finally I made him a cold but effective offer. I said I'd pay him to go anywhere, have adventures, sail the seas, study art in other countries or different parts of this one. I threw money at him. He took it with a long, hate-filled look.

This morning Bretton had gone. Seth said little but did announce plans to leave for a few days. In answer to my searching look he said, "I'm going to see if I can find my son and wish him well."

Damon left for his last graduate level year at Harvard today. I have two sons. They are as opposite as two humans can be yet rarely if ever exchanged a cross word. I'll miss Damon, never Bretton. I feel as I did years ago when the burden of a domineering, violent husband had been lifted from me.

September 15, 1892

I'm the grandmother of Amy Cale, a healthy baby girl. I can't wait to see her. A little girl in the Cale family after all this time . . .

Rebecca closed the diary and slipped it under the mattress. Lucinda's own account had proved Bretton's description of her coldness to be no exaggeration. Still, how had she lived as she did? How did she contain her dreadful secret? Did she never confide in anyone besides her diary?

Rebecca considered the Cale family. She thought of Max. If he were well enough she'd speak to him of all this. Had he suspected anything criminal in Garrett's death?

She ran through a list of other people she might question. Mrs. Anderson and Peggy were no longer here. Mrs. Anderson had passed away, and Peggy may have as well. She'd moved away after becoming a widow. Then Rebecca thought back to Lucinda's funeral. Reverend Gilmore's solemn face had shown sincere grief as he delivered the eulogy. Lucinda had never seemed religious or written of any yearning for atonement. Still, she may have confessed to the man of God at some point knowing that death stalked her.

After breakfasting with the family, Rebecca arranged for one of the nearest neighbor's boys who helped with maintenance after school and on weekends to drive her over to the church. He'd wait there while she spoke with the reverend. The man might be working on a sermon, but she'd seek him out.

At mid-afternoon, the boy, appearing shy around the lady lawyer, helped Rebecca into the sleigh. As they whooshed over snow, Rebecca squinted against the brilliant sunshine, a glittering blanket spread over the landscape.

She decided to look in the sanctuary before trying the rectory behind the church. She wanted to sit for a moment in a quiet place before interviewing Lucinda's possible confidante. The sunny day enhanced the colors of the stained-glass windows much more than on the dreary day of Lucinda's funeral.

Three large casements let in light on each side of the sanctuary. Every one depicted a Biblical story in rich leaded glass. Lucinda hadn't spared money on the windows. Rebecca studied those flanking the pulpit.

The peaceful stained-glass imagery on the right glowed in greens and blues. Its foreground portrayed a seated Madonna and child with forested mountains for a background landscape. Tenderness set the mood. Rebecca noted that the auburn-haired Mary and blond child were situated in a place more like Eagle Mountain than Bethlehem. The models bore a clear resemblance to Lucinda and young Damon.

Rebecca turned to her left. The Biblical image there surprised her. Stained glass in reds, purples, and indigos showed Judith and Holofernes at the climactic moment when the seductive, charismatic widow saved herself and her people by cutting off the besotted general's head.

Rebecca cast her memory back to the story. Didn't a maidservant wait to carry the general's head out to Judith's people? Yes, she'd seen Caravaggio's graphic painting of the scene with all three figures. But in this version a manservant with long black hair and a black beard waited, holding out what looked like a rucksack. A hunter like Seth might have used such a thing.

Rebecca studied both windows for long moments, then moved to view the two located at the church's center.

Like the first work on the right, this one glowed with a loving scene. Mary, her cousin Elizabeth, and the two toddlers, Jesus and John the Baptist, sat in peaceful contentment. Suffused and blooming with cheerful yellows, golds, pinks, and roseate hues, the picture would lift any onlooker's spirit.

Rebecca turned to the left and confronted another gruesome portrayal of murder from the Old Testament. A focused, steely-eyed Jael raised her arm to hammer the tent stake she'd positioned above the temple of sleeping Sisera, an enemy general. Rebecca searched her memory. Then it came to her. The trusting enemy general had fallen asleep and made himself vulnerable to Jael after she'd introduced herself as a simple, helpful woman offering food and a place to rest.

Again, a familiar painting of the same subject came to mind. The painting had been done by the Italian woman artist Artemisia, herself a victim of rape. Lucinda no doubt identified with both artist and subject.

She turned away from the Biblical image of blood and revenge, however righteous.

The last window on the right made her squint against its white light and clear, sunshine-filled spaces. Along with flowers flanking the banks of sparkling water, the figures were beautiful young men, Jesus and John the Baptist. In the azure sky above them a dove opened symmetrical white wings.

Rebecca turned to the left with her eyes closed, prepared to open them to another scene of bloody slaying. Instead she admired a beautiful girl dancing with veils rising around her. She swayed to charm, if not seduce, a king. Rebecca walked to the plaque below the bottom of the window frame.

"Salome," she whispered. "Of course." Salome had danced before Herod in order to be granted one wish: the head of John the Baptist.

"Lucinda Cale designed and donated these works of art to our church."

Rebecca straightened and turned. Reverend Gilmore had come from behind the sacristy and walked toward her.

"They are lovely, but she chose brutal scenes for her Old Testament portrayals." Rebecca held out her gloved hand to the minister. He clasped it warmly.

"Miss Bryan, is it not? The Cales' distinguished visitor?"

Was that said with sincerity? "I apologize for interrupting your day. I'm helping the Cales settle their mother's estate. I have a few questions for you but can certainly return tomorrow or whenever might better suit you."

The reverend smiled. "Now is fine. I have your young driver carrying donated boxes of clothing for the poor into storage, so your timing is perfect. Shall we go to my study? It's warmer there, I promise."

Rebecca had been so captivated by the windows that she'd been unaware of how the temperature in the sanctuary had fallen. As the winter sun moved lower, the stained glass of the windows dulled in dimming light. "That would be lovely."

CHAPTER NINETEEN

"I've been a widower these many years," the minister explained. "I've learned the fine, honorable, and, yes, comfortable, art of serving refreshments." He left Rebecca in his study long enough to disappear and return with rose hip tea and gingerbread cookies.

He sat at his desk, Rebecca in a chair facing him. It felt comfortable, wide and well cushioned. Chosen by a professional confidante, she thought with an inner smile, to encourage relaxed conversation.

After pouring two cups, Rebecca's host inquired as to the bereaved family. After responding to his questions, Rebecca set her teacup and saucer on his desk. Still a bit under the unsettling effect of the stained-glass windows, she began with questions about Lucinda.

"Reverend, the first time I visited your church I didn't study those artworks as I was doing when you found me today. I confess now that I've perused them in strong sunlight, I'm amazed, both by their subject matter and their beauty."

He pushed the cookie plate toward her. "Treasures each and every one. Lucinda chose the subjects . . . well, half of them in any event. At first she planned the Madonna and Child as the sole peaceful and holy addition to the brutal Old Testament depictions. She'd have put the bloody story of Jezebel in two windows instead of the pictures of Jesus and John with their mothers and the lovely picture of Our Lord being baptized by his cousin." He took a bite of his second cookie and gestured for Rebecca to have one.

She picked up and bit into a spicy treat. After an appreciative smile and a sip of tea, she asked, "They are violent scenes from the Old Testament, aren't they?"

"Indeed. I found her choices difficult to understand at the time. I objected, as did others on the church board, to such bloody stories being made a permanent part of our house of worship."

"Did she say why she wanted them?"

He shook his head. "Not in so many words. Lucinda, a young mother new to widowhood, seemed distraught when we presented our objections. Distraught and furious. She threatened to withdraw the gift of the windows, claiming she knew more than we about art. No doubt true."

Rebecca nodded. "Yes. She'd made a name for herself in the East Coast high society's art world, I believe."

"Indeed. She wanted the windows to remind men and women alike of what we are each capable of doing when desperate. Those times one is required to defend the innocent, or attack someone who has or will wrong us or ours. She pointed out that Judith and Jael were heroines to their suffering people."

Rebecca sipped her tea and pursued her line of questions. "How did she respond if someone objected to the methods of death? After all, a tent stake to the temple . . ."

"She took me aback. Others were present, so this was not in confidence. When one of the women objected, Lucinda turned on her saying, 'Oh, come now. We all know a weak woman has to use whatever is at hand to protect herself and those she loves when threatened.' "

Rebecca raised her eyebrows. "That must have been a surprise."

"Yes. An unpleasant one."

"But Jezebel never appeared."

"No. We finally compromised on only two windows showing acts of murder, both, of course, Old Testament images. The board deemed Salome acceptable because it shows the evil female's manipulation that led to the martyrdom of John the Baptist. I've wondered sometimes if we erred in that."

"Who selected the New Testament windows?"

"The board members chose the subject matter. Lucinda chose the artist who did the windows." He smiled and added, "The children in our congregation call the Old Testament ones the 'scary windows.' They called the New Testament ones the 'nice windows.' Lucinda showed little interest in the latter."

"Are the windows in any danger of the board wanting them replaced now that Lucinda can't defend them?"

"Not at the moment. After all this time, most of the parishioners who voiced objections are in the graveyard with her. Others have made their peace with the now familiar scenes."

Rebecca shifted to another subject. "Did Lucinda discuss her personal grief with you in those days?"

"No. I left the proverbial door open to offer comfort if she sought me out, but Lucinda changed in those months and years. She went away for long periods but continued to help support and maintain our little church. She attended with her boys when she resided at Eagle Mountain. Sometimes she brought guests with them."

"Did Lucinda speak with you toward the end of her life?"

"She did. I initiated the contact, but believe it brought her needed solace and guidance in matters concerning her sons, especially Bretton. We spoke three times, the last about two weeks before her death."

"How did your conversations come about? I'm interested as I'm helping the family prepare to settle Lucinda's estate. It seems she executed a Last Will and Testament that's gone missing . . . or been destroyed. Did she mention it?"

The minister refilled Rebecca's tea cup and then his own. He took a sip and leaned back.

"Lucinda and I had known each other for a very long time. Like all men, I, a lonely widower, fell a bit under her spell. She trusted me and confided many things that should remain unrepeated.

"However, the poor woman being dead, I shall share at least that she did tell me she'd drafted a Last Will and Testament that no one but her attorney, Ethan McBride in Jennings, knew about. This differed from the one destroyed in the Jennings fire. Fire destroyed the first will and killed the attorney who'd drafted it. She then spoke of the second will."

"Did she say where it was?"

"She did not. Nor did I ask. I even refrained from asking if she'd left a bequest to the church, although such reticence pained me I assure you. She did tell me her last testament would astound her heirs. And that she believed it fair. But she answered none of my questions. I think she enjoyed leaving my curiosity unsatisfied. Lucinda loved to be in control, and she usually was."

After a few more general comments about the family, Rebecca thanked the reverend and departed.

At Eagle Mountain, Rebecca greeted Claudia, then claimed the need to rest before dinner. She locked her door and lit a candle. The diary called. She pulled the comforter around her shoulders and picked up Lucinda's story again.

The next entries dealt with trips back and forth to New York and Washington, D.C., Amy's growing into such a bright little girl, and Lucinda's rising status as an artist.

September 10, 1893

I learned to my surprise and quite indirectly that after being wounded as a soldier fighting near Manila, Bretton
returned to the United States and has gone to New Mexico
to learn about pueblo and other, more modern, pottery
forms being studied there. He's never come back to Eagle
Mountain, much to my relief.

Damon saw Bretton during my youngest's recovery once
he returned to the United States. They write to each other.
I send money to cover Bretton's expenses. He's become a
sort of remittance man like unwanted English nobility. I
make it possible for him to stay away. He spends time at a
Southwest artists' colony. Damon tells me Bretton has
changed in that he now pays attention to young women,
although there's been nothing serious or lasting.

To Rebecca's surprise when she looked at the next entry, the
date indicated an entire decade had passed.

February 14, 1903

My Valentine's Day present is that Damon and Claudia
have decided to come here with eleven-year-old Amy and
three-year-old Teddy. It's a bittersweet return, with
emphasis on the bitter part. I don't know why I and mine
have such a penchant for calling disgrace down upon
ourselves. When it crosses generations it really does become
tedious.

Damon, in his eagerness to keep up with his in-laws',
the elevated Brechts', position in society, used gambling to
be seen as a man about town. To release tension I suppose.
Anyway, he lost a great deal of his and Claudia's money. If
only that were all. He didn't stop there.

In desperation to keep their status that Claudia expected,
if not demanded, my son embezzled from the Brecht Arma-

ments Company. He has disgusted and embarrassed me. This disgrace is such a reminder of my errant father. Only Damon's behavior even turned criminal. The terrible news and memories are painful and prod me to fury.

I made a special trip to New York to meet with Claudia, Damon, and the august captain of industry, Mr. Brecht. I attempted to charm him, but he wants none of any of us. The scandal became well known when an accountant, a bean counter, did in fact spill the beans. Brecht planned no mercy at first. He wanted to prosecute Damon and force Claudia to divorce him. But Damon's wife does love him. It took Claudia's prolonged hysterics to finally induce her father to cover the debt. I was actually impressed, although sobbing fits and fainting folderol were never my style. My son's wife knew how to soften her father. He remains cold and aloof, not speaking to Damon. But my first born will not go to prison.

I set conditions, however. The young couple and their children are to come and reside at Eagle Mountain, where Damon and Claudia will live a simple, quiet life. Damon must limit his drinking and indulge in no gambling. If Claudia's father imposed other rules, I don't know what they are.

Bretton is still in New Mexico. I think it a good place for him.

March 1, 1903

Amy is my love, bright and perceptive beyond her years. She's going to grow into an ethereal beauty. She'll have the boys eager to do whatever she commands . . . and later the men as well. She's been hurt by her father's public fall and resents both parents for having to leave all that was familiar to her.

Newspapers published exposés. Her friends dropped her. How I recall the sting of that in my own sudden descent into social purgatory. One boy tried to stand by her, but the move to Eagle Mountain ended their alliance.

Amy wants to know everything about my life. I told her the romantic story of how I met Garrett and how he brought me here. I'll never tell her the circumstances of Garrett's death, only that he died during a blizzard. I'm afraid I've painted him to her as something of a dashing hero, but I can't see that it will cause any real harm. Perhaps I'll tell her the truth over time.

Distracted as she'd become by everything she'd learned, Rebecca didn't talk much during dinner. She had a sense that all the unraveled threads of Lucinda's story might come together, but she also wanted to resolve things and return to Kalispell if only for a few days. She felt the need to see and talk to Max. She missed him, and he would know better than she how all these happenings affected Lucinda.

She excused herself as soon as possible and sat before the fire in her room, reviewing all that she knew about Lucinda Cale.

In the morning Claudia took Rebecca with her to Lucinda's rooms. The large bedroom stood a few doors down from the center of the upstairs hallway. Although much more spacious than Rebecca's, this sleeping area also held a simple brass bed. In fact, the whole room had a simple but elegant decor. Delicate Belgian lace curtains hung at the windows. Gleaming Dutch ceramic tiles framed the fireplace. Original paintings crowded the walls, but only one picture, a black and white photograph of an extraordinarily handsome man, sat on her nightstand.

"Garrett, of course." Claudia nodded to the photograph. "Amy found it in the attic and insisted her grandmother put it in here. Let's start with these dresser drawers. Just being in her room, the inner sanctum, makes me nervous."

Rebecca noted that Claudia's hands on the drawer handles did tremble.

The two spent the next two hours sifting through stored accumulations of Lucinda's life at Eagle Mountain. Sketches and photographs filled boxes and drawers.

Rebecca held one sketch up and exclaimed without thinking, "Why look! Here's Seth."

Claudia took the picture, studied it, and asked, "How on earth can you tell with that beard? He must have been in his thirties when Lucinda drew this. He looks like quite the mountain man with his shaggy hair, but how gorgeous. I don't think he ever wanted much except to be near her. How did you know who it was?"

"Just a lucky guess. Look at all of these baby pictures." Eager to change the subject, Rebecca held up drawings and watercolors of a chubby little boy.

"Yes, almost all are of Damon, his father's first heir. Had Garrett lived, Damon would have been spoiled. I'm afraid I haven't spoiled him. I love him, but I've been guilty of . . . insisting on having things the way I wanted and expected. Like a spoiled, silly girl."

Rebecca looked up into Claudia's face. The other woman seemed to be fighting off tears. "He adores you, Claudia. What could you have done to feel so guilty?"

"I pressured Damon to elevate our way of life, our status. He . . . he made desperate financial decisions, bad, damaging choices. As I told you, he brought shame on our families by reckless gambling. When she learned of Damon's embezzling, Lucinda considered disowning us. Father still might. I had to behave like a crazy woman to get Father to be merciful. In the end, though still enraged, Father kept Damon out of prison. He bribed people, I'm sure.

"His condition that we leave Washington until the scandal dies down, meant our move to this outpost, where Lucinda kept us under her watchful eye as though we were privates in the Foreign Legion and she the all-powerful general."

"Did you really find Eagle Mountain such a terrible punishment?"

"It might not have been except she refused to let Damon in on anything to do with her business." Claudia's voice rose, high with resentment. "She treated me as though I were a selfish featherbrain. Worse, she assumed control over Amy. She encouraged Amy to despise us, her parents. Amy transformed into Lucinda's shadow, her acolyte. I hated Lucinda for that more than for any of the rest. She just ignored Teddy."

Rebecca sensed Claudia hovered on the brink of breaking down and confiding more critical information.

She leaned toward the distraught woman. "That must have been heartbreaking. What else did Lucinda do?"

Claudia's face reddened, and she sank to the edge of the bed, giving the pillows a punch. Then she turned beseeching eyes on Rebecca. "Please, don't tell anyone what I said about hating Lucinda. I love Damon and stand with him always. But Lucinda, in a fury, once swore to disinherit Damon."

"How harsh. And your father? Will he ever forgive Damon?"

"My father remains angry and remote because I won't divorce my husband. I'm Father's only daughter, and we were once close as this." Claudia lifted a hand with two fingers tight together.

"The children and I are all he has. We do write one another, and I sense him beginning to respect my loyalty to my husband. I may in time be able to swim across that moat Father filled so wide and deep with hatred."

Claudia blinked and studied her folded hands. "I haven't been honest with you or Damon." Tears dropped onto the hand now twisting her wedding ring. "Like most powerful men, Father can be cruel. He called me aside after that terrible meeting with us and Lucinda.

"He'd taken a strong dislike to Lucinda, couldn't bear her arrogance. He claimed he had to close the meeting or wring the uppity female's neck. He's always hated outspoken women, whether or not they possess beauty or ability.

"Father had paid to uncover her past. Lucinda's father made a fortune, then lost it to gambling and drink. My father felt that Damon had inherited immoral weaknesses from both Garrett and Lucinda. Father believes in the new studies of eugenics, you know. Garrett and Garrett's father had both been brutal, frivolous drinkers, and woman chasers. He said he should have hired an investigator in New York to report on the Cale family before I married into it.

"He's also a strict Lutheran. And, besides the strict religious views, he believes the upper, middle, and lower classes should be set apart. It becomes worse and worse. He insists Damon and I repay every embezzled penny that he covered with his own money.

"Father promised not to press charges against my husband if I divorced Damon or if we paid him back. I've never told Damon the conditions of his freedom. I love him. Such a burden of debt would crush him. He might insist on a divorce to spare me a life of poverty. I don't want a divorce; I want Damon and our children. They are my future. But, unless I gain Father's forgiveness, or Lucinda left us her fortune, we'll be impoverished."

Rebecca rested her hand on Claudia's, noting for the first time that the other woman bit her nails. A sign of distress? "Would your father actually do that?"

Claudia nodded. "Father holds deep prejudices. He nurses, almost cherishes, life-long resentments. He's ruined enemies before. Frankly, repayment is all that can appease my father. Or our divorce. Without Lucinda's fortune, Damon and I will suffer."

Claudia bowed her head, breaking into sobs.

Rebecca resisted the urge to pat the lovely woman's shoulder. The understanding had taken root that Claudia was an intelligent adult who'd been patronized quite enough in her life. Those cornflower-blue eyes in the heart-shaped face didn't miss much after all.

"How else did Lucinda affect Amy?"

"In many ways. Lucinda took Amy to her office for hours every afternoon as though she were her governess. At times I crept into the closet of the adjoining room and eavesdropped. She encouraged Amy to hate us for the scandal, even for taking Amy away from some boy who, I guess, would be called her first love. Worst of all, they discussed whether Lucinda should disinherit us. Amy, in her disdain and child's ignorance, encouraged Lucinda to cast us adrift. I couldn't believe what treachery I overheard during their conversations."

At this point Claudia stood, with fists at her sides. "Things progressed against us. Lucinda drafted a will herself to replace the one that burned. She wouldn't show it to Amy but read it to her. It confirmed my worst fears. Lucinda left her entire estate to Amy. Amy whooped in joy. Lucinda shushed her and then said she planned to hide the document in a false-bottomed drawer of her desk."

"Claudia, did you destroy the will?" This time Rebecca did rest a hand on the other woman's wrist. She could hear herself breathe in the long silence.

CHAPTER TWENTY

"No. I confess I intended to, but when I slipped in after Lucinda's death to burn the despicable thing, it wasn't there. I don't know what became of it. I don't know who has it or even if it still exists. Sometimes I wonder if it ever existed."

Claudia slumped back to the bed in utter weariness. Rebecca insisted she stop working, just lie there and rest while Rebecca continued looking through Lucinda's memorabilia. But her mind raced. Trying to appear calm, she considered how this changed everything.

Claudia had every reason to hide or destroy the will. In Claudia's desperation she would be capable of doing anything. Perhaps Claudia could reveal even more. But why had Amy insisted no will existed?

"There are no baby drawings or photographs of Bretton at any age," she said to the supine woman.

"No. Not one until he grew older. Garrett's death skewered Bretton's boyhood. He's never smiling in family portraits. I think he may have found something to smile about now, though. Is something going on between you two?"

Rebecca bent over the pictures. Deciding to be honest, she looked up and said, "He's moody and secretive. Still, I'm drawn to him. We'll be spending some time together. I have to return to Kalispell to see my uncle. He made my life possible; I must see how he is. Bretton wants to come along. He says he needs to gather some art supplies, send a shipment of his art for a show in Minneapolis, and he'd like to be away from Eagle Mountain for awhile."

Claudia swung her legs off the bed and hugged Rebecca. "No matter how difficult Bretton can be I've always felt he has good in him. Look how wonderful he is with Teddy. Besides, he's such a fine-looking figure of a man. I should think any woman could put up with a little moodiness."

"What did Bretton and Lucinda quarrel about when he left Eagle Mountain?"

"That happened before we came here, but Lucinda gave me her version. Damon had been sent to New Hampshire, to Exeter, for his schooling and came back during summers. Bretton resisted that path from the first mention of it. As a boy, he followed Seth, learning everything about the natural world that a lifetime of Seth's own learning could pass on. When he wasn't with Seth, at school, or by himself, he worked in the studio watching and learning from Lucinda no matter how harsh her criticism."

Claudia shifted in discomfort. Rebecca brought her a glass of fresh water from the pitcher. Claudia sipped and continued.

"Damon made local friends, girls especially, even though he only came home for vacations. Bretton acted the lone wolf even then. Damon says Bretton broke hearts just by being oblivious.

"Then, when the time came for college, Lucinda ordered Bretton to attend Harvard, but he refused. Lucinda believed that the least he should do as a Cale was become educated enough to help Damon manage family affairs. Bretton never showed the slightest interest. He made good grades but stayed indifferent to everything but the forest and his pottery."

"That still holds true from what I've seen," Rebecca said.

"Damon loved being in on the wheeling and dealing, but Bretton never cared for it. Lucinda appealed to Seth to influence Bretton, but for once Seth refused her. That's when she really let loose. Bretton compromised, offering to attend an art school, but she'd hear of nothing less than Ivy League. She screamed at Bretton, calling him a misfit and an ingrate. She said he didn't deserve to be a Cale. Lucinda shouted that Garrett died for a worthless person who seemed determined to be a failure.

"Blind to any but her own ideas, she couldn't accept a plan different from one Garrett would have made for his sons had he lived. Seth, in his quiet way, disapproved. Lucinda remained too stiff-necked ever to apologize."

"What happened?" Rebecca pictured the angry mother as she went through the motions of searching through drawers.

"Bretton threw his clothes into a duffle bag and left Eagle Mountain."

"Where did he go?"

"Spokane. Then into the army. That led to his serving in the Philippine War. He doesn't speak about that time. We know he saw action. After a bullet entered his leg they sent him home. Once recovered, he went to New Mexico, where he continued to work with ceramics until now."

"His work seems excellent to me," Rebecca said, sitting on the edge of the bed again.

"It is. I think Lucinda started to regret trying to force him into the mold Garrett would have chosen. Bretton turned out to be more talented than Lucinda herself. His work has appeared in shows on both coasts, and he now has the one coming up in Minneapolis."

"Yes." Rebecca smiled.

"Well, if things work out for the two of you, I'll be delighted. You'll never be bored."

"Oh, things haven't gone so far yet. I've worked hard to become an attorney. I won't give that up, even for a handsome artist."

"Not for marriage. But perhaps a flirtation?" Claudia grinned and then frowned. "There's a great deal of Lucinda in him despite their battles. Still, she favored Damon in such obvious ways Bretton couldn't help but see it. We all couldn't help but see it."

Rebecca nodded and returned to looking through a collection of Italian leather gloves in grays, tans, yellows, and blues.

"Well," Claudia said, "Damon and I searched through all the nooks and crannies where Lucinda would stick a document in her office. We checked her safe after she died. Nothing there but jewelry."

"Only jewelry." Rebecca laughed as she pictured glittering diamond earrings, bracelets, and chokers shining with precious stones. She stood. "We'll just have to keep searching. Uncle Max never accepts anything less than success. It's the secret to his reputation; that and the fact that he had to have something to keep himself occupied during the years Lucinda kept turning him down. If I remain single, I might amount to something, too."

"I never wanted to be more than Damon's wife and the mother of his children. That job is still easy as far as Teddy and his father are concerned. But Amy leaves me saddened and bewildered." Claudia sat up.

Rebecca stopped to admire some French lace in one of the dresser drawers.

"I'll have to sell, or pack, or give away all her things." Claudia sighed.

"I'll help," Rebecca said. "Remember, that's the main reason why I came."

Rebecca dreamed of Uncle Max that night. He reached out to her from swirling snow, soundless mouth repeating something, but the storm tore his words away. She felt helpless.

She awakened early, dressed, laced up her leather boots, and packed her bags.

Bretton waited downstairs with a mug of coffee. As he opened the door to the outside, Rebecca noted four large wooden boxes. "Pieces to send on from Kalispell for the show in Minneapolis," he said, nodding toward them. "I'll load up while you grab breakfast."

While Rebecca ate, Damon readied the sleigh and horses, bringing them to wait on the road before the lodge. Bretton and Damon loaded the boxes and luggage behind the seats. Rebecca came out into a dawn that greeted her with salmon-scalloped clouds. Damon handed her up next to Bretton. They left Eagle Mountain and, at least for the time being, all its troubled, woeful history behind. Rebecca couldn't wait to be home to see Max.

They liveried the sleigh and horses at the incorrigible Bill Sauer's stable in Jennings. Damon would send someone to pick them up later. Rebecca and Bretton strolled to the café for a lunch of grilled whitefish. Then they boarded the train for Columbia Falls. From there the spur line took them to Kalispell.

On the journey Bretton asked Rebecca about her life in Switzerland. In turn, he described the Philippines, little concerning his war experiences, but much of the country and people. Then he spoke of the American Southwest, of artists beginning to gather there to exchange ideas, study, and create unique works of art. He admitted to being among the most ambitious honing their skills under the desert sun where ancient pueblo pottery had been created.

Rebecca asked, "Is it difficult to support yourself with art?"

Bretton gazed out their window. She wondered if her question disturbed him, but he turned back to her. "Being a novice costs in every way. Serious art devours your soul and your money. In the end, you spend hours alone but have to share and learn from others, too. The life is exciting and addicting. It takes years to develop the skills to earn a name. Mother sent checks through Damon. She paid me to stay away, and that suited me. It's going to be starvation time without that support. Or, once the estate is settled I may be fine."

Rebecca pushed, on the cusp of discovering some key to understanding Bretton. "How do other beginning artists survive?"

Bretton grimaced. "Truth be told, it's daunting without patrons or personal wealth. If you can't promote your work, if it stays unseen, you might be a genius, and it wouldn't matter. You have to mingle with moneyed collectors. Joining those circles . . ."

"So, if you inherit from Lucinda's estate, you stand a much better chance of success."

Bretton raked his fingers through his hair. "It would surely come faster. I have debts as it is. I scraped and cobbled enough together to come to Eagle Mountain, but there's little left. The absolute truth is I'll be fortunate to have enough for food on the way back to New Mexico. Now I'm spending too much on this show in Minneapolis. I have to sell there. I hated Mother at times, but her money let me buy supplies and progress in my work." He sighed. "Now you know. That's how it is."

Rebecca touched his arm. "I've seen your work. Minneapolis will be a success."

After Bretton's disclosures, they sat in silence, each mulling over implications of what he'd disclosed. But it had also made them easier with each other. They later relaxed enough to enjoy being together. Despite his troubles, Bretton told amusing stories of growing up with the wildlife and outdoor adventures that life at Eagle Mountain provided the Cale boys.

They reached Kalispell after dark. Rebecca had telegraphed

Mrs. Bracken to have Fred meet them at the depot. He helped load Bretton's crates into the wagon, then drove the weary travelers down Main Street with light emanating from numerous saloons. Ranchers, farmers, and businessmen crowded the boardwalks. The wagon moved from the commercial area into darker streets, arriving at last at Max's Victorian home.

Mrs. Bracken, her broad face rounded in a welcoming smile, declared that Max had been making decent enough progress in the hospital. The staff expected Rebecca to visit him next day. Rebecca wondered if she only imagined a slight hesitation in the housekeeper's attempted reassurance.

In spite of the late hour, Mrs. Bracken insisted on serving them in the dining room: a roast beef dinner with a merlot followed by chocolate pudding and rich coffee. Bretton and Rebecca continued their day-long conversation, with Rebecca speaking more now. She shared her perceptions of studying law under her brilliant uncle, and the challenges of establishing herself as a respected attorney, one to be taken seriously. Was it her imagination, or did Bretton begin to be less attentive?

After seeing Bretton settled in the guest room, Rebecca said her good night. They paused at his doorway and kissed, almost as a quick formality. Uncle Max's house, Rebecca decided, did not encourage romantic indiscretion. No, not at all. In her room, Rebecca pondered what she'd learned. Handsome, intelligent, gifted, Bretton needed money. The Cales had first tried to depict the family circle as a calm, respectable lake with tranquil shores. In reality dangerous currents and undertows lay beneath its surface. She sighed before reading a chapter of *House of Mirth*. Before sleep claimed her she relived the lovely day with a relaxed Bretton. At last she whispered a prayer of gratitude for the news of Max's improving health. But, she added a petition that she'd only imagined Mrs. Bracken might be withholding something about Max.

Rebecca had no nightmares that night.

Next morning Rebecca left Bretton at the house, once more the intense artist checking over and repacking his fragile creations. So far the pieces had survived the journey free of cracks or chips. He had to make sure they continued without mishap all the way to Minneapolis.

Rebecca walked to the hospital through a light snowfall. When she stopped to listen, she heard only the soft hiss of snow landing on a world made soft and white. Sunlight emerged for a moment, and each brightened flake landed on surfaces that shimmered like porcelain. Magical. Rebecca caught her breath at the sight, almost relieved when an ordinary cloud drifted in to block the sun. She needed to keep her head free of fantastic distractions. Unsure of how she'd find her uncle, she had to prepare herself for however he might appear.

It occurred to her again that Mrs. Bracken might have been too optimistic in her report the night before.

In fact, Mrs. Bracken had been almost accurate. Max sat in a high-backed wheelchair, a cane nearby. He wore a woolen robe, a soft blanket covering his lap. He appeared weary but brightened when his niece swept through the door and enveloped him in a long, loving embrace.

"Oh, Uncle Max, I've thought of you every day," she said. "I had to come and see you. You look so much better."

Max slurred his words only a bit as he said, "Rebecca, you're home." Rebecca felt relief so profound it left her limp. She understood his words as he began firing questions.

"Dear girl, start at the beginning. Lucinda's funeral?"

Rebecca pulled a chair in front of him and described the service, grateful to start there and not with her harrowing arrival at Bretton's studio. She went on to describe the family's complex relationships, including Amy's obsessing over her grandmother. She related what she'd revealed to no one else, her discovery of Lucinda's diaries. She related Lucinda's writings.

"Did she speak of me? Did she write of love for me at any time? Did she write that she considered marriage when we were young?"

Rebecca paused, then chose honesty even though she hated to hurt her uncle. "No, Max. Not once she'd met Garrett. She confessed to an affectionate friendship, but only once did she even come close to expressing what might have been. She chose the wrong man but seemed to feel that had been her destiny."

Max slumped in his wicker-backed chair, stricken with disappointment.

A pleasant, large-boned nurse entered and, seeing her patient's weary demeanor, insisted in a gentle voice that he must rest.

"Of course," Rebecca said, chiding herself for not seeing how fragile Max still remained after the stroke. "I'll return tomorrow."

In bed again, Max lifted an unsteady hand. "Wait. Before that, find Seth Dubois's file in my office. I did legal work for him. Kept meticulous notes. Indeed, I did. You'll see why. Read it, then come tomorrow. Good to have you back, dear girl." He closed his eyes, asleep before Rebecca left his room.

At home, Rebecca found Mrs. Bracken making bread. As in her girlhood, Rebecca popped a piece of dough in her mouth and started tea for the older woman and herself. While water heated, the two shared opinions on Max's condition.

"Max tires so easily," Rebecca said. She described how he'd wearied but added that the difference between when she'd left to go to Eagle Mountain and now gave her cause for hope.

"He'll mend quick enough now you're home. To stay, I hope," the housekeeper said, puffing as she kneaded and added flour to her yeast-scented dough, occasional bubbles appearing on its surface. She added that Bretton had gone to make further arrangements for when he arrived in Minneapolis and would be back sometime after dinner.

Rebecca excused herself, not wanting to reveal that she'd have to leave again, her work at Eagle Mountain not finished. "Max is well enough to assign tasks for me. I'll take that as a good sign," she said as she left the other woman scraping residual dough from her bread board. In short hours the smell of fresh baking would add to the warmth of their home, including Max's office.

Rebecca unlocked the heavy wooden cabinet containing the D's through E's. She found Seth's file with no trouble, surprised at its thickness. Goodness. For what reasons had the simple-living hunting guide needed legal help? What had he confided to Max Bryan, his rival for Lucinda? Perhaps Seth didn't see Max's unrequited love as all the rest in the Cale household did.

Rebecca could have taken the file to her own little adjoining office but instead settled down on the Persian rug, fanning the papers around her in a semi-circle.

As the sun backlit the trees outside while it lowered, Rebecca switched on electric lamps with an appreciative sigh for modern conveniences. She then read and reread the documents and notes in Seth's file.

Seth had retained Max to settle his meager estate upon his death. Max's notes of their first meeting hinted at his being amused by his unlettered old friend. Of course, Max refused to charge a retainer fee.

Rebecca paused to imagine the virile wilderness expert out of his element in the bustling frontier town. City people must have seemed confused like that to Seth when he guided them through the old-growth forest.

But she began to read what Max recorded as to Seth's unique request. Seth had placed a gold medallion on Max's desk. It showed a profile of Queen Victoria on one side and the profile of a Kootenai man on the other. Max wrote in his forward-slanting script that Seth told him his mother had given it to him when he became a man.

Max followed that with a mailing address in Quebec. An arrow pointed to a name above the address, Henry Dubois. In the margin, next to the arrow, Max wrote, "brother." Reading down the page, Rebecca saw that, in the event of Seth's death, Max had instructions to mail the medallion to Henry. Once he received the medallion, Henry Dubois would send a letter to Max. The letter would contain the rest of Seth's wishes. Seth refused to disclose at their meeting what these would be.

Max's notes indicated he'd agreed to follow his friend's odd directives.

A loose sheet in Max's handwriting contained questions. This wasn't unusual, as he had a habit of listing queries whenever he had to solve a personal or professional problem. Rebecca read on. "Seth and Lucinda? How far? How deep? Why? A serious contender? How strong? What's to be done to eliminate all competition? Is it possible?"

A tap on the door signaled that Mrs. Bracken had come to announce dinner. Rebecca scrambled to her feet and smoothed her hair. She hadn't heard Bretton return, so dinner in the dining room would probably be a solitary affair. She locked the office door rather than put away the file and joined Mrs. Bracken in the welcoming kitchen.

After dinner Rebecca returned to peruse Seth's intriguing file. What she found piqued her curiosity even more than the medallion had. Max had placed newspaper clippings in Seth's file.

An article from Kalispell's *Daily Inter Lake* described Seth Dubois's death from a grizzly attack.

The reporter described Seth suffering a gruesome mauling when on a hunting trip with prominent local attorney Max Bryan. The article quoted Max, who'd witnessed the whole thing, or as much as he could see in the moonless dark. Max related how the bear pulled Seth out of his tent and Seth's shouts and grunts as he struggled.

Max said his rifle jammed at the worst possible moment, preventing him from saving Seth. The bear dragged Seth into thickly wooded terrain rendered impenetrable in the black of predawn night. Max told how he groped on the ground to find Seth's gun but couldn't locate it in the dark. He ran back the way they'd come to summon help but met no one.

Search parties, one including Max himself, went out for three days before discovering Seth's remains: scattered bones, scraps of cloth, and hair of both bear and human. Max added how others admired Seth for putting up a good fight against his attacker. The article went on:

> Lucinda Cale, said to be distraught over her family's loss of a close friend, caretaker, and "expert mentor on matters of wilderness," claimed Seth Dubois would be irreplaceable at Eagle Mountain, perhaps for her sons most of all.

Seth's short obituary followed. His life had been a private one. He'd served the rich and famous. When they didn't require him, he spent hours alone in the forest or as a caretaker at the lodge. He never married. There were no surviving children, his only living relative the brother in Canada. Rebecca searched for additional written thoughts or observations from Max but only found more clippings from various Montana newspapers.

So that's what happened, she thought. She returned Seth's

file to the cabinet, eager to see Max in the morning to learn
more details of the death of Bretton's father.

CHAPTER TWENTY-ONE

Since Max tired and his mood darkened under the stress of too much conversation, Rebecca determined to be more patient at their next meeting. For Max's comfort she wouldn't arrive too early. Eager as she felt to learn more of Seth's terrible story, she knew she shouldn't press too much.

She worked in the office until the clock struck 10:00 a.m. She planned to walk the long way to the hospital, giving herself time to consider what she'd learned the day before, and what she still needed to know.

She strolled down the boardwalk on Main Street before turning toward the hospital. Just hours ago the town bustled with crowds seeking pleasure, money, or both. Now Kalispell stretched around her, in Sunday morning quiet, its denizens sleeping in or attending services.

Plenty of activity met her as she entered the hospital. An emergency appendectomy patient had come in who required surgery. There would be no visiting with either doctor about Max for awhile.

Rebecca proceeded to her uncle's room alone. He sat in the wheelchair again but this time faced the window to the street.

"Saw you coming," he said without turning.

Rebecca walked around to face him. She brushed back his silvery hair, dry, and more disheveled than she'd ever seen it, and bent to kiss his cheek. He gave her a steady look. "Read the file, did you?"

"All of it. What a horrible ending for Seth. And before that the strange story of the medallion. But I thought Seth's brother would have sent the sealed letter. Did you never receive it? Did you pursue the matter? There's nothing in the file about it arriving. It's not there."

"Turn me around and pull up that chair. I have a story to tell you. It's not pretty. Don't let anyone interrupt us. They don't care about privacy in this hellish place. Block the door."

Rebecca pulled her uncle's chair around and held up one finger. She wrote "A conference in session. Please do not interrupt" and removed her hatpin to secure the notice on the outside of the door. She went to the bureau and returned with a brush and comb. "I can't wait to hear, but I know you'll feel better if we tidy you up a little." When she'd finished, she brought a straight-backed chair and sat leaning toward him, eager to hear everything he had to say.

He began, "Henry Dubois sent the letter. Not one word of his own, just Seth's. Seth was a poor speller, but he knew how to go into detail. Knew how to pour his heart out. Knew what many never learn . . . how to make a full confession. A man of honor, Seth should have been treated better than Lucinda, or I, behaved toward him."

Max cleared his throat, and Rebecca brought him water to sip. When he nodded, she set it on the nightstand and waited.

"You won't find Seth's letter because I burned it. I could never say no to Lucinda."

Rebecca sat back in amazement. "You destroyed a client's letter?"

"I did, and I'll tell you why. It went back to the time of Garrett's death. Garrett, my avaricious, heartless, wife-beating friend. First he stole her from me, then he punished her with his violence. I never told you, but Garrett saved my life during the war. Sometimes I've wished he hadn't. Obligation can grow into an onerous burden, especially when gratitude turns to disdain."

"I only feel love for you, the man who saved me." Rebecca reached forward to squeeze her uncle's hand. "Is this too difficult, Max? Should I let you rest?"

"Not yet. Seth's letter revealed many things I didn't know as fact but suspected. Perhaps I didn't want to know so had never tried to learn of his love for Lucinda. He stated they were lovers, intimate lovers for many years, although Lucinda didn't remain faithful as he did. He also revealed that Bretton was the result of their affair. But there's more.

"Seth deceived Lucinda about how Garrett died. Lucinda urged him to kill Garrett to stop the beatings, the torment, the violations. Seth agreed to commit murder after she pledged to marry him if he did. He'd have done anything for that to happen. He wanted her as much as I did. He possessed her as a lover; he wanted to possess her as his wife.

"On the day of Bretton's birth, Seth intended to murder Garrett when they went into the blizzard to bring back the doctor. He'd make it look like an accident. But something strange happened. Garrett became disoriented almost as soon as they left Eagle Mountain. Sick, too. He staggered, retched, and moaned in pain. Seth, Garrett's boyhood friend, found in the end he couldn't kill him. But neither could he carry him in the blizzard.

"They were about a mile from the lodge. He settled Garrett by a gigantic old-growth pine, promising to return. Desperate to save Lucinda, he chose her over Garrett and went on for the doctor. On the way back, he went to the tree, but Garrett must have gathered some strength. Disoriented in the storm, he'd wandered off."

Rebecca leaned forward. "How did Lucinda accept that? I doubt she cared how Garrett died."

"She didn't, but Seth feared she'd reject him if he admitted being unable to kill Garrett. He kept his secret all those years."

Rebecca frowned. "Why did he tell you?"

"The need to confess the truth is strong in most of us. The irony is that he had not committed a crime. He asked me to give Lucinda the letter in the event of his death. He thought she deserved to know he hadn't kept his part of the bargain. He loved her so much he didn't want her to feel remorse for not honoring her promise to marry him."

Rebecca gave her uncle another sip of water. "You must already have been in shock over the way he died with you right there unable to save him."

"Ah." Uncle Max put a shaky hand over his eyes. "Now it's my turn at confession. Yes, I was there. We'd been hunting and talked late by the campfire. Seth said something, a slip that made me realize he knew Lucinda as only an intimate could. I hated him but said nothing. We went to our tents, letting the fire burn to embers. I lay seething. It's as if my hatred drew the beast to us.

"The bear could just as well have come for me, but it attacked Seth. I tell you now, Rebecca, because I'm tired of carrying this shameful secret. My rifle didn't jam. I hesitated. I had a clear shot but didn't take it. Seth stood, as I thought then, between me and Lucinda. Between me and all I wanted in this world. I hesitated, and my chance to rescue him passed. The bear dragged him out a good twenty feet. In the dark, I could see its hulking shape. I felt horror as I heard Seth's screams. I finally aimed at the bear and fired but missed. The grizzly moved fast, hauling Seth with it. I shot again. And missed again. The only chance I had to do the right thing came and went and will never, never, come back."

Rebecca felt as though night had fallen, a black midnight in this white, white room where she held her uncle's hand. "Oh,

Max. Anyone could have missed in the dark. I think your memory turned this into some sin of omission you may have wanted to commit but really didn't."

"No. And I did more. After his funeral, after the attention died down, I followed Seth's instructions and showed Lucinda his letter. I let her know that I knew everything, and all I wanted was her. What every man who ever met Lucinda wanted . . . to possess her."

Max paled and slumped, his eyes closed. Rebecca had seen him like this before.

She stood in alarm. "Max!" She rushed to the door and shouted, "Max is having another stroke! Help us!"

Max had, indeed, suffered a second stroke. Rebecca spoke with Doctor Amelia, then sat by her uncle's bed, reclaiming his hand even as it seemed to grow colder to her touch.

"Uncle Max," she whispered. "I'm here. Let me take care of you."

The hand pulled from her. Max pointed to the door.

"You want me to leave?" she asked, incredulous.

He struggled with a word. "Lu—Lu . . ."

"You want me to keep trying to find out Lucinda's last wishes?"

The finger swung from the door to point at her. Max gave a slight nod.

"I will if that's the best way to help, but don't you dare leave us while I'm away from you."

He gave a lopsided, sardonic smile and closed his eyes.

Rebecca sat with him for another hour. She memorized his physical appearance, distinguished even as he slackened, diminished, became distant. Then she stood, bent close, and kissed his forehead. She didn't say good-bye. She'd never said good-bye to her father because he hadn't granted her the chance. Max had assigned her work to do. That seemed to signal, at least in her hopes, that he didn't believe his time had come.

"I'll come back when I've solved all the puzzles," she whispered.

He didn't respond.

Outside the hospital she inhaled and brushed gloved hands over her face. Did her eyes tear because of the cold breeze or in her anticipation of sorrow?

At home, Rebecca went straight to Max's office. She reread the Seth Dubois file, all the while remembering Max's narration of what he'd done, or not done, and the frightening aftermath of a second stroke following his confession. It might be irrational, she thought, but Max experiencing a second stroke over his failure to save Seth made her uncle seem like another of Lucinda's victims, not the moral bankrupt he felt himself to be. Anger bordering on hatred of Lucinda rose in her. It made little sense, but Rebecca felt enraged. She slammed the file shut and hunched on her knees before the fire, the image of desolation. Why were human beings so apt to fail themselves and each other?

She stayed almost motionless for hours. Mrs. Bracken left in late afternoon after Rebecca called through the door that she wasn't hungry so no need for dinner. She'd raid the kitchen later for something light. Mrs. Bracken responded that in that case she'd visit Mr. Bryan at the hospital.

Alone in the house, Rebecca wept for her uncle, for her father, for her mother, for all of them. At some point after twilight lowered, she heard Bretton enter. In a few moments he tapped on the door, then opened it.

"Rebecca? Are you all right? Why are you sitting on the floor in the dark?"

Rebecca looked up. She saw Bretton standing in the doorway, his outline like a classical statue, only clothed. She pushed herself up and stood, shaky, but with a firm knowledge of what she needed.

"Come here to me," she said, her voice steadying but throaty from a long afternoon of tears.

Bretton stepped inside the room and turned the key to lock the door. He walked to her and enveloped her in his arms. She nestled her head on his chest as he stroked her hair.

"I don't want comfort," Rebecca said. Pulling his head down, she kissed him hard and added, "I don't want you to comfort me. I want you to take me away from all this pain. Make me not think of it."

He removed his parka and laid it on the floor. He also fetched a throw from the daybed. When he'd prepared a soft place for them before the fire, Bretton didn't speak but kissed her again. Then he began to undress her, stopping to caress her shoulder and nuzzle her throat. He kissed her bared breasts and naked skin as he peeled, unhooked, and lifted away each layer of her clothing. He lowered her, nude and trembling, then stood to remove his clothes.

He knelt before her and sighed in appreciation. "You are beautiful beyond all the art or wonders of nature under the sun or moon," he said. He lowered his long, muscular body over her, not quite touching. The flames leapt as her hands stroked his hair, his chest, his shoulders and arms. She arched as his mouth found her nipples. His hands stroked and molded her for a long time, coaxing them both to a place where bright heat, like the sudden rising of a desert sun, burst through all barriers. They cried out together, then rested apart. Rebecca wept again, but this time from relief given her as her consolation in release.

Bretton turned on his side to face her. "You'll be all right, Rebecca. Always. You have passion, intelligence, and beauty.

People will always love you."

"Thank you." She rested her thigh over his, feeling the damp heat that lingered on their sated bodies. "You did take me away. I felt, I even saw, the desert sun."

He rolled to his back and pillowed his head on his hands linked beneath it. "Come with me to see it as it hovers above the reds and yellows and oranges of the desert. I'm going back there soon. It's where I do my best work. You could come and see it for yourself. Stay with me."

Rebecca flinched, finding life complicated again so soon. "My life is here, Bretton. I'm building my practice. Justice is my passion. Max taught me how precious it is."

He kissed her again. "Ah, Justice. She has no appreciation of art."

Rebecca lifted herself and stretched the length of her lover. "She can't be influenced by beauty or anything else. She's pure. If she took off her blindfold and looked at you, though, she might not be impartial. You're like a Greek statue come to life."

She initiated their second lovemaking. Unhurried, she kissed him and exhaled against his throat. In moments they coupled, slow, tender, and rhythmic. It didn't matter where they were or what had happened in the past. It didn't matter what blessings or sorrows the future might bring. All that mattered existed here, in this passion, in this touching and joining into one being even if only for this brief moment.

They fell asleep curled into that sense of unity. Rebecca didn't wake him until hours later. Mrs. Bracken had come back but without disturbing them. She probably thought Rebecca chose to work late. It happened often enough. The lovers dressed and crept upstairs to part and sleep in their separate rooms.

Rebecca slumbered as though she had no need to awake to either responsibilities or sorrows. She slept like a woman who'd been well and truly loved.

★ ★ ★ ★ ★

Max held his own for the next two days. On the third, both doctors declared him stable and out of danger. Bretton traveled on to Minneapolis with his crates of art.

Rebecca traveled back to Eagle Mountain alone, eager to return to the challenge of finding the will. She wanted to read the rest of Lucinda's diaries, and she wanted most of all to please Max by finding the missing testament.

She arrived at Eagle Mountain in time for dinner. Claudia embraced her, and Teddy threw his arms around her legs. Amy gave a curt nod while Damon hoisted a glass of whiskey. They expressed their sympathy and concern over Max's setback.

As soon as she could, Rebecca excused herself and went to her room. She readied herself for bed, lit an extra candle, made herself comfortable, and began to read.

March 10, 1905

I've been remembering things I will never tell Amy. The gilded version of the personal history I've been recounting is a deception. The truth is dark and involves Seth's life and tragic end. My life warped into a twisting maze of deceit, fear, and passion. I loved Seth, but, of course, I used him. I've become a stranger to myself, incapable of selfless love. But, even worse, I've become the manipulative sort of woman I would have once found despicable.

I still do.

It pains me to think of how Seth died. What must have gone through his mind as he struggled against the bear? Did he smell its rank grizzly's breath? Did he feel pain? Did he think of me and how I'd miss him? Because I do. We all do and, I think, always will. What a peaceful man to die in such a cruel way.

Max took it hard. It must have been awful to be there

but unable to stop what happened.

And there was a strange coda to it all that involved Max in his attorney's capacity. Yesterday, Max came to me. He showed concern for my sorrow over losing Seth. I realized that he intuited, or had learned somehow, of our long affair.

Then Max brought out a document, a letter written by Seth in his blocky script and short declarations. Max explained how he'd come by it, then handed it to me. Its contents told everything: Garrett's abuse, Seth's and my affair, Bretton's parentage, and our plot to kill Garrett after my promise to marry Seth if he'd commit the murder.

Then he told the real facts of what happened on the day of Bretton's birth and the blizzard that directed the path, the destiny, we all had to follow. He described Garrett as disoriented and weak almost from the moment he started from the lodge that day, staggering and incoherent. The realization that his boyhood friend had been somehow rendered helpless erased all thoughts of murder. Seth, knowing I wrestled against death's grip during Bretton's breech birth back in the lodge, determined to bring the doctor back to Eagle Mountain. Seth wrote of trying to carry Garrett, then giving up and leaving him to wait. Seth succeeded in reaching Doctor Gillette.

After Garrett's death we continued along, Seth hoping to convince me to keep my pledge to marry him, me avoiding matrimony's smothering bonds. We didn't, as it turned out, become murderers, but we weren't truly happy either even though our love still existed.

Oh, Seth, I miss and mourn you. What we once had remains beautiful. I perverted all that was best in us both.

Looking up from Seth's letter, and seeing Max's yearning face, I realized what I had to do.

"Burn it," I said, handing the letter back to Max.

He hesitated, then put the letter to the flames in the hearth. As it curled to ashes in the flames Max turned to me. "I love you, Lucinda. I've loved you as long as I've known you. You're alone. Marry me. Let me be the help and protector the others could never be."

I pondered, knowing those flames meant my safety, then sighed. It seemed my life had been a line of men who wanted to save me, each as much for his benefit as for mine. Well, Max should have realized I no longer needed saving, financially or in any other way, not even from loneliness. I am slowly dying. My heart isn't just cold, it is failing. But even without the letter, Max still had learned from Seth of my plans to be rid of Garrett and my deception to keep Seth in thrall as if I'd cast a spell over him.

If I thought I had years left, I would control Max, too. Max in his love-drenched delusion would step partly into the role that quiet, devoted Seth had played. I would ensure his silence and loyalty. Once again I would use a man's love to control him, and with an artist's hands shape him to my needs. Of course he'd become my lover. Passion finally consummated would prevent any betrayal of my secrets. I'd have Max as little or as much as I wanted him. A beautiful woman can do that with almost any man, especially an older one who's waited and yearned for so many years.

I despise myself, but my craving for independence and safety from revelations of my past misdeeds would have taken firm control.

I told him I did love him and had in my own way for years. Nevertheless, my illness now made marriage inadvisable. I needed time to regain my health. I asked Max to come back if I should be well enough to send for him. He agreed. He will still come at my suggestion. I sighed. He would have made such a considerate and loving husband.

In a way, by making him betray his legal ethics, I think I've stolen his soul.

CHAPTER TWENTY-TWO

Rebecca lifted her head and rubbed her temples. How could this have transpired? Uncle Max compromised himself to possess this scheming, power-mad woman? Then she reconsidered. How could she or anyone else judge Lucinda, who'd known the horrors of being beaten, seen her child mistreated, and had been kept under the boot heel of an irrational, vicious husband?

Rebecca felt the need to move, to escape the diary for awhile. As she rose from her reading she looked out the window on the frozen scene beyond. This brooding lodge held so many secrets. What a strange, troubled place, filled with hate and silent passions and resentments.

Her thoughts circled and returned to the attic. Amy sought out that high, cold space so often with its memorabilia and antiques, tangible reminders of Cale history. The troubling attic seemed to hold more than dusty boxes and discarded clothes. What might still be discovered among its crowded bits and pieces of days long gone? Rebecca wanted to study Garrett's portrait again without interference.

Remembering the icy atmosphere under the rafters, she put on fur-lined slippers and her warm robe. She picked up a candle and matches and stole down the hall.

Rebecca peeked into the nursery just to be sure that both children were there. Teddy snored, spread-eagled on his bed. Rebecca entered the room, straightened his blankets, and stroked the little boy's cheek. What a beautiful child, she thought. How innocent. Too soon he'd join the world of adults, burdened with all their grown-up wants and desires. She wondered what Lucinda must have thought, gazing down at Bretton as he slept here.

Then she glanced at Amy's bed. To her disappointment it appeared rumpled but empty. She might not have the attic to herself.

She closed the nursery door behind her. Peering from the hall railing, she saw that the only lights downstairs were the red-orange of embers and the milky moonlight pouring in the windows. Rebecca climbed the narrow wooden steps to the attic. At the top step she froze when she heard Amy's voice.

"I'm sorry, Grandpa Garrett. I'll try to keep them from finding out. I wish I'd burned up the diaries. I planned to, but then she came. I bet she took them. Now I don't know what to do. I wish Grandma Lucinda had never written those things down. Tell me you didn't hit her. Tell me you didn't shoot the horse."

After a brief pause, Amy continued. "Grandma told me you were like the knights of old, there to serve and protect the ladies of the court. Grandma always said you were a kind person and a great man. I don't believe she made it all up. Why would she? Grandmother and I loved each other. I don't believe she ever lied to me. I decided when I read them that what she told me was true, not what she made up in those old diaries. She just invented a story in them. Maybe she meant them for a novel."

Rebecca took the final step and entered the shadowed room so crammed with personal mementos. "Amy, it's Rebecca. May I come in and talk with you? It's important that we have a private chat, and this is a good place. I know you visit your grandfather's portrait often."

Amy turned toward Rebecca and glared. "I'm already having a private conversation. You don't know what you're talking about anyway."

"Yes, I do. The truth is that your grandmother didn't make up what she wrote in the diaries."

"Grandmother told me the truth."

Rebecca shook her head. "I know it's hard at your age to see an idol shattered. Perhaps your grandmother wanted to spare you the fact that Garrett could be cruel. Maybe she couldn't bear to tell the true story except in her diary. Your grandfather, your grandmother, and Seth, too, even Max—they were just human beings. Some are kind, and some are cruel. Some people do good things, and others feel the need to inflict pain. We often don't know why people act as they do."

Amy leapt to her feet. "You spied on me! You're a spy and a liar! None of what you say is true."

"Yes, Amy, it is. Having a real conversation with this old portrait is what isn't true."

Rebecca stepped forward, struck a match on a box, and lit her candle. The illusion of Garrett's ghost disappeared. Standing beside the mirror, Rebecca saw Amy's face register shock. The child's eyes turned desperate, her face drained of color. She saw the image for the fiction, the optical illusion it really was. Amy stumbled into the real world, not a delusion that accepted her confidences.

"Amy," Rebecca spoke sharply. "You must have known deep down that it wasn't really Garrett. You've been here in daylight before. You know that what Lucinda wrote in her diaries really happened. Not the version she told you of Garrett as a knight in shining armor. Your grandfather charmed others, but he had no compass for kindness. He was a man who'd been through a horrible war. He had terrible faults, and he slid into being a violent and cruel man. He made serious mistakes."

Mute, Amy shook her head.

"Lucinda made mistakes, too. She lived under the burden of Garrett's vicious behavior. She became desperate, and desperate people often commit desperate deeds. Lucinda was a victim who fought her circumstances. Sadly, she developed into a scheming woman.

"Seth made mistakes as well. Loving your grandmother led him to make dishonest decisions. We all make mistakes. So did Seth. We all do.

"You made a mistake when you blamed Bretton for the family's problems. But it's all right. People have to learn to forgive each other. It's not easy to forgive, but you have to grow up. To face the world as it is."

"No." Amy found her voice, but it sounded rough and ugly. "Everything is spoiled. I hate Grandmother. I hate all of you. And, most of all, I hate Bretton. Why did he ever come back? I want him to go away and stay away." Amy buried her face in her hands.

Rebecca moved to soothe her. She touched Amy's shoulders, but the girl jumped. "Don't touch me. Leave me alone." She pushed Rebecca, who fell against Garrett's portrait. It crashed to the floor sideways.

The frame splintered and broke, and an envelope fell out on the floor. Amy reached to snatch it, but Rebecca, already on the floor, grabbed it first.

"What's that?" Amy demanded.

Rebecca twisted away from the girl and pocketed the letter. She had no idea what it was, but it might, she thought, be the missing will.

"I can't let you have it, Amy. I have to read it first."

"Why do you get to read it before me? This isn't your family!"

"It might be the will, Amy. I have a responsibility to investigate Lucinda's estate documents. I'm going to my room. You should go back to bed. We'll fix the portrait's frame tomorrow."

Rebecca kept tight hold of the envelope in her pocket as she rose. She stood taller than Amy, which helped her achieve an authoritative stance. She had to keep possession of this envelope and its unknown contents. Amy, and perhaps others, would be all too ready to destroy unwanted evidence. Rebecca now understood in full the dangers lurking in this moldering lodge. From now on the game had become even more serious.

"You're stealing. Nothing here belongs to you!" Amy spoke through clenched teeth, then whirled and ran downstairs. Her angry footsteps receded toward the nursery.

Rebecca sighed. "Well, I certainly botched that," she muttered. She lifted the portrait, with its damaged frame, blew out her candle, and the illusion returned. "Perhaps she's right." Rebecca addressed the elegant ghost image in the mirror. "Illusions are sometimes easier to live with than truth. But you married Lucinda. She turned into a woman far cleverer than you ever imagined. Whatever Lucinda became, you started that transformation. Nothing will change that. Now I'm going to read whatever is in this envelope."

A little alarm bell had gone off in Rebecca's head as she all but lectured Amy. She thought of the grudge she'd held against her own father for his suicide. She'd spoken of people crushed and changed by circumstances. He'd never raised his hand or voice against her. Did he kill himself believing he couldn't be the father she needed? That Max could? She thought of her anger, at one point as bitter as Amy's. It seemed to be something she didn't so much drop from her shoulders as see drift away like fog as she tried to help Amy learn about human flaws.

She paused for a moment as she looked at Garrett's arrogant stare, then closed the door behind her, leaving his image alone in the cold room crammed with the dusty stuff of forgotten memories.

Knowing she could do nothing more for Amy and eager to

peruse the mysterious find, Rebecca went to her room. She studied the writing before her, front and back.

The envelope had been addressed in a clear script to Mrs. Anderson. It appeared to have been sealed after being opened. Inside there were three letters. Rebecca opened it and read the first. It read with the formality a stranger would adopt.

June 12, 1886,
Dear Mrs. Anderson,
I recently suffered the loss of my younger sister, Peggy. She died of diphtheria and begged me in her misery to send this letter to you. She is gone, so do with this letter as you see fit. Peggy said you were the dearest friend she had in the entire world, and she wanted you to know the truth of the story. I know nothing beyond the contents of this letter. She confessed her action, and I pray for her soul every day and night. She was, at one time, a good girl.

> With gratitude,
> Ann O'Donnell

Rebecca knelt to add wood to the fire, then sat back on the floor as she might have in Max's office. Her hands shook as she unfolded the second letter.

May 21, 1886
Dear Hedvig,
You were always so kind. You were my best friend and a mother closer to me than the one I was born to. But to get to the point, I want to leave my confession with you. I don't want Seth to ever suffer for what I did. Him or any other. Seth was as much Lucinda's slave as I was Garrett Cale's. I knew about the two of them. Maids see it all. They'd sneak away to her studio. Garrett came to me in

my room. He promised all sorts of things. He said he'd divorce her and marry me. He said I'd be raised up. He never meant his promises. He snuck into the visiting women's rooms sometimes too. I know because like I said once before, us maids see it all. Now I have to tell you. I murdered Garrett Cale. Lucinda Cale was busy having Bretton. Seth and Garrett were to go for help in the storm. I hated Garrett and I saw my chance. I put laudanum, enough to kill him, in the whiskey he drank and in his flask before they left. Yes, it was enough to kill him and in the wind and cold it did. I never felt sorry. I felt glad. I had damned myself already. Still, I want to make a clean confession to be seen only by you until after I die. I think it will be soon. I'm not sorry to leave. It's been a sorry hard life. What they say is right. There is no rest for the wicked. Thank you for everything.

Love, Peggy Flynn Boyd

Rebecca read the final letter.

July 1, 1887

To whoever finds these letters,

This letter tells of the twisted lives and the dark deeds carried out in this place that became so hateful. Garrett Cale seduced and deceived my poor friend Peggy. Our conniving employer convinced the simple girl that he loved her and even wanted to make her his wife, never mind he was already married. He used Peggy, then threw her away like a rag when he tired of her. Devastated and crushed, Peggy confided in me, and I tried to comfort her. I told her I knew Garrett Cale and, to my sorrow, his father before him, both men of the lowest character. Peggy finally told me she was expecting a child, and she'd given the news to Garrett. He laughed at her and claimed the child could be fathered by anyone since Peggy was only an Irish whore who also scrubbed floors.

Her staunch Catholic parents would have disowned her. Inconsolable, she suffered and struggled against thoughts of taking her own life. Finally Peggy reached out to her married sister in Seattle. Her sister had had the opportunity to get nurses' training and married a doctor. Peggy took two weeks off. In Seattle, she obtained an abortion, comforted by her loving sister.

Still, Peggy felt damned, felt her Catholic God would never forgive her. I tried my best to convince her that God is all merciful. Over time I watched Peggy harden into a merciless woman. As her letter states, she murdered Garrett Cale. If anyone deserved to die it would be that violent, faithless, brute of a man.

I don't want Peggy's reputation dragged through the mud. She was an innocent girl swept away by an animal named Cale. Nor do I want Seth's name connected to a murder he didn't commit. I'm placing the letters in the picture frame of Garrett Cale's portrait. Someday if God wishes it so, they will be found. By then they will be a tale out of history. No one reading them will suffer. God forgive what happened in this dismal place.

Hedvig Anderson

Rebecca read and reread the envelope, and the letters, then put them inside the last diary. She climbed into bed. She couldn't sleep. Peggy's sister, then Peggy, then Mrs. Anderson had revealed so much in their letters. The night passed slowly.

Rebecca went downstairs just as Claudia opened the door to accept delivery of a telegram.

"Rebecca," she said, holding it out. "From Kalispell."

Rebecca took it with shaky hands, fearful it contained notice of Max's death. Instead Mrs. Bracken conveyed news that he'd shown some improvement and wanted to see his niece.

Another journey. Rebecca felt twice relieved. Max still lived, and his summons afforded her the perfect excuse to spirit Peggy's confession and the diaries out of the lodge. So far Amy hadn't said anything. In fact, Rebecca hadn't seen her since the night before.

Rebecca hurried upstairs and placed the diaries and letters in her suitcase. She packed clothes around them. She'd guard these hard-found objects with fierce care until all became clear about what they might mean to the problems of the Cale family.

She stood in the center of the room for a long moment, then made a slight shift in the blankets covering her bed. After she closed her room's door she also pulled out a few strands of her hair and tied them in the space between the door and door jam. These would tell her if anyone had entered or searched her room in her absence. Then she hurried to ask Damon to arrange for someone to take her to Jennings and the train.

In Kalispell that evening, Rebecca listened to Mrs. Bracken provide details regarding Max's condition.

"He seems weakened," she reported, "but he knows those around him. He can still speak. He wants to see you in the morning, the time when he has most energy. You know the man can never stop working."

Rebecca went to Max's office next and sat behind his desk. She stared at the area before the hearth where she'd lain with Bretton, remembering his body against hers. What might he be doing at this moment in Minneapolis? Then she contemplated his determination to go back to the Southwest. And that he'd asked her to go with him.

She tapped her finger on the desk, thinking of Bretton's

invitation, certainly not a proposal. She'd long nurtured plans to improve the lot of women in Montana. She could never do that as an artist's handmaiden or muse. Bretton was a Cale, perhaps too volatile to truly understand a woman's need to follow her own destiny. An independent woman would risk being "rewarded" with resentment or infidelity. Her instincts told her Bretton would not long commit all his love and attention to a woman occupied by her own demanding pursuits.

Women at Eagle Mountain led such restricted, spirit-deforming lives. Rebecca could not, would not, follow their path. She needed independence to blaze a trail for women's rights in this raw, new, beautiful state of Montana. She'd earned the right to practice law in Montana, and she'd earn the right to stay on in Kalispell as a professional woman, even at a cost.

The passionate evening with Bretton would meld in with other hidden chapters of her life. She thought of how long she'd studied and worked to be here, behind a desk in a respected law office. She would hold her and Bretton's affair as a treasured memory. But, in the end, she belonged behind this oak desk or winning trials at the Flathead County courthouse in years to come.

She sighed and pulled out the envelope, smoothed it, and reread it yet again.

She locked the letter and diaries inside Max's fireproof safe for the night. She included Seth's file. It belonged there amidst the rest of the tangle of love and betrayal that formed the strands of Eagle Mountain's history.

Max was sitting in the wheelchair when Rebecca arrived. His body had grown thinner, and he slumped a bit to one side. But his eyes retained their usual hawk's intensity, missing nothing. An old hawk, though. Rebecca reminded herself to use care in what she presented.

They embraced. Rebecca thought she sensed his strength returning. The two exchanged pleasantries before Rebecca explained how she'd been using her time.

"I don't have the will, Max, but I stumbled onto something else." She explained her discovery in the attic, including Amy's involvement.

"Spooky little brat," Max muttered. "Read what the Anderson woman wrote."

Rebecca did as he asked, then went on to read the other letters to show their exact contents.

"Confessions." The sick man spat out the word, then pushed up as straight as he could before giving Rebecca a level look. "I have one for you as well. I kept Seth's letter from Lucinda until she lay bedridden. I gave it to her on my last visit to Eagle Mountain."

"Why did you wait so long? Wouldn't her knowing that Seth couldn't bring himself to murder Garrett have lessened her feelings for him?" Rebecca braced herself for his answer, sensing she wouldn't like hearing it.

"Why did I wait? What man who loved with my depth of feeling wouldn't have withheld Seth's letter? I wanted to protect Lucinda from any investigation that might implicate her." He closed his eyes and drew a long breath before continuing. "I waited because I hoped in time Lucinda would return my love in equal measure. God knows, though, she never returned even the smallest portion of the devotion I bore for her.

"I withheld the letter because of my desperate, foolish hope that Lucinda would change. But Lucinda never altered after Garrett's death. Her life had been a series of blows, humiliations, and tragedies too brutal to overcome. She could bear no further scandal.

"I also didn't want us to experience any losses related to criminal activity by my former partner's widow, now my business partner. We're all the products of our yesteryears. Poverty and the loss of self-respect, scandal, and mistreatment did their work. They hardened that beautiful woman to stone. Weakening Seth's position might not have strengthened mine in any way. Lucinda had other lovers. She wanted no part of marriage."

"Oh, Max." Rebecca rested her hand on her uncle's.

He turned his palm up to hers. "Think of your father, Rebecca. Loss and poverty led him to end his life." Max sighed. "My adored Lucinda thought only to control everyone in her life. To lose control meant risking herself. By keeping the letter, in a manner of speaking I controlled her. She feared what Seth might have told me of their conspiracy to commit murder."

Rebecca tried not to show her disappointment and dismay at those words from the man she'd thought beyond dishonor.

Max continued. "On my life, I would never have exposed her in that way. Seth couldn't go through with murder, but he never told her the real facts of what happened. Hell, he was confused about what happened. He let her believe he killed Garrett to keep her tied to him. I let her continue in that belief to keep her tied to me. It wasn't blackmail, but it was blackmail's first cousin. A sin of omission, as the saying goes. Ironically, if she'd given me her trust, I'd have burned the letter earlier."

Rebecca refolded the letters and stuffed them in the envelope, buying herself time to think. She gazed at her uncle. "What did she say when you gave Seth's letter to her?"

"Nothing at first. Then she said, 'Max, my life warped into a lurid mix of fear and fury. I'm intense by nature. For a time my emotions distilled into pure hatred toward Garrett. Only Seth's—and your—devotion sustained me.'

"She also said, 'I have no regrets. I protected my sons and me. Garrett's beatings and degradations entitled me to his fortune. You know, he only looked human. His outside concealed an inner madness I had to destroy.'

"She sighed after that, a long, sad, exhalation."

Max sat in silence for a moment, then continued. "She wept a bit. We spoke of how we'd loved each other, albeit in different ways. We parted with tender words of forgiveness and devotion. Finally wearied, she asked me to leave. She'd drifted off to sleep by the time I reached the door. I never saw her again."

Max raised a shaky hand to his eyes. Rebecca brought him a handkerchief and fresh water.

Seeing his exhaustion, she called for help to return him to his bed.

CHAPTER TWENTY-THREE

Rebecca spent two days seeing to office matters and visiting Max. Their talk and revelations had eased him, but he still anxiously ordered her to find Lucinda's will. It seemed only that would soothe the pain of the long, difficult story of their love.

Rebecca returned to reading Lucinda's diaries.

In the undated final entries, Lucinda complained of ill health that kept her bedridden.

> I nearly weakened enough last night to ask Damon to send for Bretton. He's much on my mind of late, but instead I got a hired man to send for the young attorney in Jennings. I don't want Max or anyone else to see what my Last Will and Testament contains until I'm gone. The Jennings lawyer, McBride, will draft what I need, a will that contains my resolution to all that has plagued our house for so long.

That was the last entry in the last diary.

Elated, Rebecca murmured, "It has to be at Eagle Mountain."

She spent another day, unavoidably dividing time between her uncle and the legal matters that arose and demanded attention during his illness and her absence from the office. She enjoyed being back in the familiar setting.

Kalispell bustled day and night with small town gossip, events public and private, and the growing commerce that suggested opportunities for Bryan and Bryan, Attorneys at Law. But the unfinished business of the will now prodded her as much as it did Max. She felt eager to return to Eagle Mountain. Like a hound on the scent, she chided herself.

Rebecca took the train once more into the snowy mountains to Jennings. She hired Bill Sauer to drive her into the dark forest that enclosed the Cale family and their secrets. Once back at Eagle Mountain, Rebecca greeted the Cales and told them of Max's health. After greetings and news she went to her room. Before she opened the door she checked to see if the hair sealed by the door had been disturbed.

It wasn't there.

She found one strand broken on the floor. Someone had searched her room. Her bed blankets had been altered from when she left. The stakes rose with the evidence that someone had entered uninvited. This disturbed, but didn't surprise, her. The documents locked in Max's safe in Kalispell remained secure. She'd returned with only the diaries, wanting them with her in case she needed to refer to them. Or needed to show them to the Cales.

Rebecca unpacked. After she freshened up she locked her bedroom door and went downstairs. She sought Claudia first. As Rebecca expected from the inviting odors of meal preparation, Claudia stood in the kitchen supervising and working with the cook.

Winter's early darkness descended even before the dinner hour when the family gathered at the trestle table for beef stew and fresh-baked bread. Amy gave Rebecca an owlish glare through her glasses. The girl asked to be excused before the others finished their warm apple pie.

"Amy doesn't accept me yet," Rebecca said to Claudia when they sat before the fire later. "I tried to talk to her the night before I left, but she seemed frantic. Claudia, would you come up to the attic? I want to show you something."

"The attic?" Claudia poured cocoa from a pottery pitcher and pushed Rebecca's mug to her across the little table between them. "All right, if I can talk Damon into reading Teddy his bedtime story."

When the house quieted for the night, Rebecca and Claudia climbed the main staircase, then the narrow attic steps.

"Wait, let me go first," Rebecca said. She hurried ahead of slow-moving Claudia and turned down the wick on the oil lamp she carried so Garrett's manifestation appeared from the gloom.

"Now come here," she directed, taking Claudia's hand to guide her.

Once in position, Claudia gasped.

"You see it, too, don't you?" Rebecca asked. "Don't be frightened." She turned up the wick, turning their surroundings into the musty, familiar attic again.

"It just about scared me to death the first time I saw it. And, Claudia, Amy is a child with a big imagination and no friends close by to temper it. When I came up the last time I heard her talking to the image, to Garrett—in the dark. I think she's halfway convinced herself it's Garrett's ghost, and that he can hear her. Lucinda painted quite a picture of him, you know, and Amy is at an impressionable age."

Claudia shivered. "Let's get rid of the horrible thing right now."

Rebecca put the lamp on a table. "Let's at least move it."

With Rebecca bearing most of the weight they hoisted the heavy portrait and carried it to a corner, leaning it against the faded wallpaper of the far attic wall.

"I'll talk to Amy," Claudia said.

"Talk to me about what? What did you do with him?"

They turned to find Amy confronting them, her posture rigid, her hands in fists.

Claudia reached toward her daughter. "Amy, I had no idea that this crazy arrangement set up an illusion of your grandfather being here. It must have frightened you. It's only his portrait from a long time ago."

"It isn't crazy. This is my place. You had no right to meddle." Amy's tone vehement, she glared at Rebecca. "It was you again."

"Darling, this isn't healthy," Claudia protested. "Don't cling to something so strange. Remember Grandmother Lucinda, but don't try to imagine things, don't fantasize about Grandfather Garrett. He wasn't always—"

Amy grimaced, squared her shoulders, turned, and stamped down the stairs.

With a helpless shrug, Claudia turned to Rebecca.

Rebecca said, "She's at the age when it's hardest to give up romantic ideas about people."

Claudia nodded. "Lucinda caused some of this, not the optical illusion. That has to be an accident. But she built Garrett into something so heroic, so opposite from the truth, that Amy developed a case of idol worship of Garrett and elevated Lucinda to a goddess-like figure."

"Poor thing," Rebecca answered.

"Maybe Damon and I and the children never should have come here, even to escape shame and scandal. I don't know. Our family seems to be falling apart. Do you understand what's happening, Rebecca?"

"Only some of it," Rebecca answered.

Rebecca spent a restless night, tossing under her heavy blankets and wondering whether she'd been wrong to take Claudia to the attic. The whole family acted high strung to an unnatural degree. And Claudia expected a baby in only a few weeks.

Toward dawn, Rebecca drifted into a troubled sleep. In a

dream, she'd been sent by Claudia to look for a child's rocking horse in the attic. She climbed the stairs hearing the wind rise above the rafters. She crossed the floor to search among the chests, hat boxes, toys, and round-topped trunks. As she reached the rocking horse, a chill hit her. The air, always cold in the upper story, turned to ice. Fear tiptoed down Rebecca's spine. Her skin prickled.

She reached for an oil lamp some careless person had left burning, but, as she did, its flame went out. She stood as still as an ice sculpture, not daring to inhale. But then she whirled to face whatever threat had crept into the gloom behind her.

Standing between Rebecca and the door stood the tall, luminous figure of a woman with classic features and long, auburn hair falling in waves around her pale, bared shoulders.

She wore a light-blue evening gown with a scalloped pattern. Her skirt expanded, bell shaped, over hooped petticoats. Her bodice showed a décolletage, and her waist appeared like the point of an arrow. The younger Lucinda's eyes brimmed so full of happiness. Rebecca faced the hopeful girl who'd existed before the solemn, sharp-eyed, predatory woman in the portrait.

Beside her, just a few inches taller, one arm curving around her waist, stood the sinfully rich, sinfully handsome young Garrett Cale in his officer's uniform, a shock of tawny hair falling across his forehead. Both studied Rebecca as though expecting her to do something.

"It's you. Together. Before it all went bitter and worse." She didn't know if she spoke the words aloud. She hadn't expected Lucinda and Garrett to be so beautiful and united. She shivered, feeling the full tragedy of that youth and beauty and love spiraling into the hate and deception that overwhelmed the engaged couple.

When Rebecca jolted awake the memory of their image remained lifelike and clear, as if they'd really stood before her.

But, as she came to full consciousness, the figures wavered more and more indistinct, until they vanished in confusion as segments of dreams too often will.

Disturbed by the prospect of facing a busy day after such restless sleep, Rebecca rose, made her bed, and dressed. She'd brought extra wool shawls and jackets to supplement the heat from the stoves and fireplaces. This was deep winter, and she craved warmth in this place of unexpected chill drafts.

When Rebecca went downstairs she found Teddy sitting on the second to the bottom step kicking the one below him. His snow clothes appeared to be half on and half off. Rebecca detected a definite sniffle as she reached him.

"Why, Teddy. You look like a big, dark cloud is hovering just over your head today. What has you so glum? You're always the sunny one around here." Rebecca sat beside him. "Do you want help with your jacket?"

"Too late. I can't go out without Amy or a big person, and she left without me."

"Amy went outside already? It's barely light and freezing."

Just then they heard someone at the front door. It swung open as she and Teddy stood. Bretton strode in, smiling at their approach.

"Uncle Bretton!" Teddy waddled forward in sagging woolen pants and threw his arms around his uncle. "You're back!"

Rebecca stood behind Teddy, unable to keep from grinning. Bretton swung Teddy off the floor, then set him down with a gentle thud.

Rebecca helped Teddy out of his snow pants, then all three walked through the library and into the kitchen. Claudia and Damon were already there. As they all shared toast and eggs the talk turned to Bretton's successful show in Minneapolis. The seeds of interest for pottery with a Southwest influence had begun to flourish.

They took their time over coffee, a rare hour of peaceful enjoyment in each other's company.

Then, a hired man who'd been shoveling snow rushed up the rear walk and pounded on the kitchen's exterior door. He cried, "Fire! Fire! Somebody help!"

They flew to open the door and peered in the direction he pointed.

"It's the studio!" Claudia cried.

Bretton lunged out the door.

"Claudia, stay here," Damon ordered as he raced after Bretton. Rebecca followed but turned back as Claudia called and tossed her the brothers' parkas. Rebecca tightened the knot on her shawl and ran toward a black plume. Smoke rose against the brilliant blue winter sky.

"Has anyone seen Amy?" Claudia's voice followed Rebecca. With a sick feeling Rebecca remembered the distraught girl's reaction in the attic the night before.

That was it. The studio. The studio where the deer rack over the door symbolized Garrett at his worst and Seth at his best. The place where Lucinda and Seth met as lovers, the place where their son Bretton spent most of his time as he grew up and where he now worked and lived.

Rebecca would always remember what transpired next as happening in slow motion, as though fear had the effect of bogging everything down.

She neared the blazing cabin to see Bretton and Damon pushing their way toward the conflagration. She saw the second of two men who'd been removing snow. Gesturing with gloved hands toward the cabin, he ran toward Bretton. Bretton nodded. Then Rebecca watched him hunch his shoulders like an athlete preparing a football tackle. He dashed toward the door, where dark smoke poured out like rushing water.

"No! Bretton!" She shouted his name over and over, but the

fire's roar obliterated her words. She may as well have mouthed his name in silence.

The man who'd rushed to report the fire to those in the kitchen grabbed Damon, holding him back, struggling. When Rebecca caught up, the heat blasted her as she stared into smoke and flames gushing from the gaping hole into which Bretton had just disappeared.

"Amy went in before we saw the fire, but she hasn't come out," the first man said.

They watched, each second hammering them with the agony of apprehension. Then Bretton lurched out with Amy in his arms, both soot blackened, coughing hard, struggling for oxygen.

"She's all right. Burned her hands. Better get the doctor." Bretton sank to his knees in melted snow and ashes.

Damon took Amy from him. "Thank God she's alive." He wrapped his daughter in his own parka and ran to the lodge with her.

Amy choked and sobbed, clinging to her father's neck.

"And you?" Rebecca asked Bretton as she threw his parka over his shoulders.

Bretton winced. "I'm all right. We're a tough lot."

"Let's get you back to the house." She helped Bretton to his feet.

They walked away, neither speaking, leaving the astounded hired men to view the fire as it burned itself to ash. No one could save the cabin. It, and its history, were beyond saving. Rebecca looked back on the burning studio, once a place where Seth and Lucinda had sealed their secret love and sated their passions. Now the fates were exacting their price on the twisted Cale family.

To what end?

Two hours later, Doctor Munson arrived at Eagle Mountain. He examined Amy, cleaning and putting salve and bandages on her burns. He did the same for Bretton.

Claudia sent Teddy to play in the nursery. Amy slept in the privacy of a guest room. Over coffee with Rebecca, Bretton, and the doctor, Damon explained that Amy ignited the fire.

"Neither Bretton's nor Amy's burns are severe," began the doctor, "but, from what you just told me, your daughter should be taken out of here. She'd recover faster somewhere far away. It's partly a matter of attitude you know," the doctor advised Claudia and Damon.

"Yes," Damon agreed, "it's clear we should leave. But there's unfinished business to deal with before we're free to do that. And Claudia's in no condition to join me in finding a new residence or oversee the move of our household. We can't do it. Not at the moment."

Bretton excused himself to go to a guest room and rest. The worried mother and father walked Doctor Munson to the door while continuing to discuss Amy. Rebecca cleaned up the kitchen and then sat for awhile reliving the terrible moments of the fire. It could have been worse than the loss of the studio. Bretton and Amy could have died. She shuddered.

Her mind filled with questions about Amy's behavior and the motive behind it. Why did the girl set fire to the studio? Was she trying to die? Destroy the will? But if it were there, how would Amy know? She could find no logic to what had happened. Perhaps, that was it. No logical reason existed. Rage, but no logic.

An hour passed before Rebecca left the peaceful kitchen and went to the great room. Teddy had come down and sat on the floor, working a puzzle in front of his mother, who looked exhausted and discouraged.

"Is Bretton still upstairs?" Rebecca asked.

Claudia nodded. "His hands must hurt, and he's lost his

studio. He'll need time to recover."

Rebecca sat by Teddy. "It is a loss. Let's hope the remainder of our day will be less upsetting. Terrifying would be a better word."

Damon came in and scooped his son up, then suggested they go outside for awhile. In minutes the two bundled up and left together. Rebecca considered that spending time with sunny Teddy must be a cheerful break for his father.

Claudia wanted to talk. The worried mother wept with anguish, reliving her panic before Bretton carried Amy out of the conflagration. She admitted also to anger and disappointment when she learned that Amy set the fire.

"What madness has taken over my daughter?" she murmured, dabbing at her eyes with a kerchief that she twisted in her hands afterwards. "If she could set fire to the studio, what else might she do?"

Rebecca had no answers. The two women speculated about all that had happened and why Amy stooped to such a thing as arson. They talked until late-afternoon sunlight slanted through the windows.

Damon and Teddy came back in, and they and Claudia went upstairs to visit Amy. Rebecca tried to read *House of Mirth* by the fire until dinner, but the events of the day occupied her attention. She gave up on the novel and carried a dinner tray to Bretton. She helped him eat, his hands awkward because of the bandages.

CHAPTER TWENTY-FOUR

Rebecca departed again for Kalispell. During her week there, Max, with obvious relief, returned home. Rebecca hired a private nurse. The amiable woman and Mrs. Bracken worked out a schedule that left Rebecca free to review her caseload, knowing she'd be taking the majority over when she returned from her next visit to Eagle Mountain.

The last stroke mandated Max's retirement for all practical purposes and Rebecca's unplanned promotion to become the busiest, though not the senior, partner in the firm of Bryan and Bryan. Nevertheless, Max maintained his role as mentor, advising her in short meetings several times a day on how to proceed. Her uncle's mind seemed clear, but the elderly lawyer wearied after even brief discussions. After awhile Max would become irritable, raising shaky hands to his face in repetitive gestures.

To a distracting degree, Rebecca's thoughts centered on Eagle Mountain. Her heart never left it because Bretton Cale waited there. Or perhaps, to be accurate, he recuperated there. Had he begun to rebuild the studio? Would he leave for the Southwest with no intention to return?

On a day in mid-March, she concluded that the time had come for her to travel back to see Bretton and the family; time to resume the daunting task of finding Lucinda's will.

The stages of the trip had become almost routine for her. With the assurance that accompanies familiarity, she hired Bill

Sauer to drive her to the lodge. She warned him that if she judged he wasn't sober when he came for her at the café, she'd refuse to ride with him. In that unhappy event he would lose her business from that time on. And, she advised him, she planned to be in the area on frequent occasions, so he would lose a reliable source of paying business.

He arrived at the precise hour agreed upon. As they traveled out of Jennings, Rebecca noted for the first time a light go out in the window beneath the lawyer's shingle hung from one of the buildings. Then lights went on in the second-story windows. The lawyer had returned. He must live above his office.

"Fella name of McBride," Sauer told her.

Well, Rebecca thought, she wanted to talk to this McBride. But it would have to wait until the next day. She wouldn't arrive as late as on her first arrival at Eagle Mountain ever again.

Even if he hadn't drafted Lucinda's last will, they could use his services. As the Cales knew, given the Bryan-Cale business connections, she'd have to step away from some estate matters once they had the will in hand. Even Max had agreed. Ethics being the bedrock of their practice and reputation, they wanted to avoid even the appearance of impropriety. Rebecca meant to be as respected and trusted as Max.

Rebecca found Bretton in the great room. Amy sat apart, reading, or pretending to do so. Bretton and Teddy were the ones playing checkers tonight. Rebecca looked at the old pieces and wondered if it were the same board as the one Lucinda purchased in Omaha.

She also noted that both Bretton and Amy no longer had to cope with bandaged hands. There might be scars, but they'd both come through the aftermath of the fire with no disabling effects.

Rebecca sat next to Bretton at dinner. He reached for her

hand under the table. She felt the fine ridges of forming scars, but the hand that closed over hers held warmth.

Knowing that Bretton had a different calling, she sighed. She entertained the fleeting wish that she could meet a man who might even share her own career in life or something close to it. Did someone exist who might love her and want to live with her in Montana?

Bretton would always need freedom as well as self-discipline to create art. She found the handsome artist difficult at times, but so compelling . . . the lover she'd always remember with affection. But there would also be a little sense of relief that their meeting had not been an attempt to form a permanent alliance. A woman could burn and be consumed like a meteor in the heat of his sun.

As all slept that night, a new blizzard roiled up and surrounded them. Rebecca heard the moan of rising wind, the blast of crystalline snow against her window. She remembered the story of Lucinda giving birth during such a storm. She thought of those who lived or had lived here, the ghosts that haunted Eagle Mountain. She shivered and nestled further into her warm blankets.

In the morning, the blizzard had gained a power that made everyone uneasy.

Rebecca joined Claudia on the stairs. They went down together, discussing where they would search for the lost will during the snowbound day ahead.

Damon had made coffee, then retreated to his study, so the two women continued planning over steaming mugs at the table. Rebecca also told Claudia about Max's health and her realization that she'd be handling more cases much sooner than she'd anticipated.

Claudia listened with rapt interest until a twinge passed over her face.

Rebecca reached a hand to her friend's shoulder. "Claudia! What is it? It isn't—"

"Hush. I don't know yet. Don't say anything to anyone just now. I don't want to worry Damon in case it's a false alarm. The baby would be early, you know."

"I know, but Claudia, maybe someone should start for the doctor."

"No. Look outside, Rebecca. It would be too dangerous. Remember what happened to Garrett."

Rebecca fell silent. Memories of her own frightful experience on the day of Lucinda's funeral brought a shudder. "Of course, you're right. But you should rest now, shouldn't you?"

Claudia dismissed her concerns with an airy wave. "I'm not tired. Let's go into the great room and sit by the fire for a bit." Claudia stood.

Rebecca followed her through the library. As they walked, Claudia winced again and then staggered against Rebecca.

"Claudia, this can't be ignored," Rebecca said, her voice rising. She helped Claudia to a chair. "I'm going to find the others."

Claudia's face turned white as she gripped Rebecca's hands. "All right," she conceded. "Please hurry."

Rebecca rushed up the stairs and rapped on the door to Damon's study, opening it without ceremony. The brothers looked up from papers they'd been studying.

"What is it, Rebecca?" Damon rose to his feet as he saw her expression.

"It's Claudia. She's going into labor. You'd better come."

"Damnation," he said, slamming the file shut. "I knew I should have gotten her out of here before now. If anything goes wrong, I'll never forgive myself."

Damon and Bretton followed Rebecca downstairs. Claudia tried to hide her pain but couldn't deny it long. "Don't worry, darling. We'll be all right," she murmured.

Damon knelt beside her. "I'm so sorry, Claudia. We should have had Doctor Munson here. I'll get him."

"Let's carry her upstairs," Bretton ordered. "Rebecca, will you tell Amy and Teddy that their brother or sister is on the way, so they shouldn't expect to see their parents until that happens?"

"Can we find our way to the doc in all this?" Damon asked.

Bretton glanced at the white blanket of snow plastered against the window. "We don't both have to go," he said as he turned back to them. "I can get there by myself."

Damon groaned. "I was so sure we'd have her in town by the time she came due." He gathered Claudia into his arms and carried her upstairs.

Rebecca and Bretton exchanged worried looks.

Bretton said, "We could wait a bit. Claudia might have an easy delivery. It happens, doesn't it? But I'm the logical one to go. I should be able to bring Doc here before dark. If I don't get back in time, you and Damon will have to deliver the baby."

"No, Bretton!" Rebecca cried. "You mustn't go out into this. I—Your first idea is best. Wait to see. After all, the storm might abate."

"She's right," Damon called as he came downstairs. "Let me be the one to go. I can do it, and it's my fault Claudia is here instead of safe with a doctor in attendance. It's my fault that she's here at all." He stopped in front of them, his face anxious.

Bretton laid a hand on his older brother's shoulder. "You know I have a better chance of making it than you would. The baby has a better chance if you stay. Don't be stubborn."

Damon nodded in resignation. "I'll get snowshoes for you," he said before leaving the room.

Rebecca didn't know how to react. Claudia clearly needed a doctor, and Bretton was the only logical one to fetch him. But the fear she'd felt when he raced into the burning cabin after Amy returned. She'd lost her parents, lived with the threat of losing Max . . . whatever the future held, she didn't want Bretton to die. But what was the alternative? There was no one else.

Rebecca helped him put on his parka. "Does anyone have to go? Couldn't we who are here deliver the baby?"

"I spent more time with Seth in these woods than Damon did. I can survive out there better than my brother can. Damon has a wife and children. And he's my brother. I'm not going to let him risk his life or Claudia's and her baby's when I can do something to help them."

She couldn't help it. She spoke her thoughts aloud. "Are you certain you're not trying to erase the way Garrett died when you were born? There's such similarity—"

Bretton's eyes flashed, but he said nothing. They stared at each other as if two speechless strangers had taken their places.

Then Damon's voice interrupted. "It's all right. It's my place to go, Bretton. Mine alone. I am Garrett Cale's son, after all. I'm certain I can go and get back in one piece." He descended the stairs.

"No. Claudia needs you. Your children need you. Rebecca just asked me if I was trying to erase the way Garrett died when I fought my way into this world. I don't think so, but don't make me think it of you. Our father died; it doesn't matter how. We have to think of the living and the soon to be born."

A wail came from Claudia's room. Damon glanced up, nodded, and took the stairs two at a time to join her.

Rebecca turned from watching Damon to see Bretton in his parka, gathering up snowshoes, and putting a flask into his pocket. He gave her a long look. "I will be back, and I'll bring the doctor."

She said nothing for a moment, then smoothed her skirt and

nodded her head before raising calm eyes to him. "It's the right thing. Claudia's and the baby's lives are at risk. Be careful. Godspeed."

He pulled the parka hood up and went out, enveloped by the icy whiteness outside.

She forced the door shut against the wind and turned to see Damon coming down again.

"I know you keep brandy in the liquor cabinet," she said. "Would you like some? I believe I would."

Damon gave a shaky smile. "Please be so kind as to bring back two glasses."

She brought over the brandy and poured drinks for each of them.

Damon rubbed the back of his neck. "Damn it. Why would Bretton want to be a sacrifice to our family? No one here ever treated him right except Seth."

Rebecca turned to Damon and stated, "Your wife and children need you. Claudia needs her husband close at hand during a time like this."

A cry from Claudia's room brought Damon to attention. He quickly turned to rejoin his wife. This time Rebecca hurried after him to Claudia's room.

"It's no false labor," the distressed woman before them gasped.

"Let me help you get undressed." Rebecca brought out a nightgown and helped her friend change. She bathed Claudia's face with a cloth.

Damon took his wife's hand. Claudia clung to him, wracked with the pain of another contraction.

"It's all right, darling," he soothed her. "Bretton's gone to bring back Doctor Munson. They'll be here soon. Rebecca and I are with you."

"The children?" she asked.

"I'll tell them things are fine. Be right back," Rebecca said.

She closed the bedroom door and walked down the hall to the nursery. The image of Damon and Claudia stayed with her. Bretton had been right. Claudia, Amy, and Teddy did need Damon now more than ever.

She tucked her hair into order and smoothed her skirt before forcing a smile she hoped appeared relaxed. She could hear the children's voices. She opened the door to find Amy propped against her bed's headboard. The worn checkerboard rested on her lap. Teddy sat at the foot of the bed, considering his next move. He looked up.

"Hi, Rebecca. Where's Uncle Bretton?"

"That's partly what I have to tell you. Your new little brother or sister has started to arrive a little sooner than we expected."

Teddy grinned, but Amy jumped spilling the checkers over the floor. "Not again!" She cried, "It's happening again. It's blizzarding again, only this time it's not Grandmother Lucinda—it's Mother. Did Father go for the doctor?"

Rebecca put her arm around the terrified girl. "No, Amy, no. Your father is right here safe and warm looking after your mother."

"But the doctor isn't here. Can you help her?"

"I can help, and remember, Bretton wasn't positioned right when he was born." She stroked Amy's forehead. "This baby is following the usual proceedings as far as we can see."

"But where's my uncle Bretton?" Teddy had planted himself, legs wide apart, hands on hips in front of them.

"Your uncle—" Rebecca felt her voice catch. She cleared her throat. "Your uncle Bretton strapped on his big snowshoes and put on his big parka and went off. He'll bring Doctor Munson to your mother. Soon you'll have a new little brother or sister."

"When will they be here?" Teddy frowned in impatience.

"I don't know. Soon, I hope." Rebecca pulled the little boy to her, and he buried his face against her neck.

"She's worried about him, Teddy." With a gentle tug, Amy pulled Teddy from Rebecca's arms to sit beside her. "There's a big storm outside."

"Is Uncle Bretton being a hero again?"

"Yes," Amy answered. She turned to Rebecca. "I never told him I'm sorry about the studio. I don't know why I did that; I felt like I was someone else. Now I might never have a chance to tell him after he saved my life." Amy began to sob. "Why do I keep doing these things that are so wrong?"

Rebecca felt her own eyes fill. "You don't do everything wrong. I think he was right to be the one to go. He'll be back soon; you'll be able to apologize then."

Teddy eyed their tears and then, not to be left out, began to howl. Rebecca opened her arms, and he dove into her lap. She looked up to see Damon staring at the three in amazement.

"I'm glad to see you reassured them." He looked bemused.

"Damon, we were talking about Bretton. I'm worried, but, of course, we need the doctor."

Damon shrugged, a family gesture she'd come to recognize in Bretton.

"You're going to need my help," Rebecca said. "I'll go down to the kitchen and boil water so we can sterilize necessary things."

"Thank you. I want everything ready if the birth goes faster than we expect, but I also want to stay beside Claudia."

As Rebecca left for the kitchen, she heard Damon reassuring his children that everyone including Bretton would be fine.

Rebecca drew water from the pump in the laundry room off the kitchen and poured it into the stove's reservoir. She added wood to the stove to hurry the water to its boiling point. She also searched out clean rags and linens. As she did, she thought of how Amy had reached the age of emotional peaks and valleys. Even without Lucinda's volatile approach and manipulation, maturity vied with confusion, temper, and something of the Cale stubbornness in the girl.

She went upstairs to the sound of Claudia's groans and Damon's reassuring voice. She took wet towels from the bed and replaced them while he helped to shift his wife. He smoothed Claudia's sweat-dampened hair and spoke of how soon the doctor would be there. He added that all was proceeding as it should. Rebecca, as she carried the soiled bedding down to the kitchen, reflected that Damon might yet become a man his family could rely on in an emergency—exactly the strong husband and father they needed.

Claudia's contractions increased in strength and frequency as the hours dragged on. Damon and Rebecca conferred with her during one of her more restful intervals. All three drew the tentative conclusion that it wasn't a breech birth, just a slow one.

Rebecca spelled Damon in sitting with Claudia and played with the children when he sat with his wife. And she also paced the house as she fretted over Bretton. In the blue shadows of late afternoon with the howling wind battering the lodge, the bearskin rugs' snarling heads seemed more menacing than ever.

She warmed supper, the cook having departed for her own nearby home at the first signs of bad weather. The children came down to join her. Later that evening, Rebecca and Amy took turns reading *Treasure Island* to Teddy until the little boy's eyelashes fluttered, then closed together as he drifted to sleep. Rebecca carried him upstairs and tucked the covers around him.

She'd just reached the hallway when her candle flickered and went out. She felt her way to the stairs, noting that Amy stood by the fire gazing up at her grandmother's portrait.

Rebecca suggested they light more candles and oil lamps to

brighten the strange evening. They found several in the pantry, and Rebecca took a lighted lamp up to Claudia's room. The expectant mother lay in broken sleep. She groaned a little as Rebecca entered the room.

"How is she?" Rebecca set the lamp on the dresser.

"Resting for the moment," Damon answered.

"How worried should we be for Bretton?" Rebecca didn't want to ask but couldn't forestall the question.

"No need yet." Damon looked weary but spoke in calm tones. "They'll come soon."

Claudia cried out in the pain of another contraction. Not wanting Amy to listen alone, Rebecca left to rejoin her.

Amy sat up, reading. "How's Mother?"

Rebecca sat beside the pale girl. "It's taking awhile, but she's able to rest some of the time. Your father will tell us if anything appears to be going wrong."

"I never meant to hurt you or Uncle Bretton. I know what you meant when you said people make mistakes and we have to forgive them—forgive each other. I don't know if I can when Grandmother never could. But, Rebecca, how do people ever forgive themselves? I'm so ashamed about what I did to the old cabin."

"That's the hardest lesson of all, but the most important, I believe. I'm still working on it myself."

Amy looked up with a little smile. "I've decided perhaps it's good you're here for us after all. I hope so."

Rebecca smiled. She'd just seen a stride toward that adulthood she'd pondered earlier. "Thank you," she said. "I've been hoping to gain your respect—your friendship—and I'm so glad to hear that. Now you'd better ready yourself for bed. We'll see what the stork brings tomorrow."

"The stork! I don't believe in that nonsense. I never did." Amy cast a sidelong glance with a little of the old hauteur at

Rebecca. "Grandmother told me she had lovers. I had a friend, a boy who might have become my sweetheart until we moved. But Grandmother never told me how it all really comes about. I'm old enough to know."

Rebecca smiled and nodded. "Of course. The stork is all nonsense. I'm glad you have no fantasies. Your Grandmother saw that in you. We women need to be clear headed to progress in this century in every way. But I think it's your mother's right to discuss with you how it all comes about. She'll do that when she's less occupied. Let's not have any big discussions tonight about anything. I'm certainly not up to it. Good night, dear."

After the children settled for the night, Rebecca stayed downstairs, dreaming into the fire. She found herself remembering the dark time of losing both parents when she'd been only months older than Amy. She dozed. Nightmares of Bretton calling to her in a blizzard rose again and again. She dreamed he'd fallen in the forest and kept beating a damaged hand against a tree calling in a sort of chant, "Rebecca! Rebecca! Rebecca!"

She jerked awake in a panic. She'd experienced a repetition of Lucinda's dream of Garrett calling to her from a whiteout.

Waking to full consciousness, she heard someone beating at the front door. She called out for Damon and raced to throw it open. Doctor Munson and a stranger in a heavy parka burst in. A snow-encrusted horse harnessed to a sleigh stood with a drooping head in the drive. Bretton wasn't with them.

CHAPTER TWENTY-FIVE

"Show me to Claudia," Doctor Munson demanded, charging past Rebecca.

Damon appeared and motioned the doctor upstairs.

"What happened to Bretton Cale, the man who came for the doctor?" Rebecca's knees wobbled as she asked Doctor Munson's driver.

"Oh, he had mild frostbite, ma'am. Was all wore out. He might not have made it even a few more yards. He collapsed for awhile at Doc's. We put him in the patients' wing of the house overnight. He'll be fine. As soon as the blizzard dies down I'll run him back here. It was hard going getting Doc and the sleigh this far. If you'll excuse me I'll see to the horse."

Rebecca directed him to the barn, closed the door, and slumped against it in profound relief.

Damon appeared, put an arm around her shoulders, and suggested, "Let's get something to warm everyone up. Doc is seeing to Claudia and wanted me out of the room." Damon headed for the kitchen, Rebecca following. In a short while they emerged with a bottle of whiskey, cups, and hot chocolate. Damon poured the driver and himself each a whiskey. Rebecca noted that the expectant father's hands shook, but he maintained the composed look of a confident host.

Rebecca opted for the chocolate, then excused herself and went to gather more clean linens to take upstairs. The brusque doctor taking charge made all the difference. An anticipatory peace reigned at last.

An hour later she witnessed the birth of Bretton Cale the Second. A seven-pound baby boy wailed stout protests at his new environment. Rebecca bathed the baby, grateful for the doctor's careful oversight. Then she returned the child to an exhausted but radiant Claudia, who placed the baby at her breast. Rebecca smiled at the sweetness of that new little life.

"He's so tiny and perfect, Claudia," Rebecca whispered. "A namesake to make Bretton proud."

"But Bretton? Is he all right? I hadn't even thought." Claudia looked up from admiring her newest son.

"A little the worse for wear, they say, but he'll be fine. He's staying at Doctor Munson's until the blizzard ends. I'm sorry to say at one point I urged him to wait before going for Doctor Munson."

Claudia smiled and held out her hand to squeeze Rebecca's. "We've had enough guilt in this family. Don't burden yourself with blame. I would have done the same if Damon decided to go.

"Now, let's deal with something practical. I need your help. Could you go up to the attic? There's a wicker bassinette up there, the one Lucinda used when the boys were babies. If you'll bring it down and clean it we can put this little man in it right away."

"Of course."

"It's in the far corner as you go in. There's an old rocking horse in front of it." Claudia shifted the baby as he lay against her.

The image of a rocking horse sprang to Rebecca from her strange dream. She shivered. Then, shrugging away such strange fear, she left a candle lighted for the mother and baby. She carried the hurricane lamp to the attic. "Behind the rocking horse," she murmured to herself in the shadowed room.

Rebecca made her way through the clutter of boxes, trunks, and furniture. "Ah, here we are." She set the lamp down on a bookcase and pulled the charming old wicker bassinet out. She thought briefly of a tiny, green-eyed Bretton staring from it. "He must have been beautiful then, too," she whispered.

As she picked up the lamp, she noted the row of books on an old bookcase. They appeared to be a collection of grimy classics, yet several of them were clear of any dust. As she began to read each title she realized that these clean volumes dealt with the occult. Had Lucinda or someone else in the house taken an interest in such matters? Communing with the dead? These had been cleaned recently. Given Amy's attempts to commune with her grandmother's ghost it wouldn't be surprising. Rebecca shivered in the cold.

Four books in all had to do with the Spiritualist Movement that started in the mid-nineteenth century and continued to the present hour. The public had developed a fascination with Ouija boards.

"I wonder . . ." Rebecca muttered and began shifting sleds, skates, a milliner's frame, and old boxes around, brushing at cobwebs as she did. At last she held and lifted out what she sought. "And here you are." She held a clean Ouija board in her hands. Had someone used it of late? "Who's been using you?"

Rebecca put the books in the bassinette. She followed it with the board, adding a flat, tear drop–shaped wooden planchette. It, she knew, would have been used for pointing to the letters that arced at the board's top and the straight row of numbers across the bottom. The word *good-bye* sat centered below the numbers.

Rebecca had seen one of these before but had thought it too foolish and perhaps even too eerie to touch. She had no wish to disturb the dead. It was they who from time to time disturbed her or, to be more exact, her memories.

But who had been spending time in spiritualist activities? Should she bring this up with Claudia? Or should it be Amy? Amy had had many meetings with her grandmother. These books had old dates. At one point, perhaps after the Civil War, Lucinda may have been intrigued by the popular movement.

Lucinda lost a brother in that war. Had Lucinda's mother dabbled in spiritualism? Had Lucinda attended séances? Used a Ouija board? Perhaps in her grief she sought communication with her beloved brother. Hadn't Mary Todd Lincoln arranged for séances to take place at the White House after the death of her young son? President Lincoln had been rumored to have attended at least one or two of them while in office.

Rebecca turned the lamp down until the wick darkened. She picked up the lot and maneuvered through the attic to the stairs, descending with awkward bumps against the wall. She set the bassinette down, then went back up, retrieved the lamp, and closed the attic door. She carried her burden to her room. After removing books and board, she took the bassinette down to the kitchen, brushed dust and cobwebs from it, shook it upside down to be sure nothing remained, took a wet, soapy cloth to it, then finally carried it up to Claudia.

The mother, now delivered of a healthy second son, had given in to a well-deserved nap. Rebecca set the bassinette beside Claudia's bed and admired the little one, who lay in the crook of his mother's arm. After she'd lined the bassinette with baby blankets, she lifted the sleeping infant and laid him in it on his back. He squirmed, pursed his lips, but slumbered on. She stroked his soft cheek for a moment.

"Thank you, Rebecca." Claudia awakened, rubbing her eyes. "You'll be a fine mother yourself one day."

"Not soon. There's Max and the practice . . . perhaps someday, though."

She changed the subject. "Claudia, I found some spiritualist movement books in the attic. Did Lucinda have an interest in communing with the dead? There's nothing on the subject in the library, is there?"

Claudia nodded. "Lucinda was young during the thick of it. Peter's death destroyed their family. She developed a lifelong interest. I wanted nothing to do with the occult and told her never to involve Amy in such matters. She probably ignored me. Amy never spoke of anything like that, though."

Rebecca hesitated, then asked, "Do you ever follow Amy when she sleepwalks? I saw her in the library late one night. I couldn't sleep and came down to find a book. She came in and behaved strangely. I think she tried to communicate with Lucinda. Perhaps through her portrait."

Claudia frowned. "Lucinda must have drawn her into such activities when they closeted themselves together. There were also a few nights when they would have been here by themselves."

Rebecca sat on the edge of the bed. "Do you mind if I ask Amy about it? She isn't as angry with me as before the fire. I believe I can reach her. She might know more about the will than she's told us. As she and I visit about her grandmother I'll explain how I keep finding bits and pieces that help me understand Lucinda. Amy might confide something helpful. Or, she might just tell me where the will is and why she hasn't come forth before to tell us its location."

Claudia sighed. "It's true she hasn't been as strange or withdrawn since the fire. Realizing what she did seemed to shock her back to her senses. Perhaps her grandmother no longer imposing her influence is having an effect as well. I don't want our daughter to go back to being that impossible child you met when you arrived."

"If she is keeping unwholesome secrets we should find out what they are," Rebecca urged.

Claudia sighed. "I agree. Yes, Rebecca, please try to talk to her. I'd like to know just how far she and Lucinda went in any efforts to commune with the spirit world."

The blizzard spent itself in the night. Doctor Munson and his driver departed at dawn. Later, Rebecca helped Teddy dress, then escorted Amy and Teddy to meet their brother.

"He's so little. When can I play with him?" Teddy poked at the baby's fingers, grinning when the tiny hand closed around his thumb.

"Bretton. It's a family name," Amy said with a small smile. "I wonder what Grandmother would have thought of it."

Claudia sat in a rocker near her bed. Damon stood in a proud, protective stance behind his wife.

"Yes, dear girl." Damon stepped toward his daughter and hugged her. "We'll make sure this Bretton knows he's loved from the beginning."

"That's right. We want him to have all that's best in the Cale men with none of their dark sides," Claudia laughed. "Like our darling Teddy."

After the children left, Rebecca stayed with the baby and his parents long enough to gain Damon's permission, as well as Claudia's, that she talk to Amy about what she and Lucinda had, or hadn't, done with the spiritualist books. Damon had no objection. "I'd agree to almost anything to make sure Amy is free of any vestiges of whatever possessed her after Mother's death. And to get to the bottom of this will business," he said.

Bretton returned that day to a welcome that included warm embraces from all before Rebecca took him upstairs to meet his namesake.

She waited until the quiet time of afternoon when Teddy took a daily nap and Claudia rested with the baby. Damon had invited Bretton to go with him into Jennings to observe the current status of their mother's and Max's mining operation. Rebecca declined to go along. This seemed the perfect opportunity to talk with Amy.

The storm had left sparkling snow pillowed on the lodge pole, fir, and ponderosa branches. The woods appeared filled by diaphanous white veils as a breeze unfurled them.

Amy sat in one of the window seats in the library, gazing out at the forest's silent display.

"May I join you?" Rebecca asked.

Amy nodded and tucked up her feet, granting Rebecca room to sit. Rebecca turned, leaning into the corner of the seat so she could face the girl.

They chatted about the baby, the day's loveliness, the book Amy had been reading. Rebecca recognized the novel on Amy's lap as a favorite gothic story, *The Fall of the House of Usher* by Edgar Allan Poe. As a schoolgirl, she'd found it impossible to stop reading, even though the story of possessed children frightened her.

Seeing that Amy had been reading the novel gave Rebecca an opening, and she seized it. She started the conversation by talking about books in general. She decided to be honest with Amy as she wanted the girl to be in full agreement with what she proposed.

Rebecca told Amy how she'd discovered the books on spiritualism while fetching the bassinette for Claudia.

"They weren't dusty like the other tomes up there. Do you know who might have wanted to read them during the last while? Spiritualism was a popular pursuit during the last century and on into our day for some people. Did your grandmother revisit old interests?"

Amy hesitated. "Grandmother taught me what she knew. We studied the books together. She told me how spiritualism gave women a crucial sense of power—power beyond wealth or sex. Women could connect to the spirit world when men couldn't, because we have the strength and energy to reach beyond."

Rebecca leaned forward. "Did you and she use the Ouija board?"

Amy frowned. "Are you going to tell Mother and Father?"

"Is there a reason I shouldn't tell them? They gave me permission to speak to you on the subject. We even wondered about trying a séance to try to learn something about the lost will."

Amy pushed her glasses up her nose and blinked at the brilliant day. "It would be all right now I suppose. Grandmother and I didn't want to upset Mother by talking about such things as communing with the dead, not before the baby arrived. I know Grandmother liked to keep secrets about things she'd done in the past; but it can't bother her any more. I don't think we did anything wrong."

"Doesn't it frighten you, Amy?"

Amy stared at her, perplexed. "Grandmother would never have taught me anything that would harm me. She loved me. After all, she told me I'd inherit everything."

"Well, that would be an unusual thing with her two sons left alive," Rebecca said, raising her eyebrows.

"She promised. She read the will to me, you know. I don't know what happened to the will after that, though. Sometimes I think Mother stole it. She hated the way Grandmother and I cut her out of our private conversations. Sometimes I think Bretton took it, or even Father. Teddy's the only one I know is innocent. He's just a nuisance. Grownups cause all the real trouble."

Rebecca made an effort to stay calm. She decided to continue with the shift to Teddy.

"Well, we won't involve Teddy in any séance. The rest depends on your parents. If they say it's all right we can give it a try. Certainly these books will guide us. Maybe we'll learn something."

"Do you believe in the spirit world? Have you never tried to contact the dead? Not even in Europe? Aren't séances common there?"

Rebecca hesitated. "I did attend a séance at my school shortly before I graduated and sailed for home. It all went downhill pretty fast. I had a beau, a boyfriend you would say. His sister knew of our romance, but she also knew her parents didn't approve of me. No Americans for their titled, wealthy heir. Anyway, she pretended to be in contact with some angry noble ancestor who wanted to cause me to have a terrible accident. I've not participated in such a thing since."

"But do you believe it will work?"

"Not necessarily. But there are other things that might come up. You might remember something important, or someone else might."

"Or somebody might confess to knowing where the will is." Amy looked at Rebecca and added, "I think Grandmother will visit us. We used to be so close. She said we could read each other's thoughts. She'll say who took her will and where it is. She wants me to own everything."

To Rebecca's disappointment, Damon reported that Ethan McBride had been called away again, this time for only a few days, for a trial in Libby. It seemed their meeting was meant to be postponed indefinitely.

Damon and Claudia had hired a young woman, Alice Sloan from Jennings, to be a nursemaid to the baby so Claudia could have periods of rest. Rebecca broached the subject of the séance to Claudia and Damon that evening after Alice had seen to the children and Bretton excused himself to write letters to gallery owners. They sat in the great room under Lucinda's portrait as usual, the women sipping cocoa while Damon nursed a whiskey.

"Amy wants to conduct it. I told her I'd ask you. She and

Lucinda suspected that you knew what they were delving into, you know."

"Do you believe in these things, Rebecca?" Damon asked. He stood and refilled his glass.

"I believe in the power of wishes and suggestion," Rebecca said as he turned back. "I have doubts about those inhabiting the spirit world wanting to commune with us about such unimportant matters as lost wills. I'd think they'd want to rest in peace. Some experiments have shown that the mind can affect the body to the point that people who believe the table will be tipped put extra pressure on one side unaware of what they do. The same has been noted with a Ouija board. Fingers move bidden only by the ideas and hopes in the brain that controls them."

"But what do we hope for? That Lucinda will appear and reveal the will?" Claudia looked puzzled and uneasy with the whole idea of the séance.

"To be honest, I'm not sure. Amy now admits to a real will. She may know where it is and choose to reveal its whereabouts while we're at the séance. Or she might remember a forgotten clue under such circumstances. Perhaps something else will happen. I'm not sure. I just have a feeling that we might discover helpful information. We've hit a wall we must break through to move forward as much as we can before I finally speak with Ethan McBride."

"I suppose it would do no harm and might do some good," Damon said, taking Claudia's hand.

A log fell, scattering sparks toward the three adults. Claudia jumped. Rebecca rose, took the poker, and reassembled the burning wood, feeling its almost frightening heat.

"I don't like the idea, but if you think it will help . . ." Claudia stood with the effort of a weary new mother. "Time for me to see to our little newcomer." She rested a hand on Damon's shoulder. "I think Lucinda manipulates us still, and I don't like it. But I agree we must move forward and away from this drear place. Amy needs a normal life. I don't believe any life stays normal here. Sometimes I think we're in the spirit world, too. Lucinda seems to be with us, controlling us more than ever."

One of the reference books that Amy used to help plan the séance indicated that a round or oval table must be topped by a number of white candles divisible by three. Another stated that the number of people should likewise be so divisible. The cook was far too frightened by such "ghosty frippery." Teddy was too young, the baby out of the question, but the girl who tended him might do.

To everyone's surprise, plain-featured Alice Sloan agreed at once. "I love adventures," she announced, eyes sparkling. "I think it would be plumb fun."

"You never can predict what these quiet ones might want from life," Claudia whispered to Rebecca.

"Here's to a flair for excitement," Rebecca said, smiling. "Now we are six."

Bretton and Damon carried a parquet-topped round table down from the attic. It had probably been used at some time for board games. Now it would be covered with a white cloth and used for a different sort of gathering than ever before, Rebecca thought with an unexpected shudder.

They decided to set up the séance below Lucinda's portrait. Amy insisted that the proper and most propitious time would be midnight.

CHAPTER TWENTY-SIX

On the day the séance would be held, Rebecca and Bretton spent the afternoon walking along the lake. Their boots crunched on snow as they spoke of the night to come. Rebecca felt more uneasy than she'd anticipated. Her case of unsettled nerves confused her.

"Well," Bretton said, "we're none of us experts in such things. You have a sense that something might come out of tonight's entertainment that will help us find the lost document. You have doubts though. What if something else is called forth? The old place is spooky enough to make people jittery in the best of times."

"Oh," Rebecca said, shrugging her shoulders, "I don't accept as true that helpful spirits will come forth. It was just a thought since I, a mere mortal, can't seem to find the will. What I really believe and hope is that this approach might affect Amy. She might tell us if she's been concealing anything. It's also possible that she isn't hiding the truth on purpose but has hidden memories that the séance might call forth."

That evening Amy gave each of the participants paper and a pen. "You will be what are called sitters," she explained. "I'd like each of you to write two questions you wish Lucinda to answer. When you've finished we'll consider them together and decide what our most important questions are. Remember, we may get no responses, or they may be mysterious. In that case I will ask unrehearsed questions."

"How do we start?" Alice asked. "Don't we want to know how Mrs. Cale is doing?"

Amy nodded. "We might ask that. But the questions have to be answered with a yes or no. I will ask, 'Are you well?' "

"What if she says no? Do we ask how we can help her?" Alice looked concerned.

Amy said, "I'll ask if we can help her."

Rebecca wrote, *Did you make a will?*

Amy wrote, *Is it different from the will you read to me?*

Rebecca wrote again, *Did you destroy your last will?*

Damon asked, *Is it in your office?*

Bretton wrote, *Are you with my father?*

Rebecca studied him. How much did he know about his parenthood?

When each had penned two questions, they went through them. They settled on sticking with those that might lead to answers about the will.

By midevening, the baby had been fed at Claudia's breast, then, comfortable and calm, fell asleep in his bassinette. They placed him in the library so they could hear if he fussed. Bretton read Teddy his bedtime story, after which the little boy snuggled into his blankets in the nursery.

At midnight, following Amy's directions, they set three white candles alongside the Ouija board. It took up the middle of the table within each person's reach. A bowl with aromatic bread baked just that afternoon rested on a side table. "To attract the spirit and be a food offering," Amy explained.

Before approaching the table, Rebecca studied the room. She wanted to note every detail. If something changed, she wanted to be certain that she hadn't just misremembered her surroundings. She noted the glowing embers, the lamps turned low, how the door to the library remained open, the occasional sound of boughs soughing, and spatters of rain against the window. A night wind had risen during the spring thaw.

The sitters gathered. Amy, pale and important, sat with her back to Lucinda's portrait. Appearing strained, Damon and Claudia sat at either side of her. Skittish, but bright-eyed, Alice sat next to Damon. Bretton, with a sardonic smile, took the chair next to her. Rebecca sat between Bretton and Claudia.

Amy's eyes shone with expectation as she lit the three candles. Rebecca felt nervous, although whether from anticipation, fear, or just the strangeness of the séance she couldn't have said. Amy advised them to hold hands with those on either side. Both Bretton's and Claudia's hands felt warm. Rebecca suspected her own felt cold.

Apprehensive, she waited to see how the night would unfold. Would someone in this world or the world beyond give up vital secrets? She felt a wave of fear but dismissed it as irrational and foolish. Darwin and others had ushered in the age of science, and Rebecca welcomed it. Still, here she sat, part of a séance. She'd reached the point where she'd try any path to find answers.

Amy instructed Claudia to place her hands on the Ouija board. Next, Amy, holding the planchette that would point out the spirit's answers, intoned, "Grandmother Cale, can you hear us? Grandmother Cale, are you with us?"

Rebecca lifted her head. Her eyes met Lucinda's in the portrait. How direct they were. She seemed desperate to tell Rebecca something. But what? Was it possible Lucinda wanted to help them?

Amy had reached her third intonation when the dining room door slammed shut. "A draft," Damon muttered. They all waited in tense silence to hear if the infant had wakened, but he continued to sleep.

Amy invited the spirit again. Everyone straightened as the planchette moved Claudia's and Amy's fingers to spell the letters *Y,* then *E,* then *S.*

"Are you at peace, Grandmother?"

This time, the planchette wrote *N,* then *O.*

Claudia asked in a trembling voice, "Amy, are you moving this?"

Amy frowned and shook her head. "Don't be distracted, Mother. We won't be able to continue."

Amy asked whether there was a will. The answer came as a *Y,* then *E,* then *S.*

Rebecca studied Claudia. The new mother appeared white and shaking. Perhaps they shouldn't have subjected her to this. The candles wavered, and Rebecca heard a moaning in the pines bending outside the lodge.

Then Amy came to the question, "Is it the will you read to me?" After a long hesitation, the planchette spelled out *N O.* "Did you make out a new will?" The planchette hesitated, then moved with rapidity to the letters *Y E S.*

Amy shot Claudia a look of suspicious anger. She muttered through clenched teeth, "Stop it, Mother. I know what you're doing."

Claudia's voice shook. "I'm—I swear I'm doing nothing."

"Grandmother," Amy's voice rose as she asked, "did you hide the new will?"

Claudia stood and flipped the Ouija board. "This has to stop! This is wrong." Tears glistened, and she brushed them away.

"Mother! Sit down. We can't stop now. We have to thank Grandmother."

Claudia sat. "All right, if that's how we can end this. If this is how we can be out from under her at last. Even after Lucinda's death I can't be free of her dominating presence."

The séance ended with Amy giving a muttered "thank you" to her grandmother. Amy studied Claudia with a strange brightness in her eyes. The girl had gone white except for red splotches on each cheek. Without another word she stood, then ascended the stairs. Rebecca stood and rubbed her arms, surprised at how tense she'd been. Her eyes following Amy, Rebecca had no doubt the attic would have a visitor before morning.

Rebecca went for a walk the morning after the séance. At first she regretted ever suggesting such a thing. How foolish, she thought, to have been so influenced by Damon's and Claudia's troubled girl. Amy most likely ended the séance because of anger and disappointment at Claudia's disruptive behavior. Did her silence after the séance signal shock or acceptance that she might not be the sole beneficiary named in the missing will?

Rebecca pondered Amy's strange serenity given the Ouija board's message. Claudia may have moved the planchette for her own reasons. Yet, if so, what motivated her? Was she afraid to see her destruction of the will revealed? Had she moved the planchette? Rebecca had heard that certain mediums had been debunked in books that explained how they moved the planchette with trickery.

But why would Claudia do that? She claimed she couldn't find the document that left everything to Amy. Could she have knowledge of a new will? If so, where would she, or where would anyone else, even Lucinda, have put it?

Rebecca spent the day searching and observing the family. At one point she sought out Claudia, who sat in the rocker in her room nursing the newborn.

"I can't stop puzzling over the séance. What's your reaction to it?" Rebecca asked.

Claudia shook her head and gave a rueful little laugh. "That séance. I haven't seen such theatrics since drama club."

"Drama club?" Rebecca had a sudden insight. "Claudia, the séance?"

Claudia gave a small, inscrutable smile. "Just an observation. Of course, it frightened all of us, didn't it?"

That night, feeling a renewed need to roam through the house, she carried a lamp downstairs. The family, the cook, and a handyman had all gone to their homes. Alice Sloan now slept in the nursery with the children.

Rebecca paused before Lucinda's portrait. Studying it, she looked into those intense, almost intimidating, eyes. She'd always thought them cold, but now she wavered. Did the eyes try to speak? Ask for help?

There were so many hiding places in this lodge, home to familial discord and secretive unhappiness. And why would Lucinda hide her own will anyway? But Lucinda loved to control others. She must have imagined the family scrambling about trying to find the document. Perhaps she imagined Max in on the scramble. He'd kept the truth of Garrett's death from her long enough.

"Where did you put it, Lucinda? And why?"

Rebecca lifted her lamp above her head. Lucinda's green stare intensified, seeming to seek Rebecca. Then it struck her. In this dismal place, letters that contained revelations had once been secreted behind a portrait. Why not again? Rebecca strode to the library and returned with a ladder.

She set the lamp on a table and climbed to take the portrait down. That proved a heavy, awkward business, but she managed. When she reached the floor, she turned the picture around. A thick, heavy envelope had been squeezed between the painting and its frame. It looked almost demure, tucked there. She pulled it out and read the words *Last Will and Testament*.

Her hands shook. Her heart thudded in her throat. At last the question of the will would be settled. For a moment she felt only relief. How she longed to leave this appalling place. How she yearned to tell Max that the search was over, that they could turn the estate's probate over to the appropriate lawyer, Ethan McBride. Rebecca planned to control the situation until such legal reinforcements could be located and brought to Eagle Mountain.

Replacing the portrait proved an awkward struggle. Sweating, with arms shaky from the strain, she lifted it and hooked its backing over the nail on the wall. As a final step, she straightened the painting. Once down on solid footing, she put the ladder back where she'd found it.

It would be crucial that the testament's seal remain unbroken. No tampering with evidence. It had to be clear that there'd been no changes to it once it had been sealed. She slid the document under her mattress that night. Despite her gnawing curiosity, reading of the will must wait. Tomorrow she would, she hoped, meet Ethan McBride, Attorney at Law.

Rebecca dressed in a plaid wool dress with a fitted jacket, put up her hair, and descended the stairs early the next morning. She'd explain to the family that she'd found the will. She'd determined that no one should read it until an attorney with no ties or claims to the Cale fortune could be retained to handle the estate. Therefore, they had to send for the Jennings lawyer who she believed drafted the will. He should be present before it could be opened. If their luck held, he'd be available to come that day.

Astounded when Rebecca announced the search for the missing will to be over, the family expressed puzzled amazement over its hiding place.

"Mother could never have managed to put it there," Damon said.

"Amy?" Claudia turned to her daughter.

Amy ignored the implication and asked, "Mother, did you

destroy the will that left me everything?"

"No," Claudia insisted. "How can you say such a thing? I swear I didn't."

At three that afternoon, Damon and Ethan McBride rode up to the house, McBride astride a skittish young appaloosa mare. The men dismounted and turned their horses over to a hired man. Claudia welcomed her husband and their guest into the lodge and made introductions.

The attorney wasn't as young as Rebecca had expected. He had a long, good-humored face and stood a good six inches above everyone else in the room. She noted his intelligent brown eyes.

"Would you like something to eat? I know it's a long trip." Rebecca took McBride's coat and hung it up. It smelled of fresh air.

"No, thank you. If all of you are ready, I see no point in delaying the reading of Lucinda's elusive Last Will and Testament. I drafted it for her."

"I wondered if you had," Rebecca said.

"Yes, she sent for me some time ago. I arrived on the day she wanted me to, an occasion when all you family members were in Kalispell. She wanted it done in secret and at once."

"Well, she certainly had her way," Damon said with a wry smile.

"We did it all in that one day," Ethan went on. "She absolutely refused to let me have a copy for my office files as is customary. I left the original with her. There were no copies, and she insisted we burn all the rough drafts."

"That's curious," Damon responded. "Well, we're more than ready for the reading. We can all fit into my office. Come on, everybody."

They went in a group. Rebecca, beside Ethan McBride, grew aware of Bretton walking close behind her. She turned and smiled in an attempt to be reassuring. But his expression, like Damon's beside him, had turned anxious.

Damon arranged chairs in a semi-circle before the desk. Rebecca handed the will to McBride, who sat behind Lucinda's desk. Claudia and Amy entered last. Bretton closed the door. The lawyer removed glasses from his vest pocket and proceeded to put them on halfway down his nose with maddening slowness.

Rebecca had to stifle a knowing smile despite the tension. With moves like that, he could win any jury to his side. That little bit of showmanship would always help a trial attorney's cause.

McBride took a brass letter opener and broke the seal on the envelope. Before he began to read he explained that Lucinda had wanted no witnesses to the will, so through the long and painstaking day, with his advice, she had written it all in her own hand, as he advised her that holographic wills would stand with no witnesses. He explained there were periods of writing and periods of rest. He cleared his throat and began to read from the document.

Last Will and Testament

I, Lucinda Bordeaux Cale of the Cale Lodge, also known as Eagle Mountain, in the County of Lincoln, State of Montana, being of sound mind do hereby declare this to be my Last Will and Testament, hereby revoking all former wills and codicils heretofore made by me.

I

I direct that my just debts and funeral expenses shall be paid by my personal representatives hereinafter named, as soon as conveniently possible after my death.

Parts II and III appointed Bretton and Damon as Lucinda's co-personal representatives, and listed her many properties and investments.

Part IV of the will, stated in simple, straightforward language, revealed what at least some of the family's future would hold:

It is my wish that all of my real and personal property, wherever situated, including, but not limited to, the above listed real and personal properties shall be divided share and share alike among Damon Garrett Cale, Bretton Bordeaux Cale, who is the natural son of Seth Dubois and me, and Amy Cale, who has been such a comfort to me in my days of decline.

Part V expressed Lucinda's desire that her body be transported to New York and buried in her family's plot in a designated cemetery overlooking the Hudson River.

Part VI contained her dated signature notarized by Ethan McBride on September 7, 1905.

Ethan pulled out a few more sheets that seemed to surprise him. Another document in Lucinda's hand had been placed in the envelope as well. The lawyer said, "Now I see why she didn't want me to seal the will before I left. It appears she made an addition." It read:

I apologize to Amy for letting her believe she would inherit everything. For a time that felt right, and it was my way to use wealth, once beauty fled, to manipulate even those I loved. After much thought, and with one long conversation with my spiritual advisor, the good Reverend Gilmore, I realized it would not do to bypass my sons. It is not what either of their fathers would want, or any reasonable person. I must be even-handed. Perhaps I was a little afraid of some final quarrel or upset, and I don't think my heart could have borne up under such a thing happening between my beloved granddaughter and me. I took the coward's way of nondisclosure. But Amy, my love, you are a wealthy woman now. I trust you to manage your inheritance with care. I saw that intelligence and wisdom in you from the beginning.

I loved all of you. We became mutual disappointments at times, but forgiveness, in the end, must prevail. No one knows better than I the emotional link between love and money.

I want all of you to leave here as soon as possible. I trust that you will respect these, my last wishes. Abandon everything except your personal items and clothing. Close the door and take yourselves from this place of deadly deceptions and dark desires. It is my wish that this accursed lodge never be inhabited by any person or people again, especially those descended from me. I wish it to molder and return to the forest and its creatures. They alone may find happiness here.

It is also my wish that Bretton Bordeaux Cale read my journals, which are to be found in the three volume set of *The Decline and Fall of the Roman Empire* by Gibbon, located in the library at Eagle Mountain.

I wish my sons to know that in the end I loved them both, and that I regret the pain I caused by my past actions and painful silence.

I add here that I am going to seal this document and with the last of my strength and determination place my testament in the most appropriate place where one of you has found it if you are reading this. I don't want anyone to know the truth of the final settling until I am safely beyond this troublesome life. It is my life, sad, at times even bad, but lived as I could in this place.

Silence followed the reading. Amy stood and walked with straight-backed dignity from the study.

Bretton approached Rebecca. "You have the journals, don't you?" His voice sounded husky.

"Yes." She rose and faced him.

"Give them to me, if you please. It's about time I saw them." His eyes were hard.

"I'll retrieve them from my room." She turned to McBride. "Are we finished here?"

"We are. Of course, you'll want to read them at once, Mr. Cale." McBride's voice sounded smooth and assured. He'd read the astonishing will and Lucinda's addition, her codicil, with professional poise. He continued now to handle matters with tact.

Bretton gave Rebecca a level look. "You knew almost from the beginning, didn't you?"

His anger made her defensive, but she kept her tone smooth. "I couldn't just give them to you outright. You'll understand when you read them. I didn't have all the information yet. Perhaps I was waiting for Lucinda's permission. After all, it was Lucinda's story to tell. I found her diaries while searching in the library for her will. I read them and revealed their contents only to Uncle Max. He said there had to be a will. That we should wait until we found it to disclose the private diaries. He agreed that Lucinda had the right to tell you the truth about your father in her own way."

Damon interrupted, "Where's Amy?"

"She slipped out," McBride said, rising. "She may need time to herself. All of you must feel shaken."

Damon nodded. "Shaken, yes. But, thank providence, Mother did right by all of us."

Claudia tucked her arm through Damon's. "I'm finally in agreement with your mother. We've all had enough. Please, Damon. Our family should leave, and I, too, thank God that we're finally free to do it. We were never meant to be here. No one should be here. We'll be able to repay Father at last."

Bretton cleared his throat and frowned. Rebecca left the room and in moments brought back the journals. She handed them to him saying, "Read them to understand her. You've seen enough of the world to know the value of compassion."

Bretton took the journals and turned to leave the room without comment.

Three days later the family had packed. Rebecca finished consulting with McBride over estate matters as they applied to Max's interests. All seemed in order except that she hadn't really had a private talk with, much less a chance to say good-bye to, Bretton.

Everyone had agreed to leave Eagle Mountain at the same time that afternoon. Before lunch, with nothing more to do, Rebecca strolled outside.

Sunlight sparkled in little explosions over fresh snow. Ravens' wings whirred overhead. She walked toward the place where it all started, where she'd first met Bretton

Cale. She'd not been back since the fire. The studio stood in ruin, a jagged, blackened reminder of Lucinda's troubled days, and of her loves and family. Snow had drifted gray around the soot-encrusted kiln. Part of two walls stood, hollowed shells that would soon crumble.

Rebecca stepped through the door frame. The ceiling and shelves had all collapsed. The cot stood with its burned mattress. Blackened shards of pottery lay half-buried in snow and ashes. She shuffled through, picking up and tossing them away. One of the little demons grinned up at her from the snow. She bent to grasp it.

"They're called kiln gods," a voice behind her said. "They're just for fun."

Rebecca dropped the figure and turned. Before she could speak he was holding her in his arms. She melted into his embrace, and for the longest moments neither moved.

He pulled back at last and smiled. "That's better. Not quite a replica of our first meeting here."

"Are you free of your past? Did the journals help you understand your mother?"

"Yes. I know now what she suffered. What's the adage? 'To understand is to forgive.' It's a relief, and you made it happen. I thank you. You have something of her passion and stubbornness, only you're kinder . . . softer. I'll ask one last time: Come with me to New Mexico? Be my muse?" Bretton cupped her chin in his hand. "Is the answer yes?"

"I'll always have a place, a tender place, in my heart for you. But it wouldn't go well for us. Be assured, I'm not meant for the Southwest or the artist's life. I have my own work. I want to be a successful attorney. I want to break a path for women to vote, to have a place in the professions. I have Uncle Max to think of, and an office and household to run."

He sighed and looked away. "I had to try."

She nestled in his arms. "Tell me you understand."

"I'm trying. I do. I believe I do." He kissed the top of her head, then her forehead and her mouth.

This time she pulled back, brushing away tears with a rueful smile. She turned to go back to the lodge before common sense conceded to the pull of her heart that didn't quite want to let Bretton go. He caught up, and as they walked they spoke of inconsequential things, the journeys ahead, the family, Max and his health, all while avoiding each other's eyes. When the two reached the lodge, they saw their luggage waiting by the gate. They traveled in separate buggies back to Jennings.

They would never see each other again.

EPILOGUE

The driver slowed her 1945 Packard on the dusty road. She stopped at the ruins of what had once been a lodge. Rebecca McBride turned off the car, sat a moment, and climbed out. Still slim and erect, she wore her white hair short now. Smoothing it in the old gesture, she made her way closer to what had been Eagle Mountain Lodge.

She paused in front of the lodge. Through broken windows she could make out ragged drapes and the patchy, crumbling mounts of trophy animals. Moss covered the walk and clung to the sagging shingles, walls, and gate. She could sink her fingers into it, it had grown so thick.

Rebecca saw that the roof had caved in the middle. Garrett's portrait no doubt suffered the effects of rain and snow. One attic window had broken as a fallen tree crashed through it. Rebecca thought of the family, and herself, as they'd been that winter in 1905.

Everything had changed. Max died within months after contracting pneumonia, leaving Rebecca a wealthy woman at the head of her own law firm. After a year of meetings that became visits that became courtship, she'd married Ethan McBride. He joined the firm, making it Bryan, McBride, and McBride, Attorneys at Law. They'd run a fine, equal partnership in every way. In addition to the practice, she'd helped Montana women achieve suffrage in 1914 and served six terms in the state legislature. She'd born two sons, one lost to them in the recent war, a searing grief. The other now taught in the School of Law at the University of Montana.

The great influenza pandemic claimed Damon's and Claudia's young Bretton. Damon, who suffered greatly over his son's death, died of a heart attack in 1920. Claudia remarried two years later and lived in New York, taking part in community theater productions. Amy never married but became a writer and philanthropist. Teddy grew into outrageous good looks and charisma. He became a movie star first, then a director and producer. And Bretton. Bretton had gone to New Mexico. He'd moved as an artist from pottery to painting. His style changed American art.

As Rebecca stood before the house, a raven swooped out of the broken attic window. It veered toward her, then rose and disappeared over the spires of the forest into the west. The wind rose, and a thousand sighs lifted and fell. There had been so many deceptions and desires born, realized, and vanquished here. She and the others had been flawed mortals. The phrase that came to her to describe them was "all too human."

Rebecca returned to the Packard more than ready to drive back. Ethan would be waiting.

ABOUT THE AUTHOR

Karen Wills lives with her husband just a few miles from her beloved Glacier National Park in northwest Montana. She loves to write, hike, read, and visit with family and friends. She is also an active volunteer for social justice. Karen has practiced law, including representing plaintiffs in civil rights cases. She also taught English and writing on the college and secondary public school levels, including on the Cheyenne River Sioux reservation in South Dakota, and in the Inupiaq Eskimo village of Wales, Alaska. She's encountered bears, both grizzly and polar, and still believes passionately in the value of wild creatures and country.

The employees of Five Star Publishing hope you have enjoyed this book.

Our Five Star novels explore little-known chapters from America's history, stories told from unique perspectives that will entertain a broad range of readers.

Other Five Star books are available at your local library, bookstore, all major book distributors, and directly from Five Star/Gale.

Connect with Five Star Publishing

Visit us on Facebook:
   https://www.facebook.com/FiveStarCengage

Email:
   FiveStar@cengage.com

For information about titles and placing orders:
   (800) 223-1244
   gale.orders@cengage.com

To share your comments, write to us:
   Five Star Publishing
   Attn: Publisher
   10 Water St., Suite 310
   Waterville, ME 04901